Plain Perfect

A Daughters of the Promise Novel

BETH WISEMAN

A Man of His Word

A Hearts of Middlefield Novel

KATHLEEN FULLER

THOMAS NELSON
Since 1798

NASHVILLE   DALLAS   MEXICO CITY   RIO DE JANEIRO

Plain Perfect

BETH WISEMAN

To Reneé Bissmeyer,
my best friend.

Glossary

ach—oh

Aemen—Amen

appeditlich—delicious

baremlich—terrible

boppli—baby or babies

daadi—grandfather

daed—dad

danki—thanks

Deitschi wege—Dutch ways

Die Botschaft—a weekly newspaper serving Old Order Amish communities everywhere

dippy eggs—eggs cooked over easy

eck—special place for bride and groom at the corner of the wedding table

Englisch or *Englischer*—a non-Amish person

fraa—wife

guder mariye—good morning

gut—good

haus—house

hochmut—pride

in lieb—in love

VIII   BETH WISEMAN

Kapp—prayer covering or cap

kinner—children or grandchildren

kinskind—grandchild

mamm—mom

mammi—grandmother

mei—my

naerfich—nervous

Ordnung—the written and unwritten rules of the Amish; the understood behavior by which the Amish are expected to live, passed down from generation to generation. Most Amish know the rules by heart.

Pennsylvania Deitsch—Pennsylvania German, the language most commonly used by the Amish

redd-up—clean up

riewe—red beets

roasht—traditional main dish at an Amish wedding, consisting of cut-up chicken and stuffing

rumschpringe—running-around period when a teenager turns sixteen years old

rutschich—squirming

schnitzboi—snitz pie

schnuppich—snoopy

verhuddelt—confused

wedding nothings—dessert reserved for weddings; fried pastries sprinkled with confectioner's sugar

wunderbaar—wonderful

ya—yes

yummasetti—a traditional Pennsylvania German casserole

1

LILLIAN PEELED BACK THE DRAPES AT THE FRONT WINDOW and squinted against the sun's glare. She'd called the taxi almost an hour ago. If her ride didn't show up soon, she would have to forego her plan and spend another night with Rickie. Biting her lip, she worried if she had enough cash to change her flight if she didn't make it to the airport on time.

She lowered the drape and paced the living room in Rickie's house, silently blasting herself for ever moving in with him in the first place. Her stomach writhed at the thought of one more day under the same roof with him. And yet her window of time for her departure was closing, she realized, glancing at her watch.

She tugged at the drapes again. Relief fell over her when she saw the yellow cab pull into the driveway. Snatching her red suitcase and purse, she bolted for the door, shuffling toward the driver as he opened the trunk.

"Please hurry," she said to the driver, handing him her suitcase.

The driver stowed her luggage without comment and was climbing into the driver's seat when she saw Rickie's black Lexus rounding the corner and heading up the street. Her heart sank.

"Where to?" the driver asked.

"Bush Intercontinental Airport," she answered. "Hurry, please."

As the driver made his way down Harper Avenue to make the long drive to the northwest side of Houston, Lillian watched out the rearview window. Rickie's car slowly neared the house.

The cab driver turned at the corner. She'd made it. A clean getaway.

Irma Rose Miller couldn't help but notice the bounce in her husband's steps. The cancer kept him down and out on most days, but not today. Today Lilly was coming, and his anticipation and joy were evident.

"*Danki,*" Jonas said as Irma Rose poured him another cup of coffee.

"You're welcome."

Her tall husband, once muscular and strong as an ox, sat hunched over the wooden table between them. His healthy load of gray locks and full beard were now thinning and brittle. Dark circles under his eyes and sunken features revealed the many sleepless nights of pain he had endured over the past few months. God had given her husband of forty-eight years a challenging road to travel, and he was making the trip with dignity and grace.

"Our Lilly will be here this afternoon." Jonas smiled and raised the cup to his mouth. His hands trembled, but his eyes twinkled with a merriment Irma Rose hadn't seen since the first mention of their granddaughter coming to stay with them. She hoped he wouldn't be disappointed. They hadn't seen the girl in seventeen years, since she was ten years old.

Irma Rose stood to retrieve some doughnuts from a pan atop the wooden stove.

"It will be *wunderbaar gut* to have her here."

Irma Rose placed two doughnuts on her husband's plate. "*Ya*, that it will. But, Jonas, you must keep in mind how different our ways are. We will seem like foreigners to our *Englisch* granddaughter."

"These doughnuts are *appeditlich*," Jonas said.

"*Danki*. But, Jonas, you need to prepare yourself. Sarah Jane raised Lilly in the outside world. We don't know her. As a matter of fact, we don't know exactly how Sarah Jane raised her."

The thought twisted Irma Rose's stomach in familiar knots. It had been hard enough when her daughter chose to leave the Old Order Amish community at the age of eighteen, but even more difficult when she wrote to tell them she was in a family way soon thereafter . . . with no husband.

"She was a glorious child," Jonas said. "Remember how quickly Lilly learned to ice-skate? What a joy she was. What a *gut* Christmas holiday we all had."

Irma Rose shook her head at her husband's ignorance of the obvious. Lilly wasn't a child anymore. She was a grown woman. Jonas had talked about that last Christmas together until the next season came and went. When Sarah Jane and Lilly didn't show up the following year, he merely shrugged and said, "Maybe they will visit next year." And each Christmas thereafter Jonas anticipated a visit that never happened.

Jonas never uttered a negative word about Sarah Jane's choices. But she'd seen the sadness in his eyes when their daughter left home, and she knew the pain dwelled in his heart over the years. But he only said it was impossible to always understand God's direction for His children—their child. Their *only* child. The good Lord had only seen fit to bless them with one. A beautiful daughter who had chosen a life rife with hardship.

Irma Rose had prayed hard over the years to cleanse herself of any discontentment with her daughter. Sarah Jane's choice to leave the Amish faith was prior to her baptism and church membership. Therefore the community never shunned her daughter. She had chosen to avoid visits with her parents. From the little Irma Rose gathered over the years, Sarah Jane and Lilly had lived with friends and moved around a lot.

An occasional letter arrived from her daughter, to which Irma Rose always responded right away. More times than not, the letters were returned unopened. It was less painful to assume Sarah Jane had moved on and the postal service returned the letters. Although sometimes it cut Irma Rose to the bone when she recognized her daughter's penmanship: *Return to sender*.

She was thankful her last letter to Sarah Jane wasn't returned. She couldn't help but wonder if the news about Jonas's cancer had prompted her granddaughter's visit. When Lillian's letter arrived over a month ago, Irma Rose had followed her instructions not to return a letter but to call her on the telephone if at all possible. She wasted no time going to the nearby shanty to phone her granddaughter. The conversation was strained and the child seemed frantic to come for a visit.

"I'm a teacher and when school is out in May, I'd like to come for a visit," her granddaughter had said on the phone. "Maybe stay for the summer. Or maybe even longer?" There was a sense of urgency in the girl's tone.

Irma Rose feared her faith was not as strong as her husband's and that a tinge of resentment and hurt still loitered in her heart where Sarah Jane was concerned. She didn't want any of those feelings to spill over with her granddaughter. She would need to pray harder.

As if reading her mind, Jonas said, "Irma Rose, everything will be fine. You just wait and see."

———

It wasn't until the plane was high above the Houston skyline that the realization of what she'd done hit Lillian. After landing in Philadelphia, she caught a train to Lancaster City and hopped a bus to Paradise, which landed her only a few miles from her grandparents' farm. She was glad there was a bit of a walk to their property; she wanted to wind down and freshen up before she reacquainted herself with her relatives. Plus, she'd had enough time on the plane to wonder if this whole thing was a huge mistake. Her mom hadn't wanted to be here, so why think it would be any better for her?

Not that she had much choice at this point. She had no money, no home, no job, and she was more than a little irritated with her mother. When her mom had begged Lillian to loan her money, Lillian reluctantly agreed, with the stipulation she got her money back as soon as possible. But her mom had never repaid a loan before. Lillian didn't know why she thought it would be any different this time, and she was determined to move away from her "boyfriend" Rickie. So Lillian quit her job and made a decision to distance herself from her mother and Rickie by coming to a place where she knew neither of them would follow: Lancaster County.

Lillian shook her head, wondering if she was making a bigger mistake by coming here. She didn't know if she'd ever understand what ultimately drove her mother from the Plain lifestyle. From what she read, it rarely happened—Amish children fleeing from all they'd ever known. The circumstances must have been severe to drive her mother away.

Although . . . it didn't look so bad from Lillian's point of view, now that she was here. Aside from having a dreadful wardrobe, she thought the Amish men and women strolling by looked quite content. They seemed oblivious to the touristy stares. The women wore simple, dark-colored dresses with little white coverings on their heads. The men were in cotton shirts, dark pants with suspenders, and straw hats with a wide brim. Box-shaped, horse-drawn buggies were abundant.

Ironically, it all seemed quite normal.

She took a seat on a bench outside the Quik Mart at the corner of Lincoln Highway and Black Horse Road and watched the passersby. Clearly, Paradise was a tourist town, like most of Lancaster County, with everyone wanting to have a look at the Amish people. Watching them now, she wondered if the Amish were all as peaceful as they appeared. Despite her initial thoughts, she decided they couldn't be. Everyone had stress. Everyone had problems. Surely the Plain People of Lancaster County were not an exception.

But they could have fooled Lillian.

Samuel Stoltzfus gave hasty good-byes to Levina Esh and Sadie Fisher and flicked his horse into action, hiding a smile as his buggy inched forward. The competitiveness of those two widow women! First Levina had presented him with her prize-winning shoofly pie. Not to be outdone, Sadie quickly offered up her own prize-winning version. Stalemate. The two of them had stood there glaring at each other while he tried to think of ways to escape unhurt . . . and unattached.

He might have to rethink his shopping day. Both women knew he went to the farmer's market on Thursdays . . .

Once he cleared town, he picked up the pace. The road to his farm near the town of Paradise was less traveled, and he was particularly glad of that on this day. It was a glorious sunny afternoon, perfect for a buggy ride through the countryside. Pleased he had chosen his spring buggy instead of his covered one, he relished the warmth of the late afternoon sun. Rachel had loved this time of year, when spring gave way to summertime and all the world felt full of promise.

God's soil was tilled, and he had planted corn, alfalfa, and grain. Life would be busy as he awaited the bountiful rewards of spring's labor. There was the garden, with peas to pick. The strawberries would be ready. Lots of canning and freezing. Much time went into preparing a garden for harvest.

And Rachel's garden had always been lush and plentiful. Gardening was work for the womenfolk, but Samuel had done the best he could the past two years. He was thankful his sisters took care of most of the canning and freezing.

He closed his eyes, his shoulders lifting with his sigh. He missed Rachel the most this time of year.

Lillian felt like a fool. Didn't "down yonder a spell" mean right down the road? The friendly Amish boy had pointed down Black

Horse Road and uttered those exact words when she'd asked for directions to her grandparents' farm. She'd thought the walk would do her good—help her shed some of the calories she ingested while sitting at the Quik Mart with a large cinnamon roll and cola.

Evidently, she'd mistranslated "down yonder a spell." There wasn't a farmhouse in sight.

She really should have considered the strappy sandals she was wearing before opting to venture down the road to nowhere. Her capri blue jeans and short-sleeved, pink-cotton shirt were good choices, however. The clement sun mixing with a soft breeze made for a perfect day. An excellent day for a walk . . . if only she'd worn better shoes.

Setting her red suitcase on the grassy shoulder of the paved road, she plopped down on top of it and scanned the farmland surrounding her. It was so quiet. Peaceful. She could only hope that some of the peacefulness the Amish were known for would rub off on her during her stay. She needed it. Life had not been easy on her the past few years.

Her mom's idea of parenting had left much to be desired— jumping from one man to the next, looking for something she never seemed to find. All the while she'd toted Lillian along. Lillian had grown up changing schools, saying good-bye to friends, and continually hoping Mom's next boyfriend would be better than the last. At the first chance, Lillian had bailed on the situation, telling herself she could do better.

Despite her good intentions, she'd ended up close to follow-ing in her mother's footsteps. After putting herself through college while living with three other girls in a small apartment, she'd landed a teaching job. There were boyfriends, and she'd definitely made her own share of mistakes.

But always, something had whispered to her that there was another way to live. Sometimes she'd listened, sometimes not. But she never felt comfortable enough to ask herself just where that voice was coming from—she just didn't know enough to form an opinion. She didn't listen to the voice when it cautioned her not to move in with Rickie. But when the voice became too strong to ignore, she knew it was time to get out of that situation.

Despite the complete lack of religious upbringing, she always suspected there might be a God looking down on her. But in light of her mom's thoughts on church, she couldn't ask her about it. Her mother seemed angry at religion. While she heartily encouraged Lillian to attend various churches with her friends when she was a child, she herself would have no part of it. It was a huge contradiction in parenting, and Lillian didn't understand it to this day.

Now, knowing the Amish to be solid in their faith, Lillian decided it might be best to keep her suspicions about God to herself around her grandparents.

"Guess I better get moving and find out how far 'down yonder a spell' really is." She jumped off the suitcase, gave it a heave-ho, and started back down the paved road, gazing to either side where the acreage stretched as far as she could see. The sun pressing down on the horizon left her a tad worried about how much farther the farm was.

———

"Whoa, boy!" Samuel yelled to his horse. The animal slowed his pace to a gentle trot, bringing the buggy alongside an *Englisch*

woman cumbersomely toting a bright-red suitcase. She was minus
a shoe . . . if you called a flat-bottom sole with two small straps a
shoe. Certainly not a good walking instrument.

"Can I offer you a ride?" He pulled back on the reins and
came to a complete halt, as did the small-framed woman. When
she turned, he was met by radiant green eyes in a delicate face.
Delicate, that is, until she grimaced and blew a tendril of hair out
of her face.

Then she smiled, and her face transformed, lighting up like
the morning sun. He was momentarily struck dumb.

It didn't matter. The woman was focused on his horse. Deserting
her suitcase on the side of the road, she stumbled over to Pete
and reached out to stroke his nose without so much as a "May I?"
Thankfully, Pete was a gentle giant.

"He's beautiful," she said, glancing briefly in Samuel's direction, eyes sparkling.

He cleared his throat. "*Ya.* And a fine work horse too."

What an interesting woman this was. Unafraid. And beautiful, he had to admit. He watched as her long brown hair danced
in the wind, framing her face in layers. She wore no makeup
and seemed lacking in the traditional *Englisch* look, although her
brightly colored blouse and calf-length breeches certainly gave
her away. A tourist, most likely. But a tourist walking alone down
Blackhorse Road?

The woman's mouth curved upward in delight as she cooed
over Pete. The horse gently snorted, nudged her, and she laughed
heartily, her head thrown back. It was a thoroughly enchanting
scene.

Suddenly uncomfortable at his thoughts, he straightened

and coughed. It was enough to bring the woman's attention back to him.

"I would love a ride!" With a final kiss on the old horse's muzzle, she went back for her suitcase. "Where should I put this?"

"*Ach*, my manners." Samuel jumped out of the buggy and made his way to the woman. "Let me." He took the suitcase from her, quite surprised at how heavy the small bundle was. After stowing it behind the double seat, he offered his hand to assist her into the buggy.

"Thank you." Now she was studying him . . . seemingly from head to toe. At her open glance, he felt a flush tint his cheeks.

"I'm Samuel Stoltzfus," he said, extending his hand but avoiding her questioning eyes.

"I'm Lillian Miller."

Her hands were certainly that of an *Englisch* woman, soft and void of a hard day's work. The Plain women in Lancaster County tilled gardens, shelled peas, kneaded bread, and a host of other necessary chores uncommon to *Englisch* women from the city. City women's hands were not only smooth and manicured, but pleasing to the touch.

Returning to his seat, he started up the buggy again. The woman was obviously tired and happy to be resting; with a slight groan she stretched her legs out. He found his eyes wandering her way and silently remonstrated himself.

"Where are you from, Lillian? Or, more important, where are you going?"

"I'm from Houston."

"*Ya*, Texas," he said, slightly surprised. They didn't usually get

Texans walking the roads out here. "Lots of farms in Texas. What brings you to Lancaster County, Pennsylvania?"

"I'm coming to stay with my grandparents for a while." She smiled. "They're Amish."

Amish? He was once more at a loss for words. Not to worry— the *Englisch* woman wasn't.

"Actually, I guess I'm Amish too," she added.

Discreetly glancing at her *Englisch* clothes, he wondered how that could be so.

"My grandparents are Irma Rose and Jonas Miller. I'll be staying with them for a while." She looked his way as if waiting for a response that never came. "I'd like to adapt myself to the Amish ways. I need a peaceful, calm lifestyle away from the city. Anyway, I've decided to be Amish for a while."

Samuel had been trying to connect this vivacious outsider with the staunch Irma Rose and Jonas he knew, but these words jostled him out of his musings. "You'd like to be Amish for a *while?*"

"Yes. Although I don't plan to wear one of those dark-colored dresses or white caps like the women I saw strolling by earlier."

In spite of himself, Samuel chuckled. "Do you even know what being Amish means?" He didn't mean the remark as harshly as it sounded.

Lillian slanted her eyes in his direction, as if slightly offended.

Unexpectedly, the buggy wheel hit a rut. With an *oomph*, his new friend bounced in her seat. She was a tiny little thing. Luckily, she didn't catapult right off the seat and onto the pavement.

"Yikes!" she said when her behind returned to the seat. And then she giggled. As Pete's ears swiveled back to catch the commotion, Samuel couldn't help but grin. The woman's enthusiasm was contagious.

He decided to drop the subject. He knew Irma Rose and Jonas well enough to figure they'd set her right about being Amish and what it really meant. Samuel reckoned they'd have their hands full with their granddaughter.

As Samuel righted the buggy, he asked, "When is the last time you saw your grandparents?" He hadn't even known Irma Rose and Jonas had a granddaughter.

"When I was ten. Seventeen years ago. It was the first time I saw snow. *Real* snow." Her eyes twinkled from the memory. "Anyway, I know things will be different from what I'm used to. But I can live without television. There's too much bad news on TV anyway. And I know Amish women cook a lot. I'm a great cook." She shrugged. "I'm a hard worker in general. I know Amish get up early and go to bed early. I know they work hard during the day. And if that's what it takes to feel peaceful and calm . . . I'm in!"

Samuel found her enthusiasm charming, no matter how misdirected it was. "Lillian, I'm sure Irma Rose and Jonas will appreciate you helping with household duties, but it will take more than chores and giving up worldly things to provide you with the peacefulness you're lookin' for."

"Well, it's a start," she said, sounding optimistic.

As for that . . . who was he to argue?

Lillian remembered the Christmas visit with her grandparents at their farm, especially the snow. Unlike the icy mix of sludge found rarely in her hometown state, snow in Lancaster County glistened with a tranquil purity. Almost two decades later, she could still recall the towering cedar trees blanketed in white and ice skating on the crystalline pond in her mother's old ice skates.

There were few presents. She remembered that. And while she recollected her grandparents as warm and loving, she also remembered the tension between them and her mother. Her grandfather had kept the mood festive, suggested the ice-skating, and seemed to make it his mission for Lillian to have a good time—even carting her to town and back in his gray, horse-drawn buggy. It had been the highlight of her trip.

"I remember liking the way my grandparents talked," she recalled to Samuel. "I didn't understand a lot of things they said. Things like '*Outen* the lights until sunrise when we'll *redd-up* the house.' And 'It wonders me if it will make wet tomorrow.' Mom translated those to mean *'Turn out the lights until in the morning when we'll clean up the house'* and *'I wonder if it will rain tomorrow.'*"

"That would be right," Samuel said.

Grandma and Grandpa both spoke another language she'd later found out was *Pennsylvania Deitsch*. Lots of times they would comingle their language with English. "*Danki, Sarah Jane, for bringing our little* kinskind *for a visit*," her grandfather told her mother that Christmas. To which Sarah Jane Miller forced a smile and nodded.

"*Grandma, why are you and Grandpa wearing those costumes?*" Lillian recalled asking her grandparents.

Grandpa had just laughed and said, "*It is our faith, my* kinskind.

We wear these plain clothes to encourage humility and separation from the world."

At ten, Lillian had little understanding of what that signified. Except somewhere in the translation she knew it meant they couldn't have a television or a phone. Several times after their one and only trip, Lillian had asked her mother if she could call her grandparents. Mom reminded her that Grandpa and Grandma did not allow phones at their house.

"Evidently, my grandparents came to Houston a couple of times before our visit at Christmas, but I don't remember," she told Samuel. "That Christmas was my last trip to Lancaster County and the last time I saw my grandparents. Until now."

"I reckon Irma Rose and Jonas are really looking forward to seeing you."

"I hope so."

Lillian tried to keep her gaze focused on the road in front of her. But her eyes kept involuntarily trailing to her left. Samuel Stoltzfus was as handsome a man as she had ever seen in the city. His plain clothes did little to mask his solid build and appealing smile each time she glanced in his direction. But it was his piercing blue eyes Lillian couldn't seem to draw away from.

"So, how long have you been married?" *Nosy, nosy.* The astonished look on his face confirmed her worry. She was crossing the line. "I'm sorry. I just noticed that you have the customary beard following marriage." She'd done her research before arriving here. "And . . . I was just . . . curious." *And curious why? He's Amish, for heaven's sake.*

"I'm not married. I'm widowed."

"Oh," she said softly, thinking how young his wife must have been when she died. " I'm so sorry. When did your wife die?"

"*Mei fraa*, Rachel, passed almost two years ago," he answered without looking her way.

"Again, I'm so sorry."

Samuel continued to stare at the road ahead. "It was God's will."

There was no sadness or regret in his tone. Just fact. Lillian knew she should leave it alone, but . . . "I'm sure you miss her very much."

He didn't glance her way. "There's Irma Rose and Jonas's farm," he said, pointing to their right. "I better take you right up to the house." He coaxed Pete down a long dirt drive leading from the road to the white farmhouse.

"Oh, you don't have to do that. I can walk." She wondered if Samuel Stoltzfus was ready to be rid of her.

His eyebrows edged upward beneath his dark bangs and he glanced at her shoeless foot.

Point taken. "A ride to the house would be great."

As Pete trotted down the dirt driveway toward the farmhouse, reality sank in. This would be her new home for the summer—or however long it took to accomplish her goal. At first glance, every-thing seemed lovely. Neatly mowed, prodigious fields were on either side of the lane, and the white fencing in good repair. But unlike the farms she passed on the way, there were no signs of new life planted. It wasn't until they drew closer to the farmhouse that she spotted a small garden off to her left enclosed by a wire-mesh fence. Parallel rows of greenery indicated vegetables would be forthcoming.

There was a large barn off to her left, the paint weathered and chipping. Another smaller barn to her right also was in need of a fresh paint job. She recalled the barns they had passed on her journey down Black Horse Road. Most were a bright crimson color.

The white farmhouse appeared freshly painted, but with flowerbeds absent of flowers or shrubs. They must have been beautiful at one time. But now they—and the rest of the yard—lent an air of neglect to the farm.

A wraparound porch with two rockers looked inviting. But while the idea of curling up with a good book in one of the rockers was appealing, Lillian knew it was the inside of the house and its inhabitants she feared most. Her grandma had seemed pleasant enough on the phone, but what if she and her grandfather were too set in their ways to make room for her? And what if she couldn't adjust to their ways? No electricity meant no hair dryer, curling iron, or other modern conveniences she considered necessities. How would she charge her cell phone? And she couldn't imagine a summer without air conditioning.

Grimacing as the thoughts rattled around her head, she reminded herself why she'd come. She'd had a month to consider all of these factors. She thought she had. But as her fantasy of leaving everything behind for *this* became absolute, her tummy twirled with uncertainty.

She was still attempting to envision her new way of life when Samuel brought Pete up next to a gray buggy parked on one side of the house. Samuel moved quickly to get her suitcase from behind the seat and extended his hand to help her out of the buggy. Towering over her, he promptly released her fingers.

"Thank you for the ride. Maybe I will see you again." She

could only hope. But his lack of response as he quickly jumped back in the carriage left her wondering.

Lillian waved good-bye and watched until horse, buggy, and man were back on the paved road. She knew she was stalling. Her grandparents would be strangers to her, and she would be a stranger to them. Yet they had encouraged her to come and stay with them. *"For as long as you like,"* her grandmother had said.

Striving to cast her worries aside, she turned around, picked up her suitcase, and headed up the walk toward what would be her new home . . . for a while.

2

"The boppli is here!" Jonas exclaimed. He closed the window blinds and staggered to the door to welcome their granddaughter.

"She's hardly a *baby*, Jonas. She's a grown woman." Despite her confident tone, Irma Rose fiddled with her apron strings as she followed her husband.

"Irma Rose, there's no need to look so *naerfich*. I reckon things will be just fine. The Good Lord will see to it." Jonas winked at her as he reached for the doorknob.

"I can't help but be nervous, Jonas. We don't know this girl," she whispered.

Jonas flung the door open and walked onto the front porch. Irma Rose followed her husband and noticed immediately that the young woman before them looked nervous as well. But, as was his way, Jonas plowed through the tension by making a joke.

"Irma Rose, this poor girl must have walked here all the way from Houston, Texas," he teased, his eyes narrowing in on his granddaughter's shoeless foot. "First thing to do is get her some proper walking shoes."

Irma Rose shook her head at Jonas as she scooted past him and toward the stranger in her front yard. Jonas didn't move. Hunched over, he kept his hands on his hips and continued studying the girl's feet with a wide smile.

"Welcome, Lilly," Irma Rose said. She embraced her grand-daughter for the first time in seventeen years.

"Lillian," the young woman said as she awkwardly returned the hug. "I go by *Lillian* now."

"Oh, I'm sorry. We called you Lilly when you were young and assumed . . ."

"It's okay. I just grew out of 'Lilly.'"

"Well, Lillian—" Irma Rose began. Jonas interrupted her.

"I like *Lilly*. I am going to call you Lilly," he said firmly, with a boyish grin still plastered from ear to ear.

"Now, Jonas, if she prefers to be called *Lillian* . . ."

"No. I like *Lilly* better," her husband insisted. "Now, Lilly, let's get you into the house. We've got warm brownies and lemonade ready for you."

"Jonas!" Irma Rose tried to intercede. She often wondered if her husband's various medications had caused his already strong personality to escalate over the past few months. Sometimes he seemed to swing whatever way the wind was blowing and other days . . . Well, it was either his way or nobody's way. Today was clearly the latter.

"Brownies and lemonade sound great," Lillian said. She shot Irma Rose a soft look, assuring her Jonas's persistent ways didn't offend her.

Irma Rose watched Jonas struggle to tote the bright-red suit-case up the porch steps. She knew better than to assist him. His determined look left no question that he wanted to appear as much a man as he had ever been to his granddaughter. Irma Rose knew he'd pay for it later.

"Whatcha got in this thing . . . bricks?" he asked as he maneuvered through the front door ahead of the women.

Irma Rose studied the suitcase with curiosity.

"Mostly books," Lillian said, grabbing the suitcase from Jonas. "I like to read. I was an English teacher for several years . . . until recently."

Irma Rose considered asking Lillian what *"until recently"* meant, but stopped short, sensing regret in her granddaughter's tone. Perhaps Lillian had been fired from her job and had nowhere else to go. Or some other such embarrassing situation.

Lillian took in her surroundings and was pleasantly surprised. Not remembering much from her last visit, she'd built up an image in her mind. But the room was not as sparse as she'd envisioned. Dark-green blinds that were drawn halfway up covered the windows, and the whitewash walls were bare. But lovely furniture was placed throughout the room, including two high-back rockers with blue cushions, an oak sideboard and matching hutch, and a shelf that held four lanterns. Intertwined between the lanterns was a leafy ivy plant that was draped across the length of the shelf. There was even a worn brown recliner in the corner. No television, of course. The aroma of freshly baked goods lent even more warmth to the room.

Following her grandparents into the kitchen, she noticed the same dark-green blinds covering the windows. Unlike the den, there was definitely a focal point in this room: the wood-burning stove nestled against the far wall, the keeper of the fabulous smells permeating throughout the house. This room was more of a step back in time.

"Welcome to our home, Lilly," her grandfather said, beaming. She couldn't help but smile at his gleeful energy. Her grandmother was another story. Irma Rose seemed guarded and hesitant. Even her hug felt strained. Lillian knew she herself was partly to blame for the tension.

"Thank you for having me." She glanced at the pan of brownies atop the stove. Normally, she would shy away from such caloric luxuries, especially since she'd already blown it for the day with the big cinnamon roll she wolfed down earlier. But her grandmother offered her the biggest brownie in the pan. She accepted, deciding the walk had evened out the caloric playing field again.

"Lillian, Jonas and I already ate supper. We eat at four-thirty. But I saved you some chicken and mashed potatoes."

As her grandmother headed toward the refrigerator, Lillian shook her head while trying to quickly swallow the above-average bite of brownie. "No, no," she said, gulping the last of the warm dessert down. "This brownie is fine for me."

"I should have offered you some supper, I suppose, before brownies," her grandmother said, sounding regretful. She returned to one of the long wooden benches facing Lillian.

"Propane gas, Lilly," her grandfather belted out, seeing her eyes go to the gas bottle next to the refrigerator. "We use propane. No electricity. No connection of wires to the outside world."

"Oh." Lillian glanced upward at the gas lantern hanging above the table.

"We have an indoor bathroom," her grandmother added. "In case you were wondering."

"Yes, I remember that." The old outhouse was still outside, but she remembered indoor plumbing from her last visit.

"How did you get here, after your plane flight and train ride?"

Lillian recalled her journey with fondness. "I took a bus to Paradise and then Samuel Stoltzfus brought me in his buggy."

It was hard to miss the look of bewilderment on both their faces.

"Really?" her grandmother asked, her eyes lighting up with interest.

Lillian shrugged. "I guess he took pity on me when he saw me walking down the road with only one shoe on. I must have looked a mess. But the Amish boy in town said this farm was 'down yonder a spell.' Uh, it was considerably farther than I thought."

"Samuel Stoltzfus is a *gut* man," her grandma said. "He was a fine husband. His son works here in the afternoon on most days. Now that school is out, he's able to put in a few more hours. He chops wood, mows . . . the things Jonas and I can't get to anymore."

"That's a shame about his wife." Lillian took a sip of her lemonade.

"You talked about Rachel?" Grandma seemed surprised.

"Not much."

"It was God's will," her grandfather said softly.

"I guess." Lillian said and got questioning looks from both her grandparents. It didn't seem like God's will to take a man's wife at such a young age. "She must have been young. How'd she die?"

"The cancer got her, just like it's gonna get me," Grandpa said matter-of-factly and seemingly with no bitterness.

"Maybe not," Lillian said, not looking at him. She knew her grandfather had bone cancer and that it was a painful way to go. Grandma had mentioned the cancer in her last letter to Mom. The thought of anyone going through that kind of agony bothered her immensely.

"God has blessed me with a *gut* woman in Irma Rose. It's God's will that she will have to bury me first."

"Now, Jonas, you don't know that."

"She's right, Grandpa. They come out with new treatments all the time for cancer patients." Surely her grandpa would be open to every available option.

It felt strange to call her grandfather "Grandpa," but what else should she call him? That's what she'd called him when she was ten. The look on his face told her that he picked up on it and was pleased.

It seemed even stranger to call her grandmother "Grandma." Lillian felt sure Grandma had some strong reservations about her being here. And that was fair. Lillian had her own strong reservations about being here. Her worldly ways were as foreign to them as the lantern dangling above the table was to her.

It was a tiny bedroom, and Lillian slept like a rock. She probably would have kept sleeping if her cell phone hadn't started ringing. She peeled back the quilt on her bed and reached for the phone atop the nightstand.

"Hello."

"Are you okay? I didn't hear from you." The connection was a bit crackly, but adequate.

"Hi, Mom. I didn't know I was supposed to check in."

"How is your grandpa?" Mom went on, ignoring Lillian's irritated tone.

"He seems okay. He looks a lot older than Grandma, who by the way seems okay too."

"Well, I still can't imagine why you would want to go and live there, Lillian. You will never make it in their world. I'm staying with Paul, and he said you're welcome to come stay here."

"Mom! Why would you do that? Paul treated you like dirt when you were dating him before!" Lillian sat up and pushed back tangled strands of hair. "Why do you keep choosing the wrong men?" Wondering if this wasn't the pot calling the kettle black, she was determined to learn from her mistake with Rickie.

"Lillian, things are different now."

"They're always *different*, Mom."

"Just come home."

"I don't have a home, Mom."

"I will get you back all the money I borrowed, Lillian. I promise. Then you can start fresh somewhere. Although I think it was a mistake leaving Rickie. He took such good care of you."

Lillian threw herself across the bed in disgust. *If you only knew.* "Why don't you just come here, Mom? Spend some time with your parents and find some peace." She knew it was a safe request. Her mother would never come, nor did she want her to.

"Is that what you're doing, Lillian? Looking for *peace*?"

Lillian bristled. "I don't know what I'm looking for, Mom. I just needed to get away, and I'm broke."

"Well, I hope you find what you're looking for."

"I wish you meant that."

"You're my daughter. Of course I mean that. But just remember that you have options. You can always come and stay with Paul and me and—"

"Good-bye, Mother. I'll talk to you later." Hanging up on her was better than enduring a full-blown fight. It was too early in the morning. She pulled the quilt over her head and buried her face in the pillow.

"Shame on you, Irma Rose," Jonas whispered with a chuckle as he passed her in the hallway outside Lillian's room. "That looks like eavesdropping to me."

"I was just wondering if the child was still alive. It's nearly seven o'clock. She missed breakfast hours ago. And she's either talkin' to herself or she's on a portable telephone." She continued to press her ear against the door.

"I'm going to hope it's a mobile telephone," Jonas said jokingly, then paused. "Give her some time, Irma Rose. I think our Lilly has had a hard life. God sent her to us for a reason. You can't expect her to give up all her worldly possessions overnight."

"*Ya*, I know. I really do, Jonas. But she said in her letter that she wanted to find peace in her life. If she meant that, I'd think she might try to live our ways while she's here. You're probably right, though. It's going to take her some time."

As Jonah kissed her on the cheek and headed down the hallway toward the bathroom, Irma Rose stood there trying to shift doubt to hope. Just because Sarah Jane wasn't happy here didn't mean Lillian couldn't be.

"Is that Samuel's son outside?" Lillian asked her grandma as she sat at the kitchen table eating a bowl of oatmeal. The blinds were open, and she could see the boy chopping wood off to the side of the barn. She wished her grandfather would join them. Felt like less tension when he was around.

"*Ya.* He's been a huge help ever since Jonas got down." Her grandma walked to the window and watched the boy. "He's a fine lad."

"His father seems like a nice man too."

"*Ya.* He's been a good father to the boy since his *mamm* died."

Lillian saw her grandma taking note of her attire. Blue jeans and a white T-shirt. She'd purposely not packed any of her flashier clothes and had thought her attire plain enough, but Grandma seemed to have her nose turned up a tad.

"I hung some dresses on the peg in your room. I thought they might be more appropriate for our community."

Lillian had seen the dresses the night before. She couldn't help but cringe at the thought of having to wear them and wondered if Grandma intended her to do so. Evidently. Plain dark-colored dresses that would hit her about mid-calf. *Ugh.* She was more comfortable in her own traditional attire. Plus, blue jeans seemed much more practical for farm life. Although maybe Grandma would be embarrassed to introduce her to the community dressed in blue jeans? Might bring forth questions Grandma didn't want to field. She'd think about it, but for now she decided it best to change the subject.

"I'm sorry I slept so late this morning. I know you get up early

and we have lots of chores to do. I don't want you to think I'll
do this every morning—sleep late. I was just really tired from
the trip. But I'm a pretty good cook if you'd like for me to cook
supper tonight."

Grandma straightened the black apron atop her dark-brown
dress and turned to face Lillian. Her sheer exhaustion was apparent, along with doubt Lillian could do the job. "Well, I wouldn't
know how to act if I was given a break in the kitchen." She
paused and considered the idea. Then shook her head. "It's a mite
challenging to cook on a wood-burning stove. And Jonas likes to
have things a certain way. I don't know . . ."

"I'll be glad to give it a shot, Grandma. Cooking is the one thing
Mom did really well, and I learned early on how to prepare a meal.
You said you and Grandpa eat at four thirty. I can have it ready."

"Your *mamm* is a *gut* cook?"

Lillian sensed her need for a *yes*. "She is. She said she learned
from you."

Grandma's face flooded with emotion. "And she taught you to
cook . . . like *we* do?"

"I suppose I didn't know it at the time, but yes. I made my
first shoofly pie when I was nine. And I know how to make apple
butter." Lillian was about to tell her grandma those types of
delicacies were few and far between, but when she saw the elated
look on her grandmother's face, she held her tongue.

"There are a few meats in the freezer above the refrigerator.
We keep the bulk of our meats in a freezer at Kauffman's Market
in town. And there's plenty of canned goods in the basement.
You'll see them long 'bout the far side on some shelves. If you
need anything extra, I—"

"I'm sure I can find everything. I just might need you to show me a little bit about cooking on this woodstove." Lillian studied the ancient piece of equipment. "Take a break, Grandma. Let me help you some while I'm here."

Lillian washed her cereal bowl, thinking how worn out her grandma looked. Twice she'd heard her up during the night with her grandpa. It sounded like he was vomiting. She'd thought about going to see if she could help, but her grandpa seemed like such a proud man, and she didn't want to embarrass him.

"I think I'll go introduce myself to David," Lillian said as she dried her hands on the dish towel. She headed toward the door, then impulsively turned around. "Grandma, is Grandpa okay this morning?"

"Your *daadi* had a bad night. He ate a little breakfast and went back to bed."

"What about chemotherapy? Would that help him?"

"He's chosen not to have any such thing."

"If it's an option, did he consider it?"

"He's on medications for the pain. Jonas says it's God's will and that he will ride it out at home, as best he can."

"Oh," Lillian said. She wanted to argue that God—if there was a God—would want him to fight. But it seemed she and her grandmother might be moving in a positive direction amid very different worlds. Offering to prepare supper earned her some points. She hated to rock the boat, especially about God.

"You start work early," Lillian said when she walked up behind the boy busily chopping wood. The sun was still working its way upward, and dewy droplets speckled Lillian's tennis shoes as she walked across the freshly cut yard. "I'm Lillian."

David removed the oversized glove on his right hand and extended it. "Nice to meet you. I'm David."

As he removed his straw hat with his other hand in a polite gesture, David's traditional bangs fell forward and his bobbed haircut came into view, a lighter shade of brown than his father's. He had inherited Samuel's handsome square jaw and natural good looks.

"I'm Jonas and Irma Rose's granddaughter." Lillian moved toward the boy and shook his hand.

"*Ya*, I know," he said, smiling. He put his glove back on and motioned for her to step aside as he drew the axe back and swung at the log centered before him.

"Oh, they told you about me?"

"No, my *daed* did." He placed another log on the pile and prepared for another split.

Lillian waited for him to swing the axe before she spoke. "Really? So, your dad mentioned me?"

"*Ya*."

David looked about eleven or twelve years old. Old enough to interpret any interest she might have in his father. She'd have to be careful. "Did he tell you I came here all the way from Texas?"

His expression shifted to contemplative, and his tone took on a hint of mischief. "He said you were real pretty, like my *mamm*." Grinning, he heaved another log on the pile.

The compliment made her stomach flip. "I'm sorry about your mother," she said softly.

"It was God's will."

She grimaced, thankful the boy's back was to her. How could they all accept tragedy as simply being *anyone's* will? His mother must have been in her twenties when she died of cancer. How horrible to be taken from your husband and child at such a young age, whatever the motivation of a suspected Higher Being.

Knowing it was best to leave it alone, she said, "Well, I just wanted to come and introduce myself. I'm sure I'll be seeing you around."

David nodded and tipped his hat in her direction.

Samuel finished plowing for the day and headed to the house to clean up before picking up David. He wondered if his son had met Irma Rose and Jonas's granddaughter. He wondered how her first day had gone without the modern conveniences she was used to.

As he bathed, thoughts of the *Englisch* woman filled his mind. Reaching for the bar of soap, he pondered what would bring an outsider into their world. To be *Amish for a while*, she'd said. Interesting. Maybe trouble had found her. The *Englisch* Samuel knew always seemed to seek out Amish ways when they were in trouble. Although her spirited laugh led him to believe the woman didn't have nearly a care in the world.

It had been a long time since he'd laughed.

Samuel knew it was always best to keep a comfortable distance from the *Englischers*. And practicing separation from the rest of the world came easy to him . . . most of the time.

Lillian was glad she'd offered to prepare supper that evening, but she was exhausted from the daily chores that Grandma evidently struggled with every day. Normally a night owl, Lillian felt sure she'd hit the bed by sunset. Otherwise, she'd never make it up by four-thirty to start all over again. Her face twisted in disbelief that she hadn't thought out more carefully her choice to come here. And this was only day one.

But given the day's events, preparing supper was the right thing to do. She had watched her grandma take numerous trips up and down the stairs to take care of her grandfather, patiently instructing Lillian as to the daily chores in between. The dark circles under her grandmother's eyes were testimonial to her exhaustion, but she never complained.

Grandma obviously enjoyed the hard work, taking pride as she instructed Lillian on how to use the treadle machine for sewing, how to fire up the gas-powered washing machine, the proper procedure for hanging clothes on the line, and which strawberries were ripe for picking in the garden. Grandma had also managed to knock out three loaves of homemade bread and bake a rhubarb pie while Lillian watched.

She'd said she didn't want to overwhelm Lillian with too much work on her first day. Surely she was kidding.

"I'm on a light load," her grandma had said earlier that afternoon. "I thank the Good Lord for sending us David to help with the outside chores. And we gave up our milk cows when Jonas got too sick for us to milk twice a day. And goes without sayin' that we don't harvest the fields anymore. We have a small garden and plenty of meat in the freezer. And the *gut* people in our district never let us go without."

Lillian was worrying what the next day would bring when Grandma offered up the information. "Tomorrow, we'll add some canning to the other chores, and we'll see 'bout picking some peas," she'd said merrily. "We'll start out slowly."

Forcing an enthusiastic smile to match her grandma's eagerness, Lillian wondered if she'd even make it to sunset this evening.

After locating a rump roast in the freezer, along with some potatoes and carrots, Lillian was now topping off the meal by preparing a salad, along with laying out some applesauce and jellies, which Grandma said was a necessary part of every meal. In between one of her many trips upstairs, Grandma had laid out one of the loaves of homemade bread on the table.

As the roast and vegetables simmered atop the wooden stove, Lillian wondered if coming here had been a bad idea—for several reasons. Evidently her grandfather was sicker than she suspected. Sickness made her uncomfortable. Cancer made her even more uncomfortable. People with cancer died. And death . . . well, death was something she hadn't come to terms with.

"Lillian, it sure does smell *gut* in here." Grandma had returned from another trip upstairs. Her hair was in the traditional bun beneath her white prayer *Kapp*, and several strands of gray had fallen forward.

"I hope you like it." She took a break from chopping the tomatoes for the salad and checked on the roast. "Grandpa's having a bad day, isn't he?"

Her grandma took a seat on the wooden bench and rested her

head in her hands. As if sensing Lillian's fears, she said, "*Ya*, he is. But they're not all bad days. Some days he does real *gut*. Then he gets down for a spell. Maybe tomorrow he'll be better."

Lillian didn't say anything. She was at a loss for words.

"Ah, there is Samuel to pick up the boy." Grandma nodded toward the window. The blind was open, and Lillian looked past the blooming begonias along the windowsill above the sink. She heard the clippity-clop of hooves and then Samuel directing Pete with a "Whoa, boy."

Foregoing her preparation of the salad, Lillian bolted toward the screen door, then turned back to face her grandma. "I thought maybe I'd invite Samuel and David for supper. Is that okay?"

Grandma's face scrolled into a questionable expression and Lillian feared she might be going to nix the idea, so she added, "Or, maybe, since Grandpa isn't feeling well today, it might not be a good day for . . ."

"I think that's a nice idea," her grandma interrupted. "I'll finish the salad. You go talk to Samuel and the boy."

"Great!" She flew out the door to catch Samuel before he carted David away.

Irma Rose dragged her tired body off the bench and started slicing the tomatoes. She peered out the window as Lillian jetted off toward Samuel and David. The glow in the girl's eyes had been unmistakable at the mention of Samuel's name. Now, her brow furrowing, Irma Rose watched her granddaughter near Samuel. Widowers Samuel's age were rare in their Old Order district. Choosing not to remarry by now was even rarer. It had been almost two years since Rachel's passing. Samuel should have already found a good Amish woman and remarried. That's the way it was done—to move on as quickly as possible. She'd hate to see a good man like Samuel get distracted.

Tending to a farm and raising a child was more than a full-time job. Samuel needed a good woman. An *Amish* woman. But as she watched her *Englisch* granddaughter through the window, laughing with Samuel and David, pangs of worry gnawed at her insides.

Samuel looked distracted indeed.

3

SAMUEL HEARD THE SCREEN DOOR OF THE FARMHOUSE slam and looked up to see Lillian darting across the yard toward them. He helped David stack the last of the chopped firewood, but his eyes remained on the *Englisch* woman.

"She's real pretty, Pop. Just like you said."

Samuel glanced over at his son, who was also watching the approaching woman. "And *she's* very different from us, David."

"And *we're* different from her," David said shrugging. "So?"

Samuel didn't say anything but waved at Lillian as she drew nearer.

"Hello!" she called out, catching her breath as she came to a stop before them. "I thought you both might like to stay for supper. I cooked a roast."

The woman was clearly proud of her work in the kitchen, and her bubbly spirit made the offer tempting. He and the boy hadn't eaten roast in a long time.

"Roast sounds real *gut*," he said. He put a hand on David's shoulder. "Are Jonas and Irma Rose up for it?"

"Grandma said you are both welcome."

"What do you think, David?" Samuel asked.

36

"Are you kidding me? That'd be a real treat. *Danki*, Ms. Lillian!"

"Go get cleaned up, David." Samuel motioned David toward the watering pump near the barn.

"How old is David?" she asked.

"He'll be twelve come August." Samuel started toward the farmhouse.

Lillian's face registered a variety of questioning expressions, and he assumed she must be curious about the Amish ways.

"I suppose he has a few years, then, before his *rumschpringe*," she said confidently, as if to impress him with her Pennsylvania Deitsch. Although . . . she was looking a bit too smug . . .

"What's a *rumschpringe*?" he asked.

Her face went blank. "Oh, I'm sorry. Maybe I pronounced it wrong or got it confused with something else. I thought it was when an Amish person turned sixteen and ventured out to explore the world, leading up to courtship."

She looked so confused, but he was having fun. He nodded thoughtfully. "Hmm, never heard of it."

As they neared the front porch, she turned toward him and planted her hands firmly on her hips. "Well, I could have sworn that's what *rumschpringe* was and—"

She caught sight of his face. "Are you messing with me, Samuel Stoltzfus?"

At her expression, he couldn't help but laugh.

"Shame on you," she fussed. But her eyes twinkled.

"I might be Plain, Lillian, but I do have a sense of humor, no?" He opened the door and motioned her inside ahead of him, grinning all the while.

Lillian placed the platter of roast surrounded by potatoes and carrots on the table. Grandma brought the salad and some chowchow. Once they were all seated—all but Grandpa—Lillian enthusiastically motioned toward the food, "Dig in!" She was anxious to see how everyone liked the meal.

All three of them stared blankly at her.

"Did I forget something?" She didn't think so.

With a significant look, her grandmother bowed her head, followed by Samuel and David. *Ouch.* Chagrined, she lowered her own head as Grandma blessed the food.

Following the prayer, Samuel seemed to sense her embarrassment and gallantly began a conversation. "David, it's been a while since we've had such a fine meal laid before us." He winked at Lillian. *Or did he?* It was quick, but she sure thought it was a wink. Her stomach flipped again. She could feel a blush building in her cheeks.

"*Ya,* Ms. Lillian, this is a fine meal," David said, stuffing a bite of potatoes in his mouth.

"Thank you, David. I wish my grandpa was well enough to join us, but he—"

They all heard a loud, gruff voice at the bottom of the stairs. "The smell of *gut* food and the promise of *gut* company ain't gonna keep me away."

"Jonas, I declare," Grandma reprimanded. "You should have let me help you down those stairs."

Giving her an incredulous look, he asked, "What for?" When he reached the kitchen, he rubbed his forehead and looked hard at Lillian and then at Samuel. "What have we here?"

Feeling the need to defend her invitation, Lillian began rambling like a crazy person. "I, uh, invited Samuel and David for supper. David has been working so hard, and I figured Samuel probably worked hard all day too. And . . . and . . . maybe a good meal would be good for both of them. And I haven't had anyone to cook for in such a long time. And, uh, Grandma looked tired. And, by gosh . . . I don't know much about sewing, working in a garden, or much of the Amish ways . . . but I can cook!"

Lillian drew in a breath and held it. She wanted to crawl in a hole. Forks halted midway to mouths. No one was moving or talking. They were all just staring at her as if she was nuts. Maybe she was.

Grandpa's tired face rolled into the biggest smile Lillian had ever seen. "I *meant* . . . what have we *here*? What's for supper?"

Samuel and David sat motionless. Lillian glanced at her grandma, pleading for assistance.

"Lillian prepared supper, Jonas. She cooked a roast with potatoes and carrots."

"Our Lilly can cook?" Grandpa took a seat at the chair on the other end of the oblong table, across from Grandma.

"She's a *gut* cook too," Samuel said.

"*Danki*," Lillian said sheepishly.

"*Gut!* You're learning the *Deitsch wege*," Grandpa said. He helped himself to a slice of roast. "I told you, Irma Rose. The girl will come around to our ways in no time."

Lillian suspected her grandma doubted any type of transformation was in the works.

A distant trill sounded. *Oh, crud!* There couldn't have been a worse time for her cell phone to start ringing. Maybe no one had noticed.

"Is that a telephone I hear?" David asked, glancing toward the stairway.

"It's probably Mom." Lillian said sheepishly as the phone continued to ring. She hoped it was Mom and not Rickie. Mom being the lesser of the two evils. "I'll get it later."

Her grandmother looked up at her and started to say something, then hesitated. Lillian assumed Grandma was about to reprimand her for having the phone in the house, but evidently that wasn't what was on Grandma's mind.

"How is . . . um . . . how is your *mamm?*" Grandma looked back at her plate and shuffled her food around a bit.

"Same as always," Lillian said, knowing it was an undignified response. "I mean, she's fine."

Grandma nodded. An awkward silence followed. Everyone ate.

It wasn't long, though, before Grandpa spoke up. "So how was your first day, Lilly?"

"Well, I slept too late. But otherwise I tried to help out the best I could."

"Lillian had a *gut* first day. Cooking supper was a mighty big help too." Grandma smiled in her direction as she took a bite of carrots. "And the meal is delicious."

"*Appeditlich* it is!" Grandpa said. "But tomorrow maybe you should go to the neighboring town of Intercourse. There is lots to see in town, and you can pick me up some of that special root beer I like."

"Sure, that'd be great."

Lillian looked up to catch Samuel gazing in her direction. Then felt another set of eyes on both of them. She shot a look in Grandpa's direction. He was grinning like a fat cat.

"Maybe Samuel can show you around? It's a far piece to town and I don't think you'd better be headin' off in the buggy so soon." He lifted his chin slightly, putting the question to Samuel.

It was hard to miss the look Grandma fired in her husband's direction. But before she could say anything, Samuel stepped up to the plate.

"I'd be happy to show Lillian around."

Irma Rose began clearing the dishes, watching Samuel and David thank Lillian for the meal and say their good-byes. She feared trouble was brewing—a concern that intensified as she watched Lillian head out the door with them toward Samuel's buggy.

While the thought of Samuel and their granddaughter developing a courtship was a farfetched notion, stranger things had happened in their district over the years. And now, thanks to her husband, a date was set for the following afternoon. She couldn't help but think of what the Good Book said: "Be ye not unequally yoked together with unbelievers: for what fellowship hath righteousness with unrighteousness? and what communion hath light with darkness?"

Someone would have to be pretty thick to miss the looks going on between Lillian and Samuel. They'd taken a bit of a fancy to each other. She would like nothing better than to see Samuel settle down with a good woman and for Lillian to settle down with a good Amish man and become part of their community. But such things just didn't happen. As much as she'd like the chance to make up for her failures with Sarah Jane, she knew anything more than a friendship between Samuel and Lillian was wrong. They were just too different. She'd need to keep a close eye on this and pray about it.

Lillian watched Samuel and David climb into the box-shaped gray buggy, which was unlike the topless two-seater she'd ridden in with Samuel the day before. What was it about Samuel that piqued her interest so? The fact that he was Amish and mysterious to her way of life, or the fact that she was wildly attracted to him?

Not that it mattered much either way. She planned to be Amish to some extent—to avoid the use of modern conveniences, work hard, and find some sort of peace in her mixed-up mind. A quiet lifestyle far away from Rickie and her mother, void of the complications of the city, would bring her peace. She'd just wait for it to come. In the meantime, having a new Amish friend would be nice. But nothing more than that.

"See you at four-thirty tomorrow?" Lillian asked, reaffirming their plans for Samuel to pick her up the following day.

"What about me?"

"You can come too," Lillian said quickly, thinking it would seem less like a *date* with David along. She glanced at Samuel.

"David, you have evening chores to do." Samuel settled into his seat and prepared to give Pete a flick of the reins.

"I promise I'll get them all done." The boy glanced at Lillian, his eyes coaxing her to come to his defense.

"We don't have to stay too long, Samuel, if David needs to get home to do his chores."

Looking defeated by the two of them, Samuel nodded.

"Then I will pick you and David up at four-thirty when he finishes his chores here. Since it's suppertime 'bout then, we can eat at the Family Cupboard Restaurant between Bird-In-Hand and Intercourse, if you want. Me and David treat ourselves every couple of weeks anyway. They sell the homemade root beer Jonas talked about near there. "

"Sounds great."

"*Danki* again for supper!" David yelled as Samuel turned the buggy around and headed down the dirt drive.

———

"I like Lillian, Pop," David told his father as they both walked up the stairs to bed.

Samuel started to tell his son he was sure Lillian was a fine woman but not to get any ideas.

David caught his hesitation. He nudged his father in the arm and snickered. "You like her, too, no?"

Samuel knew where his son was heading. "Of course I like her. She seems like a fine woman."

"No. I mean you *like* her," David said as he reached the door to his bedroom.

Might as well nip this right now, Samuel thought. "David, listen to me. The *Englisch* woman seems nice enough, but don't be gettin' any ideas. It's not like that. We're just gonna show her around town. She's Jonas and Irma Rose's *kinskind*, and it's a favor to them."

He could tell by the grin on David's face that he wasn't buying it. "She's funny. She's got lots of energy. And she sure is pretty."

"David, I already told you . . . Lillian is not like us. So get any crazy notions out of your head, boy." He tried to keep his tone firm. Last thing he needed was for his son to take a fancy to an *Englisch* woman. No question, the boy needed a mother. But while Levina and Sadie might not fit the bill, Lillian was certainly no better for him and his son. Maybe agreeing to show Lillian around town tomorrow was a mistake.

In an attempt to practice the Amish lifestyle and help Grandma more, Lillian got up and headed downstairs for breakfast at four-thirty. She cheated, though, setting the alarm on her cell phone. That was the one modern convenience she wasn't ready to give up—it was her only connection to the outside world. But the phone was slowly losing the charge.

She didn't hear Grandma get up with her grandpa during the night, and she was glad to see him joining them for breakfast.

"*Guder mariye*, Lilly," he belted. His jolliness so early in the morning warmed her heart. But then she saw Grandma's disappointment at her choice of attire. What was the problem with blue jeans and a T-shirt? *Scowl away*, she thought. *I'm not wearing one of those frumpy dresses on the peg upstairs.*

"Why doesn't my bread look as pretty as yours?" Lillian asked that afternoon. She and her grandma stood in the kitchen making bread.

"Maybe you didn't knead it enough."

"I sure *thought* I did. I pounded on that dough till my elbows couldn't take it anymore."

Grandma smiled. "I've had years of experience, Lillian. You'll get it with time. It's only your second day here and the first time to make bread, no?"

"Yeah, but I've always thought of myself as a pretty good cook." She glared down at the lopsided mound before her and frowned. "I'm sure disappointed in this bread. Might have to feed mine to the birds or something."

Grandma laughed. "The bread is fine, Lillian. I'm sure it tastes mighty *gut*." She patted Lillian on the arm.

"Where's Grandpa?"

"He's resting."

"Did he have a better night last night?"

"*Ya*, he did." Grandma popped another loaf into the wooden stove. "As I said, he has *gut* days and bad days."

"Grandpa's funny. He makes me laugh."

Her grandma closed the door on the stove and turned to face her. "You're a lot like him, Lillian. You have the fire in your belly, a zest for life."

Hmm. A compliment from the woman who seemed more than a little apprehensive she was there . . . with her blue jeans and cell phone in tow.

"Why did my mom leave, Grandma?"

Lillian wished immediately that she hadn't brought up the subject. The pain registered instantly on her grandma's face.

"Your mother was of age to choose whether or not to seek baptism into church membership. She chose to seek out the world." The tone in her voice indicated she'd rather not elaborate.

"But isn't that pretty rare?"

"'Train up a child in the way he should go: and when he is

old, he will not depart from it,'" her grandma said softly. "I suppose we failed."

"It was her choice, Grandma. That doesn't mean you failed." Lillian took a seat at the kitchen bench, hoping her grandma would take a break and do the same. But she stayed occupied at the kitchen counter, rinsing dishes and avoiding Lillian's gaze.

"Your mother wasn't shunned, Lillian. She could have come to visit any time." She paused. "But we saw very little of her over the years. I wrote letters to her, but . . ."

"Mom made a lot of bad choices over the years, Grandma. It's just hard for me to understand how she grew up in such a faithful home and then turned from it. She never even took me to church."

Her grandma bent slightly over the sink, shook her head, and reached for her chest as if Lillian had stabbed her in the heart.

"I mean, I went to church with friends when I was growing up. I just didn't have any formal religious education."

This wasn't going well. The woman remained hunched over the sink, and Lillian was afraid she might be crying. "Grandma?" she said softly. "I didn't mean to upset you. I just have a lot of questions where my mother is concerned."

Her grandma slowly turned to face her. "As do I," she said softly, forcing a half smile before changing the subject. "Now, let's get this next loaf of bread into the oven."

―――――

Lillian headed to the woodpile where David was diligently splitting wood.

"Your dad should be here soon." She walked up behind David, who was stacking the chopped logs.

The boy spun around. "Hi, Lillian." Breaking from the chore at hand, his eyes were dancing with curiosity.

"What is it?" she asked as he stared a hole through her.

The boy hesitated, tilting his head to one side, pushing back his straw hat. "What's it like out there?"

Oh, boy. This was probably an area she shouldn't be delving into. How much had his father told him? She didn't want to speak out of place.

She said the first thing that came to mind. "Complicated."

"Huh?"

"It's complicated *out there*." Lillian said, letting out an absent-minded sigh, briefly reflecting on her own life. "And people just aren't always nice to each other."

"Why?"

"That's a good question."

She could tell David's young mind was awhirl. But his next question caught her completely off guard. "Do you have a boy-friend?"

"No," she answered, thinking about Rickie and surprised he hadn't called her by now. Knowing her brief good-bye letter had probably left him reeling, it was a welcome relief he hadn't con-tacted her.

"Why aren't you married? You seem kinda old."

"I'm twenty-seven. Is that *old*?"

David chuckled. "I guess not too much. Do you want to get married?"

"I don't know." Lillian frowned. She had watched her mother

survive two bitter divorces, and the whole marriage thing had left a bad taste in her mouth. "Maybe."

David cocked his head to one side. His amazing blue eyes— just like his father's—squinted thoughtfully as he pondered a question he quite obviously wanted to ask her.

"What?" she asked, while wondering where Samuel was. It was after four-thirty by now.

"If Irma Rose and Jonas are Amish, why aren't you?"

"I'm *kinda* Amish," she said sheepishly. "I mean, my mother was raised Amish, and my grandparents are Amish." What a dumb answer, even in response to an eleven-year-old boy.

"I don't think you can be *kinda* Amish."

"I'm living on an Amish farm with my Amish grandparents. I gave up modern conveniences, and I even made bread today." No response from her young friend, who clearly needed more. "And I want to feel peace in my mind and in my heart."

He stared blankly at her. "Oh."

As he continued to study her, Lillian could tell there was more coming. "Why do you wear those boy breeches?"

Lillian glanced down at her blue jeans. "Well," she began, "I guess that's why I said I'm *kinda* Amish. I'm working on it . . . slowly."

"Oh."

Hoping that had satisfied him, she glanced down the dirt drive toward the road and looked at her watch. "Wonder where your dad is? It's almost five o'clock."

"I better get cleaned up." She watched while David stowed the axe near the woodpile and headed toward the water pump by the barn. As he splashed water on his face, she thought about what his life must be like. So Plain. So uncomplicated. How she wanted that for herself.

"My *daed* is never late," David said, drying his hands against his trousers as he met her near the farmhouse.

"He's late today." She smiled and took a seat in one of the wooden rockers on the porch. David sat down on the porch step.

"Hum," he said after a while. "Hope nothin's wrong."

"Probably just running late."

The sound of a running horse carried across the field. Lillian and David moved toward the yard. As Samuel's buggy peeled around the corner and onto the driveway, she figured he was rushing because he was late. But as clods of dirt flew from the speed of the horse's hooves and Samuel's face came into focus, Lillian knew this was more than trying to make up for lost time. Something was wrong.

4

SAMUEL SLOWED PETE TO A STOP. "WE HAVE TO HURRY, David," he yelled without addressing Lillian. "Ivan said Lilly's birthin's gone breech."

"Huh?" Lillian asked David. Instinctively she followed him to the buggy.

"Lilly's our cow!" The boy picked up his pace. Lillian continued right behind him.

"I'm sorry, Lillian," Samuel said as she reached his side of the buggy. "We'll have to schedule our trip to town for another day."

"Your cow is delivering breech?" She leaned in toward him, scoping out how she was going to crawl into the backseat. "I've never seen a cow giving birth. Can I come? And who is Ivan?" She paused. "And your cow's name is *Lilly*?"

Samuel's mouth twitched to one side and his brows drew inward. He was either irritated or amused. She wasn't sure. When he finally did open his mouth to speak, she was fairly certain he was going to deny her request to go see Lilly the Cow have her baby. But luckily, David had other plans.

Hurriedly, he jumped out of the passenger seat of the buggy and motioned for Lillian to crawl into the backseat, requiring Samuel to exit the buggy in order to fold the front seat forward.

Samuel moved with hesitancy, so she wasted no time crawling in the back. She didn't want him to change his mind.

David was barely back in the front seat when Samuel motioned Pete to make a U-turn and head down the dirt drive. Once they reached the road, it was full-speed ahead.

"Wow," she said, more to herself than anything. She had no idea the buggy could move so fast.

Samuel wondered what Ivan would say when he showed up at his farm with an *Englisch* woman. A chatty *Englisch* woman, at that.

"Where are we going? To your farm? Is Lilly your cow or Ivan's cow? Now, who's Ivan? She'll be okay, right?" Lillian paused and drew in a breath as she grabbed on to the back of the seat to steady herself from the increasing speed. "*Lilly*. Lilly will be okay, right? And her calf too?"

"I don't know about Lilly yet," Samuel responded.

David started giggling before Samuel could attempt to answer the rest of her questions. Samuel feared what the boy might say. Rightfully so.

"You have the same name as our *cow.* Jonas calls you *Lilly.*" His son turned around to face her, snorting with delight, and Samuel wondered if the boy was offending her. But then Lillian laughed.

"Yep! I certainly do," she said. "And the first time you make a *mooing* sound toward me, we're gonna have a problem." She playfully poked David's arm, and he grinned. "Now, who is Ivan?"

"Ivan is my older brother, and we're going to his place," Samuel answered, pleased to see his son enjoying her company but a little worried just the same. "Some of our cattle graze on his land." He glanced briefly over his shoulder. Her face was aglow with anticipation.

"I've never seen a cow give birth before," she said. "I hope everything goes okay for Lilly. Thank you for letting me tag along."

Letting you? Samuel didn't know he had a say-so. He hadn't had the time to waste arguing with either of them. He had a cow in distress.

"There's Ivan's place." He pointed to his brother's farm toward the left.

"This will be a first for me," she repeated.

Samuel didn't see what all the fuss was about.

Lillian wondered why she rambled on like a silly teenager every time she was with Samuel. She made a mental note not to do that any more, then concentrated on her surroundings.

Ivan's farmhouse looked a lot like her grandparents' farmhouse—white with a large porch. Although amongst the greenery were flowering blooms, unlike at her grandparents' place. She'd assumed Grandma had given up gardening when Grandpa got so sick. Maybe planting some flowers would be a good project for her to undertake at their own farm—to brighten the place up. She'd heard that gardening brought peacefulness.

As they pulled up the dirt driveway, Lillian honed in on a man in a straw hat hovering over a cow out in the pasture. Standing beside him was a woman dressed in a brown dress and black apron. The traditional white *Kapp* held her dark hair in a bun underneath. They waved as Samuel's buggy drew near.

"Poor Lilly," David said, suddenly realizing the gravity of the situation. "Bet she's in a bad way 'bout now."

"She's hurtin' for sure." Samuel hopped out of the buggy and folded the seat up. He extended his arm to help Lillian step down. She noticed his strong hands.

She must have misgauged how far down the ground was because falling into his arms was an unplanned action that caught them both off guard. His arms around her waist . . . her head burrowed against his firm chest . . .

However, Samuel moved fast, freeing himself of any contact with her like she had a contagious disease he didn't want to contract.

"I'm sorry," she sheepishly said. "I guess I lost my footing."

"No harm done," he replied nonchalantly. But Lillian caught his eyes veering in his brother's direction. He cleared his throat. "Better go tend to Lilly."

She followed him to the pasture, where David was already leaning down beside the ailing animal. The cow made an agonizing sound. Maybe witnessing the birth of a calf was a bad idea—especially one that was having this much trouble entering the world.

"Calf is backwards, hind end first with both hind legs bent," Ivan said as he leaned down beside David. "Gonna have to turn it around and pull it out. I got some baling twine right here that we can tie around the limbs once we get it where it needs to be. It's gonna take both of us, Samuel, to pull."

Ivan looked up as if just noticing Lillian.

She smiled. "Hi. I'm Lillian." She offered him her hand. He rose slightly to reciprocate but didn't follow through. Instead he eyed his hands, which were clearly not fit for shaking, and shrugged. He glanced at Samuel and then at the woman standing nearby.

"I'm Ivan. This is *mei fraa*, Katie Ann." The woman nodded politely but didn't move from her spot a few feet away.

"This is Jonas and Irma Rose's *kinskind*," Samuel said, looking slightly uncomfortable.

Both Ivan and Katie Ann looked surprised. "I didn't know Jonas and Irma Rose had a granddaughter," Katie Ann said. "How long will you be visitin'?"

"I'm not sure. I'd like to find out more about the Amish lifestyle since I am Amish," Lillian answered. "Amish by birth," she added, noticing the confused looks on their faces.

Ivan and Katie Ann turned to Samuel, apparently waiting for further clarification from him.

David spoke up before anyone could gather their thoughts. "She wants to feel peace in her mind and heart." He nodded his head up and down as if to tell the others that it was a fact and didn't warrant further discussion. But when they all looked like they might have a thing or two to throw into the conversation just the same, poor Lilly let out a wail of a *moo*.

"You goin' in or me?" Ivan asked his brother. "This ol' girl ain't gonna be able to take much more."

"I'll go in, turn the calf, and get it right," Samuel said. "Then we'll tie on with the twine and pull. Lilly won't have the strength."

Go in . . . ? Lillian watched as Samuel rolled up his sleeve and soaped up. *No way.*

She cringed as she watched him go to work. Poor Lilly had been in distress before, but this new sound escaping from her was indicative that his arm was in a place it didn't need to be. It was a gut-wrenching, agonizing, horrible, mooing sound. And she could swear the cow's eyes were rolling back in her head.

"Stop!" she finally said. "Stop! She can't take any more."

They all looked at her with sympathy, but it was Katie Ann who walked to her side and spoke up. "They gotta do this, Lillian. Otherwise, the calf will die."

Death. She was suddenly very uncomfortable. This was a bad idea. "No, no . . . of course," she said. "I know they have to do this. But can't you give her something for the pain?"

Ivan and Katie Ann looked at each other.

"I mean, don't they have drugs for this type of thing?" she asked, when no one commented.

Samuel continued working. Now he called out. "Ready. Give me the twine."

Lillian looked at Katie Ann. This couldn't be right.

"They gotta hurry and get that calf out, and it would take poor Lilly too long at this point," Katie Ann said. "It's the only way to try to save them both."

Lillian watched as David stroked the cow's head. "It's okay, girl. Everything is gonna be just fine."

"Ivan, I'm ready," Samuel said, standing up with a double strand of twine in his hand.

Ivan grabbed the twine with his brother. Lillian couldn't believe she'd opted for this type of adventure.

It seemed like an eternity of pulling and tugging. And all the while poor Lilly voiced her objections. But when two front legs emerged, followed by a tiny little calf's head, it was a sight to see. And Lillian was thrilled.

Ivan brushed past her and briefly inspected the calf. After he nodded to Samuel that all was well, Lillian dropped to the ground to welcome the new baby.

"Hello," she said softly as she stroked the slithery, wet skin. "Look at you." What an amazing event. She had just arrived in Lancaster County and already she had witnessed the miracle of birth. Fabulous. Just fabulous. "You are so beautiful," she said, leaning in closer to the new baby. "Welcome!" Ah. It was a good feeling. A peaceful feeling.

"Look, guys!" When no one responded, she looked toward them all, huddled near Lilly's head. She knew immediately what was wrong. "No," she said softly. "No."

"Poor girl just couldn't take it," Ivan said, patting David on the shoulder.

"No," Lillian repeated softly. "What about her calf?"

Samuel sat down beside her. "The baby is *gut*," he said with a tenderness in his tone she hadn't expected.

She looked at the mother cow. Someone should close her gaping eyes. She'd never gotten to see her calf.

"Some things are just His way and not meant to be," Samuel said, still in a soothing tone.

"*Whose* way?" Lillian blurted, tired of them writing off everything as God's will around here. *Don't say it*, she thought.

"God's," Samuel said as he gave her a questioning look.

That was enough. She'd had enough about God's will. First it was God's will that Samuel's wife died so young. Next it was Grandpa's cancer. She would tell them exactly what she thought about God's *will*.

She was prepared to do just that when she glanced at David.

His face registered a pain far greater than her own. He was struggling to fight back tears, and his eyes were pleading with her. Pleading for what, she wasn't sure. She walked to where he was sitting near Lilly's head and sat down beside him.

"Where there's life, there's death," he said softly with a maturity beyond his years. He tried to choke back any sign he might possibly cry.

"Yes," Lillian replied as she looked into his young eyes, unhardened by worldly ways.

It was a quiet ride back to Irma Rose and Jonas's farm. Samuel's heart hurt for David and their friend. Understandably, David was taking it pretty hard. He'd had Lilly for four years. He'd been there when she was born. When she'd grown, Samuel had wanted to take her to auction, but David wouldn't hear of it. He was attached to the old girl, so Samuel didn't push it.

His new *Englisch* friend, on the other hand, didn't even know Lilly. But she was taking it hard too.

"Here we are," he said as he pulled in front of Jonas and Irma Rose's farmhouse.

"I'm so sorry," she said, shaking her head.

"Sorry for what?" Her voice was the saddest thing Samuel had ever heard.

"About Lilly." She shook her head again. "I know it was just a cow. And I didn't *know* the cow. But it made me incredibly sad just the same."

"There's no need to be apologizin', Lillian," he said, finding it a bit odd she'd react this strongly. "With so many farms in

Texas, I'm surprised you've never seen a calf birthed. And this happens sometimes. The momma dying."

"I live in the *city*," she said with a hint of irritation.

Samuel shrugged.

As he stepped out of the buggy, their eyes met before she hopped down. How beautiful she looked, he thought, even with her sad eyes. She looked lost on a whole bunch of levels.

"I promise I won't fall this time," she said, forcing a smile as she stepped out of the buggy with ease. "Thank you for allowing me to come with you."

Samuel nodded and watched her walk to David's side of the buggy.

"I'm sorry about your cow, David."

David nodded his head. "*Danki*, Lillian." Then to Samuel's surprise, David hugged his new *Englisch* friend. Alarms began going off in Samuel's head.

Lillian avoided David and Samuel for the next two days. She was embarrassed about her reaction to Lilly's death. It was understandable for David to be so upset. It was *his* cow, and he was a child. But she was unsure what Samuel must think of her at this point. He definitely gave her funny looks sometimes. Still, after busying herself in the kitchen with Grandma for two days, she was ready to venture out. She needed a break.

As Grandma had warned, they had incorporated more activities into their daily routine. Lillian felt like a professional canner at this point. They'd made red-beet jelly, rhubarb jam, apple-cider jelly, and apricot preserves. It was somewhat tedious at first and she had to learn which recipes required hot packing and which ones required cold packing, but she had to admit, she was enjoying it. And to her surprise, she enjoyed the lengthy conversations with Grandma.

She especially enjoyed hearing how her grandparents met and about their wedding—an all-day affair that sounded incredible.

"Your *daadi* Jonas was a handsome man," Grandma said proudly. "And he still is in my eyes." Her eyes twinkled when she spoke of their younger years. Although Lillian noticed her grandma avoided any conversations having to do with her mother, even when Lillian tried to nudge the conversation in that direction.

The canning came easy. And she was getting the hang of the bread making. The sewing was another story. Getting the treadle machine to function at the right speed while trying to sew a straight line—or worse, a curved line—was a challenge. She felt relieved when Grandma said that might be a chore she'd keep for herself.

"Grandma, I think I'll go to town today." She held up a loaf of bread ready for the stove. "Hey! This one looks much better."

"*Ya*, much better. I told you that you'd get the feel of it." Grandma accepted the bread and headed for the stove. "It's a long walk to Intercourse and Bird-In-Hand. It would take you half a day on foot. You and Samuel didn't plan another trip?"

"Uh, I haven't actually talked to them since Lilly died."

Grandma closed the door of the wooden stove and turned to face her. "I would take you myself, but it wonders me if Jonas would be doin' well unattended."

"How far is it?"

"It's a good piece. You go up Black Horse Road, cross over Lincoln Highway into Beiler's Bed and Breakfast drive. Use it as a throughway to get to Leacock Road. Just keep goin'. When Jonas is havin' one of his better days, we'll saddle up Jessie and you can practice driving the buggy."

"Really? That would be great! Jessie is a beautiful animal." Lillian went to the barn every afternoon and lavished attention on the horse. And how fun it would be to drive the buggy to town.

Grandma's face twisted. Lillian knew exactly what was causing her displeasure.

"Maybe you ought not ride the buggy dressed that way, Lillian."

She watched as her grandma scanned her attire from head to toe. It was the same as it was every day—blue jeans and a T-shirt. Today, a red T-shirt. And Lillian still didn't see a problem.

Oh, I see. You'll let me drive the buggy if I wear one of the frumpy dresses on the peg upstairs. No deal.

"Well, I'll be walking today, anyway," she said, turning away from the woman before she told her exactly what she thought of those dresses. All the Amish women wore them. There was no sense of style, little choice of color. And they hung halfway to the floor! It was the one Amish custom she was not going to partake in. Wasn't the fact that she didn't wear makeup or jewelry enough? *The blue jeans stay.*

"Glad to see you have some better walking shoes." She pointed to Lillian's tennis shoes. "We can talk about learnin' you how to handle Jessie on another day when Jonas is feeling better." Her brows jutted upward as if wanting a commitment that Lillian would indeed wear the dress at some point in the future.

Time for a change of subject. "I thought maybe I might plant some flowers in the flowerbeds and around the trees in the yard," she said. "Is that okay with you?"

Grandma lit up. "I think that would be *gut*. I've been telling myself to make time for tending to the yard. But with Jonas and all . . ." She shrugged and glanced upstairs. "We have accounts in town. You can charge the flowers, and there's a scooter in the barn you better use. It was your *mamm*'s. The towns of Paradise, Bird-In-Hand, and Intercourse are close enough together to use a scooter. Lots of Amish use them. It's much too far for walkin' on foot." Her tone indicated she was willing to forget the blue jeans for now.

"That'll be fun. I'll use the scooter and get some flowery plants in town."

"You won't be able to tote much back. There's a basket on the front of the scooter, though, that you can use for carryin' your buys."

"Maybe I'll get a ride back from some nice Amish person, like I did on my way here." She thought of Samuel, starting to regret avoiding him for the past couple of days.

Grandma rubbed her hands on her apron, her mouth pursing in obvious indecision.

"What, Grandma?"

"Samuel came callin' for you yesterday."

"Came calling? When?" *And why didn't you tell me?*

"He came to the door yesterday. Him and David both," she said, sounding fearful she'd made a mistake by not telling Lillian. "You were resting upstairs."

"I was reading a book." Her tone was indicative of her frustration at not being told she had a visitor.

Grandma began to pace across the wooden slatted kitchen floor. "I was worried that you might have taken a fancy to him." She shrugged. "I don't want to see you get hurt."

Lillian chuckled. "Grandma, I can take care of myself. And, I assure you, if Samuel 'came callin', he was only being friendly. Maybe he wanted to apologize for not being able to take me to town," she speculated. "Did you think he might have taken a fancy—so to speak—to *me*?"

"Oh, *ya!*" Grandma belted. "Yes, I did. And it worried me too. The both of you are very different." She shook her head.

"It's okay, Grandma," she said smugly, feeling a newfound sense of pleasure that Samuel had come looking for her. "It will be fine."

"*Ach*, I know that *now*. Katie Ann came by earlier to bring me some vegetables from her and Ivan's garden. She explained to me that Samuel was courting Levina Esh. She saw them having lunch today." She waved her hand. "It just feared me for a minute that he might be thinking of courting you. I saw you both laughing together the other day and my mind ran amuck about it. But now I know it was just silly thinkin' on my part."

"Oh," Lillian said softly. "That's wonderful for him . . . and *Levina*." She whipped around and headed toward the screen door. "I'm off to town."

As the door slammed, she bolted down the porch steps, feeling anything but wonderful.

5

Samuel was admiring the craftsmanship on a fine Amish table he hoped to purchase someday. Someday when he had a wife and more children. The shop was his favorite in Bird-In-Hand, and his friend Big Jake was a mighty fine woodworker. But the table was too big for just him and David. Maybe someday he would see fit to make the purchase.

"Why don't you just buy that table, Samuel?" Sadie Fisher asked as she approached Samuel. "You've been eyeing that thing for months."

"Hello, Sadie," he said, not feeling up to making small talk. He'd done enough of that with Levina earlier in the day when she pinned him down for lunch. No more going shopping on Thursdays for him.

"How've you been, Samuel?"

"*Gut*, Sadie. And you?"

"*Gut, gut*," she said, taking a step backward and eyeing him up and down. "Samuel Stoltzfus! You are thinning up. Do I need to come over and fix you and David some of my special meatloaf? And maybe a lemon meringue pie for dessert?"

"No need, Sadie," he said, forcing a smile. "Me and the boy do just fine."

Looking only a tad defeated, she said, "Oh, I think my cookin' would plump you right up. It's just what you and David need." She leaned closer to him and grinned.

There couldn't have been a better time for Lillian Miller to pull up on a scooter.

———

"Hello, Samuel," Lillian said, out of breath as she approached him and Sadie. He was glad to see her happy. Last time he'd seen her, she was a mess. "I don't know what Grandma was thinking. It was a long way to get here, even on a scooter." She curled her bottom lip, blew upward, and cleared a strand of wayward hair dangling across her face.

He glanced at Sadie and then back at Lillian. The two women seemed to be waiting for an introduction. There was a tension in the air he couldn't quite put his finger on. He should have never hesitated. He should have introduced them right off. Lillian beat him to the punch, though.

"And you must be Levina?" Lillian asked. "I'm Lillian Miller." She extended her hand to Sadie.

Samuel cringed when he saw the fire blazing in Sadie's eyes. He opened his mouth to make the correction, but Lillian wasn't through. "My grandma told me how the two of you were a couple—or 'courting' I believe is what she said. And she also said—"

"This is Sadie!" he quickly interrupted when he saw Sadie's mouth draw up and her hands land on her hips.

Lillian dropped her extended hand. "Oh . . ."

What she was smiling about, Samuel would never know.

"My grandma said you came to see me yesterday. I'm sorry I missed you. I was upstairs reading." Lillian's smile broadened. "Maybe you could come by later?"

Sadie ripped him to shreds with her piercing eyes. And yet, for the first time since he'd known her, Sadie Fisher was speechless.

Once again, his *Englisch* friend was not. "I just want to apologize again about the other night, the way I carried on when the cow died. How's the little calf, though?" Her eyes lit up, and Samuel couldn't help but smile.

But venom was spewing from Sadie's direction. Ignoring Lillian, she turned to Samuel. "Samuel Stoltzfus, exactly who *are* you courting these days?"

"I'm not courting *anyone*," he said cautiously, glancing back and forth between the two women. Although he kept his focus pretty much on Sadie. She was mad as fire and a mite scary looking.

Lillian spoke up first. "Uh, I'm sorry if I caused a problem. I just—"

"I best be gettin' on," Sadie interrupted, making sure her voice drowned out Lillian. She straightened her apron and held her chin high as she allowed herself a long hard look at Lillian. "Nice to meet you, Lillian," she finally said and walked off. No, *stomped* off was more like it.

"Sorry," Lillian mumbled when Sadie was out of earshot.

"For what?"

"Uh, for messing things up with your lady friend."

"Sadie and Levina are both widows in our district. And I am a widower. Need I say more?"

Of course he needed to say more.

"So, which one is it? Sadie or Levina?"

"Neither," he answered. "Why does it interest you so much?"

He reached up and stroked his beard, sporting a curious smile. He was dallying with her. Her insides flipped, and her cheeks took on a tingly sensation, which she knew meant they were red as her T-shirt. "It doesn't," she snapped in a much too defensive tone.

"Coulda fooled me."

"Well, aren't you a little full of yourself, Samuel! I believe you are the one who came to see me yesterday." She shot him a catty smile.

"David wanted to make sure you were doin' okay. You were so upset when Lilly died." His expression shifted to a look of concern, and he leaned down toward her as if to see if she really was all right.

"I'm fine. And, as I said, I'm sorry for my emotional display."

"No apology necessary." He tipped his hat. "Well, we're in town. Want me to show you around?"

"I guess," she said, unsure what she wanted from the handsome Samuel Stoltzfus. "I actually want to buy some flowers. Grandma said she didn't have time to do much gardening with Grandpa so sick. I thought it might be nice to brighten the place up."

"Do you know anything about planting flowers?"

"How hard can it be? Dig a hole and put them in."

He shook his head. "It's May. Do you know what *kind* of flowers to plant this time of year?"

"Uh . . . I guess not."

"Come on. I'll help you."

Two hours later, Samuel helped Lillian load flats of colorful foliage into his buggy.

"How exactly were you going to get all this home, since you scooted all the way here?" He lifted the scooter up and placed it in the backseat.

"I knew you'd come around and give me a ride," she said in a playful tone. Her eyes flashed alongside her smile.

Something twisted in Samuel's gut. He shook his head as she handed him a flat of flowers to store in the back of the buggy.

"What?" she asked.

"Nothing," he mumbled, suddenly reticent.

"Oh, come on," she said, poking him lightly on the arm. "Must be *something* on your mind."

He shook his head. "No, nothing." After loading the last of the flowers, he walked around and opened the buggy door on her side.

"*Danki!*" she said as she hopped in. There was that childlike enthusiasm again—a quality he found mighty attractive.

Which was the whole problem. Lillian Miller stirred things in him better left alone. She was beautiful. She was interesting. And she was off limits.

It was almost four-thirty. He better pick up the pace to get her home and pick up David.

"Jonas, the three of them are *still* sittin' out by the barn," Irma Rose said as she peeped out the window. "They've been out there almost three hours. Since right after supper. For goodness sakes, what could they have to talk about for so long?"

"Irma Rose, you might be gettin' thick around the midsection, but I didn't think you were gettin' thick in your head too." He chuckled. "Our young *kinskind* is being courted by Samuel. Now quit your spying."

She was glad Jonas was having a good day, but his sharp tongue was about to get him in a mess of trouble.

"Ouch, Irma Rose." Jonas snickered. "You're hurtin' me with that look you be givin' me."

"This is serious, Jonas. Samuel is courting Levina Esh. Katie Ann saw them having lunch today. It isn't proper for him to be spending so much time with Lillian." Their *Englisch* granddaughter didn't even go to church. And she couldn't see fit to wear a more appropriate outfit either. Lillian was a high-spirited, lovely child. Irma Rose wanted nothing more than for her to be happy. But she had seen Samuel and the boy suffer. This just had trouble written all over it.

"Are you sure Samuel is courting Levina? Both those widows—Levina and Sadie— have been chasin' that Samuel for a long time." Jonas chuckled. "He don't seem to want to be caught by neither of 'em."

"Katie Ann sure saw fit to tell me about their lunch today."

"That don't mean they're courtin'." Jonas shook his head.

"It just scares me, Jonas. I don't want to see our Lillian or Samuel and the boy get hurt." She took another peek out the window.

"Irma Rose," Jonas said in a softer tone. "It ain't up to you."

"I know." She walked away from the window. "But I'm still going to worry."

Lillian was impressed with how little it seemed to take for Samuel and David to be happy. Their Plain, uncomplicated lifestyle provided them with everything they needed. Despite her worldly ways, she'd never been able to achieve the one thing they seemed to possess in abundance: peace.

The one thing both father and son talked about with pride was their love of the land and sense of stewardship to care for God's creation.

"Tilling God's earth and providing plentiful crops is an important part of our lives," Samuel said now. "With more of our farmers having to venture out into the *Englisch* workplace, some of us are still blessed to harvest our land and enjoy the fruits of our labor."

Lillian thought hard about what he was saying. "Tomorrow, I'm going to plant all those flowers I got in town today," she said.

"It'll be nice to see some flowers here again."

"What are we going to do tomorrow, Pop?" David enthusiastically asked, as if assuming the three of them would spend time together.

Evidently, that was *not* Samuel's plan. "David, you've already missed today's chores. I think it'd be best if we headed home tomorrow after your work is finished here." Samuel lifted himself from the tree stump he was sitting on. "As a matter of fact, maybe we can salvage some chores tonight."

"But, Pop—" David protested, only to have Samuel interrupt him.

"Lillian, please thank Irma Rose again for that fine meal."

She stood up from the wooden chair she had placed in the

front yard earlier. "I will," she said softly, trying to mask her disappointment.

Hot and cold. One minute Samuel was warm and kind and seemed pleased by her presence. The next minute, he was formal and withdrawn. Just like earlier today, in town. Yet despite his quiet demeanor on the ride home, they'd had a good evening, laughing and talking about all sorts of things. She felt like after tonight she knew him and David much better.

And yet . . . hot and cold. Samuel could turn on a dime.

"*Ya*, we best be on our way, David," he said as he extended his hand to Lillian. "Bye, Lillian."

His tone was curt, as if forcing distance between them. But as she latched onto his hand, she thought she felt him hold it longer than normal. Maybe she was just imagining that.

Samuel could sense that something was on David's mind. He hadn't said a word since they left Lillian. He pulled back on the reins and slowed Pete to a trot. "It was a mighty fine meal, *ya*?" he asked.

The boy nodded but kept staring ahead.

"Something on your mind?" He slowed Pete even more, to allow a chance for the two of them to talk. Once at home, they'd need to work on the chores they had let go to spend time at the Millers' farm.

David shrugged. "Nothing, I guess."

Samuel wasn't convinced. "You like Lillian, don't you?" He suspected whatever was on David's mind had to do with her.

"You like her too!" The boy's tone was defensive and bordering on angry.

"Of course I like her. She's a very nice person, and—"

"No, I mean you *like* her, and you don't want to admit it!"

"Whoa, boy," Samuel instructed Pete as they pulled into the yard. He turned to David, surprised at his son's tone of voice. "Boy, what is goin' on in that head of yours?"

Children start getting rebellious at this age—he remembered his own temperament at that period. But David had never taken such a sharp tone with him before.

"I think you should court Lillian." He turned and faced Samuel with a look that almost demanded he consider the notion.

Samuel opened his mouth to reprimand the boy for thinking *he* could choose a courting partner for his pop. But seeing the look in David's glassy eyes stopped him short. Clearly the boy had taken a hard fancy to Lillian.

Another reason they should stop spending time with the woman.

"David," he began slowly, "it wouldn't be proper. She's from a worldly place, and it just wouldn't be right." He shook his head.

The boy instantly cheered up, obviously sensing Samuel's defenses were down. "She's gonna come around, Pop. You'll see. It's just gonna take her some time to learn about our ways. She wants to make a change. Maybe we can help her."

"It's not that easy, David."

David crawled out of the buggy and turned to face Samuel, who was still sitting and pondering his son's words. He seemed to be waiting for his dad to go on, to give him a better reason not to pursue a courtship with this woman who was so different from them.

His son knew to reject pride, arrogance, and haughtiness. The boy had been studying the *Ordnung*. How could he explain to the boy that submitting to the will of God does not come easily to an outsider? It wasn't always easy for an insider.

"'Come out from among them, and be ye separate, saith the Lord,'" Samuel said, hoping to remind the boy of their need to resist influences from the outside world.

David smiled. "'And be not conformed to this world: but be ye transformed by the renewing of your mind, that ye may prove what is that good, and acceptable, and perfect, will of God,'" he responded proudly. "Lillian just needs our help to find her way. That's all. We're not conforming to *her* world, we're just giving her a hand to renew her spirit and find that peace of heart and mind she wants."

Samuel stared at his son with a combination of admiration and fear. Where had the boy learned of such things at such a young age? It was a maturity way past his years. But leave it to a boy his age to find a loophole in the Scriptures. "It's not that easy." Samuel repeated softly. But David was already on his way into the farmhouse.

───※───

It was nearing eight o'clock when Lillian headed upstairs. She knew Grandma and Grandpa were already in bed. As she plopped down across her quilted counterpane, she looked around her small room. "Sure would be nice to watch some TV," she whispered. Glancing at the dark-colored dresses on the peg, she frowned. Sadie had sported one of the Plain dresses—a dark green one—while she was goggling all over Samuel earlier.

Lillian realized she'd certainly messed things up for any potential courtship between Samuel and Sadie. She wasn't having much regret about it. The more time she spent around Samuel, the more time she wanted to spend with him. She just wasn't sure if the feeling was mutual.

A familiar trill. She grabbed her cell phone on the first ring, hoping she hadn't wakened her grandparents. She was glad she'd thought to borrow a shopkeeper's electricity to charge up the phone while she browsed in the market today—awkward, to be sure, but he hadn't seemed to mind. And she just wasn't ready to part with this last modern convenience.

"Hi, Mom."

"Lillian, how are you?"

Something was wrong. Lillian could tell by her mother's tone. She'd heard it before, way too many times. "What's wrong, Mom?"

"What makes you think something is *wrong*? I just called to check on you . . . and your grandpa."

"I'm fine, and Grandpa had a pretty good day today." She waited for her mother to get to the point.

"Good, good."

When her mother didn't offer up the reason for the call, Lillian decided to step up to the plate. "Mom, I want to know why you left the Amish faith and chose to go out on your own." She knew her tone was demanding, but she needed an answer.

"Lillian, I have too much going on to get into this with you right now." Mom's tone was equally as sharp.

"You've *always* had too much going on to talk to me about it, Mom. And Grandma doesn't seem to want to talk about it either."

"You asked your grandma about it? Don't do that, Lillian," Mom exclaimed.

Realizing she struck a nerve with her mother, she went on. "I will ask her again if you don't tell me what happened. Because I know *something* happened, Mom."

"I chose to leave, Lillian. That's all. It was my choice to choose baptism into the church or to leave the Old Order district."

"Then why do I get the impression there's more to it than either you or Grandma are telling me?"

"I have no idea." Her tone was still sharp, and once again Lillian could tell they were heading down a bad road. "Now, tell me about your grandfather. Is he in a lot of pain?"

"Why don't you come see for yourself, Mom? He's *your* father." It was a mean thing to say, especially since she knew her mother wouldn't come. And even more so, if she was honest with herself, because she didn't want her mom there.

"Did I raise such a hateful child?"

"*Raise?* Is that what you're calling it these days?"

"Lillian, let's don't do this. Why does everything have to be a fight with you?" She could hear her mother's voice crack, but she wasn't sure if it was for effect. There was another reason for her mom's call. She just hadn't gotten to the point yet.

"I don't want to fight with you, Mom."

"Sweetie, I don't want to fight with you either. The reason for my call was to check on you and your grandparents, and also to tell you that I'm mailing you a thousand dollars. I know I owe you much more, but I have sent you what I could for now, to help you while you're there."

Lillian silently hung her head.

"It might be a couple more weeks before I can send you some more," her mother went on when Lillian didn't respond. "My new job at the employment agency pays commission for every placement. It turns out I match up employees with employers quite well."

"Thanks, Mom," Lillian said. Guilt rose to the surface. Why couldn't she just once give her mom the benefit of the doubt? Probably because history had a way of repeating itself. Sarah Jane Miller had filled her life with promises and disappointments. She was certain the phone call was because her mom needed something from her.

"Now, I have to go get ready for dinner. Paul is taking me to the new Italian restaurant in town. Things are going fabulously well with us." Her mother paused. Lillian closed her eyes, shook her head, and sighed. "Anyway, the offer still stands for you to come and stay with us, sweetie."

"I like it here, Mom."

"What about all the things you've had to do without? Television, for starters."

"I miss TV sometimes, but I stay busy. I've learned how to make homemade bread and jellies, and I even sew a little. There's tons to do around here. Tomorrow I'm going to plant some flowers. And Grandpa is a hoot." She laughed, thinking about some of the things her grandfather said sometimes.

"You're a lot like your grandfather," her mother said lovingly.

"That's what Grandma says." *Odd.* Was this turning into a

normal conversation? Maybe this would be the new norm. That would be a welcome change.

"Your grandma? She's well?" Her mother's tone resonated with the same sense of hesitation Lillian heard when her grandmother asked about her daughter.

"She's tired a lot from taking care of Grandpa."

"Are you wearing the Amish dresses?" Her mother chuckled, which hit Lillian the wrong way. She might not want to wear the frumpy dresses, but she didn't want her mother making fun of them either.

"No. But Grandma sure wants me to." She glanced at the three dresses on the pegs—dark blue, dark green, and a deep purple. "It's hard to picture *you* wearing them."

"I didn't know any different. They are a far cry from the black pants outfit I will be wearing to dinner. Which reminds me, I need to go get ready."

The conversation was going so well. It felt good to have a normal one with her mother. Maybe she would go out on a limb. "Mom, I met a man here."

"Really? So soon?" Lillian could hear shower water turn on in the background. She knew her time was limited.

"His name is Samuel. Samuel Stoltzfus."

Lillian heard the shower water shut off. "Lillian, listen to me," her mother said, pausing. "That is an Amish name. Please tell me you don't have a crush on an Amish man."

Oh, how quickly her mother's tone changed. "Yes, he's Amish," she said firmly.

"Oh, Lillian! That will *never* work."

"First of all, we're just friends, Mother." She was twenty-seven years old. And, based on the choices her mother had made, she shouldn't have to defend her own.

"Well, keep it that way."

It appeared Lillian was going to defend her own choices after all. "I might. I might not. I really like him. And his son, David."

"Oh, great. There's a child involved too?"

"He's eleven. He's a great kid, and—"

"Lillian, I have to run. Paul is calling from downstairs for me to hurry. I'll talk to you soon."

Her mouth was still open, midsentence, when she heard the line go dead. The false pretense of a normal conversation with her mother was nice while it lasted, but she could have predicted the final outcome.

The next morning Lillian swore she smelled smoke as she headed downstairs for breakfast. She looked at her watch. "Oops," she whispered. It was almost six o'clock. She'd probably missed breakfast. Cereal would have to do. Grandma was already headed to town by now.

That is *smoke I smell.*

Reaching the kitchen, she came to a sudden halt when she saw Grandpa casually puffing away on a cigar at the kitchen table.

"Grandpa! What are you doing?"

"Nothing like a fine cigar after breakfast." He flicked ash into a nearby coffee cup, his eyes twinkling with mischief.

"You can't do that . . . can you?" Amish people didn't smoke.

He chuckled. "We grow tobacco, my little Lilly. And some of us older folk partake in a cigar from time to time."

"Oh." She watched him take another puff. "But that's not good for you. I mean, you're sick. Maybe you shouldn't be smoking." She walked closer to him and frowned. "Does Grandma know about this?"

He sat up straighter on the wooden bench. As he held the cigar in one hand, he blew smoke and stroked his beard with the other hand. "Might be best not to mention it to her." He smiled with the sneaky satisfaction of a child.

"She's going to smell it." Lillian crossed her arms and shook her head.

"*Ya!* You'd think so! But every time she goes to town, I have me a smoke. Been smokin' me a cigar like this for months when she's afar. I open the windows and the doors." He pointed to the three open windows in the kitchen and the open screen door.

"Well, I could smell it coming down the stairs. Why don't you go on the porch?" Lillian knew she shouldn't be encouraging him.

"It's more comfortable in here, and near the coffee. Besides, I think Irma Rose has a bad nose. She don't smell good. I passed some gas the other day that would have knocked over a large cow. She didn't even give a flinch." He laughed as he took another drag.

Lilly blushed. "But, Grandpa, it's not good for you. You're sick and shouldn't be smoking."

"Lilly, I'm going to the Good Lord—soon. Ain't nothin's gonna change that." He grinned. "Just hope I go on a day when Irma Rose is in town, so I can go with a cigar in my hand."

"Grandpa, you might live many more years." She could only hope. The thought of him not there put her stomach in knots.

"Not gonna happen, my Lilly. I'm on my way out the door."

"Don't say that!"

He lifted his hairy chin, pushed back his straw hat, and gave her a hard look. With the cigar dangling from one side of his mouth, he said, "So, tell me about Samuel."

He clearly wanted to change the subject. And she supposed if it was going to get changed, she was glad it was to Samuel.

"He's nice. I like David too." She reflected on the hours of talking and laughing the three of them had shared the night before. It was nice. Although, based on Samuel's reaction, it might not be happening again.

"He's a fine man. The boy is a hard worker." He winked at her, the cigar still dangling to one side.

She wasn't sure how much to say. "Yes, he seems like a good father too."

"Gonna be spending more time with him?"

"Uh, I don't know. I'm sure I'll see him around." It was a vague answer but a truthful one.

"Well, it appears you'll be seeing him tomorrow."

"What? When?"

"It's his turn to have church service at his farm. You will be goin' to church?" His tone was an assumption she would be in attendance.

One thing at a time, though. "You have church service at a *home*? How did I miss that? I knew service was held every other week, but I must have missed the fact that it was at home."

"'God that made the world and all things therein, seeing that he is Lord of heaven and earth, dwelleth not in temples made with hands,'" he said. "*Ya,* we have church service in folks' homes. We each take a turn 'bout every ten months."

"Oh." She thought for a minute about the opportunity to see Samuel and where he and David lived. "I guess I can go."

Grandpa eyed her up and down. "Don't make a lick o' difference to me, but your Grandma sure would be pleased if you'd wear one of them dresses upstairs."

She frowned. "They're just not for me, Grandpa."

He sat quietly for a few seconds. "Maybe just give it some thought," he suggested.

Suddenly his face took on a fearful expression and he stuffed the cigar into the coffee cup. "Quick! Start fanning the room! Dump this out!" He handed her the coffee cup. "My hearing must be off too! I usually hear Jessie's hooves before he hits the dirt drive. Look at that! They're already in the yard!"

She grabbed the coffee cup and dumped the contents as instructed. Grandpa moved faster than she'd seen him since she arrived, waving his arms about, pushing the smoke toward the open windows. She watched with amusement at his wholehearted effort to keep his secret. Then, shaking her head, she said, "I'll go outside and try to stall Grandma. I'll show her the flowers I'm going to plant today."

With her grandpa still flailing his arms wildly around the room, she moved toward the open screen door. "I still think you shouldn't smoke," she whispered before she walked onto the porch.

"Hurry, child! Or Irma Rose will have my hide!"

6

LILLIAN HAD BEEN STARING AT THE DRESSES ON THE PEGS for nearly ten minutes. She needed to make a decision soon. She glanced toward the bed, where she'd laid out the only dress she brought with her: a blue one, but much shorter and *way* more stylish than the ones on the peg. All the other women would be wearing dresses similar to those Grandma had put in her room. Maybe it would be best not to stand out.

She pulled the dark blue dress from the peg.

"Grandma's already in the buggy, Lilly!" Grandpa yelled upstairs. "You comin'?"

Changing quickly, she ran down the stairs to see her grandfather sporting a wide-brimmed straw hat and a pair of suspenders she didn't remember seeing before. His eyes lit up when he saw her.

"You'll make your *mammi* very happy, Lilly."

"Feeling good today, Grandpa?" she asked. He seemed to be walking a bit taller this morning.

"It's a good day to go to church," he said, pushing back his hat and taking another look at her. "What a fine Amish woman you make."

"Thanks, Grandpa."

He made his way slowly down the porch steps and across the

front yard. A little wobbly, but all in all Grandpa seemed to be doing well. She stayed close by, occasionally offering her elbow for support. Grunting a little, he heaved himself into the driver's seat of the buggy while she went to go lavish a little attention on Jessie before they took to the road. "Hello, boy," she whispered as she stroked the horse's snout.

"Look at our Lilly. How 'bout that?"

Lillian poked her head around Jessie's. Grandma was sitting in the buggy and had her hands to her mouth as if overwhelmed by what she saw. After a moment's pause, she took a shaky breath. "I think you should drive us to worship this fine morning," she said, scooting off the seat. "I'll sit in the back. Jonas get up and push that seat forward so I can crawl in."

"Bossy, bossy," he snickered.

Thrilled, Lillian joined her grandpa in the front seat. With Grandma settled in the backseat, Grandpa handed over the reins. Lillian glanced over her shoulder. Grandma's hazel eyes shone with vivacity. If that's all it took for her to gleam like that, Lillian knew she should have worn the Plain dresses way before now. After all, they were just dresses.

Before she catapulted Jessie into action, Lillian reached into her apron pocket and pulled out the little white prayer covering she had stuffed inside. Hurriedly she wrapped her long brown hair into a tight bun and secured it with a hair band from her wrist. It was a last minute choice to bring along the hat, but she was glad she had. Her *Kapp* wasn't properly ironed, but she might as well wear the entire get-up.

She twisted in her seat and gave her grandma an "All set?" look. It warmed her heart to see the smile that stretched across the older woman's tired face.

"*Danki*, Lillian," she whispered.

Lillian smiled as she gave Jessie a giddyup. Why hadn't she just worn the silly dresses sooner?

As if sensing the women were having a moment, Grandpa lightened the mood. "Let's kick up some dirt, Lilly! Let ol' Jessie stretch his legs. Give a gentle flick with the reins. Jessie will do the rest."

Doing as her grandpa suggested, Lillian carefully maneuvered the buggy down the dirt lane to the main road. Then she looked at Grandpa again. He grinned and nodded.

"*Ya!*" she yelled, which thrust Jessie forward so fast Grandma fell backward against the seat.

"Thata girl, Lilly! A *wunderbaar* day to feel the wind in our face," Grandpa said as Jessie got comfortable in a quick gallop.

"Jonas, the Good Lord will still be there when we arrive!" Grandma yelled, regaining her composure as she adjusted her *Kapp*. "This is Lillian's first time to drive the buggy. She might not feel comfortable moving along so fast."

"Sure she does. Pick it up, Lilly! Another gentle flick of the reins."

Lillian glanced at her grandma, who was preparing herself for another increase in speed. But when she smiled in Lillian's direction, Lillian took that as the go-ahead and did indeed pick up the pace.

"Yee-ha!" Grandpa wailed.

Samuel's mother and two sisters, along with Katie Ann, had been busy readying the farmhouse for church service since the early-morning hours. Samuel, Ivan, and David were setting up tables and benches inside and out to prepare for the meal after worship.

"How did you meet the *Englisch* woman?" Ivan asked Samuel as they carried a bench from the barn.

"She was tryin' to find her way to Jonas and Irma Rose's farmhouse. She was walking along the road with only one shoe." He chuckled at the memory. "I gave her a ride."

"Is she planning to study the *Ordnung* in preparation of baptism? She is, after all, Amish by birth." Ivan placed the bench beside the long wooden table.

"I don't know. She says she wants to live a peaceful, quiet life for a while."

"Hmm, I see. The worldly ways of the *Englisch* are so different." Ivan shook his head.

"*Ya.*" Samuel wasn't clear about Lillian's plans, but he knew her heart was filled with compassion and kindness. That much was evident in the way she interacted with David, the way she reacted when the cow died, and her overall desire to lead a good life free of complications. Although misdirected in her attempts at finding such peace, Samuel knew her motivations were of God. She just didn't know it yet.

"Isn't that Jonas and Irma Rose coming up the drive?" Ivan pointed toward the dirt road leading to Samuel's farmhouse.

Samuel looked up. "That's Lillian driving," he said to his brother. "And . . ."—his heart did a somersault—"she's dressed in Plain clothes."

"It's a far cry from the boy breeches she wore when I saw her last." Ivan tipped back his straw hat and strained to have a better look at the approaching buggy.

"*Ya,*" Samuel whispered, too stunned to say much else. He was pretty sure he'd heard her say she'd never wear one of the traditional Amish dresses.

As the buggy came to a halt, Samuel stifled a grin. Irma Rose's hair looked like she'd been through a tornado. Loose gray strands fell forward from beneath her *Kapp,* and she looked a tad pale. Lillian was sporting the same messy hairdo, but seemed to be bursting with pride.

"*Guder mariye!*" she yelled as they pulled up. "I drove the buggy!" Her contagious laugh even prompted a smile from Ivan.

"Good morning to you too," Samuel said as he walked toward the buggy. "How was the ride?" he asked Irma Rose.

"Lillian did a fine job," she said, stabbing strands of hair back under her *Kapp,* housed underneath a black bonnet. She drew in a deep breath, an obvious attempt to gather her composure.

Jonas popped out of the buggy. "I don't think I've been that fast in a buggy since my *rumschpringe!*" He paused and drew in a cleansing breath. "What a ride. And what a glorious day for worship." He shook Samuel's hand and made his way to one of the benches to take a seat.

Lillian slid off her seat and pushed it forward so Irma Rose could crawl out of the back. Samuel helped her out of the buggy. "Thank you, Samuel," she said, offering him a half smile. She headed toward Jonas, presumably to also take a rest after their adventurous ride.

Lillian couldn't have looked more beautiful. The crisp morning air tinged her cheeks a rosy pink, and her eyes were aglow with a passion for life. Her heavenly smile enhanced her dimples. In spite of his earlier resolve to keep things simple between them, he had to admit he felt strangely weak in the knees. He couldn't have been happier she'd chosen to attend worship service at his house on this fine Sunday morning. It was going to be a good day indeed.

As he had welcomed the others, Samuel extended his hand to her. "You look . . . lovely," he said. Surprised he'd verbalized the thought, he searched her eyes for a reaction. Her gaze met his, and she gave his hand a gentle squeeze.

"Why, *danki*, Samuel."

Samuel could hear faint rumblings and voices in the background, but he couldn't seem to decipher anything. The feel of Lillian's hand in his, the way her eyes connected with his . . . He was lost in her world.

"I dressed Amish," she whispered as she let go of his hand.

"And a mighty fine Amish woman you look." He couldn't seem to walk away from her, even though he heard someone calling his name.

"I think your brother is calling you," she said, obviously pleased she was diverting his attention.

He turned to see Ivan waiting for his help to carry another bench. "*Ya, ya.* Make yourself at home," he said to her and reluctantly made his way toward Ivan.

Samuel certainly seemed smitten with her this morning, and Lillian couldn't shake the smile he'd brought to her face. The way he held her hand and the look in his eyes left no question in her mind: he was glad she was here. She headed to where her grandparents were sitting. Grandma stood up right away.

"Let's head in with the other womenfolk, Lillian, and give a hand with the meal preparations." She grabbed Lillian's hand and continued holding it all the way into Samuel's kitchen.

"Hello," Lillian said softly when she entered the room. In addition to Katie Ann, there were two other younger women, and another woman about Grandma's age. They all paused at their respective chores and waited for an introduction. She was under the spotlight, no doubt.

"This is Lillian, *mei kinskind.*" Grandma's tone was proud. It touched Lillian's heart. Grandma gave her hand a squeeze. "And, Lillian, this is Mary Ellen, Samuel's sister." She pointed toward a woman about Lillian's age, who nodded in her direction. "This is Rebecca, another of Samuel's sisters." The slightly older woman also nodded and smiled. "And, this is their *mamm,* Esther."

"Lillian and I have met," Katie Ann spoke up. "Welcome to our worship service."

Lillian nodded. "Thank you for having me." She glanced around the kitchen, which mirrored her grandparents' kitchen, with the same white walls, table and bench, and wood-burning stove. Samuel's mother continued to study her as the other women returned to peeling potatoes, buttering loaves of bread, and arranging pickles on a tray.

"What church district do you come from?" Esther Stoltzfus finally asked.

"Uh, I don't come from any church district," Lillian said, unsure how Grandma would like for her to answer.

Grandma held her chin high. "Lillian comes to our district from the city—from Houston."

Esther looked confused.

"Lillian, maybe you could help me get the butter bread ready?"
Katie Ann asked.

Grandma seemed relieved with the change of subject.

It was a church service unlike any church service Lillian had ever
attended. Not that she had attended very many. The men and
boys sat by themselves in one room, and the women and girls sat
in another room. There was a central room in between where the
preaching took place. Since it was almost completely in German,
Lillian understood very little of the two-hour service.

Her back ached from the backless bench. There was no organ
or music, just songs that were sung unusually slow. When the
service was over, the men left first, then the young women, and
lastly the older women. Lillian tried to follow tradition as best
she could.

Despite the awkwardness of the whole event, she came away
from the service feeling a sense of fellowship and calm. While
some of those in attendance gave her questioning looks, everyone
was friendly. Sadie Fisher, however, didn't acknowledge her presence. She'd noticed the young woman sitting on the same row, at
the far end from her. As they exited the service and moved
toward the kitchen, Lillian caught Sadie watching her, but the
woman quickly turned away when their eyes met.

Samuel, on the other hand, locked eyes with her several times.
Each time, a smile swept across his face.

The men began to seat themselves at the benches outside
while the women started to carry out trays of food. It seemed
incredibly old-fashioned to her the way the women waited on

the men. She had never seen Grandpa so much as serve himself a cup of coffee at home. And Grandma never seemed to mind tending to his every need, on good days or bad. Nor did these women seem to mind that the men were eating first. So she followed suit and helped carry out food trays and pitchers of sweet tea.

"Hi, Lillian."

After placing a pitcher of tea on the table, she gave David a hug. "Hi, David. How's it going?"

"*Gut*," he said.

Frowning, she pointed to a large bowl on a nearby table. "I canned some of those, but I have to tell you, I don't care for them."

"Those are *riewe*. Red beets. They're *gut*."

"Yuck. I don't think I'll be having any of those. But I'm going to have lots of that pie." She nodded her head toward one of the many desserts lining the table.

"That's *schnitzboi*. Snitz pie," he said grinning.

"Well, I'm going to be sure and have some. Where's your Pop?" she asked, looking around for Samuel. "Eating with the other men?"

David didn't say anything.

"What are you snickering about?" she asked playfully.

"Oh, nothing." He nervously kicked at the grass.

"It's my Amish outfit, isn't it?" Maybe it just didn't work for her, like she suspected. Although his father had sure seemed happy to see her wearing the traditional dress.

"No, that's not it. I think you look Plain."

"Well, *Plain* is good, right?"

Ignoring her plea for acceptance, he said, "Pop's in the barn.

He asked me to take him some sweet tea. But *you* can take it to him if you want." He reached for a glass of tea on the table and pushed it in her direction, still grinning.

She accepted the tea and winked at him. "I think I will." She walked toward the barn. "Save me a piece of that pie!"

"I will."

Samuel filled Pete's trough with oats. "There's a mighty crowd takin' over the house, ol' boy. Maybe I'll sit a spell with you." Knowing he should get back to the group with the extra chairs he'd been sent to retrieve, he took advantage of the opportunity to sit quietly for a minute. Taking a seat behind his woodworking bench, he eyed the many uncompleted projects. So much to do and so little time. Between caring for the boy, farming the land, and the many other chores necessary to keep the farm running, his favorite pastime was quickly becoming a thing of the past.

He picked up a birdhouse modeled after a plan his pop gave him before he died. It would be a fine home for the redbirds, if he could ever finish it.

He didn't hear Lillian walk into the barn. When he looked up, she was there.

"David said you wanted some tea," she said, handing him the glass.

"*Danki.* David could have brought it out here."

She remained quiet as he took several big gulps. He set the glass down, fearing he'd hurt her feelings with his comment. "I mean, I hate for you to have to get away from the other folks to bring me tea."

"I don't mind."

"What did you think about the church service?"

"Long." She sighed. "And my back's a little sore."

"The benches take some gettin' used to."

"But it was nice. I didn't understand most of it, but there was a certain something in the air. I don't know. I guess maybe a fellowship. It was like one giant family. I didn't really have a family growing up. It was just me and Mom."

"I reckon we're like one big family in most ways. Do you plan to study the *Ordnung* while you're here?"

"That's like the order of conduct, right?" She pressed her lips together and thought for a minute. "I guess if I'm really going to live the Amish life while I'm here, I should."

"It's not easy, Lillian. Especially since you come from worldly ways. Don't you miss television, electricity, and all the other modern conveniences?"

"Of course I do. But I don't miss living by myself and being afraid to go home alone at night. I don't miss my mother's reckless behavior and always needing something from me. I don't miss the busyness, the constant fast pace. I don't miss—" She caught her breath as vivid and painful memories of Rickie stabbed at her insides. "I don't miss a lot of things. All my life, I've sensed there was something else for me. I just didn't know what."

"Is this the something else you've been looking for?"

"I hope so. I don't know. I just know that I've felt lost for a long time, and something about being here, living with Grandma and Grandpa"—she paused—"and meeting you makes me believe maybe it is."

Alarms began to ring in Samuel's head. His fascination with

her aside, he knew it would be best to get things right in *both* their minds if they were going to stay friends.

"Lillian," he began.

"Yes?"

"I hope you find what you're lookin' for." She nodded and seemed to be waiting for more. "I mean, truly living our ways would mean a lot of studying and acceptance of God's will. It's not just about wearing the clothes, gardening, making bread, getting up early, or making quilts."

"Hey! I haven't thought about quilts. I want to learn that too."

She was missing his point. "Our way of life is *here*, Lillian." He held his hand to his heart. "It's a faith we carry without doubt and a way of life we practice with humility and selflessness."

"I know," she said as if trying to convince him.

He shook his head, realizing any feelings he had today at seeing Lillian in her Plain clothes were best put aside. No matter her intentions, they lived in two different worlds.

"Why are you shaking your head?"

It was time to clear the air. "I like you, Lillian. And I would like to be a friend to you." He hesitated; she seemed to hang on his words. "But for it to be anything more between us isn't possible. David seems to have taken a fancy to you, and I don't want to see the boy get hurt by an *Englisch* woman with no sense of our ways."

———

A little presumptuous of him, Lillian thought, as she weighed her options. There were two ways to play this. One, she could save face and say she completely agreed and then change the subject. Or two, step out on a huge limb and see if Samuel could practice what he was preaching.

Choosing option two, she said, "I think maybe *you* have taken a fancy to me, also, Samuel Stoltzfus." She lifted her chin and shot him a curious grin.

His eyes widened.

Sensing his shock at her comment, she decided not to back him into a corner where he might choose to not even remain friends. "But . . . okay," she said.

"Okay, what?" He pushed back the rim of his straw hat as though trying to see her better.

"We'll be friends. Nothing more. And we'll make that clear to David as well."

"I think that's a fine idea. I'll talk to David, so the boy doesn't get any misconceptions 'bout us spending time together."

"That's perfect. You and David are the only friends I have here, and I'd hate to lose that." She leaned forward a bit. "So . . . *friend*. Wanna come have another talk by the barn tonight?"

"There's chores to do and I think—" He stopped midsentence when his eyes met with her pleading gaze. "I reckon it would be all right. David and I will come over after suppertime, though. I don't want us to wear out our supper welcome with Irma Rose. Plus, that will give us time to catch up on some chores around here."

"Sounds good. I better head back. I'll see you and David later."

It was nearing six o'clock when Samuel walked downstairs that evening. David was at the kitchen table generously helping himself to leftover butter bread and pickles.

"David, Lillian asked us to come by this evening to talk for a while."

The boy grinned. "You're courting her."

"No, David. Lillian is a friend. Anything else wouldn't be right. I want you to understand that."

With the same maturity beyond his years that Samuel had noticed before, his son said, "I know our ways are different from hers, Pop. But she's here, and she's learnin' our ways. Whose to say God won't work a miracle? Maybe she'll realize she'd like to become Amish."

"David, you know that doesn't happen very often—an *Englisch* man or woman converting. And even if they choose our ways, most can't stick to it. I've told you before: don't be gettin' any silly notions in your head about Lillian. Now go get cleaned up, and we'll just go visit for a while."

Mischievously, David said, "Ivan is picking me up any minute. I told him after church service I would spend the night with him and Katie Ann so I can help him paint the fence starting early in the morning. Didn't he tell you?"

Samuel felt a slight pang of panic. Most of the time he'd spent with Lillian had been with David in tow. Safer that way. "Uh, no. No one told me."

The boy choked down a piece of bread and jumped up from the table. He reached the window and stared into the sunset. "Here comes Ivan now."

Samuel followed his son to the window and saw Ivan's buggy

coming up the driveway. "What am I going to tell Lillian? I told her we'd come for a visit. I didn't know you were going with Ivan."

David spun around on his way to the door. "Guess you'll have to go visit her all by yourself, Pop."

It wasn't right. Going to see Lillian by himself would seem like he was courting her. But if he *wasn't* courting her, then why was he worried about it? It was just a friendly visit, after all.

So why couldn't he control the buzz of activity in his belly at the thought of being alone with her?

7

LILLIAN CONSIDERED CHANGING OUT OF HER AMISH DRESS and back into her blue jeans, but she didn't. As she roamed the yard inspecting her gardening efforts from the previous day, she heard the screen door slam. Grandma took a seat in one of the wooden rockers on the front porch.

"The yard looks *gut*, Lillian."

"*Danki*, Grandma. It was fun planting all these." She waved her arm around, motioning toward her work.

She thought back to Samuel's comments about nurturing the land and how work could be healthy and enjoyable. Planting the flowers didn't seem like work, and it certainly brought her a sense of calm. She noticed she felt the same way after a successful day of baking, or when she mastered a particular sewing task. It was a sense of accomplishment, but there was something else too.

"How's Grandpa feeling?"

"He's resting. I'm thankful he was able to attend worship this morning, but I think he's paying the price about now." She shook her head. Lillian could see the worry in her tired eyes, magnified by dark circles underneath. "The *Englisch* doctors in town changed his medication. Seems to give him a boost of energy, but then he's down and out in the evening hours." She shook her head again.

"I'm sorry I didn't finish my other chores in time to help you with supper." She paused. Grandma was shaking her head as if it didn't matter. But Lillian knew she was going to have to start taking on more chores around the house and try to complete them in a more timely manner. Otherwise, Grandma was going to end up sick right alongside Grandpa.

"Grandma, I think maybe I should just make it a point to cook the meals. That includes breakfast. I've been getting up early, and I've seen what Grandpa likes to eat for breakfast. Why don't you start sleeping in a little bit, and let me handle the cooking?"

As if she didn't hear a word Lillian was saying, Grandma said, "Child, what are you watchin' for down that driveway?" She strained to see down the dirt drive.

"Huh?" Lillian was anxious for Samuel and David to arrive, but she didn't think she was that obvious.

"Are you waiting for Samuel and David?" Grandma wrinkled her nose.

"Oh . . . They're just coming by. For a quick visit." She shrugged her shoulders to signify it was no big deal.

Grandma's lips pursed together and she gave her granddaughter a stern look. "Now, Lillian," she began slowly. "You'd have to be thick as pea soup not to see that you and Samuel have taken a fancy to each other. But you need to be very careful. There's a child involved here, and it seems to me that the boy has taken a fancy to you as well."

So, it wasn't just her imagination. Samuel *did* like her a little more than he was willing to let on. Even Grandma had picked up on it. "We're just friends, Grandma. That's it."

In a tone indicative she wasn't buying it, her grandmother said, "*Ya.*"

"Really. We've talked about it." Lillian took a seat in the other rocker. "We're just going to be friends, and Samuel said he'd talk to David about it."

In spite of her obvious concern, Grandma chuckled.

"What?" She watched her grandma shaking her head.

"You've talked about it?" Grandma's face grew serious. "Lillian, if you've *talked* about it, then the notion for courting must be in both your heads. And you need to know it would be devastating to the community, and to Samuel and David, if he fell *in lieb* with you. You *aren't* Amish and it could cause a world of trouble for Samuel." Her mouth twisted as if biting on a sour grape.

"What?" Lillian couldn't believe what she was hearing. "Grandma, first of all, we barely know each other. No one is *in love.* We're just friends. And I would never allow Samuel to get into any kind of trouble."

"You say that now, dear. When two people are attracted to each other, reckless decisions can be made."

"I know all about reckless decisions, Grandma. I watched Mom make a whole slew of them over the years." She looked away, trying to avoid certain memories that crept into her dreams at night. Her own reckless decisions had stemmed from her attraction to Rickie. But unlike her mother, she refused to allow herself to keep making the same mistakes. She blinked her eyes, shook her head, and turned back toward her grandma. "I like it here. So I don't see why Samuel and I can't be friends."

A worried look still scrolled across the older woman's face. "I didn't say you couldn't be friends, Lillian. I'm sayin' you are both treading into dangerous territory. I'm pleased as punch you like it here and want to stay on for a while, but to live among us is to learn our ways and to give up many things you're used to having. Most people come here looking for something they don't find."

Lillian's chest grew heavy. "Don't you want me here?" She realized just how much she wanted to be here.

"Your *daadi* and I want you here very much." Grandma smiled, but the worry quickly returned. "But running away from something isn't always the answer either."

Lillian thought for a minute and tried to ignore the lump forming in her throat. Maybe Grandma was having second thoughts about bringing her into their community. "Grandma, I'm not running away *from* something—I'm running *to* something. There's been something terribly amiss in my life."

"Do you think you've found that something in Lancaster County?"

"I do, Grandma. Or at least . . . I might have. These last few days have been wonderful. But if you don't want me here, I would understand. I know I have a lot to learn." Tears were building, and she didn't want Grandma to see her cry. Then she'd feel obligated to say she wanted Lillian there.

Grandma reached over and cupped her hand over Lillian's. "Lillian, there is nothing I want more than for you to live with us—for as long as you like." She paused. "But the *something* you are running to won't be found through gardening, cooking, or making bread." She looked at Lillian's blue dress and black apron. "Or by wearing our Plain clothing."

"That's what Samuel said."

Grandma looked shocked at first that she and Samuel had

such conversations. But then she softened. "Well, Samuel's right. Find God, Lillian. The rest will follow."

Find God? And exactly where had He been hiding all her life? She'd tried praying, waiting to see if an all-powerful Being really existed, but her prayers had gone unheard. When she and her mother slept in the car when she was twelve, where was God then? Where was God when her mother begged the landlord for just one more day to pay the rent? When Rickie strode into her life and trapped her in a twisted maze of good and evil, why didn't this Supreme Being show her a path to safety sooner?

Find God. She had looked for God. And while she hadn't ruled out the possibility Someone had helped her through some tough spots, she hadn't ruled out the possibility it was all just coincidence either.

As if reading her mind, Grandma said, "Try to find *not* what the Lord has done for you, but what *you* have done for the Lord."

Lillian pondered her statement for a minute. What could she have possibly done for God when she wasn't even sure He existed?

But if He did exist . . .

Suddenly, it was as if every bad thing she'd ever done was rising to the surface and demanding to be heard. There was an inner conflict going on inside her head she didn't understand. It was confusing.

"Grandma, I want so badly to feel a calmness inside. I want so badly to live a good life." Her heart was heavy. "It's just hard for me to understand why sometimes things happen the way they do." She brushed away a tear.

"There, there, child," Grandma said, again reaching over and placing her hand atop Lillian's. "Some things are just God's will."

There it was again: God's will. That was the part she had the biggest problem with. "But I have doubts, Grandma. I have doubts, and I know that's not right. How can I find God with all these doubts in my mixed-up mind?"

Grandma lifted Lillian's chin up. "I think this is a very good start."

As Samuel turned onto the dirt driveway leading up to Jonas and Irma Rose's place, he'd made up his mind to stay only a few minutes. He'd say *hello*, talk briefly about church service, admire the flowers he knew she'd planted the day before, then be on his way. But all that changed when she met him at his buggy in the front yard. He didn't think he'd ever seen a more fragile-looking creature. Tears stained her rosy cheeks, and her eyes glazed over with emotion. Towering over his *Englisch* friend, he softly asked, "Lillian, what is it?"

She shook her head.

Idle chitchat wasn't on her agenda. Something had her all awhirl. "Lillian?" he asked again.

"I'm sorry, Samuel," she said, dabbing at her eyes.

"Did something happen?" Maybe Jonas had a bad spell. "Is it Jonas?"

"No, no." She took another swipe at her eyes. "Just ignore me. I was having a talk with Grandma . . . a talk about God. I just got kind of emotional and a little upset."

Wondering if this territory was best left alone, he asked, "What got you upset?"

"I have so many doubts about God, and I don't have a relationship with Him. And I want to, Samuel. I really do. But I
don't know how to go about it."

She was clearly waiting for answers. And he didn't have any.
It wasn't his job to show Lillian the way to God. *Unequally yoked.*
The phrase pounded away in his head. Missionary work was not
part of the Amish way. Steering clear of nonbelievers in an intimate way—friendly or otherwise—was.

When he didn't respond, she turned her back toward him.

"Lillian?" he asked, unsure what to say or do.

After a few seconds, she turned back around. "Let's don't do
this," she said after taking a deep breath. "I had a conversation
with Grandma that got me thinking about things. About God.
And then you got here. You just caught me during an emotional
moment. Let's talk about something else."

"*Ya,*" he said relieved. They'd talk about something else for a
short while, and then he was hightailing it home. He shouldn't
be there in the first place. The *Englisch* woman was mixed up, all
right. She was a downright mess.

But a beautiful mess.

What a whiny baby. Lillian hardly knew the man and yet she had
gotten teary in front of him twice. Once over a cow and now
about her lack of faith. She frowned as he followed her to their
spot on the side of the barn. From now on, cheery conversation
was in order.

"Sadie didn't acknowledge me at church service today," she
said without thinking first. Not exactly cheery conversation.

"She was jealous." Samuel seemed to regret the comment the minute he said it. He glanced away when she met his eyes with a look of surprise.

"Really? Why would she be jealous? You and I aren't courting." She should have avoided empahsizing the word *courting*. He looked uncomfortable.

As silence formed a barrier between them, Samuel changed the subject. "The other evening we spent most of our time talking about life here. Tell me about yourself, Lillian. Tell me about your life before Lancaster County."

She watched him place his straw hat on the stump nearby. His flattened hat hair did nothing to take away from his stunning looks. As she watched him stroking his beard, she tried to envision the face underneath. "What do you want to know?"

"Whatever you're comfortable telling me." He shrugged.

"Hmm, let's see." She'd made so many mistakes. Surely he didn't want to hear about her failures. Better to focus on the positives in her life. "I was a teacher in Houston. I wanted to make a difference in the lives of children, help them see their potential and feel good about themselves. I love kids."

"Well, David sure likes you."

"He's a great kid. You've done a good job with him."

"*Ya*, he's a *gut* boy. But, I can really only take credit for the past couple of years. Before that, I give credit to his *mamm*. After Rachel died, I've done the best I know how."

She wanted to know more about Rachel. But before she could say anything, he said, "So tell me more."

"I guess saying I'm a lost soul trying to find my way would sound a little dramatic." She cringed and forced a half smile.

"Less dramatic would be to say I needed to get away from my mother for a while, and I had a bad breakup with my boyfriend." She paused and looked up to see him hanging on her words. "So I'm trying something new."

"What happened with your boyfriend?" he asked.

This was veering away from the cheery conversation she'd hoped for earlier. She shrugged, unsure how much to tell Samuel.

"Did you love him?"

"I thought I did."

He was waiting for more. There was so much more. She hesitated, but the look on his face was kind and encouraging. "Rickie was great in the beginning. Very loving and kind."

His eyes were intently focused on her, and she wished she could finagle her way out of this conversation. She'd make it brief so they could move on to something else. "Then he just changed."

"What do you mean?"

Closing her eyes, she pushed the vivid details of her and Rickie's last confrontation out of her mind. She was far, far away from him and didn't want to dredge up the memories. "He just changed," she repeated as she shook her head. "I should have never moved in with him."

"You lived with him? And you weren't married?"

"It was a horrible mistake. I should have never moved in with him," she repeated. She meant it, but why all of a sudden did she feel like Samuel thought less of her with this confession?

She prepared herself for a turn in his attitude toward her, but he surprised her. "All of us make mistakes. God forgives us for those mistakes." His tone was gentle and kind.

Lillian shook her head. "He wouldn't forgive me, Samuel. I've made too many mistakes. I try to be a good person and live a good life, but I keep falling down. I've tried so hard not to make the mistakes my mother made. And yet, somehow, I let Rickie creep into my life. He wasn't good for me."

Samuel tilted his head to one side; she felt as though he was staring right through her. "Of course God would forgive you, Lillian. All you have to do is ask Him. The important thing is to get up when you fall down, and it sounds like you have."

"You make it sound so easy, Samuel."

In an unexpected gesture, he reached over and briefly patted her hand. "Maybe you should try it."

Something was going on inside her. Something she couldn't get a grasp on. All this talk about God and forgiveness stirred emotions inside that she wasn't familiar with. Grandma and Samuel—both so solid in their faith . . . Maybe there was something to it all.

Suddenly she felt cheated out of whatever insight they both seemed to have.

"I can't help but wonder how different my life might have been if Mom had just stayed and raised me here." Would she be privy to the same strong faith Samuel and Grandma had? She cringed at the thought of some of the situations she and her mother had endured over the years.

"Do you know why your *mamm* left?"

"No, I don't. Mom won't talk about it, and I don't think Grandma and Grandpa really know. I guess I'm looking for answers in several areas."

"Where's your father?" He balanced both elbows on his knees and leaned forward. Facing him, she did the same—putting their faces about a foot away from each other. As darkness closed in around them, she could see Samuel's features illuminated with interest.

"I don't know." This was another painful subject. Somehow they'd gone offtrack in an effort to keep things upbeat.

"We don't have to talk about this," he said softly, as if sensing it caused her discomfort.

"It's okay. I don't know where my father is because I don't know *who* my father is. Mom said she doesn't know. But she's lying. She does this thing with her eyes and nose when she's lying." She blinked repeatedly and crinkled her nose, to show him. "Like that."

He smiled broadly, amused by her imitation, which lightened the mood.

"I know. It looks funny. But I'm telling you, that's how I can tell she's lying. I can recognize a lie immediately. I've heard plenty over the years."

"It sounds like you had a hard childhood."

"Let's just say my mother wouldn't have received the Mother-of-the-Year award."

His bewildered gaze made her wonder if talking so intimately with him was a mistake. She'd probably shared too much about Rickie. And she'd barely touched on that painful part of her past. He probably had the perfect childhood. Great parents. A wonderful family. She, on the other hand, didn't know who her father was, had duplicated her mother's legacy by living with a man she wasn't married to, and wasn't even sure she believed in God.

"Parenting is a hard job." He pushed back his windblown

bangs and wiped his forehead. "So, if you weren't really *in lieb* with Rickie, have you ever been truly *in lieb*?"

Samuel had a way of changing the subject when he felt it was time to move on. Where was he going with all this? And if they were just going to be friends . . . why was he so interested? "No, I don't think I have," she said, realizing it was heartbreakingly true. She looked at the ground.

"It's a *wunderbaar* thing to be *in lieb*," he said.

She looked up at him. He looked as if he were a million miles away, presumably with thoughts of Rachel. She couldn't imagine losing someone so dear. Placing her hand atop his just felt very natural.

Samuel knew he was in dangerous territory. Somehow his plan to keep the visit brief and be on his way hadn't panned out the way he intended. But the feel of her soft hand resting on his gave him comfort. Her touch ignited senses in him that he had buried along with Rachel. His blossoming friendship with Lillian was confusing. Wonderfully confusing.

Underneath the moonlit sky her face was radiantly aglow, as if the clouds parted solely for her benefit and bathed her in the magic of the night. He tried to put his apprehension at ease and just enjoy the moment. It had been a mighty long time since he'd felt this good. But as he attempted to bask in the present, visions of Rachel began to flash through his mind. How he'd loved her and missed her. The feel of her soft skin. Her passion for life.

Lillian had that same passion.

Scolding himself for comparing the women, he gently pulled

his hand from underneath Lillian's and sat up a little straighter, leaning away from her. Surely God would help him steer clear of such temptation. To hold hands, no matter how calming the effect, wasn't right.

As Samuel pulled his hand away, Lillian worried if perhaps she'd crossed a line she shouldn't have. Cupping her hand over his had been an unplanned expression of mild affection that just happened. She didn't mean anything by it. But she didn't recognize the emotion she was experiencing. It wasn't a physical longing, but a yearning of the heart. Her need to be close to Samuel was overwhelming.

"What are you thinking about?" she asked, fearful her small gesture might have caused him to withdraw. There was so much she wanted to know about him.

He shrugged. "I reckon I was just thinking about a lot of things."

"Rachel?" she asked softly, hoping he would open up to her. But he shook his head. "Not so much."

His expression said otherwise, but Lillian wasn't going to push it. She decided to change the subject this time. "Are you curious about the outside world? I mean, have you ever been tempted to walk away from all this?"

"I know all about the outside world. During my *rumschpringe* I was allowed to experience the *Englisch* world. I watched television, went to movies, rode in cars with *Englisch* friends, drank beer, and kicked my heels up at the local dance hall." He paused. "You look speechless. And one thing I have learned about you is that you're usually not without somethin' to say."

She looked away, feeling a little embarrassed. "Yes, I tend to talk a lot."

"That's a good thing, though. You have a bubbly spirit."

"Which means I talk a lot."

Samuel reached beside him and retrieved his hat. Placing it atop his head, he stared intently at her. He gave her the strangest look, and Lillian couldn't decipher it.

"Just because I choose this life doesn't mean I don't know what's out there." He swung his arm toward the highway. "I hope you find what you're looking for, Lillian."

Jonas stumbled around the kitchen until he found some leftover butter bread. A slice of bread and some lemonade was in order. Irma Rose would be fit to be tied if she knew he'd made his way down the stairs by himself so soon after taking his pills. But he was hungry, and the poor woman was snoring so loud he didn't have the heart to wake her. The Good Lord had seen fit to give him the cancer, but he knew his wife was plumb worn-out from tending to him all during the night. She shouldn't have to be caring for him during the sleeping hours. Some things he could do for himself. A man should be able to walk down the stairs and get a slice of bread and some lemonade if he wanted them.

As he filled his glass up, he thought he heard voices. The wooden door in the kitchen was open, and he hobbled to the screen door. "Well, well," he whispered as he spotted Lilly and

Samuel out by the barn. "Looking mighty cozy." Jonas sighed. Irma Rose would have a fit about now.

Feeling a little light on his feet, Jonas headed back toward the lemonade pitcher he had left on the table. He topped off his glass and took a big gulp. Having another look outside, he couldn't help but share some of his wife's worry about Samuel and Lilly. They'd have a hard road ahead of them should they start court- ing. Straining to get a better look, he chuckled. If they thought they *weren't* courting, they were fooling themselves.

Knowing Irma Rose might stir and be all wound up he was gone, he finished off the butter bread and put the lemonade back in the refrigerator. Taking a step into the den, he looked up at the stairs. Going up was a mite more challenging than coming down. And it sounded like he had bees in his head. *Buzz, buzz, buzz.* A bothersome noise, getting louder by the second.

He reached for the back of the wooden rocker to steady him- self. Seemed like his legs were turning to jelly, and the bee noise was getting louder and louder. He took another couple of steps. *Just need to get back in bed, that's all.*

As everything went dark, he never felt his lanky body slam onto the wood floor. Nor did he feel it when his head caught the corner of the rocker. And he couldn't feel the rush of blood spill- ing into a pool beneath him.

8

Lillian responded to Samuel's comment about finding what she was looking for by simply nodding. The tone of his voice indicated he might not be interested in playing much of a role in that process.

As he stood up, presumably to leave, Lillian tried to think of something to say, something that might make him stay. She wasn't sure, but Samuel seemed hesitant to go.

Say something. Anything. He appeared to be waiting for her to come up with a reason for him to linger. But maybe she was reading him wrong.

Before she could come up with anything, a loud noise from inside the house caused them both to redirect their attention.

"What was that?" she asked, turning toward the porch.

Samuel began to move toward the house. Lillian was right behind him. Sensing something was wrong, they both burst into a run, taking two steps at a time up the porch steps. As they moved through the kitchen, Lillian heard her grandma calling her name repeatedly.

"Grandma!" she answered, never slowing her pace behind Samuel as they entered the den.

Grandma was hurriedly making her way down the stairs toward her husband. "Lillian!" she yelled. "Lillian, help!"

The three of them rushed to Grandpa's crumpled figure on the wood floor. Grandma gently lifted his head. Tenderly cradling it in her lap, she brushed back his blood-soaked hair. "Jonas, wake up," she cried. "Oh, Jonas. Oh, Jonas, wake up." She looked up at Lillian and Samuel. "Lillian, he won't wake up. My Jonas won't wake up. Oh, Lillian . . . *do* something."

Lillian was frozen, legs glued to the floor. So much blood. Grandma's agonizing cries echoed through the old house, and Lillian felt like she might pass out. One thought consumed her. *Is Grandpa dead?*

Samuel ripped his shirt from his body before Lillian had time to gather her thoughts. Applying pressure to Grandpa's head, he turned to face her. With a calmness Lillian found incredible, he firmly said, "Lillian, bring me some wet towels and then go get your portable telephone."

"Jonas," Grandma cried. "Please, Jonas. Wake up, my love."

"Now, Lillian!" Samuel yelled, bolting her into action. She retrieved a wad of towels from the kitchen drawer and soaked them with water from the sink. Dropping the towels into Samuel's hands, she looked down at Grandpa. His mouth hung open, and his face was pasty white. He was dead. She just knew it. This couldn't be happening. She was just getting to know him.

"Not yet, God. Not yet," she silently prayed.

"Go get your telephone, Lillian," Samuel said, holding the wet towels against the gaping gash in Grandpa's head. "Hurry."

She bolted up the stairs, continuing to pray. Aloud she repeated, "Please, God, don't let him die. Please, God, don't let him die."

She repeated the prayer all the way back down the stairs, whispering as she neared the threesome. Samuel was holding his hand out for the phone. He grabbed it, fiddled with it, and handed it right back to her.

"I don't know how this works," he said, frustrated. Then he rattled off a number and instructed Lillian to dial it. When it started ringing, she handed it to him.

"Mr. Pierson, this is Samuel Stoltzfus. I'm out at Irma Rose and Jonas's place, and we need some help. Can you bring your car out here? Jonas is hurt, and we need to get to a hospital." He nodded and set the phone down as he turned his attention to Irma Rose. "He's on his way."

Lillian watched the way Samuel calmly handled a crisis. She, on the other hand, was fighting waves of panic, and she still worried she might faint. She sat down on the floor beside Grandma and put her arm around her. The woman's cries softened. But as she rocked back and forth stroking her husband's face with hands covered in blood, Grandma's lips moved in prayer. If ever there was a time to pray, it was now.

Lillian closed her eyes and pleaded with God for her grandfather's life. If there was a God, he wouldn't let her grandpa die.

———

"What's all the fuss about? Irma Rose, why in the world are you crying?" Jonas reached up and touched his head. Samuel sighed, feeling the relief wash over him. Lillian let go with sobs she must have been stifling the whole time, and Irma Rose looked toward the heavens and whispered softly, "Thank you, Lord."

"I think you gave the ladies a scare, Jonas," Samuel said,

continuing to apply pressure to Jonas's head with the wet towels. "Mr. Pierson is on the way with his car, and we'll get you to the hospital."

Jonas looked around at the three of them before honing in on Irma Rose. "You know I *hate* hospitals, Irma Rose. I'd rather you just fix me up here."

"You silly old man," she blasted. "I can't fix you. You need a doctor." She shook her head in exasperation. "What in the name of the Good Lord made you come down here by yourself?"

Samuel glanced at Lillian, who was still crying. Discreetly he reached for her hand and gave it a quick squeeze.

Jonas was glaring at Irma Rose as if he'd like to rip her head off. "I was hungry!"

"Why didn't you get me from my sleep then?" Irma Rose demanded, patting her eyes.

Ignoring his wife, Jonas looked over at Lillian. "Lilly, why are you crying?"

Lillian wiped her eyes. "You scared us, Grandpa."

Jonas patted her hand. "Thought I was dead, didn't ya?" Then he chuckled.

"That's not funny, Grandpa!" Lillian's tone of voice made it clear she was not amused.

"You scared us all, Jonas," Irma Rose belted out. "From now on, if you get a hankering for a late-night snack, you get me or Lillian."

"*Ya,* I'd have starved to death waiting on one of you."

Samuel tried not to laugh. He glanced at Lillian, who was also fighting a trembly grin. He was glad she'd stopped crying. Always a joker, Jonas was turning a bad situation around, with everyone laughing to keep from crying.

"You were snoring so loud, Irma Rose, the house could've fallen down and you wouldn't have taken a notice." Jonas turned his attention to Lillian. "And our *kinskind* here was busying herself with other things." He looked at Samuel and grinned.

Lillian picked up on the curious stares all around them at the hospital. True, they were all covered in blood, but she heard the occasional whispered, "Oh, look, they're Amish." She supposed it would have been worse if they were somewhere other than Lancaster County, where so many Amish lived.

"Thank you, Mr. Pierson," Samuel said, shaking the man's hand.

Lillian could tell right away the men shared a friendship. So Samuel had friends who weren't Amish. And a good thing too. Mr. Pierson had arrived within minutes of Samuel's phone call, and without his help it would have been difficult to get Grandpa up off the floor.

"I'm glad you called, Samuel. Any time I can help you folks, you let me know." The gray-headed man smiled. "I'm going to go call Mrs. Pierson and let her know everything is all right."

As they waited for Grandpa to get his head stitched up, Lillian looked at Grandma seated nearby. Her head was tilted back, and she appeared to be sleeping. Samuel leaned against the wall, looking as haggard as she felt.

"Thank God he only needs a few stitches and that he's okay otherwise," Lillian said to Samuel as she stood beside him. *Yes, thank God.* She had prayed, and Grandpa had lived. It worked.

When Samuel didn't respond, she asked, "Are you okay?" He didn't look okay.

He took a deep breath and blew it out slowly. "I haven't been here since Rachel died."

Instinctively, she reached for his hand. And as her fingers brushed against the top of his hand . . . he pulled away. And it stung.

Samuel recognized Ms. Morgan behind the desk. The nurse had stayed with him and Rachel right up until the end. For weeks, the woman had tended to Rachel's every need. Samuel hoped she wouldn't recognize him.

He scooted slightly away from Lillian. He should have never squeezed her hand when they were on the floor tending to Jonas. She had just looked so sad and scared at the time, and it was nothing more than a comforting gesture. But he needn't have her thinking his action was an open invitation for affection—particularly *public* affection.

Glancing at Lillian, he feared his deliberate action had hurt her feelings. She'd been through enough on this night. He didn't want to add to her upset, but this touching of the hands needed to stop. It wasn't proper, and it roused feelings in Samuel he shouldn't be having. Especially right now, only a little ways from where he'd said good-bye to his beloved Rachel in a small room down the hall.

"Samuel?" The tenderness in her voice warmed his heart and frightened him just the same. "I know it must be hard for you to be here. If you need to leave . . ."

He wasted no time accepting an excuse to leave before he said or did something he'd regret.

"I'm glad Jonas is going to be okay," he said abruptly. "Tell

Mr. Pierson I needed to head on home. I'll take a taxi cab. He'll wait for you all and take you home." His emotions were flailing and he needed out of there.

"Okay," she said. "I don't know what we would have done if you hadn't been there, Samuel. Thank you so much."

Samuel nodded and took a step away from her and toward the exit door. He'd almost made a clean getaway when he heard her call his name.

"*Ya,*" he answered, turning reluctantly.

"Maybe you'd like to come over for supper tomorrow night? You and David." She paused when he didn't answer. "As a repayment of sorts for all you did tonight." She smiled as warmly as he'd ever seen.

He looked at her a moment, then shook his head sharply. "*Danki,* Lillian, but I can't." The woman was frustrating him, confusing him, and he was irritated with himself for allowing her to do so.

Her pleading green eyes made it mighty hard to walk away. But he did.

Irma Rose might close her eyes from time to time but seldom her ears. As Lillian plopped down beside her in the waiting room, she opened her eyes and looked at her granddaughter. She had heard the sharpness in Samuel's tone when he declined the supper invitation, and it saddened her to see her granddaughter unhappy. But it was bound to happen. Samuel was content with his world, willingly locked into his life among the Plain folk, and he was a smart enough man to recognize what was happening between the two of them. Probably best he put an end to anything before it got started. It would be more painful for both of them down the road if he didn't.

"It takes a strong man to walk away from something he might want but knows isn't right by God."

Lillian tucked her head in embarrassment, "You heard?"

Irma Rose patted her leg. "I did."

"It was just an invitation for a meal. But the way he spoke to me was rather harsh."

As Irma Rose suspected, her granddaughter was hurt. "Be true to yourself, Lillian. There's a spark between you and that Samuel, and it has nowhere to turn but into flames. And if it had continued, you'd both have been burned far worse than you are now."

"It's not what you're thinking, Grandma. We talked about it. We were just going to be friends."

"*Ya*, so you say. But I saw him squeeze your hand at home when we were tending to Jonas. And I saw you reach for his hand a few minutes ago." Wondering if she'd already said too much, she went on. "Has he kissed you yet?"

"Grandma! Of course not."

Lillian's incredulous look screamed guilt. If they hadn't kissed, she imagined it wasn't for lack of wanting on Lillian's part.

"Lillian, we might be Plain and not know much about worldly things, but we love and we have desires, just like the rest of the world." She could only assume her granddaughter was no longer pure. Living out in the world, she was bound to have succumbed to things that would be unheard of in their Amish community. There was no judgment. It was just a fact.

"Samuel isn't wise about worldly ways, nor are your *daadi* and me. Temptation to step astray is unheard of in our community. We live by the *Ordnung*."

Lillian's face took on a flush, and her eyes filled with tears. Irma Rose regretted instantly that she'd clearly said something to hurt the girl's feelings. "Lillian, I just meant—"

But her granddaughter interrupted her. "You think I'm *seducing* Samuel. You think I'm filled with impure thoughts and tempting him to go against his beliefs!"

"That is not what I said, Lillian. What I meant was—"

"Grandma, you really don't know me at all. I'm nothing like my mother." And with that the child stormed off, leaving Irma Rose with a heavy heart.

Irma Rose knew Lillian spoke the truth. She *had* been fearful Lillian would pull Samuel into her world, in every way. Apparently she'd been wrong.

After four days of not seeing Samuel and barely speaking to her grandma, Lillian decided it was time to make amends with everyone. Grandma had tried repeatedly to apologize for anything she might have said to hurt her feelings, but Lillian had made little effort to recognize her attempts. She and Grandma had continued on with their daily chores, often side by side, but the tension was thick. Samuel had come to the door asking about her the day before, and she refused to come downstairs.

Today was a new day, and she was going to start fresh.

"Grandma," she said as she walked into the kitchen early that

morning. "I told you I'd make breakfast. Sit down and I'll do it."
She gently pried the spoon from Grandma's hand and began to
stir the eggs.

"You haven't had much to say to me, Lillian. I'm feeling badly
about things," Grandma said. She sat down on the bench at the
kitchen table.

"I'm sorry. I got my feelings hurt, and I should have talked
things out with you."

"I am sorry, Lillian. For me to presume that by living out in
the world you had not made good choices was wrong of me."
Lillian turned around to see her grandma shaking her head.

"Oh, I've made bad choices, Grandma. Make no mistake. But
I've tried to avoid some of the same blunders I watched my
mother make over the years." She had to accept responsibility for
her bad judgment when it came to Rickie. But she planned to
better her life by learning from the experience, as opposed to
reliving the pattern via a repetitious string of men who were
wrongly suited for her—as Mom did.

Grandma seemed to be in deep thought, a place she retreated
to anytime there was mention of her mother.

"I want to study the *Ordnung*. I want to learn everything about
living Amish. Maybe it would help me to get my mind right."

"Lillian," her grandma began, then paused. "Nothing would
please me more. Please don't take offense by what I am about to
say . . ." She hesitated again.

"What, Grandma?" Lillian stopped stirring the eggs and
turned completely around.

"Just do it for the right reasons."

"You mean not for Samuel, but for myself?"

"*Ya.*"

"I am. And I'm going to talk to Samuel and set things right with him as well. I want him to know I'm not interested in anything more than friendship with him and that there is no reason why we can't get back on track with that." And she meant it. She'd had a few days to realize that she needed to realign her proiorities. Lancaster County represented a new beginning. She wanted to get back to making the right choices.

"Well, hello there," she said to David later that afternoon.

"Hey, where've you been?" he asked. His tone indicated his feelings might be hurt.

"I've just been thinking about things," she said as she followed him to the barn. "Whatcha doin'?"

He was carrying a cardboard box with a lid on it. "These are old newspapers I found in the other barn. They were getting wet, though, so I was moving 'em in here."

"Are there any more? Want some help?" She eyed the box, thinking maybe she'd catch up on the history of Lancaster County when she had some spare time.

"That was the last box. There were three of them." He pointed at two other boxes stacked nearby. "This barn stays dry. The other one has a few leaks. Pop says we'll fix those one day for Jonas and Irma Rose."

"Speaking of your pop, here he comes." She watched as Samuel maneuvered Pete onto the dirt driveway. "David," she said hesitantly. "Do you think it would be all right if I talked to your pop alone for a minute?"

"I think if it will make him stop being so sad, then *ya*." David shrugged and turned to walk off.

"David, wait," she said, realizing things didn't seem the same between them. He turned around and faced her, and the look on his face confirmed her suspicions. "Things are just complicated sometimes, you know?"

He seemed to be thinking as he glanced up to see his pop getting nearer. "I reckon sometimes grown-ups make things complicated that needn't be."

"*Ya,*" she whispered as he walked off. "You're probably right."

Samuel was glad to see Lillian waiting for him in the front yard. He smiled with newfound confidence as he approached her. He had done a lot of soul-searching and prayed for answers over the past four days. He was creating problems that need not be there and worrying about things he shouldn't. They'd discussed the terms of their friendship, and there was no reason they had to stray from that. Being attracted to Lillian didn't mean he had to act on it.

"Hello, Samuel," she said as he walked to where she was sitting in the grass.

"I tried to talk to you yesterday. I feel badly about speaking so harshly to you when I left the hospital." He sat down in the grass beside her.

"I think I understand, and there are some things I want to clear up." She paused, then started to wave her hand in front of her nose.

"What?" he asked as she edged away from him.

"You smell like you've been rolling in manure, Samuel

Stoltzfus." She crinkled her nose as he sniffed at himself, feeling highly embarrassed.

"I came straight from the fields spreading manure, and the wheels from the plow probably slung some my way." He went to stand up, but she put a hand on his arm.

"No, sit down. I can take it." She giggled, but quickly removed her hand. "I just wanted to tell you that I think maybe you have the wrong impression about something, and I want you to understand that—"

"No, Lillian. Me first," he interrupted. "My chores aren't the whole truth as to why I said I couldn't come to supper. I've been worried that maybe you and me were moving in a direction that might not be right in God's eyes. But I've prayed hard about it, and I think maybe it's still His will for us to be friends." There. He'd said it. Now, with the Good Lord's help, he'd live the life God meant him to live and be the man he knew he should be.

"That's exactly what I wanted to tell you."

Samuel sighed with relief.

"Only, I have one more thing to tell you. I'm going to be studying the *Ordnung*. Grandma is planning to teach me everything about the Amish faith. And I just want to make it clear to you that I'm doing this for *me*, no other reason. I seem to have gotten sidetracked from my original plan when I came to Lancaster County: to find a sense of who I am and my role on this earth. I don't understand about God, or having a relationship with Him. But I *want* to understand. And I prayed to God to let Grandpa live. And it worked."

It worked? She wasn't exactly fully on the road to becoming Amish, but she at least had a foot on the path. So instead of arguing that her motivation for prayer was still misdirected, he said, "I think that's a fine idea." Studying the *Ordnung* would be good for Lillian. And they seemed to be clearing the air about some things.

———

"What's your pop and my Lilly have their heads together about?" Jonas asked David as he took a seat in the other rocker on the front porch.

"Not sure," David said.

Jonas strained to have a better look. Lilly had been moping around ever since they came home from the hospital. He didn't know what had happened, but he was hoping they'd fix whatever it was.

"I brought you boys some sweet tea," Irma Rose said, walking onto the porch toting two glasses. She looked out toward Lillian and Samuel. "Nice to see them talking again," she said as David attempted to get up and give her his seat. "Keep your seat," she said, smiling. "I can see better standing up."

"Pop's seemed kinda down lately," David said.

"Well, our Lilly has been in a *baremlich* mood too." Jonas shook his head.

"Definitely not herself lately." Irma Rose sat down on the porch step.

"They'll both be better now," David said. "They just have to get things uncomplicated."

"What do you mean, David?" Jonas asked him, curious where the boy's mind was.

"Lillian said her world was complicated. And by coming here, she's complicated my pop's world. She didn't mean to. It just happened." The boy shook his head and frowned. "They're both just making things complicated for themselves, and they needn't be. It's all real clear to me."

"What's clear?" Irma Rose asked.

The boy took a sip of his tea and said proudly, "She's my new *mamm*. Her and Pop just haven't figured it out yet."

Jonas knew his eyes were bugging out of his head. But he also knew a person wouldn't have to look far to find eyes gaping even larger than his own. You could've mistaken Irma Rose for an owl. She sat motionless, eyes bulging, speechless.

"Take a deep breath, Irma Rose," Jonas said, hoping his wife wouldn't say too much to the boy. He had to agree with David. Samuel and Lilly were making things too complicated. One day at a time. Once Lilly completed her studies of the *Ordnung*, there was no telling what the Good Lord might have in mind for them. But if they took to courting, it would be a long road to travel. He hoped they both survived the trip in one piece. He hoped Irma Rose would survive it. The woman was looking a tad pale.

"Well, David, stranger things have happened. I'm sure God will guide both your pop and our Lilly in the right direction," Jonas said as he reached over and patted poor Irma Rose on the hand.

David smiled. "He already has."

9

"WHAT DO YOU MEAN THERE IS NO EQUALITY OF THE sexes?" Lillian asked Grandma the next morning as they began to tackle the *Ordnung*.

"It's very clear in the Bible, Lillian." Grandma dried another plate and handed it to Lillian to put in the cabinet.

"It actually says in the Bible that women are to be subservient to men?"

Grandma looked confused, and Lillian realized she didn't understand the question. "The women serve the men, so to speak?" she translated.

"'He is the image and glory of God: but the woman is the glory of the man,'" Grandma said with pride. "'For the man is not of the woman: but the woman of the man. Neither was the man created for the woman; but the woman for the man.'"

Lillian sat down at the kitchen table, pondering the biblical reference. "I might have some trouble with this one, Grandma. Relationships should be an equal partnership." She shook her head. "I've noticed the way the Amish women always sit in the back, eat last, and wait on the men hand and foot."

"We are proud to do so. We don't question the Bible." Grandma placed another plate in the cabinet and took a seat at the kitchen

126

table across from Lillian. "It is our job to care for our husbands, the children, and the home."

"I understand that, and that part is fine. But to say there is no equality just doesn't seem right."

"The man is the ruler of the home."

Lillian chuckled. "Now Grandma, you seem to have a pretty strong thumb on Grandpa."

Playfully Grandma said, "*Ya*, but Grandpa doesn't know that." She paused. "But in our early years, things were different. And I'm still proud to do for your Grandpa, even in his silliness."

"When I get married, my husband is going to have a clear understanding that we are entering into a union as *equals*."

"*Ya*, as long as you don't marry an Amish man," Grandma said, tilting her chin upward. "To marry an Amish man, you would say in your vows that the man is the head of the household and that you are his helpmate."

"Who made this rule?"

Grandma seemed taken aback. "Why, God, of course. We don't question the Bible, Lillian. Let's move along."

Lillian was still wrestling with the literal interpretation of this particular Bible reference when Grandma continued, "The two most important things to understand are our rejection of *hochmut*, which is pride and arrogance, and that we are not forward, self-promoting, or assertive. We let things be."

Grandma folded her hands together and sat up a little straighter. "For example," she pressed on. "It is perfectly fine for us to ride in automobiles. But to own such a means of transportation would be arrogant and prideful. There are so many different kinds of cars. All the choices of price, color, and accessories could cause us to be competitive—which would be a breeding ground for arrogance and pride. We have to watch our young folks when they go through their *rumschpringe*. Many times they add radios in the buggies or opt to install flashy trinkets, which distinguishes one from the other. That is not acceptable in our way of life."

"Okay," Lillian answered softly, realizing Grandma was enjoying her role as teacher. However, this topic was clearly non-negotiable.

"And when I say we let things be," she added, "that means we accept all things as being God's will. The *Englisch* often mistake our passiveness as not caring. That's not true. We do care. But we believe God will resolve a situation in a way that's best for all concerned."

As if checking items off on a mental list of things to teach Lillian, Grandma continued. "Our children become adults when they are baptized and make a lifetime vow of obedience to the *Ordnung*."

"How is the *Ordnung* different from the Bible?" Lillian didn't know a lot about the Bible. But at least the Bible was a book that could be studied. So much of the *Ordnung* was unwritten.

"Let me see how I can explain this so you will understand," Grandma pondered, pausing. "You really can't compare the *Ordnung* to the Bible, Lillian. We believe in literal interpretation of the Bible. Meaning we don't question it. That belief is part of the *Ordnung*, which is our governing system. The *Ordnung* is a means of making sure we all live by the Scriptures in the Bible."

"Shouldn't all the rules be written down for people to study and to prevent misinterpretations?" *You'd think over the many years someone would have done that.*

"The *Ordnung* varies from district to district. Governance is local."

"So why aren't the rules for the *Ordnung* in this district written down and studied?" Lillian had spent the better part of her life studying written texts, all the way through college. She'd made a career out of teaching others to do the same.

"We just know them," Grandma answered. "We begin learning the order of conduct in the *Ordnung* at a young age. It's passed down from generation to generation."

Seeing there was no hope for a written study guide, a practical question popped into Lillian's head. She knew the rule but hoped it could be bent. "Grandma, I don't understand why we can't cut our hair. It seems to me that as busy as we are, it would be a lot easier to manage, and—"

Grandma vigorously shook her head; it appeared that there was no questioning this rule. "No, no, no, Lillian. 'But if a woman have long hair, it is a glory to her: for her hair is given her for a covering.' This is in Corinthians, Lillian. We do not cut our hair."

Grandma abruptly jumped up. "I have something for you, Lillian. Wait here."

It was a couple of minutes before she returned from upstairs. Rejoining Lillian at the table, she handed her a black book. "Is this for me to keep?" Lillian asked. She'd never owned a Bible.

"It is. And you'll notice an inscription inside from me and your grandpa." Bouncing back in time, she said, "I bought it when you were born."

Lillian read the inscription: *This Holy Bible presented to Lillian Miller by Mammi and Daadi.*

"I've dreamed about this day." Grandma's eyes grew moist. "I'd hoped that maybe someday you'd come callin' for the Lord. I'd meant to give it to you when you were here last. You were young, but I meant to send it after you left." She shook her head. "And I forgot."

"Thank you, Grandma." Holding the book gave Lillian an unfamiliar sense of hope.

"You seem to need words to study," Grandma offered. "Study the Bible, Lillian. It is the contents of this book that we live by. To understand the *Ordnung*, you must first understand God's Word."

"I will, Grandma." She blinked back her own emotions.

The lesson continued for the rest of the morning while they baked extra loaves of bread for a sick friend of Grandma's. With a full plate of her own, Grandma never complained and always volunteered to help those around her.

For the next several weeks, Samuel and David ate supper once a week with Lillian, Irma Rose, and sometimes Jonas, when he was well enough. Lillian always cooked, and much of the menu came from Samuel's garden. It was the highlight of Lillian's week. Finally, she had a family. A *real* family. David and Samuel had become as much a part of her little group as Jonas and Irma Rose.

"How are your studies of the *Ordnung* coming along?" Samuel asked one evening after supper.

Lillian handed him and David each a piece of shoofly pie. "It's a lot to learn, but I'm getting there. It's hard because so much of the *Ordnung* isn't written down. Everyone here starts learning at such a young age and I guess it just sticks. I'm trying to absorb and store all the information as best I can."

She thought it best not to mention her constant questioning of their ways. Grandma spent much of their morning sessions exasperated by Lillian's inability to just accept complete obedience to God's will without all the questions. But with strained patience, Grandma continued to instruct her daily about the code of conduct they all lived by. She realized how hopeful Grandma was that she'd choose their ways.

"She's a fast learner," Grandma said, placing a piece of pie on a plate. "I'm going to take this upstairs to Jonas."

After waiting until Grandma was out of earshot, Samuel asked, "How is Jonas? I noticed he hasn't been at supper the past two weeks."

"I don't think he's doing so well," she said, taking a seat on the bench beside David and across from Samuel. "He's been in bed a lot during the day too. It's hard on Grandma. I've offered to help her with Grandpa, but she insists on taking care of him all by herself."

"Men are funny about things. Maybe Jonas wouldn't be comfortable with you tending to him," Samuel said.

"Well, he's going to have to get over that, or I'm afraid Grandma's going to just wear herself out."

"*Ya*, it's hard when you're a caregiver."

"You took real good care of my *mamm*," David said to Samuel.

"I did the best I could."

Samuel often looked uncomfortable at the mention of Rachel. Lillian sure wanted to know what the woman looked like and more about her. But she'd never know. Samuel offered up little information about Rachel and she'd learned the second commandment forbid photos: *Thou shalt not make unto thee any graven image, or any likeness of any thing that is in heaven above, or that is in the earth beneath, or that is in the water under the earth.*

She had been studying. And putting on her Amish attire had become as natural as brushing her teeth in the morning. But to go without *any* pictures the rest of your life . . . That particular rule, like several others, seemed to take things too literally. But literal interpretation of the Bible was the Amish way. There was no picking and choosing of the rules.

"It must be hard not to have any pictures to remember her by," she said, resting her chin in her hands. She glanced back and forth between Samuel and David. "I don't like that rule."

"I remember exactly what she looked like," Samuel said softly and in a tone she seldom heard him use. He seemed a million miles away with thoughts of Rachel.

Lillian's stomach twisted. For all her honest efforts to keep a healthy distance from Samuel, the thought of him having loved someone *that* much bothered her immensely.

"*Ya,* me too," David said, lost in the same world as Samuel.

"But wouldn't it be nice to have a picture of her?"

Both of them looked at her like she was crazy.

"We have a picture of her," Samuel said. He pointed to his head.

"It's not the same." She shook her head and paused. "When I have children, I want to have pictures of them growing up."

"It's not our way, Lillian," Samuel said, as if there was no room for further discussion.

"Do you want *kinner*?" David asked with a keen interest.

"Lots of them." She loved children. "And I'm going to be a much better mother than my mother." The mention of children caused her to reflect on her students at Northbrook High. She'd regretted having to leave her teaching job.

"I don't think she did such a *baremlich* job," David said.

Lillian nudged her shoulder against his and smiled. "*Danki,* David."

"I think you'll make a fine *mamm*." David glanced at Samuel. "Don't you, Pop?"

Samuel looked uncomfortable. "I'm sure she will," he said.

Lillian found the awkward way he made the remark touching.

She is so good with David.

There was no doubt in Samuel's mind Lillian would be a good mother someday. It was hard for him not to occasionally fantasize about a life with her. With each passing day, he found her more beautiful and more interesting. He'd allowed the occasional fantasy to float around in his head, but he always followed it up with a dose of hard reality. Lillian usually did or said something to remind him of their many differences or brought up one of the Amish "rules" she didn't agree with. She seemed to be going through all the motions by learning the *Ordnung*, attending worship, studying the language, reading the Bible, and following community traditions. It was just a mighty big change for her, and he had serious doubts she'd choose a life in their world. Her ideas about pictures were a good example.

"Why did your *mamm* leave here?" David asked.

"David!" Samuel said, reprimanding the boy. "That's *schnuppich.*" He knew it was a painful subject for Lillian.

"No, it's not snoopy," she said, pausing. "I don't know why she left. I think something happened, though. Something *big* that no one wants to talk about."

"Like what?" David pushed.

"David," Samuel warned. The boy should have no interest in such things. Plus, the look on Lillian's face told him that her bubbly spirit was taking a nosedive.

"I don't know." Her lips folded into a frown. But, in a forced effort, she sat up a little straighter and smiled. "And I'm starting not to care. She made her choices, and I'm making mine."

Her statement was strong, but Samuel knew it wasn't true. She cared a lot.

Lillian walked Samuel and David to the buggy, as had become the norm each time they came for supper. David always needed to go back into the house for something—either to go to the bathroom or because he'd forgotten his hat or needed a drink of water. It was always something, and he wasn't fooling anyone. Lillian could see right through his forgetfulness and last-minute potty breaks. His intent was for her and Samuel to spend a few minutes alone. And she had to admit: it was a welcomed gesture on young David's part.

This night in particular, David stayed gone longer than usual. Maybe it was the full moon, or maybe it was the way Samuel was looking at her, but Lillian's heart was bursting with emotion.

Despite their initial attraction, they'd pushed impure thoughts aside and a special friendship was blossoming. She was just about to tell him how much she enjoyed their weekly suppers when he hit her with a piece of news.

"I know staying for supper has become a regular thing on Wednesdays," he said, sounding hesitant to continue. "But next week David and I will be eating supper elsewhere." His gaze shifted from her to David, who was slowly making his way back to the buggy.

She was disappointed, but tried not to sound as let down as she felt. "All right," she said, and then added, "But you know you're always welcome to change your mind."

"Change his mind about what?" David asked as he walked into earshot.

Samuel crawled in the buggy and shut the door, motioning for David to do the same thing. "I was just telling Lillian how we wouldn't be havin' supper here next week."

David let out a big sigh. "*Ya*, we have to have supper with Sadie Fisher." He shook his head in obvious disappointment, but Lillian doubted his unhappiness equaled her own sense of displeasure.

No wonder Samuel hurried into the safe haven of his buggy; probably afraid of her reaction. The thought of him having supper with anyone other than her—much less Sadie Fisher—was a hard blow. But she kept her thoughts to herself. She and Samuel weren't courting. How could she justify such jealous thoughts?

"It's even worse we have to go on a picnic with her the next Saturday," David said as he frowned and continued to shake his head.

"What? A picnic?" she asked, foregoing her plan to keep her thoughts to herself. "How cozy," she added sarcastically, shooting a look of disapproval at Samuel.

"She kept asking to cook for me and the boy," Samuel said defensively, "so I finally accepted her kindness." He shrugged, signifying he owed her no further explanation.

Kindness? There was nothing *kind* about it. She bit her tongue so hard it hurt. When she didn't respond, Samuel added fuel to the fire.

"The elders think I should at least give courtin' Sadie a try. So she's cooking supper for me and David next week. And we're going on a picnic the following Saturday."

"*Courting?* You're going to court her?" Her tone was demanding and laced with angry bewilderment.

"I don't know, I just . . ." He paused briefly, but his tone firmed up. "*Ya*, I am." As he sat up a little straighter, his look challenged her to argue.

Trying to stare him down, she was having a much harder time controlling her emotions. She knew what that meant: tears were not far behind. "Fine," she said. She turned her back and walked briskly toward the house. "Just *fine*."

———

"I told you she'd be real mad, Pop," David said as they headed toward home.

"No need for her to be. We're only friends." Samuel really didn't want to have this conversation with his son. He knew exactly how the boy felt about Lillian. And how David felt about Sadie.

Maybe Sadie wasn't the one for him and David, but Samuel knew he needed to go through the motions, at least.

Whatever it took to keep Lillian from creeping into his dreams at night.

But Lillian's reaction to his news only made him want to be with her that much more. She was as jealous as she could be, and it warmed his heart. And to have such notions made him wonder if he was doing right by Sadie. His intentions were mostly in the right place. But was he really being fair to her? Agreeing to give it a try because the elders thought it was a good match didn't seem the best way to approach a courtship. If he was true to his heart, he'd have to admit that courting Sadie would distract him from the person he really wanted to be with but couldn't have.

Samuel refused to set himself and his boy up for heartbreak if Lillian chose to leave the district.

"I'd rather be havin' supper with Lillian next week," David snapped. "And I sure don't want to go on a picnic with Sadie either!"

Samuel stopped the buggy with a sharp pull on the reins. He turned to face his son, whose face was shriveled into a scowl. "I did not raise you to speak to me in that tone, David." He'd never heard his son use such an angry voice. Yet another reason he needed to put some distance between not only him and Lillian, but *David* and Lillian. The boy was way too attached to her.

Samuel prepared to reprimand the boy even more, but stopped when he saw David's scowl shifting into a look of hopelessness. As his son's eyes clouded with tears, he hadn't the heart to scold him further.

"I miss my *mamm*," he said softly, turning to face Samuel.

"I know."

"And if you court Sadie, I'll miss Lillian." His tone pleaded for Samuel to reconsider his plan.

He gave Pete a flick of the reins and bolted back into a trot down the dark dirt road. How could he tell his son how much he'd miss Lillian, too, and still make him understand that it was best to put some distance between them? He didn't want to send the boy mixed messages.

"Please don't court Sadie, Pop. Please!"

In a tone harsher than Samuel had ever used with the boy, he said, "This talk is over!"

Lillian was glad her grandparents were upstairs asleep. She lit the propane lantern above the kitchen table and rummaged around for a snack. Grabbing some butter bread and a glass of tea, she plopped down on the bench and stuffed herself silly. It was misery eating, she knew. And she didn't care. "I'll just be a big fat Amish woman," she whispered angrily, stuffing another piece of bread in her mouth. It was a flippant statement, and she was glad no one was around to hear it. One thing she'd learned since her arrival was that all the hard work allowed for extra calories. It was a healthy balance.

How could Samuel even think about courting Sadie? She shook her head. It was fine being friends with him as long as it was an exclusive arrangement. Sharing him with the likes of Sadie Fisher was another thing. And this was worse than just breaking their friendship bond. He was actually going to pursue a romantic involvement with Sadie. Courting to the Amish meant a prerequisite to marriage. Surely Samuel was not considering marrying this woman? She shoved another piece of bread in her mouth.

"How's my Lilly?"

She hadn't heard Grandpa come down the stairs. "Grandpa!" she scolded. "You're supposed to get me or Grandma before you come down the stairs by yourself."

He waved her off and took a seat across from her at the kitchen table. "I was hungry."

"Well, you should have gotten Grandma up."

Frowning, he whispered, "She's cranky, Lilly, when she gets woke up." He leaned in and helped himself to a piece of the bread she had piled on a plate. "Hungry?" he asked sarcastically, eyeing the mound before her.

"I'm eating my misery away," she said, stuffing in another piece of the moist buttery bread.

"And what does my Lilly have to be miserable about this fine evening?"

"Samuel is going to court Sadie Fisher," she said around a mouthful.

"*Ya*, I heard there's a rumor about that going 'round town." He shook his head. "And this makes my Lilly feel like she has to eat a loaf of bread?" He shot her a questioning grin.

"I know how things stand with Samuel and me, Grandpa. Really, I do."

"Do you now? Because it sounds to me like you're jealous." His grin transformed into a look of disapproval. "And jealousy is a sin, Lilly."

"I'm not jealous, Grandpa. There's no reason to be. Samuel can certainly court whoever he wants. We share a friendship. Nothing more."

"Who you tryin' to convince, Lilly, me or you?"

"Well, of course I know we're just friends. It's just . . . well, if he's courting Sadie, I won't get to see him and David as much. We're buddies. That's all. Samuel and I agreed it was best to keep it that way."

Grandpa smiled broadly. "My silly little *kinskind*. I may be a Plain man who's been married longer than I remember, but the only two people who don't know you and Samuel are *in lieb* are you and Samuel."

"We're not in love, Grandpa! But we have a special relationship."

Grandpa frowned, as if he knew she was lying. "A courtship with Samuel would be filled with challenges," he said. "But the Lord sometimes makes the good things worth the struggle."

"Well, there's no courtship going on with me. He's courting Sadie."

"Maybe that's for the best, then," he said softly.

"How can it be for the best when—" Stopping abruptly, she knew what she'd almost done.

"When *what*, Lilly?"

She looked down at the half-eaten loaf of bread and sighed. Was she fooling herself by thinking she could remain friends with him? If the thought of him courting Sadie sent her into this much of a tailspin—well, perhaps she *did* have feelings. But no one had to know. "I just got used to having them around. They've become like family."

"*Ya*," her grandpa said as he sat up a little taller and stroked his beard. "They surely have."

It took a couple of days for Lillian to adopt a more mature attitude about the prospect of Samuel and Sadie courting. After a good cry, she concluded that at this point in her life she wasn't worthy of Samuel's affections. It was only right he should seek someone better suited for him and David. So after keeping her nose in the air and ignoring Samuel those first two days, she spent the rest of the week making polite small talk when he arrived to pick up David—if she happened to be outside when he showed up. Funny thing, she always seemed to be outside when he arrived.

But she made it a point to stay in the house when she heard Samuel coming up the drive to pick up David the following Wednesday. As she peeked out the window, her heart was breaking. The thought of Samuel and David spending an evening with Sadie was almost enough to make her run outside and beg them not to go.

The temptation was mounting when she heard her cell phone ringing upstairs. Knowing Grandpa was sleeping, she jetted up the stairs two at a time. Grandma met her at the top of the stairs with a frown. "Sorry," she whispered, offering her grandma a sheepish smile. She'd meant to turn it off and just check messages to save her battery. Charging her battery in town was a hassle, and she knew it irritated Grandma to hear it ringing in the house. Although her mother hadn't called her in weeks—not since she'd called and said she was sending Lillian money. Money that never arrived.

"Hello," she said breathlessly into the phone.

"I miss you."

She sat down on the bed and pushed back her hair. She recognized the voice immediately. "Hi, Rickie."

"Did you hear me, Lillian? I miss you." His humble tone filled her with memories. In the beginning, things had been so good between them. It took a while for him to show his true colors. But he did. More than once.

As if reading her mind, he went on. "There's nothing we can't fix, Lillian. I want you in my life, and I'm willing to do whatever it takes to make things right between us." He paused, then continued when she didn't respond. "It's been weeks, Lillian. I've left you alone like you asked in your letter. And that was really hard. I wanted to call you so much, but I thought if I gave you some time, you'd come around. Come home, Lillian. Please. I promise—"

"Rickie," she interrupted before his tone tempted her to believe him. She knew better. "I've started over in a new place. I have a new life."

"I know," he said. "And I think that's great. Putting some distance between us has made me realize how much I love you. Please, Lillian, come home."

"I *am* home, Rickie." And she realized she meant it. Her feet were firmly planted, and she wasn't going anywhere.

"Then I'll come to you. I'll get on a plane tomorrow. Your mom said you're in Lancaster County with your grandparents."

She'd specifically told her mother she didn't want Rickie to know where she was going. *How could she do that?* "No, Rickie!"

"Just for a short visit," he pushed on. "We just need some time together to sort this out."

Rickie was a born salesman. He might sell expensive cars for a living, but he wasn't about to sell her his story that he was a changed man. "No," she repeated.

An uncomfortable silence brewed, and Lillian said, "Rickie, I need to go."

"Is there someone else?"

She didn't say anything.

"Oh, I see," he said after a while.

"There's no one else, Rickie. But I've changed my life."

"I heard. Your mom said you're living with the Amish. Surely you haven't become one of them?"

She would have flown through the phone line if she could have. How dare he say *them* as if they were from another planet? "As a matter of fact, I have," she said firmly. She wasn't sure if this was true, but she hoped it would deter Rickie.

"So you're all into God now?" He sounded disgusted.

Her first instinct was to yell at him, to defend her actions. But . . . *That isn't the Amish way.* As soon as the thought registered in her mind, she realized it stemmed from the hours of time she'd spent with Grandma studying the *Ordnung*. She had a long way to go, but some of it was sinking in. The way she might have handled Rickie in the past no longer seemed appropriate.

"I'm learning to live a different life, a better life. I think the way to do that might be through God."

She could hear him yelling at her choice of lifestyle, but it became fainter and fainter as she realized the implications of what she just said, and the fact that she *meant* it. She *was* giving God a shot . . . for the first time in her life. Trusting that He was there.

"Good-bye, Rickie," she said softly, and she hung up the phone.

When she returned downstairs, she gazed out the window in the den. Samuel and David were gone, and Sadie would be cooking for *her* family tonight. A combination of bitterness and despair crept through her like a virus, targeting her heart and landing in the pit of her stomach. She'd grown to love Samuel and David, and with that love came a new sense of unselfishness unfamiliar to her. How could she deny Samuel and David a life with someone who might be better for them?

"I'm trying, God. I'm trying to have faith. I'm trying to live a good life. Please help me to trust that You will provide what's best for me," she whispered, "and for Samuel and David."

She felt a hand on her shoulder.

"Grandma, I didn't hear you come downstairs. Is everything okay?" She was embarrassed that Grandma might have heard her praying. She wasn't entirely comfortable with her evolving relationship with God.

"*Ya*, Jonas is sleeping soundly," Grandma said, sighing. "He isn't feeling well."

Her gray hair was bound tightly in a bun on her head. Deep wrinkles spiderwebbed from the corners of her eyes and trailed downward, burrowing into sunken pale cheeks. The circles under her eyes were more prevalent than usual, and her stance indicated sheer exhaustion might cause her to surrender to gravity at any minute.

"Grandma, you can't go on like this. You have to let me help you with Grandpa." She grabbed her grandmother's elbow and walked her to the nearby rocker. All the while Grandma was shaking her head.

"Why not?" Lillian asked.

"Your *daadi* is a proud man, Lillian. Sometimes he gets down in a bad way. He wouldn't want his Lilly to see him like that." She kept shaking her head.

"Irma Rose!"

Grandma jumped when she heard him calling, but Lillian gently grabbed her shoulders. "Grandma, let me go to him. I can handle it. You have got to get some rest."

She watched her Grandma eyeing the staircase as if it were Mount Everest. "But he might need—"

"Whatever it is, I will handle it. Go have a snack or something. I'll take care of Grandpa."

Before Grandma could refuse, she headed for the staircase. Halfway up the stairs he cried out again. But it wasn't Grandma's name or Lillian's name he was calling. Lillian froze in her tracks on the staircase, her legs trembling.

10

FORCING HER FEET TO MANEUVER UP THE STAIRS, LILLIAN eased into her grandparents' bedroom, dimly illuminated by one small lantern on a nightstand by the bed. On a wooden hutch across the room there were at least a dozen pill bottles, a pitcher of water, a glass, and a Bible. Grandpa was tucked under a brown-and-red quilt, his eyes closed. His thinning gray hair was tousled and flattened against a feather pillow, and his breathing was labored, his mouth opened wide.

Taking a seat on the wooden chair beside the bed, she said, "Hi, Grandpa." She reached over and touched his arm.

Twitching his pale face, he slowly opened his eyes and smiled. "Sarah Jane," he said softly. She'd hoped maybe she heard him wrong when she was walking up the staircase.

"Grandpa, it's Lilly," she said. She gently squeezed his arm and leaned in closer to make sure he could see her clearly.

"I've missed you," he said tenderly.

"I saw you at breakfast this morning, Grandpa."

"*Ya, ya,*" he whispered. "Is the pond frozen up? Reckon we'll have to shine your skates up."

"Grandpa, it's summertime," she said hesitantly, resisting the urge to cry. *What is wrong with him?* He'd been frail since she arrived, but his mind was always sharp as a tack.

He laughed. "I'm a silly old man. I know you're a might too old to be skatin' on the pond." He leaned in close and his eyebrows lowered as he reached over and gently clutched her arm. Gazing hard into her eyes, he said, "You'll be breakin' your *mamm's* heart if you leave us, Sarah Jane. I know something's goin' on with you. Talk to your Pop."

"Grandpa," she whispered, "it's Lilly."

He was looking right through her with a glassy expression. "It's the *Englisch* man, ain't it?"

"What?"

"*Ya.* Your *mamm* ought not know 'bout this, Sarah Jane. But I reckon' I've seen the newspapers you've been stashing in the barn. The *Englisch* man writes of worldly ways, Sarah Jane, things best not learned. And you ought to stay away from him."

Her mind was awhirl, thinking about the boxes David moved into the barn. "What *Englisch* man?" she asked.

Grandpa released his grasp on her arm and pushed back gray bangs that were too long and had fallen forward. Swiping his brow, he frowned and shook his head.

"Grandpa, what *Englisch* man?" she asked again. But, he closed his eyes.

"Grandpa?"

Within seconds, the labored breathing returned, and she realized he was fast asleep. Lillian sat quietly for a few minutes, until she heard footsteps coming up the stairs. She turned to see Grandma entering the room.

"What did he need?" she asked.

"I don't know." Lillian paused. "He thought I was my mother."

Grandma patted her shoulder. "It happens. I reckon it's those pills the doctor gives him." She waved her arm toward the hutch. "Sometimes he thinks I'm *his* mother."

"Does he just snap out of it?" She hoped so.

"*Ya.* He mostly acts up like this right after he takes the pills."

"Oh," she said softly, contemplating whether or not to share the conversation with her grandma. Deciding she wasn't up for such a discussion, she excused herself.

───────

She barely choked down her breakfast the next morning. After cleaning up the kitchen, she told Grandma she was going to the barn to brush Jessie and lavish a little attention on him for a while. Giving her loose strands of hair a final tuck under her white *Kapp*, she asked, "Need me for anything else right now?"

"You go on," Grandma said. "I'm going to take these *dippy eggs* on up to Jonas." She poured a glass of orange juice and toted everything up the stairs.

On the way to the barn, Lillian pondered on what Grandpa had said the night before. Between that and thoughts of Sadie cooking for Samuel and David, she hadn't gotten much sleep.

"Hello, Jessie," she said, prying the barn door open. Giving the horse a quick stroke on the snout, she made her way to the stacked boxes in the corner and heaved the top box down to the dirt floor. In the dim light of early morning, she saw *The Intelligencer Journal, November 2, 1980* folded neatly on top. Lifting the newspaper up, she could see the box was filled with past issues.

Why did Mom save all these? And what Englisch man was Grandpa referring to?

The Intelligencer Journal was a daily publication. But upon further inspection, she noticed they were all thick Sunday editions. *Why only Sunday papers,* she wondered.

The Budget was the choice of newspaper for the Amish in Lancaster County—the national Amish publication coedited by both the Amish and English. Grandma read *The Budget* every Wednesday. Grandma also read *Die Botschaft*—strictly for Old Order Amish—every week. But she'd never seen *The Intelligencer Journal* in the house.

Placing one of Jessie's saddle pads on the dirt floor, she took a seat with the November 2 issue of *The Intelligencer.* She scanned the headline. "U.S. President Jimmy Carter and Ronald Reagan Debate in Cleveland, Ohio."

"Wow," she whispered as she flipped through the pages to the entertainment section. *Star Wars: The Empire Strikes Back* and *Friday the 13th* were movies featured at the theatres. Both movies were made before she was even born. "Sailing" by Christopher Cross was the top record. And everyone wanted to know who shot J. R., evidently from some TV show named *Dallas.* The headline said the November 21 conclusion was expected to draw more viewers than any other show in TV history.

She set the paper aside and retrieved the next issue in the box. *November 9, 1980.* Ronald Reagan won the presidential election in a landslide victory. The NASA space probe Voyager 1 made its closest approach to Saturn and sent the first high-resolution images of the world back to Earth. And people were still talking about who'd shot J.R.

While all this was fascinating, why did her mother save all these papers? Clearly, it had something to do with an *Englisch* man who wrote about worldly events, as Grandpa put it. Continuing to flip through each Sunday edition, she looked for something each issue had in common.

After an hour, she was starting to doubt the newspapers had anything to do with anything. But July 27, 1980, offered up a clue. As she had been doing, she scanned the front page headlines. "Former Turkish Prime Minister Nihat Erim Killed by Two Gunmen in Istanbul, Turkey." And "Pope John Paul II Visits Brazil—Seven People Crushed to Death in Crowd."

No wonder the Amish didn't read the daily papers and stuck with *The Budget* and *Die Botschaft*. Bad news was everywhere.

The most interesting items to her were what movies were showing and the top albums. She scanned the entertainment section and almost closed the paper when something in the columns section caught her eye. Actually, not the column itself, but the inscription beside it. She couldn't be sure, but it looked like her mother's handwriting. *Daniel and Sarah Jane forever.*

She pulled the newspaper closer to her face to get a better look. Daniel Foster looked to be in his late twenties. Maybe thirty. Although it was hard to tell from the black-and-white photo above his column, he looked to be a handsome guy. Sporting clean-cut short hair and a pair of large, gold-rimmed glasses, he smiled above his column, entitled "Outside the Box." She read:

The road to happiness is filled with paths of self-discovery. One slip, and you can end up going down the wrong path with no map to guide you back to the main road. How do we as individuals choose which road will fulfill our destiny with the least amount of challenges? Are we born into a predetermined plan? Is it fate? Or do the choices we make render us capable of creating our own destiny?

These are questions I have pondered. In the end, I believe we create our own destiny. But notwithstanding an occasional trip down the wrong path. The key is realizing when it's the wrong path and having the courage to do a little backtracking until you are back on the road to the life you were meant to live.

Were all his columns this *heavy?* She grabbed the next paper and read:

Dreams are the manifestations of our daily thoughts. Although some dreams might seem like they came out of nowhere, that's not true. We have but one mind, and the thought processes—whether in waking hours or asleep—belong to us exclusively. So the next time you have a bizarre dream that makes no sense, take the time to dissect it. There might be a message in there somewhere.

Lillian tossed the paper aside and went on to the next issue, thinking about her mom reading the columns twenty-eight years ago. Clearly, his message had intrigued Mom.

Religion and spirituality—are they one and the same? I think not. I know people who are religious and who lack a shred of spirituality. Then there are those who never attend church but possess more spirituality than most . . .

She read at least ten more columns. Two of the ten had hearts drawn around them. All thought-provoking in some way, she could see why her mother would have a crush on the guy. But she wasn't naïve and she'd done the math. Her mother would have been eighteen in 1980. Mom left the Amish community in 1981. Lillian was born in 1981. Could this guy be her father?

Her heart was pounding against her chest. Maybe, just maybe, she'd be able to find her father. He was handsome, a good writer, deep, and apparently spiritual.

Her heart raced faster. Finally, after all these years . . . just maybe.

There was only one way to find out.

———————

"Hi, Mom," Lillian said. She'd retrieved her cell phone and headed back to the barn without Grandma's knowledge.

"Lillian, what a surprise. Is everything okay?"

"Yeah, everything is fine."

"I know you're probably wondering about the money, Lillian. I had it all ready to put in the mail to you, and I—"

"It doesn't matter, Mom," she interrupted. "I want to talk to you about something else."

"What's that?"

"Who's Daniel Foster?"

The line was silent so long, Lillian wondered if her mother was still on the other end. "Mom?"

"Yes, I'm here."

"I found the newspapers in the barn. I read his columns, and I saw where you wrote—"

"Lillian!" her mother interrupted hastily. "I don't know where you're going with this, but just leave it alone."

Her mom's voice was quivering, and Lillian knew she'd hit the nail on the head. "He's my father, isn't he?" She knew her tone was demanding, but she'd been denied any knowledge about her father because her mother had refused to discuss it, always saying she just didn't know who he was. Lies. All lies. She knew exactly who he was.

"Is *he* why you left Lancaster County? Is he, Mom? I have a right to know who my own father is. It's him, isn't it?" She realized her voice rose to a near yell.

"Lillian. Please let this go." Her mom was crying, but Lillian pushed on. She felt it was her right to know.

"Mother," she said sharply. "You said you never knew who my father was. If you covered this up for all these years . . . That is *so* wrong. You owe me this."

"I was young, Lillian. I was just so young." She was crying full force now.

Lillian softened her tone. "Mom, please. Please tell me. I'm trying so hard to start a new life. I'm trying so hard to find answers and fill the voids. This is part of the process for me. You have wonderful parents. You can't deny me the right to even know who my father is." Her own tears began to flow as she realized she needed to know, but at the same time was afraid to know.

"DNA does not make a person a parent, Lillian."

Confirmation. "Oh, Mom. So Daniel Foster is my father."

"Yes."

Lillian grabbed her chest, sure that her heart was going to leap through her skin. "Why didn't you ever tell me?"

When her mother didn't answer, Lillian went on. "Is that why you left Lancaster County? You were pregnant with me? Why didn't you tell someone? It would have been hard, but I don't think Grandma and Grandpa would have—"

"Shunned me?" her mother interjected with a sharp tone. "No, Lillian. They would not have shunned me in the traditional sense because I wasn't baptized. But I was eighteen years old, and I had premarital sex with an *Englisch* man. Reprimanding by the community would have been equally as harsh as a shunning. I couldn't have stayed. The embarrassment for your grandparents . . . I just couldn't stay. It was best to leave and never say anything."

"All these years, Grandma and Grandpa never understood why you chose to leave the district." She paused. "And what about me, Mom? You let me believe that you didn't know who my father was. How could you do that? How?"

"Lillian," Mom cried, "you don't understand."

"Then explain it to me!"

"I made a horrible mistake and I didn't know what to do. Daniel gave me some money, and I left to start a new life."

"Why couldn't you have started a life with him?"

Mom wept harder. "He wouldn't have me, Lillian. He wanted nothing to do with me or having a baby. Daniel said he would deny the entire thing, that I would be an outcast in my community, and that it would be best for me to leave town."

"And you never saw him again? Did he ever see me? Did he know you had a girl?"

"I never heard from him or saw him again. Please, Lillian. Now you know. Let it go."

"I'm going to find him. He'll want to meet me after all these years. I'll find him, Mom, with or without your help."

Sobs were vibrating through the phone lines. "No, Lillian. It was a long time ago. Please don't do this. I doubt he even still lives near Paradise."

"Mom!" she cried. "That's three miles down the road. I could have bumped into him on the streets in town. How could you not have told me?"

"Lillian, leave it alone."

"Good-bye, Mom."

She hung up the phone, nervous anticipation flooding over her, commingled with fury and sympathy for her mother. As angry as she was with Sarah Jane Miller, hearing her mother relive that painful part of her past pulled at her heartstrings in an unfamiliar way.

Samuel eyeballed a big wooden table outside a shop in Paradise. It wasn't as nice as the one in Intercourse—the one he would buy someday. He wondered if that day would ever come. Lately his visions of the table in his kitchen came with a detailed picture of him and David sitting at the table with several other children—and Lillian cooking supper. It was a notion he couldn't seem to shake.

Telling Sadie the night before that a courtship wasn't going to work had been hard. Extra hard when she started to cry. But carrying on with her when he couldn't shake his feelings for Lillian wasn't fair. Not even the elders could push him into a courtship with someone he didn't think he could ever love. And it wasn't fair to the boy either.

He'd rather hold out hope that maybe Lillian could find her way to the peaceful way of life she was longing for. That maybe she'd find God in her heart. She'd so lovingly accepted him and David into her heart. Why was it so hard for her to accept God's will in her life? It wasn't his way, but maybe he should help her more. After all, she'd had no upbringing that would teach her such things.

It was a difficult situation—compounded by the fact he could list all the reasons Lillian wasn't right for him and David. But the bottom line was she brought out feelings in him he'd only ever had for Rachel. And allowing himself to indulge usually resulted in guilt. Guilt that he shouldn't have such thoughts when Rachel was the love of his life. He still dreamed of her. Only now, not as often. It was both comforting and worrisome when Lillian showed up in his dreams more often than Rachel these days.

As he continued to fantasize about a life with Lillian, he caught a glimpse of her out of the corner of his eye. Was she looking for him? She was sure looking for something. He headed toward her.

She appeared frazzled. Her hair looked like she'd been on another high-speed buggy ride, tousled and dangling about her beautiful face. But something was wrong. Her eyes were swollen and registered an uncharacteristic seriousness.

"Hello," he said as he walked up to her.

"Hi, Samuel," she said with little emotion. He was being punished, which he probably deserved. He'd need to set her straight about Sadie right away.

"What are you looking for?"

She shot him a look that confirmed what he suspected, and didn't answer. Yeah, she was mad all right.

"Are you not speaking to me?" he asked, leaning down.

"Where's Sadie?" she blurted out. "I figured the two of you would be planning your picnic for Saturday."

He grinned. He couldn't help it. She was jealous. And it felt so good. "*Ya*, the picnic," he teased.

"What are you grinning about?" She put her hands on her hips and attempted to stare him down with her big green eyes. Swollen eyes.

"What's wrong?" he said, changing the subject. "I can tell you've been crying."

"Don't worry about it," she said harshly. "I'm fine."

"You don't look fine."

"Well, I am."

"What do you think would be good to take on a picnic?" He was toying with her, and in light of her current mood, he knew he was stepping on thin ice.

"Samuel Stoltzfus, what you and Sadie decide to take on your picnic is of no concern to me." She leaned in and cut him down to the bone with her look.

"You like tuna salad, don't you?"

"Who cares what I like. Go ask Sadie what she likes!" Her tone was getting really mean. Better tell her.

"Why would I ask Sadie what she likes when it's you I'm taking on a picnic on Saturday?" He shot her a wide smile, hoping to cheer her up.

"What?"

"I told Sadie last night after supper that I just wasn't going to be able to court her. It just wasn't right to even try."

Her hands dropped to her side and her look softened, but he still had a sense something was wrong. "Oh," she said softly. "And why's that?"

A loose strand of hair was sweeping across her face. Wanting desperately to push it back into place, wanting an excuse to touch her . . . he did nothing.

"It just didn't feel right."

"But I thought that's what the elders wanted?" she asked, backing away from him somewhat.

"In the end, the elders want me to be happy. I have to make choices that are best for me and David."

She smiled, but not the fullface smile he was used to seeing from her. "Are you asking me to go on a picnic with you and David on Saturday?"

"Nope," he said, playing with her again.

Those hands landed right back on her hips, and she opened her mouth to say something . . . but stopped, straightened her apron, and took a deep breath instead. Samuel thought he better tell her the truth. "I'm asking you to go on a picnic with me. Alone. David will be helping Ivan do some work out at his place."

"Oh," she said softly.

"And me and the boy have more vegetables than we can ever eat. I thought we might bring some for supper tonight, if you think that would be all right."

"That's fine."

She lacked the enthusiasm Samuel hoped for. Not that he expected her to run into his arms for changing his mind about Sadie. But . . . something more than this.

"Lillian, what's wrong?"

She motioned for him to follow her. Away from a group of tourists chatting in the street, she sat down on a wooden bench outside a small Dutch bakery. He took a seat beside her.

"I just found out who my father is," she said, fighting tears.

"And I'm going to find him and meet him. I'm sure he's wondered about me all these years, like I've wondered about him. I think it will help me to put some things behind me, so I can have the life I'm looking for." She paused and looked him hard in the eyes. "And, Samuel, yes, I'm trying to find a place for God in my heart. I have a lot to learn, but I'm working very hard to find my way. Finding my father will fill a void I have in my life."

It was music to his ears that Lillian was working to accept God into her life. And if it would help her to make peace with her father, well he was all for that.

"He lived right here in Paradise. Evidently, he and my mother had a love affair. She became pregnant with me and knew people in the district would look down on her, so she left. I don't know why she couldn't have told me sooner." A tear rolled down her cheek as she shook her head.

His need to comfort her was overwhelming. But he didn't move. Fantasizing about Lillian was a safe secret he could live out in his dreams. The reality of actually touching her, even as innocent as that might be, would imply intentions he was still unsure of.

"That was twenty-eight years ago. He was a young writer who worked for *The Intelligencer Journal.* Who knows where he might be now."

"*Ya,* that's true," he said as he continued to fight the urge to put his arm around her, offer her hand a squeeze . . . something. "So, what's his name?"

She sighed. "I'm still in shock that I have his actual name. And I can sort of put a face to the name, from the picture in his column. It's just all very surreal."

"Do you want me to help you find him?" It wasn't his way to pursue anyone or anything outside the district, but if it would fill the void in Lillian's life and help her to move forward, then he was going to help her.

She sighed, looking down at her hands in her lap. "His name is Daniel Foster."

Samuel tried not to react, but he was stunned. Grimacing, he shifted his position on the bench. How in the world would he tell her that she wasn't going to have to look very far for her father? Not farther than about twenty yards. Samuel could see Daniel Foster's shop from where they were sitting.

11

LILLIAN WAS THINKING ABOUT THE SUPPER THEY'D HAVE later, about their picnic on Saturday, about finding her father, and what her future might hold. Hopeful thoughts were flying around in her head. It seemed odd when Samuel jumped up and began to pace in front of her.

"What's wrong?" she asked. He was nervous as a cat.

"I don't exactly know how to tell you this, Lillian." He paused and sat down beside her again. But the words didn't come.

"Samuel, you're scaring me. What is it?"

"Daniel Foster," he said softly.

"My father. What about him?"

Samuel removed his straw hat and ran his hand through his hair. Placing it back on his head, he began to stroke his beard as if in serious thought. Lillian couldn't help but notice his huge arms underneath the blue shirt and the way his suspenders draped across his solid chest.

"What?" she asked again. "Samuel, what is it?"

"Lillian, stay calm."

"Samuel, you better just tell me whatever's on your mind because you are *really* scaring me!"

"Daniel Foster is standing right over there." He pointed toward their right.

Lillian jumped up and peered in the direction he was pointing. "What?" She sounded confused.

"He owns that shop," he said hesitantly, knowing it would be a blow to her to find she'd walked past her father's shop dozens of times in the past couple of months.

"What?" she asked again, staring down Lincoln Highway.

Samuel stood up and reached for her arm, fearful she might take off running in that direction. That probably wasn't the best plan. He watched Daniel arranging a table full of wares right outside his antique store. "He's the owner of Outside the Box," he told her.

"The name of his column," she whispered. "I've been in that shop." She pulled away and headed toward her father. The closer they got, the faster she moved.

"Wait, Lillian." He grabbed her arm and brought her to a halt. "Have you thought this through?"

She turned briefly to face him. "No, I haven't thought it through. But I've imagined a million times what it would be like to meet my father. I can't wait another minute." She picked up her pace again.

Samuel knew very little about Daniel. Besides exchanging friendly greetings over the years, the only thing he knew about the man was he'd been married for a while but later divorced. As they neared the store, he couldn't help but wonder if Lillian was entering a hornet's nest.

Lillian was bursting with anticipation. Part of her wanted to run into her father's arms and tell him how long she'd waited for this moment. However, about ten feet from the store she stopped. Her mother's words flooded her like a rushing river. *"He wouldn't have me, Lillian. He wanted nothing to do with me or having a baby. Daniel said he would deny the entire thing, that I would be an outcast in my community, and that it would be best for me to leave town."*

That was a long time ago though. Surely he had wondered over the years if he had a daughter or a son. So many times she'd wondered if she had brothers and sisters. So many questions.

"Lillian, this might not be the best time—"

"I'm not waiting. I've waited my whole life." But her feet weren't moving. What would she say? She scanned the table full of antique trinkets and household items on the display table outside the shop. A FOR SALE sign hung in the window. Maybe he was retiring. People bustled by her, seemingly in slow motion.

"Are you sure about this, Lillian?" As Samuel shook his head, clearly indicating *he* wasn't sure about it, she wondered how this moment had crept up on her so quickly. Years of imagining, dreaming. And now, all in one day, she'd discovered who he was and where he was. Swallowing hard, she stood stiffly in place watching the man arrange items on the table outside his shop.

Her father. Standing not ten feet away from her.

It wasn't just her life that would be changing forever, but his too.

Placing her hand on her chest, she took a deep breath. Her heart was beating much too fast. She could faintly hear Samuel—

"Lillian, are you okay?"—but she couldn't peel her eyes from Daniel Foster. Maybe Samuel was right. Maybe she needed to think things through and plan things out.

But she knew she wouldn't. She was going to meet her father. Today. Now. Her lifelong vision would be a reality in a matter of minutes.

Gradually, she uprooted her feet and eased her way forward. She'd only taken a couple of steps when she stopped. Realizing this was the most important moment in her life to date, she sidestepped to the wall of the shop next to Daniel Foster's, leaned against it, and closed her eyes. She could feel Samuel next to her as she attempted to block out the noise of passersby, cars, the clippity-clap of horse hooves, and the conflicting voices rambling around in her head. *Stay. Go.*

God, she prayed silently, pressing her eyes closed even tighter, *I don't know You very well. And it might be wrong of me to ask for Your help right now. But this is so incredibly important to me. Please help me to say the right things and to accept whatever it is that's Your will.*

Her plea for help and guidance sent a flood of emotion running through her. Fighting tears, she went on. *I'm so sorry. I'm just so very sorry for all the things I've messed up in my life. Please help me to do this right.*

It seemed wrong to ask for His help when she'd been absent from Him her entire life. Was it a selfish request? Did He even hear her?

No sooner than the thought registered did she feel a sweeping wave of courage. More profound was an unfamiliar sense of guardianship surrounding her, as if Someone wrapped her in a blanket of protection and love. *Is this You?* she silently asked.

As a tear trickled down her cheek, she allowed herself to feel the glory of prayer. "Thank You," she said as she opened her eyes and wiped the tear from her cheek.

She looked over at Samuel standing by the wall next to her. His eyes were closed. Was he praying for her? She watched him intently, presumably offering up prayers on her behalf. This moment on the busy sidewalk of Lincoln Highway would be with her a long time.

"Are you ready?" he asked, opening his eyes.

"I am."

Side by side, they eased their way toward Daniel Foster.

"Good afternoon," the man she now knew to be her father said. "Can I show you anything in particular?"

"We're just having a look," Samuel said when she didn't respond.

Lillian could see he still resembled the picture. He was a handsome man. His dark hair was now salt and pepper and receding, and he had replaced his gold-rimmed glasses with smaller ones that hung low on his nose. Considerably shorter than Samuel, he still towered over her. He had a friendly smile, and Lillian knew right away that everything was going to be fine.

"I'm Lillian Miller," she said, wondering if the name Miller would ring any bells. Maybe she should have planned this conversation out. Too late. She was there and waiting for any recognition from him.

"I'm Daniel Foster." He extended his hand to her as though she was any new customer wandering up to his shop. "Welcome to Outside the Box."

It had been twenty-seven years and there were tons of Millers. She'd have to be more clear. "My mother is Sarah Jane Miller."

Instantly Daniel took a step backward. His smile faded, and
he gave her an odd look she couldn't decipher.

"I, uh . . ." She stumbled. "I . . . think you're my father."

Samuel was stroking his beard and pacing slightly. Daniel just
stared at her.

"I'm so happy to finally meet you," she went on. "I've waited
my whole life for this moment, and I didn't think I'd ever find
you. And, here you are, three miles from where I'm living with
my grandparents. It's just so good to meet you." She instinctively
stepped toward him.

"What do you want?" His tone was more than abrasive and
sent chills up her spine, halting her in her tracks.

"I, uh, don't want anything. Just to know you." She felt
Samuel gently touch her arm. It gave her little strength; her knees
were buckling with the weight of the moment. "You still look a
lot like your picture from the column you wrote years ago. I see
you named your store after it." She was rambling. "Maybe we can
have a cup of coffee and get to know each other when you have
time and—"

"I don't know you. I don't want to know you. Whatever your
mother told you is a lie. Sarah Jane Miller has lied to you." He
took a step back.

"So you do know my mother, then?" she asked, resisting the
urge to cry. "Are you my father?" It was a simple question that
she felt deserved an answer.

"I just sold my shop; I'll be moving from here in two weeks.
If you try to find me, I'll call the law on you." His face drew into
a raging scowl, and his posture became aggressive. He leaned
forward as if he might dive for her.

Every wonderful fantasy she'd had about meeting her father was stolen from her in less than a minute. On instinct, she stepped back from him. She wanted to run. To go back. To start over. Resisting the urge to flee, she spoke again.

"Sir, I'm not here to cause you any trouble at all."

"Is it money you want?" His fists were clinched at his sides and he stared her down as if she were threatening his life.

"No!" she said emphatically. "Of course not."

"Lillian, let's go," Samuel gently took her elbow and attempted to guide her away from him.

"Yes, I think you better go," the man said. The man who couldn't *possibly* be her father.

"But, I just . . ." The words weren't coming. The fantasy was over. She now understood why her mother had chosen to avoid even an informal community shunning. She'd never felt more abandoned in her life. A bastard baby, with a father who didn't care if she was alive or dead.

"Lillian, let's go," Samuel said again, pulling her farther away from Daniel.

She yanked free of Samuel's hold. As a tear rolled down her cheek, she walked toward her father. He didn't step back this time. She couldn't read his expression, but she was not going to leave without letting him know how she felt.

"I dreamed about meeting you my entire life. I dreamed about this moment since I was a little girl. In a few short minutes, you have not only denied me my dream of what it would be like to meet you, but you've discarded me as if I were dirt." She stepped closer to him, and this time he did step back. "Well, I'm not dirt. I am a wonderful, vivacious woman. I'm smart. I graduated from high school at the top of my class, and I went to college and became a teacher. I am a fabulous cook. I care deeply about other people." By now she was sobbing almost uncontrollably, and she struggled to form the words so he could understand her. "I'm sorry that you won't have the opportunity to know me."

She paused. His expression softened, and the water forming in the corners of his eyes pushed her to go on. "So go ahead and toss me aside. It's certainly your choice. But I am a good person, and it will be your loss."

And with that, she spun around and ran down the sidewalk.

———

Samuel kept up with her until she was away from the crowds. When she crossed the highway and headed down Black Horse Road, it appeared she might keep running all the way home. He grabbed her arm. "Lillian, stop," he said. "Did you come in the buggy?"

She pulled free, shook her head and kept on walking until she was a good piece down the road. "Well, I brought my buggy. I have to go back," he yelled. She waved him on and didn't stop. "I'll be back to pick you up."

Fast as he could run, he headed to where he'd parked his buggy and got on his way. A few minutes later, knowing he was going a bit too fast through town, he still gave Pete an extra flick of the reins. It didn't take long to catch up with her.

"Get in," he said, guiding Pete to a stop.

She wouldn't look at him as she crawled into the buggy. It didn't seem like she was going to stop crying any time soon. Maybe he needed to just let her get it all out.

"I'm sorry," he said softly.

She didn't say anything and continued to stare off into the pasture. When he passed Irma Rose and Jonas's farm, she spoke up.

"Where are we going?" She swiped at her eyes.

"To my favorite place."

Samuel hadn't been to the overlook since Rachel died. He used to go there when he wanted to be by himself—just him and God. He'd never taken anyone there. Not even David. Today he was going to take Lillian. She needed all the spiritual guidance she could get right now, and Samuel knew God would be waiting there for her with open arms to comfort her in her time of need. Aside from the incredible view of the valley below, it was where Samuel felt most connected to God.

She'd stopped crying by the time they reached the overlook. He helped her out of the buggy and toward the edge of the cliff. "Don't get too close to the edge," he said as he pulled her to the ground with him. "Let's sit here a while."

For a split second, a hint of happiness swept across her face. "This is the most beautiful place I have ever seen," she said before placing her hands over her face. She started to cry again.

"I'm so sorry, Samuel."

"What do you have to be sorry about?" he asked, turning to face her.

"That I cry a lot."

"I think I heard you say earlier that you care deeply about others," he said. "That's nothing to be sorry about."

"Thank you for being here with me."

As he watched her staring at the ground, fiddling with a

blade of grass, he worried how she was going to handle all this. But one thing he knew for sure. He wouldn't let her handle it alone.

"There's nowhere else I'd rather be," he said.

***

Samuel's words warmed Lillian's heart, and his presence eased her pain somewhat. The meeting with her father had been a setback. A painful, heart-wrenching setback. But now she knew. She'd put it behind her and move forward.

"There's something about this place, Samuel. It's very . . . I don't know. I mean, it's beautiful here, but there's something else. It's very calming. Serene. It's like I feel . . . I feel . . ."

"God?" He asked.

She speculated for a moment. "Yes, I suppose that might be it." She recalled the feeling she'd had while she prayed before meeting her father. She'd had the same feeling then.

"And that's only the beginning. I have my strongest sense of Him here too. But one day you'll take that feeling with you everywhere you go. When that happens, it will become easier for you to accept things as God's will."

"It's hard for me to accept what happened earlier as God's will. I would think God would have preferred things to go differently." She cringed and shook her head as the memory of her father's look and words came flying to the forefront of her mind.

"We don't question God's will."

"That part is hard for me. And I want to, Samuel. I want to accept all things as God's will." She paused. "And I'm working on it."

"I can see that. It'll come, Lillian. Talk to Him. But more important, listen to Him."

"What do you mean? I've said my prayers, but I've never heard a response."

"Are you sure?"

"I've never heard God talking to me." She shook her head, quite sure of that one.

"Ever have a thought or feeling and wonder where it came from? A thought that just seems to come out of nowhere, or a comforting feeling?"

"Sometimes." She recalled again how she'd felt when she prayed before she met her father. Leaning against the storefront wall, she'd felt an overwhelming sense of calm. "Is that God?"

"I believe it is. I think some people are so busy talking to God that they forget to listen too." He bumped his shoulder gently against hers. "I'm sorry about what happened today, Lillian."

He'd changed the subject again, as she had gotten used to. "I'm sorry too," she said. "Sorry for me. Sorry for you. And sorry for my mother."

Wow. It was the first time she'd thought about her mother since all this had happened. For the first time, she saw her mother in a whole new light—as a young Amish woman who got involved with an *Englisch* man, got pregnant, was afraid of becoming an outcast in her community, and decided to venture out into a world she knew nothing about. Maybe there was enough compassion in Lillian's heart to forgive her mother for her childhood.

"Are you gonna be all right?" he asked.

"It's not the storybook reunion I'd hoped for by any stretch of the imagination. But I'll have to put it behind me. Now, at least, I know. I'm not completely sure how I feel about all of it, but . . ."

As she and Samuel sat together at the overlook, Lillian trailed off, trying to push the events with her father out of her mind. While she knew it would take a long time for her to completely heal, a new sense of calm and peacefulness seemed to be slowly seeping into her heart. It was a welcomed feeling. For the next hour they sat at the overlook. Mostly they were quiet.

"I'm sorry that Sadie cried when you told her you wouldn't be courting her," David told Samuel on the way to Lillian's that evening.

"How'd you know she cried?"

"I heard her from upstairs."

"I thought you were sleeping."

"Nope. But Pop, she just wasn't the one. You know that, *ya*?"

Samuel nodded, unclear exactly what he thought these days. But he knew it wouldn't be right to court Sadie.

"Well I'm glad we're going to Lillian's house for supper. I like being around Irma Rose and Jonas too."

Nodding again, Samuel wondered if Lillian was feeling any better. Time healed so many things. Time and God. But it had only been a few hours. A blow like this would take a long time for her to get over. He knew all about pain, healing, and the time it took.

As his thoughts drifted to Rachel, David came out of the clear blue with a direct question not suitable for a boy to ask his pop.

"Are you going to marry her?" David's eyes grew wider and wider as he waited for a response.

"Not right for you to be asking me that, boy."

"But it could happen?"

Samuel could handle his own feelings, even if they were all mixed-up. His thoughts about a life with Lillian were his secret. But, he knew what was right and wrong. "No, David. I've been tellin' you for weeks that Lillian and I are friends. Just like she's a friend to you."

"But she's studying the *Ordnung*."

"So do a lot of people who come from worldly ways. And I think the *Ordnung*—and God—will help Lillian to find her way. But outsiders don't stay, David. It's rare. So you need not be thinking about things that may not happen."

This was exactly what Samuel feared—David getting too close to Lillian. And he sure couldn't be telling his son that he had allowed himself to get too close to her.

"But it *does* happen sometimes. Besides, aren't people good friends before they get married?"

Samuel glanced at his son. The boy's youthful optimism caused him to briefly contemplate the possibility. "I guess, David. It does happen sometimes. And, *ya, gut* marriages start out with friendship first."

Nonetheless. He shook his head as doubt resurfaced.

Lillian was glad to see Grandpa down for supper. She'd prepared one of his favorites: roast with potatoes and carrots. The events of earlier that afternoon weighed heavily in her heart, but her family was all together. It was cause for happiness and she refused to let Daniel Foster take that away from her.

"Boy, what are you *rutschich* about?" Grandpa asked David when they all sat down to eat. Unless there was a problem with his meds, Grandpa never missed a beat.

"Jonas, leave the boy alone. He's not squirming," Grandma said.

"*Ya*, he's *rutschich*. And grinning like he's got some business for sharing. What's on your mind, son?" Grandpa leaned an ear inward, waiting for an answer.

"David, why don't you give the blessing," Grandma said as she shushed Grandpa.

They all bowed in prayer.

"Dear Lord, thank You for this food before us and the many blessings You have given to us. Thank You for the land that provides us with this fine food, and we know all things are God's will. *Aemen*."

"*Ya*, God's will. *Aemen*. Thank you for that offering, David," Grandma said.

"And one more thing!" David said, bowing his head again. As everyone else hastily lowered their heads, he added, "*Danki* for bringing Lillian to Lancaster County and for Pop deciding not to court Sadie. *Aemen*."

All eyes shot to Samuel, whose embarrassment—and anger— were apparent. Planting clenched fists slowly on the wooden table, he scolded his son with his eyes to the point Lillian feared a trip to the woodshed for David when they got home. That wasn't fair, though. It was such a sweet thing for him to say— about *her*, anyway.

Grandpa chuckled, but quickly stopped when Grandma fired him a look like she might take *him* out to the woodshed for a lashing. As Grandpa pursed his lips together and frowned, Lillian tried to lighten the mood.

"I'm glad God brought me here, too, David." She reached across the table and patted his hand. "That was a very sweet thing to say."

Maybe that would keep him out of trouble with Samuel. But by throwing out the fact that Samuel wasn't courting Sadie in the same breath as his comments about her . . . Well, it *was* cause for speculation by all of them.

It took him a few seconds, but Samuel's scowling look softened and his fists unclenched. *Whew.* Maybe David was in the clear.

Grandma still had a visual hold on Grandpa, warning him not to speak. But as was Grandpa's nature, he spoke anyway. He was looking down when he said it, almost in a whisper, as if a tiny bit afraid of Grandma. But everyone heard him loud and clear.

"Don't know why you kids keep hee-hawing around and don't just take to courtin'." He shrugged.

"Jonas Miller!" Grandma snapped. "This is not your place to talk of such things!" She turned to Samuel. "It's his medications, Samuel. Makes him all cuckoo."

Samuel nodded and opened his mouth to say something, but Grandpa beat him to it, turning toward Grandma. "Irma Rose, if you don't quit blaming them pills for everything I say, I'm gonna stop takin' 'em!"

"Don't take that tone with me, Jonas Miller!"

David's eyes widened in amusement. Glancing at Samuel, Lillian was glad to see him suppressing a grin. He winked at her.

Everything was going to be just fine. And she wondered if maybe, just maybe, Samuel might be toying with the idea of them actually courting. It was always hard to tell with him.

"Irma Rose—" Grandpa prepared to fire back, but stopped and cupped his hand to his ear. "Somebody's here," he said, leaning back to see out the window.

"Jonas, watch yourself. You're gonna fall right over," Grandma said.

"We expecting company? It's the supper hour," Grandpa growled as he shoveled another load of roast onto his plate, seemingly fearful he might not get his share.

"Jonas, I declare. There's nothing wrong with your appetite, 'tis for sure." Grandma wiped her mouth with a napkin, indicating she'd get the door.

"I'll get it, Grandma," Lillian said as she stood from her place on the bench, which was next to Samuel. She smiled in his direction, glad to see he wasn't going to take offense at Grandpa's comment.

Smile still on her face, she contemplated the evening's excitement as she pulled on the wooden door and peered through the screen door. What she saw turned her legs to rubber. Suddenly she was struggling not to suffocate on the air around her. Air poisoned by the past that now found her.

"*Rickie*, what are you doing here?"

12

"ARE YOU GOING TO LET ME IN?" RICKIE ASKED, GRINNING as he studied her from head to toe.

Lillian opened the screen door onto the porch and closed both doors behind her. She couldn't believe Rickie was actually here. Always perfectly groomed, his neatly clipped blond hair accentuated his golden tan. Deceptively charming deep blue eyes scanned his surroundings. Dressed in khaki pants and a yellow golf shirt, he appeared to be the epitome of the perfect man. His looks were undoubtedly what had attracted her to him in the first place. Oh, how he had fooled her, though.

"What are you doing here?" she asked him again between clenched teeth, not wanting anyone to see him.

"That is not your best look, baby," he said, shaking his head and taking in her Amish attire. Him calling her *baby* turned her stomach. "I know you said you've started a new life, and I can see that—but it's hard for me to understand how you could just leave without even talking to me first. That's cold, Lillian. I provided you with a home. I've taken care of you. How could you do this?"

"Taken care of me?" she asked in a loud whisper. "Go home, Rickie. You should have never come here."

Ignoring her, his eyes darted over her shoulder. "Going to let me come in and meet your grandparents?"

"No. We have company tonight. You just need to leave!" Panic was starting to set in. She didn't want any of them to see the kind of person she used to be with. It was hard for her to believe she ever dated Rickie, much less lived with him.

"Lillian, I came a long way to talk to you," he said. "You owe me that much. I love you, and you just took off."

"You know why I left, Rickie." She glanced over her shoulder. The faint voices coming from inside crippled her thought process. Somehow she needed to get rid of him, at least for now. "We can talk tomorrow," she said as she backed up toward the porch door, hoping he would venture back to his rental car.

"Lillian, please," he begged, standing steadfast. "I know I made mistakes, but do you realize what a mistake you've made by coming here? You can't possibly want to live this life. When you get this God thing out of your head, I'll be waiting for you to come home." Walking toward her, he added, "But I won't wait forever, Lillian."

She took a step backward. "I don't want you to wait for me at all, Rickie. It's over. You should have never come here!"

She heard the rustling of feet inside. She dreaded introducing Rickie to anyone.

"I don't believe you, baby," he said, closing the gap between them.

"Don't call me that! I'm not your 'baby.' Please, Rickie, just . . . go home. I don't love you." She held her arm out to keep him at a safe distance.

"What's wrong with you?" His voice spiked up a notch. "And

what's with the freaky clothes? Have they brainwashed you or something?"

How dare you. But fighting with him would only heighten the risk of someone coming out on the front porch. She needed him to just go. "If you'll leave now, I promise we will talk tomorrow. Where are you staying? I'll call you in the morning."

"Lillian, it's only five o'clock in the afternoon. I'm *not* going to wait until morning to talk to you."

"Then let me at least finish supper with my family. I'll call you when I'm done. I can meet you in town or something."

"Fine," he said as he turned to head down the porch steps. He'd almost hit the grass when he called over his shoulder. "Change your clothes too. You look ridiculous."

Her pulse quickened. Thoughts of tackling him to the ground raced through her mind. But he was leaving, and that's all that mattered. She made an about-face and opened the screen door about the same time Grandpa opened the wooden door.

"Who's our company?" he belted out, causing Rickie to spin around and head back up the porch steps.

"Hello, sir, I'm Rickie." He extended his hand, and Lillian's panic settled in even further when Grandpa eased past her and shook his hand. "I'm a friend of Lillian's," Rickie added.

"It's suppertime. Come in and fix yourself a plate." Grandpa turned to go back in the house, obviously anxious to get back to his roast more than anything else.

"Thank you, sir," Rickie said, making his way past Lillian. She flinched as his arm brushed against hers.

"Lilly, come make the proper introductions," Grandpa said over his shoulder.

A sense of dread accompanied her as she followed Grandpa and Rickie into the house.

"This is a friend of Lilly's," Grandpa said, resuming his place at the table. "David, maybe you could scoot that rocker from the den over here to the table for this man."

"No, thank you, sir. Actually, I ate on the plane. I just came to see Lillian." An arrogant smile swept across his face—the same smile that had won her over in the beginning but now was making her stomach turn. "I need to make her realize how much I've missed her." He paused. "I don't want to interrupt your Amish dinner."

Lillian wanted to gag. The look on Samuel's face was one of confusion mixed with irritation.

"I imagine it's about the same as an *Englisch* dinner," Grandpa said sarcastically, still stuffing roast in his mouth. "Lillian, best you introduce everyone to your friend."

Grandma's facial expression resonated with sympathy. David seemed oblivious, or was just as preoccupied with the meal as Grandpa.

"Uh, Rickie, these are my grandparents, Irma Rose and Jonas." She pointed to each respectively. "And this is Samuel and David."

Samuel stood first and shook Rickie's hand, followed by David.

"Nice to meet all of you. I see you really don't use any electricity, just like in the movie *Witness*."

Lillian wondered if anyone saw her cut her eyes in Rickie's direction. Could this day get any worse?

"Well, we don't shoot at people like I hear they done in that movie," Grandpa said. "Or protect shot-up detectives. Right silly, if you ask me."

Lillian was still standing near the doorway, hoping she could coax Rickie back out the door—and then out of her life forever. Mom was going to hear about this.

"David, I reckon we better be on our way," Samuel said, standing up. He walked directly to the hat rack and retrieved his hat without even looking in Lillian's direction.

"No!" she blurted out. "We haven't had dessert."

"Me and the boy have chores to do. *Danki* for supper," he said, still barely making eye contact. "We'll let you and your friend catch up." The way he said "friend" revealed more than just a slight irritation.

"Nice to meet you both," Rickie said, nodding at Samuel and David as they headed toward the door.

"Likewise," Samuel responded, almost pushing David through the doorway.

"I'll be right back," Lillian said in a frenzy, leaving her grandparents with Rickie. That in itself was probably a mistake. No telling what Rickie might say. Or Grandpa, for that matter.

"Samuel, wait," she said, scurrying down the porch steps.

"David, tell Lillian thank you for supper and go wait for me by the buggy."

"*Danki*, Lillian," David said hesitantly, as if he knew something was wrong.

"Don't go," she said, touching Samuel's arm. "I thought you and David might stay for a while."

"Your company came a long way to see you."

"He should have never come here," she said firmly. She wanted to throw herself into Samuel's arms, a place she knew would be safe.

"*Ya* . . . but he *is* here." He raised his brows as if asking her what she would do about it.

"Not for long. As soon as I go back inside, I'm going to make sure he gets on the next flight home."

"I have to get David home, Lillian."

She could hear the remorse in his voice, and she worried to what extent he was feeling it. Did he regret leaving so early? Did he regret ever befriending her in the first place?

As he turned to walk toward the buggy, Lillian followed him. "Samuel."

He turned around to face her. "*Ya.*"

"Thank you again for being with me today."

Samuel shook his head and then gazed intently into her eyes. "Lillian." He paused. "I'm glad I was there for you today."

She definitely sensed there was a "But" coming.

"But, you have . . ." He hesitated.

"I have what, Samuel? Just say it." Although she wasn't sure she wanted to hear it.

"A lot of things going on that I don't understand. All this with your father, the problems with your mother, and now this. These are all worldly conflicts I'm just not used to." He shook his head again.

The regret was still evident in his tone. In a defensive explosion, she tried to redeem herself. "What my mother did is *not* my fault. What my selfish father did is *not* my fault. And Rickie showing up here this way is *not* my fault. Are you going to punish me for these things I have no control over?"

He gently grabbed her shoulders and leaned down. "Lillian, I'm not punishing you for anything. I'm just being honest and telling you I'm not used to all this."

She didn't know what to say. It seemed no matter how far she traveled, drama was determined to follow her.

"Make peace with all the confusion, Lillian," he said softly. "It's the only way you'll find the happiness you're looking for."

"I'm trying! I found my father, which answers a lot of questions. I understand a little better about why my mother left here, and I broke up with a boyfriend who is a jerk! He should not be here."

Samuel didn't say anything, instead looking over her shoulder. She clenched her teeth as she slowly turned around.

"A *jerk*?" Rickie was standing on the porch step and had clearly heard her last remark.

Lillian glanced back and forth between the men. Samuel dropped his arms to his side. Rickie folded his arms across his chest.

"Exactly what's going on here?" Rickie went on. "Are you involved with this Amish guy or something?" His voice deepened to a growl as he spoke—a sound she'd grown to recognize and fear.

"He is my friend, Rickie."

She clasped her hands together and momentarily closed her eyes. *Please God, don't let Rickie hurt the people I love*, she silently prayed.

"Are you *praying*?" Rickie asked, a disgusted look sweeping across his face. "Give me a break!" As he came flying down the porch steps, Lillian instinctively backed up. His eyes were ablaze. "Get in the car, Lillian. I'm taking you home," he said softly as he forcefully grabbed her arm above the elbow and began dragging her toward the car. "We will get all this straightened out at home, sweetie."

Lillian glanced over her shoulder at Samuel, who hadn't moved. His feet were firmly planted in the grass a few feet from the porch steps as he watched Lillian's life unraveling. She looked around for David. To her horror, he was standing by the buggy as Samuel instructed, taking it all in with a look on his face Lillian would carry with her for a long time.

"I'm not going with you, Rickie," Lillian said as she tried to wiggle out of his grasp.

"Oh, but you will. Did you really think I wouldn't come get you?" He spun her around to face him, tightening his grip on her arm. "I just wanted to enjoy my freedom for a little while." He chuckled.

"You'll never get me on a plane, Rickie," she said.

"Oh, I know that. But I'm going to get you back to my hotel room. I don't know who you think you are! Leaving me a cheesy little note and walking out of my life without so much as a warning! This is something we need to talk about."

"I've had one too many talks with you, Rickie."

"Well, you've got one more talk coming," he threatened, opening the car door. "And quit looking over your shoulder. Do you really think that Amish guy is going to come to the rescue?" He snickered. "His kind would let someone shoot up the place, rape his wife, and kill his dog without doing anything. They're *passive*." He paused and glanced briefly at Samuel as if to confirm he was indeed still in the same spot. "Now, get in the car, Lillian," he growled. "We are going to talk."

"No, Rickie. I'm not going." She struggled to pull away, looking toward Samuel. She knew Rickie was right. No matter how strong her friendship with Samuel was, she knew he would remain non-assertive. She was not going to make it any harder on him by begging him to help her. Plus, she couldn't bear the thought of Rickie going after Samuel—and David having to witness such a horrible event.

Rickie swore. "I left my cell phone in the house. Get in the car, Lillian, if you don't want any trouble for your new friend. I'll be right back."

She crawled into the front seat. The car door slammed shut, along with her hope. Facing forward, she couldn't look back at Samuel. She just couldn't. Resting her head in her hands, her body trembled with the realization of what was happening. She'd just take it, one more time. Then she'd come home. She'd be humiliated, but she'd survive. Somehow she always survived.

"God, give me the strength," she said aloud, "and please get Rickie out of my life forever."

After a while, she wondered what was taking Rickie so long. She slowly turned around, still unsure if she could bear to look at Samuel. No one was in sight.

Sitting up a little straighter, her eyes darted across the yard toward the house, then to her right, her left. Where was he?

David was nowhere in sight either. Where was Rickie? Her heart raced, fearing a confrontation between Samuel and Rickie. She opened the car door and bolted out.

She was running toward the house when the screen door swung open. Grandpa walked out on the porch holding a glass of tea as if he had not a care in the world. At the same time, she heard the clippity-clop of Pete's hooves and watched as the buggy spun around. David was driving.

"Grandpa! Where's Samuel?" She scrambled up the porch steps in time to catch the strained look on Grandma's face before Grandpa closed the door behind him. She turned to watch David galloping down the dirt driveway. "Grandpa!"

"Samuel thought it best for David to run over to Ivan's for a bit. Katie Ann has a shoofly pie she made 'specially for them. He'll be right back."

Confusion. Panic. Where was Samuel? She saw Grandma peek out the window. Her face resonated with pity. Lillian wondered if Grandpa was utilizing his authority as head of the household, instructing her to stay in the house—for her own safety.

"Grandpa," she said frantically, gently grabbing his arm. "Where is Samuel?"

"Why, he's in the woodshed right here beside the house." Grandpa took another sip of tea.

"What?" She turned to venture in that direction, but Grandpa stepped forward.

"Lilly, I think it best if you come sit with your ol' Grandpa on the porch." His expression turned solemn. "Do what your *daadi* says."

"But, I—"

"On the porch, Lilly." Grandpa pointed to one of the rockers, taking a seat in the other one himself.

She reluctantly sat down. "Grandpa, listen to me. Rickie is not a very good person. Samuel could be in trouble. I have to go to him." She looked toward the woodshed.

Grandpa tilted his head back and stared into the yard. "Lilly, you will have to trust your grandpa and do as I say," he said firmly, before cutting his eyes in her direction. "And we will not speak of this again."

A rustling to her right drew her eyes. There came Samuel, walking side by side with Rickie. As they reached the front of the house, Samuel headed toward the porch and Rickie walked to his car. Rickie never looked her way. Samuel said nothing as he walked up and took a seat on the porch step.

"I'll have Irma Rose bring you something to drink," Grandpa said to Samuel. "We'll have us a nice glass of tea. David should be back shortly."

"Samuel, what—" Lillian started ask.

"Maybe you'd like something cold to drink, Lillian?" Grandpa interrupted as the three of them watched Rickie's car ramble down the dirt drive. Rickie looked none the worse for wear, but something had happened to make him tuck his tail and run.

Lillian turned back to look at Samuel. His face was as solemn as Grandpa's.

"Samuel, are you all right?"

Before he could say anything, Grandpa spoke up one more time. "He looks mighty fine to me." His look left no question in Lillian's mind that there were to be no more questions. Now . . . or ever.

"Who was that man, Pop?" David asked Samuel when they pulled into the driveway.

"You heard Jonas," he said. "An old friend of Lillian's."

"Pop, I'm almost twelve. I know what's going on."

"Do you, now?" Samuel brought Pete to a halt and hopped out of the buggy. David followed him into the house.

"It's her old boyfriend," David said, watching Samuel light the lantern above the kitchen table.

Samuel eyed the kitchen, again picturing the table at his favorite shop. As was the case recently, the image in his mind included Lillian. But it was hard not to have doubts that such a notion was ever going to happen. The thought of Lillian being involved with the likes of that Rickie fellow brought on a rage that was not in line with his upbringing.

As Samuel poured him and the boy each a glass of cold milk, David said, "I didn't like him. I saw the way he tried to drag Lillian to the car. He's not a *gut* man."

"Only the Good Lord can pass judgment, David."

Samuel reflected on the judgment he himself had just passed on the man out in the woodshed.

"*Ya*, I know."

Samuel regretted the boy saw as much as he did. Especially Rickie pulling Lillian to the car like a rag doll. Sending David to Ivan's was a good move. The boy needn't ever know why Rickie hightailed it back to the city. For that matter, no one ever had to know. But Samuel would know, and he'd have to live with it.

It was hard for him to imagine what life must have been like for Lillian, living with a man like that. He imagined things must have been even worse behind closed doors. No one to see him doing her harm. Cringing, he recalled her fearful expression when Rickie dragged her off—a look that shifted from dread to compliance to embarrassment, all in a split second. Her face had revealed a painful past not fit for any human being. Lillian would never cause harm to another person. It sickened him to envision anyone hurting her. That Rickie fellow sickened him for sure.

He couldn't help but worry how many more skeletons from Lillian's closet might show up in Lancaster County.

Grandma and Grandpa were sitting at the kitchen table when Lillian walked back into the house.

"Mighty fine mess we had here, Lilly," Grandpa said, uncharacteristically somber. "I don't think we'll be seeing that pretty *Englischer* again."

"I hope not, Grandpa." Lillian hands trembled as she poured herself a cup of hot tea and took a seat beside her grandma at the kitchen table. "I'm sorry about all this."

"*Ya*," Grandpa said. "We will put this behind us. No talk of it again."

Grandpa spoke with a conviction Lillian hadn't heard before. Grandma had temporarily taken her place as a traditional Old Order Amish woman, allowing Grandpa to rule the roost. Her expression was distant and staid.

"I hope Samuel will still want to be friends after all this," Lillian said, fighting tears.

Her grandparents didn't answer, as if they were harboring the same thought.

"I think I'll head upstairs," she said finally, feeling defeated by the events of the day. She barely heard her grandparents wishing her a good night's sleep as she headed up the wooden steps. She was almost to the top of the stairs when Grandpa called to her. "Lillian."

"Yes, Grandpa?" She turned around, not sure if she wanted to hear what he had to say. His voice still resonated with the same somberness.

"God does not judge us by the actions of others," he bellowed. "And me and your Grandma don't either."

Lillian tried to muster up a smile. She nodded, turned back around, and headed upstairs feeling embarrassment and regret. Everything she'd been working to attain seemed to be teetering toward failure. Feeling herself curl up into the place she often went after an encounter with Rickie, she realized she could either allow herself to revert back to the person she used to be—or fight for the peaceful life within her grasp.

"Guess who showed up on the doorstep this evening, Mom?" Lillian asked her mother when she answered the phone.

"Lillian, I think Rickie deserves another chance, and that's the reason I told him—"

"Mother! I decide who I am going to be with. You made a terrible mistake sending Rickie all this way!"

"Rickie is a very nice-looking, well-mannered man with a good job, Lillian."

"He has you so fooled, Mom."

"Is this about the Amish man?" Her mother's tone resounded with disapproval. "Are you not giving Rickie another chance because of this other man?"

"It has nothing to do with Samuel."

"You should give him another chance."

Sensing her mom's complete and utter disappointment in her, she considered setting her straight about Rickie. But her mom had introduced her to Rickie, and she knew her mother would blame herself. Yet again, Lillian found herself in a role reversal, feeling the need to protect her mother. But she wondered when her mom was ever going to be a mother to *her*.

Still, she and her mother had sufficiently hurt each other enough over the years, and she wasn't going to rub this in her face. Besides, she felt humiliated that she'd let it go on for as long as she did.

She recalled the parting of ways between Samuel and Rickie, wondering what exactly had happened out in the woodshed.

"Samuel and I are just friends, but Rickie could never be the man Samuel is."

"Oh, Lillian! I can hear it in your voice. You've fallen for this Amish man." She heard her mother's sigh.

Lillian took a deep breath and decided to change the subject. "I met my father today."

No response. "Well, Mom?"

"I'm trying to imagine what that must have been like," her mother replied.

Lillian thought back to her meeting with Daniel Foster. Shattered dreams. Suddenly, she didn't want to talk anymore.

After a while, her mother said, "I'm sorry, Lillian. I really am."

Again she didn't respond.

"I was hypnotized by Daniel's writing. He was wise about the world. He was forbidden. Just like Eve, I bit the apple. When he found out I was pregnant with you, I saw his true colors. Sweetie, I tried to warn you about him. Did you tell him who you were? Was he horrible?"

"Yes, I told him who I was. And yes, the whole thing was horrible." She paused, trying to imagine what it must have been like for her mother. "I suppose it was horrible for you, too, Mom. But you should have told me much sooner who my father was."

"I just wanted to protect you. How did you find out about the newspapers? I can't believe they're still in the barn after all these years."

"Grandpa thought I was you one night. He said he knew you were saving newspapers, and it would be best to stay away from the *Englisch* man. I had already seen the boxes of newspapers, so I looked through them. You made little notes beside some of his columns."

She heard a sniffle on the other end of the line.

"Mom?" she asked when there was no reply.

"How is Grandpa?" Now Mom was changing the subject, but she was also crying.

"He's okay, most of the time. I think his medicines cause him to get confused at night sometimes."

And, then, as if it had been building for years, Sarah Jane Miller wept uncontrollably. Lillian had never heard her like this. Thank goodness she hadn't told her about Rickie. "Mom? Are you okay?" Her own tears began to build. "Mom?"

"I'm so, so sorry, Lillian. I'm sorry I've been a bad mother. I'm sorry I didn't tell you about Daniel." She wept harder. "I miss my *mamm* and *daed* so much."

It was the first time Lillian had ever heard her mother speak any *Pennsylvania Deitsch*. It was the first time she remembered her mother apologizing for the way she had raised her.

"I miss them so much, Lillian," she went on. "And I'm so sorry for everything I've put you through."

Lillian tried to gain a level of composure before she said anything. The whole day had been an emotional disaster. Now she just felt sick about everything. She needed a hug. Oddly, she needed her mother.

"Mom," she said softly, choking back sobs. "You're not a bad mother. You made mistakes. We all do. I'm sorry for everything you went through."

"You don't have to try to make me feel better, Lillian. I know what kind of life I've led and how it affected you."

But I want to make you feel better, a little voice screamed. *I really do.* "It's okay, Mom." She sniffled and attempted a smile. "Besides, I think I turned out pretty good. And you get some credit for that."

"Oh, I don't know about that."

"Well, I do. Remember when I was in first grade and all the kids were going to the roller skating rink? We didn't have any money, and I knew that, but I wanted to go so badly. It was Cheryl Henston's birthday party. Remember?"

"Yes, I remember," her mother responded softly.

"I knew you pawned something important to get me a new outfit and a present to take to the party." She paused. "And Mom, I remember you singing to me when I was little. I remember you hugging me, bandaging scrapes, brushing my hair—" She stopped when she heard her mother sobbing again.

As Lillian's own cries of forgiveness leaped forward, she realized she'd been so busy thinking about the ways her mother had wrecked her life, she hadn't stopped to realize all the good things her mother had done. It wasn't as if she forgot the good things. She just had allowed the bad things to dominate her memories.

"I love you, Lillian. I'm sorry about telling Rickie where you are."

"I love you, too, Mom. I really do."

"Give your grandpa an extra big hug from me."

Both of them still crying, Lillian hesitated before saying, "Mom, why don't you come give him a hug yourself?"

"Oh, I can't face them, Lillian. I just can't. Do they know about Daniel? Did you tell them? They knew who he was back then. He lived in Paradise. Do they know?"

"No, no, Mom. They don't know. It's up to you to tell them if you want to. But either way, come to Lancaster County. Come see your parents."

She pleaded several more times with her mother, and her mother's response was consistent: "I just can't, Lillian. I can't."

The next morning, Lillian awoke with puffy eyes. It had taken effort to talk to God before she fell asleep. She couldn't help but feel like He had let her down. And she could feel doubt about His existence creeping in. But she had prayed just the same, like she had been doing each night.

She'd prayed for her mother: "Please God, help me and Mom to both make good decisions and heal from the bad ones. And help us to be close, the way mothers and daughters should be. Please help Mom to find the peace she is looking for and keep her safe."

She'd prayed about Samuel and David: "I pray that maybe there is a place for me in Samuel and David's life, God. Please keep them both safe."

Next were Grandma and Grandpa: "I'm so thankful for my grandparents and the relationship You've given me with them. So very thankful. Please keep Grandpa in my life. I pray his medications will keep him from being in pain and that he'll be able to live many more years. I pray that Grandma will get more rest, and that we will continue to grow closer. I've learned a lot from her."

Those were the easy ones. Much harder was to pray for Rickie: "I pray that Rickie will find his way to You and make the changes necessary for him to live a good life." That was all she could muster up on Rickie's behalf.

Her father was the toughest of all and she kept it simple: "Please let me forgive him."

She had put all her worries in one big bubble and blown it up to heaven for God to handle. Her last words before falling asleep were, "I'm putting it all in your hands, God."

This morning, as she forced herself out of bed and dressed, she wasn't sure if Samuel would show up for their planned picnic around noon. She wouldn't blame him if he didn't.

As Samuel guided Pete down the dirt driveway a few minutes before noon, he still worried if Lillian would be able to shed her worldly ways and past boyfriends. He had spent several long, sleepless hours last night raging with bitterness at the thought of that Rickie fellow. And several more questioning his feelings for Lillian. Now those concerns resurfaced.

But as he neared the farmhouse, he saw Lillian sitting on the front porch. And he realized one thing was for sure: despite everything, no matter her past, he couldn't stay away from Lillian.

She ran to meet him. As he stepped out of the buggy, she stopped right in front of him. "I was afraid you might not come."

"I invited you on a picnic. Why wouldn't I come?" he said, feeling a little guilty that he considered not showing up.

"Because of yesterday, I thought you—" she blurted out.

He forcibly shook his head, hoping they could put things behind them. "Let's forget about it." He paused. "You look different."

It was true. She glowed with a radiance that made her more beautiful than she already was. How was that so? He'd expected she'd still be a mess.

"I look just the same as I always do," she said beaming. She scanned her outfit and pointed toward her feet. "Right down to my black leather shoes!"

Seeing her so lighthearted set Samuel's heart and mind to rest. It was going to be a good day after all. Something was different, all right. He wasn't sure what. But he need not pay it any more mind. His heavy heart from the prior night, along with his worries, were beginning to wash clean.

"The picnic basket!" she said. "How can we have a picnic without any food?" She ran back into the house, returning with a large basket in one hand and a small knapsack in the other.

"I invited you on the picnic. I should have brought the food," he said, thinking back to when Lillian had offered to pack the basket. "What's that?" He pointed to the knapsack.

She smiled. "It's a surprise." She handed him the basket but kept hold of the knapsack.

"What kind of surprise?" he asked, intrigued.

She winked at him. "You'll see."

13

LILLIAN FELT LIGHT AND CAREFREE AS SHE AND SAMUEL exited the buggy and walked toward the lake. It was a beautiful summer day without a cloud in the sky, and the clouds in her mixed-up mind were slowly clearing as well. And Samuel was with her. Despite the horrors of the previous day, she wanted to face her future with hope and determination. She'd come too far to let Rickie or Daniel Foster deter her efforts.

"What are you thinkin' about?" Samuel asked, walking alongside her.

"What a beautiful day it is." Her eyes twinkled. "And how lucky I am to have you for a friend. Plus, I'm clearing the baggage in my heart that I've carried around for such a long time. I'm breathing in the blessing of this new day."

"We can talk about yesterday if you want," he offered, apparently regretful he'd avoided the subject earlier.

"No. I think I've figured out a way to put it all behind me."

Obviously curious, he nodded. As they moved closer to the lake, he asked, "What'd you think? Is this a good spot?"

"Perfect," she was quick to say. "It's beautiful here." And it was. The "lake" looked more like a large Texas pond. Tall pines surrounded them and a small pier edged across the water.

"It's quiet here most of the time. The tourists don't know it's here."

"Well, this is a great spot. Let's go get the blanket and picnic basket."

"And you can tell me what's in that bag," he said as they returned to the buggy. His eyes widened hopefully.

"I told you it's a surprise," she teased. "First we dine on this fine meal I have prepared—tuna-salad sandwiches, potato salad, some nasty beets, and funnel cakes for dessert. And, *ya*, I made the funnel cakes."

Samuel spread the blue and gray quilt on the ground. Lillian set the picnic basket on the quilt but kept guard over the knapsack, giving him a grin.

He was glad to see it. It had been a rough couple of days, especially for her. The sight and sound of her carrying on the way she was today reminded him of the first time he'd met her, toting the red suitcase and laughing up a storm. What a beautiful mess she'd been.

Now, as he watched her dishing out their lunch onto paper plates, he thought about how far she'd come. She looked Amish, and she sounded Amish. And she had gone a long way toward learning the *Ordnung* and some *Pennsylvania Deitsch*. She just might make it if she didn't let her old life get in the way.

They settled down to eat, chatting about nothing in particular, each of them careful not to bring up unpleasant topics. Lillian frowned when all of the food was gone. "I don't think I made enough. I should know by now how much you eat."

"I'm plenty full. It was the perfect amount. And tasted mighty fine too."

Shining with delight, she stowed food containers, plates, and the like back in the picnic basket.

"Now, let's have a look at the surprise in that bag." He rolled his eyes toward the heavily guarded knapsack.

Looking a bit embarrassed, she explained, "It's not really that big of a deal. Just something I wanted us to do . . . together."

"You've got all my attention."

"You might think it's kind of silly, but it's something I want to do." She reached for the bag and opened it. First thing she pulled out was a gardening spade.

"Are we digging a hole?"

"Yep. We sure are."

"Hmm . . . Mind if I ask what for?"

Leaning her head to one side, she shot him a serious look. "To bury this." She held up the knapsack.

Samuel sat up a little straighter. "Do I even dare ask what you've got in there? It's not like a dead critter or something, is it?"

"Yes, it's a dead animal, and I'm going to perform a pagan ritual."

He couldn't believe his ears.

She slapped him playfully on the arm. "Samuel! I'm kidding." She was eager to press on. "But we have to dig a hole."

"How big a hole? And more important, what are we burying?"

"Stop looking so scared," she said, letting out another round of giggles. "I have a few things I want gone, that's all. It's symbolic of a new beginning for me. No dead animals, I promise."

"What's in there?" He reached over and attempted to have a peek.

She quickly snatched the bag and pulled it to her chest. "You'll see," she said, once again embarrassed. Whatever the girl had the notion to get rid of, it sure seemed important to her.

"What about over there for your hole, where there isn't any grass?" He pointed to a nearby patch of ground.

"Perfect!"

He heaved himself up and offered her a hand. Once on their feet, he shook his head. "I sure am wondering what you're up to."

"You'll see," she said, heading toward the grassless spot a few yards away.

———————

She watched Samuel digging her hole, his muscles bulging beneath his blue cotton shirt. His physical strength was evident, but it was his emotional strength she found most attractive. In addition to his unquestionable faith in God, his faith in her seemed to be growing. And his extreme sense of discipline did not overshadow his ability to enjoy life. He was able to play and have fun, but he took his responsibilities as seriously as his faith. Hard work was part of the Amish lifestyle, and Samuel worked harder than most. His role as David's father only added to his attributes.

A few inches down, the ground was moist, and it wasn't long before Samuel had a hole in the dirt about two feet deep and a foot wide. "Big enough?" he asked, wiping his brow.

"*Ya.*" Still toting the knapsack, she went to retrieve the quilt from where they had eaten. She spread it beside the hole and motioned for Samuel to take a seat, then joined him. As she reached into the knapsack, she glanced his way and smiled. "As I said, this might seem silly to you. But it will help me to move forward."

"If it's important to you, then it's not silly at all."

She reached into the bag and pulled out the first item she planned to discard. Retrieving the small diary, her thoughts traveled back to a time when she was fourteen—a mixed-up teenager harboring hateful thoughts about the life she was forced to live because of her mother's decisions. With no extras and living in a run-down shack, she'd saved her occasional lunch money to buy the diary. Absent of hopes and dreams, woeful accounts of her daily challenges filled the small book. Her plan: to show it to her mother someday and say, "Read this, Mother, and don't shed a tear because I have shed enough for both of us."

Samuel sat patiently as she scanned the pages. February 3, 1995—a particularly painful day. She silently read:

Dear Diary, today is possibly the worst day of my life. I haven't seen Mom in two days. She has a new boyfriend. There's no food in this place we call a house. And Mitzi died. I buried her in the backyard. I don't know what happened. I found my precious kitty lifeless on the front porch. She was skinny, but I'd been feeding her whatever we had in the house. I don't think that's why she died. Her eyes were open and her white and black fur was wet. She wasn't breathing, though. I brought her in the house and cried for almost two hours. I loved her. When Mom never showed up, I just dug a hole in the backyard and put her in it. I don't know much about God, so I didn't really say any prayers or anything. Then, it started to rain, so I went back in the house. This was a very bad day.

She jumped forward to July 23:

Dear Diary, something is wrong with Mom. I don't think she's drunk, but something else is wrong. She's slurring her words. I'm not sure if it's drugs or something. I told her I was hungry, but she just cried and mumbled something I didn't understand.

September 12:

Dear Diary, I'm feeling very sad because I want to go to the dance at school. Henry Webster will be there, and I really like him. I think he likes me too. But Mom says I can't go. It costs five dollars to get in. I don't have anything to wear anyway. I hate my life. I hate my mom.

Lillian cringed, recalling the events of that year. Hard to believe it was thirteen years ago. So much had changed. She had changed. And her mother had changed as well. Continuing to allow the bad memories to override the good memories was only hurting her. After her recent conversation with her mother, she knew the only way to continue along in her quest for peace was to replace resentment with forgiveness. She tossed the book into the hole.

"I forgive you, Mom," she said softly.

Samuel's expression was solemn, but he offered her a comforting smile and nodded his head. She reached into the knapsack for the next item. Opening the envelope, she pulled out the newspaper clipping she had cut out the day before. Studying the young face of her father, she read his column—such heartfelt insights on the page. Why couldn't he have made a place for her in his life?

She glanced at Samuel, who was studying her actions intently. He acknowledged that he saw the clipping, and she tossed it in the hole.

"I forgive you, Daniel Foster."

She blinked away tears, determined not to cry. If she continued to weigh herself down with the years behind her, she would never be free to experience the life before her with joy and happiness. The peaceful life she longed for—a life where she didn't harbor any resentments—was within her grasp. Releasing the burdens of her heart, forgiving those who hurt her, and turning her life to God would free her soul to be the person she wanted to be.

She reached into the bag.

"Are you sure about this, Lillian?" Samuel asked when he saw her retrieve the next few items. His forehead creased with worry.

"*Ya*, I am. This represents all my worldly clothes, along with a few other things." She folded the blue jeans and placed them in the hole, followed by a bag of makeup, several pieces of costume jewelry, a small battery-operated radio, and two books she no longer felt were suitable reading material. Some of the jewelry was from Rickie. She didn't see the need to mention that.

There was one thing left in the bag—her last tie to the outside world. As she pulled out her cell phone, Samuel said, "What about talking to your *mamm*?"

"I'll do what everyone else here does. I'll go to town and use the pay phone, or the shanty at the Lapp farm."

Samuel seemed leery about the cell phone, her final separation from the outside world. The lines in his forehead became more evident.

"It's fine," she replied as she tossed the phone atop the pile. "Grandma hates that thing. She winces every time it rings."

Samuel knew that giving up her worldly items and forgiving those who hurt her was all part of Lillian's plan to move forward in her new life. But he also knew it wasn't easy for her. Just like it wasn't going to be easy for him to add his own piece of the past to the pile.

"Okay, that's it." She twisted her hands together in a nervous sort of way. He reckoned he'd feel nervous in her shoes too.

"Wait," he said when she reached for the spade, preparing to refill the hole. He reached into his pocket. "I have something to add."

He'd been thinking about it the whole time he watched her giving up her worldly possessions and letting go of the things that haunted her. The item in his pocket didn't haunt him, but it would be equally as hard to give up.

He pulled out the wallet-sized picture of Rachel and handed it to Lillian. The edges were worn, but her face as beautiful as ever.

"Samuel," she whispered, as if she couldn't believe her eyes. "But I thought . . ." She paused, looking at the photo. ". . . pictures aren't allowed."

"I'm not perfect, Lillian." He thought back to the day his

Englisch friend Carl Johanson from the supermarket gave him the picture a few days after Rachel died. "We don't have to tell anyone about this," Carl had said as he slipped him the picture of Rachel. Carl adored Rachel and evidently had sneaked in a picture when she wasn't looking, knowing she had the cancer real bad and that someday Samuel might want it. He'd carried it in his pocket ever since. No one knew he had the picture, not even David.

"She's beautiful, Samuel," she said, taking note of the woman's exquisite facial features. Her eyes were a warm hazel color, and her tightly wound hair a honey-brown shade. "Wow." She handed the picture back to him.

He took one last look at the woman from his past, then looked at Lillian. Her face was as serious as he'd ever seen her. And she'd never looked prettier.

Slowly, his hand made its way toward the hole. But Lillian's hand was quickly on his arm. "No, Samuel," she said, shaking her head. "No."

"She's part of my past." His arm wavered over the hole in the dirt. "And pictures aren't allowed."

Lillian disagreed. "It's not the same, Samuel. Rachel is a wonderful part of your past, someone to remember. You loved her, and she's David's mother. I don't want you to ever forget her. I would never allow you to mix her picture with these things I want to bury forever." She continued shaking her head in a very determined way.

Samuel froze. He wasn't sure what to do. His hand held fast to the picture, still hovering over the hole. The whole while he watched Lillian make peace with things from her past, he'd thought burying the picture would be the right thing to do. He wanted to be able to move forward too.

"Put the picture back in your pocket, Samuel," Lillian instructed, guiding his arm away from the hole. "We won't tell anyone. But I think you need to keep the picture."

"I reckon it's not right, though."

"It'll be our little secret." Her eyes sparkled with warm sincerity.

As he placed the picture back in his pocket, his gaze locked with hers in mutual understanding.

That night at supper, with her entire family assembled at the table, David offered the blessing, and everyone dug into the feast Lillian had prepared. She'd mastered *Yummasetti*, a traditional Pennsylvania German dish—ground beef, Amish noodles, bread, butter, onion, peas, chicken soup, mushroom soup, sour cream, and lots of cheese. Her city life would have sent the high-calorie meal straight to her thighs, but there was always enough work here to keep a nice sense of balance when it came to worrying about weight gain.

Everyone loved the meal, and she'd even made rhubarb pie for dessert.

"Our Lilly has turned into a fine Amish cook," Grandpa announced. "*Appeditlich!*"

"It's real *gut*, Lillian," David said. Although Lillian noticed he'd been awfully quiet since he came in from his chores outside. Maybe he felt left out, knowing she and Samuel had spent the day together.

"Are you ready to start school soon?" she asked. "Let's see, you have two more years left, right?"

"I reckon," David said softly, barely looking up. Lillian

glanced at Samuel, who shrugged slightly, also sensing David's solemn mood.

Lillian knew Amish children only attended school through the eighth grade. Weeks ago, Samuel had shown her David's school. The one-room, red schoolhouse was within walking distance of every child who attended. There were rows of wooden desks facing a long blackboard. There were no televisions, computers, or any other type of electronic equipment. It was like stepping back into another time period. Samuel explained that Amish teachers taught lessons in English.

Reflecting on her trip to the schoolhouse with Samuel, she thought about her twelve years in public school, plus her four years in college. In her mixed-up world, teaching had been the one goal that had remained constant. Once again, she recalled her regret at having to give up her teaching job.

"What are we gonna do when young David returns to school?" Grandpa asked. "We've become mighty dependent on him 'round here."

"David will still come around after school," Samuel said. "And Jonas, I'll do whatever I can to help too."

Grandpa sat up a little straighter. "*Ya*, well, I've been feelin' downright well here lately. Whatever medical concoctions those *Englisch* doctors are given' me tend to make me wanna tackle that yard with the push mower."

"Jonas, you will do no such thing!" Grandma snapped.

"Irma Rose, don't go bossin' me." His tone was equally firm. "I know yard work is for the womenfolk, but I'm gonna do it since I ain't been able to do much else."

"If I catch you mowing that yard, I'll do more than boss you,

Jonas Miller." She shot him a look that would've had everyone else at the table cowering, but Grandpa just sat up even taller.

"After I be done mowing the yard with the push mower, then I'm gonna go after the repairs to that hog pen. Thinkin' about takin' on a few hogs this next year."

"Jonas! We have more than we can say grace over to take care of 'round here. I'm pleased as punch you are feelin' better, but you can get those crazy notions out of your head."

Lillian glanced at Samuel, who was trying not to laugh. Even David was stifling a grin. When Grandma and Grandpa got going, it was always an amusing display of misdirected affection.

"I'll do whatever I want," Grandpa muttered, diving into some rhubarb pie.

Grandma rattled off a bunch of *Pennsylvania Deitsch* Lillian didn't understand, but Samuel and David looked shocked. And Grandpa didn't say another word.

As the men ate their rhubarb pie and began their own conversation, Lillian and her grandma cleaned the supper dishes.

"I think I smelled cigar smoke in here this morning when I returned from the supermarket," Grandma whispered. "Do you think that grandpa of yours would be silly enough to be smokin' with his bad health?"

Lillian figured Grandpa was in enough trouble for one day. She shrugged.

Whispering again, Grandma said, "Those medications have his mind all amuck. Do you know what he told me last night?"

Whatever it was, Grandma looked appalled. Her lips pursed together as she leaned in close to Lillian's ear. "He said he wants to have more *kinner*," she groaned in exasperation. "Now, is that not the silliest notion you've ever heard of in your life? First of all, Jonas knows the Good Lord was only able to bless us with one child. I couldn't have any more. Secondly, has that silly ol' man looked in the mirror lately?"

Lillian tried not to smile. Grandma was clearly upset.

"He's just been saying and doin' the craziest of things. It's those pills." She glanced over at her husband and frowned. Swiping a plate dry with the cup towel, she placed it in the cupboard.

Grandpa didn't notice. He was well into his second piece of rhubarb pie, as were Samuel and David.

"Well, at least he's feeling better," Lillian said, trying to cheer up Grandma.

"And I praise God for that. I just wish it wouldn't make his mind so cluttered, where he's not thinkin' like he should be."

As they whispered to themselves in the corner of the kitchen, Grandpa interrupted them. "Oh, Irma Rose and Lilly!"

"What, Jonas?" Grandma asked with a sigh. She glanced his way.

"I almost forgot to tell you both somethin'."

"What, Grandpa?" Lillian asked.

"No tellin'," Grandma whispered under her breath. She turned her back to dry another dish and place it in the cupboard.

Lillian watched while Grandpa swallowed his last bit of rhubarb pie. A big smile stretched across his wrinkled jowls. "Sarah Jane will be here on Wednesday."

Grandma spun around, sending the plate in her hand crashing to the floor.

14

LILLIAN PULLED THE BROOM FROM THE PANTRY AND BEGAN sweeping up the pieces of the broken plate. She'd begged her mother over the phone to come to Lancaster County. Had she finally decided to make peace with her parents?

"While you were out tending to your pretty flowers in the yard, Lilly, that noisy portable phone kept ringin' this morning," Grandpa bellowed. "It took me a few tries, but I finally was able to talk into it." He paused. "I told Sarah Jane she needed to come for a visit. She'll be here on Wednesday."

He made the statement as nonchalantly as if he saw his daughter all the time. When no one said anything, he went on. "Lilly, I say you prepare a special supper for your *mamm*. Show her what a fine Amish cook we've turned out 'round here. Said she'd be here by suppertime."

"Jonas, are you sure about this?" Grandma asked in a skeptical tone.

"Irma Rose, our Sarah Jane will be here on Wednesday." His announcement left no room for argument.

It was quiet for a bit before Samuel stood up to retrieve his hat from the rack. "That's great news, Jonas," he said, placing the hat on his head.

"*Ya, gut* news! Isn't it, Irma Rose?"

"Of course," Grandma said. Emotion flooded her face. "That's *wunderbaar* news."

"I'm going to walk Samuel and David out," Lillian said, not wanting to voice her concerns in front of her grandparents.

Once they were outside, Lillian told Samuel and David, "I begged my mother to come see her parents. She was adamant about not coming. I wonder what Grandpa said to change her mind?"

"Whatever he said, I think it's great she's coming," Samuel remarked.

Lillian shook her head. "You don't know my mother. She probably just *said* she would come. Grandpa is so excited about her coming, and she'll probably never show up. That will break his heart."

"People change their minds," Samuel said. As they headed to the buggy, he continued. "Think positive. It'll mean the world to Jonas if your *mamm* comes for a visit."

"It'll mean *everything* to Grandpa. And that's what worries me." She paused. "And another thing: Grandma said Grandpa has been saying all kinds of crazy things lately, mostly due to his medication. What if he didn't even talk to her? I'd better go into town tomorrow and use a pay phone." A guilty feeling swept over her; she was beginning to regret disposal of that one worldly item. How much easier it would be to walk inside and call her mother from the comfort of her bedroom.

"Pop, did you tell her about next weekend?" David asked, changing the subject.

"I was gettin' around to it." He turned toward Lillian. "I

know you've been around my *mamm* and the rest of my family at
church services, but they want to have a big shindig next Saturday
and have you, Irma Rose, and Jonas to the house for supper.
They know me and the boy eat supper here a lot, and I think
they'd like to do something for your family."

Lillian got along well enough with Samuel's family, but she
knew they still regarded her as the *Englisch* outsider. Conversation
was always polite, but limited. Neither his two sisters, nor
sister-in-law had allowed her into their inner circle. Several
times after church service she'd tried to make conversation
with them. They were cordial, but guarded. His mother barely
acknowledged her.

"And, of course, your *mamm* is welcome too," Samuel added.

"I wouldn't count on her being here."

"You never know," Samuel said optimistically. "People
change."

She started to say, "Not my mother." But that would be the old
Lillian talking. She had to admit: people could change. She had
changed. And she had buried any bad thoughts she'd harbored
about her mother in a hole by the lake. Plus, she'd had some hard
but good conversations with her mom lately that helped her see her
mom in a new light.

Her eyes glistened with hope. "I pray she does come." And she
meant it. She just doubted it.

The next day, she set out to go talk to David. She sensed something was bothering him. It was a beautiful day for a walk and it
was an off Sunday. Alternating Sunday worship services was one

of the "rules" she wasn't about to argue with. While the service always left her with a sense of fellowship and heightened spirituality, it was incredibly long.

Walking down the dirt road toward Samuel's farm, she reflected on the events of the past few days. Deep in thought about her mother, she heard a buggy approaching from behind. She spun around and watched the buggy slowing down.

Of all people . . .

Sadie Fisher let out a "Whoa, boy" that any man would have been proud of. As she coaxed her horse to a stop, she yelled, "Need a ride?"

She didn't really. However, Sadie's expression was nonconfrontational and it seemed safe enough.

"Heading to Samuel's?" she asked, guiding her horse back into motion after Lillian crawled in.

"*Ya.*"

"I heard you were learning the *Ordnung* and some *Pennsylvania Deitsch.*" Her tone was neither sarcastic nor condescending.

"Yes, I am."

"Are you thinking of converting and staying in our community?" Again, her tone wasn't bitter.

"I'm learning as much as I can so I can make a good decision." *Why does this seem like dangerous territory?*

"That sounds like a *gut* plan." Sadie issued a pop of the leathery strap and picked up the pace.

Lillian didn't know what to say. The woman was being nice. She just nodded.

"It's no secret I was hoping to marry Samuel someday."

Uh oh. Here we go. "Maybe you still will," she replied.

Sadie shrugged. "*Ach*, don't be silly. He took a fancy to you, and I'm happy for the both of you."

"What?" She didn't mean her response to sound as surprised as she was. "No, no," she added. "We're only friends."

"Sure you are."

The woman didn't seem the least bit jealous or upset. Maybe it was a trick.

"I'm actually on my way to Samuel's as well."

Ah ha! She knew it.

"Levi Zook's barn burned down and a barn raising is planned for Saturday. I was going to let Samuel know, so he wouldn't make any plans."

"Oh," Lillian responded, wondering how that would affect the family shindig planned for both their families on the same day. She had heard about the Amish barn raisings. The whole community participated and framed and roofed-in a barn all in one day.

"And I know Jonas isn't well, but it'd be nice if you were able to come help tend to the menfolk."

Sadie's tone was sincere. She didn't seem to harbor an ounce of resentment that Samuel and Lillian had become friends. "I'd be glad to help," Lillian replied.

As they pulled onto Samuel's driveway, Sadie asked, "Can I tell you a secret?"

"Sure." What kind of secret could she have to tell her?

Lillian took in Sadie with fresh eyes. Sadie was a feisty red-head with ivory skin and sky-blue eyes. Tiny creases in the corner of each eye hinted she might be a few years older than Lillian. She was tall and thin. Her striking appearance was unique to the

Old Order district. Lillian had noticed almost all the women had dark hair and olive complexions.

"I've been writing letters to a man in Texas."

The look on Lillian's face must have revealed her shock.

"Not to worry—he's an Amish man. I'm going to travel there to meet him!"

"Really? Is that allowed?" Lillian wasn't sure. "I'm from Texas," she added.

Skipping past her latter comment, Sadie said, "*Ya*. My husband died three years ago and Samuel was my only prospect for marriage here. My biological clock is ticking, as the *Englisch* would say." She glanced at Lillian and smiled for the first time. "I have no bad feelings about it, Lillian. Once I found out that Samuel carried no interest, I rested my efforts."

Lillian doubted Sadie's biological clock was ticking too much ahead of her own. She knew the Amish started their families early. She couldn't help but wonder why Sadie had no children. It wasn't proper to ask.

"How did you meet him?" Lillian knew there were scattered, small Amish districts in Texas.

"His family traveled here for my cousin's wedding. That's how I found out 'bout him. His wife also died about three years ago. But he wasn't able to attend the wedding. So I haven't actually met him. We've just been exchanging letters. No one knows, either, except for my cousin."

They were now parked in front of Samuel's farmhouse. Lillian could see David on the front porch. "Sadie, I have to say I'm a little surprised that you're telling me your secret."

Sadie shrugged again. "I guess I wanted to show you I wasn't going to stand in your way." She kept going over Lillian's protests. "But I'll ask that you keep it to yourself for now, if you don't mind."

"Sure. I won't tell anyone."

Sadie nodded. "Listen. I don't reckon I need to come in. Can you just let Samuel know about the barn raising?"

"I will. And I'll come help."

"That would be *gut*." Sadie guided her horse in the other direction. Before she pulled out, she yelled out the window. "Lillian?"

"*Ya?*"

"Come for a visit anytime. I'd love to hear all about Texas." She smiled and headed down the road.

Lillian decided she liked Sadie. Who would have ever thought? An unlikely friendship, but one Lillian felt she would pursue.

By the time Lillian reached the front porch, Samuel was outside with David. "And to what do we owe the pleasure?" Samuel asked as he walked toward her.

"Actually, I came to see David."

"*Ya?*" David asked, sounding alarmed.

"I wanted to talk to you. How about taking a walk with me?" she asked.

"Can I, Pop? I did most of my chores."

"You can do the rest when you get back," Samuel said, firing a questioning look in Lillian's direction.

Offering no explanation, she smiled at Samuel and motioned for David to walk beside her. Halfway down the driveway, she said, "Something was bothering you at supper last night. Anything to do with me?"

"No," he said. Although he didn't deny something was wrong.

Lillian thought for a minute and decided honesty would be best. "I thought maybe you were upset that your Pop and I spent the day together without you. Most of the time, it's the three of us together."

David shrugged, but didn't say anything.

"*Ya*, that's it, isn't it?"

"No. That would sound like I was a kid."

"You are a kid."

Once on the main road, she said, "I think me and your pop are just trying to get to know each other better. Is that okay with you?"

"*Ya*, I reckon so."

"Sometimes me and your *daed* might want to spend some time alone, getting to know each other." She paused. "But it doesn't mean that I don't still want to do things with you. Like this—our walk. This is our time to talk. So there will probably be times when it's just me and your *daed*, or just you and your *daed*, or just me and you. See what I mean?"

"*Ya*, I know."

He seemed to understand. Maybe he just needed to hear it from her. "So, everything is okay?"

Before David had time to answer, they both heard a blaring noise coming from down the road. As the buggy drew closer, Lillian was surprised to hear music blasting from within it. That certainly wasn't allowed. As the speeding buggy came frighteningly close to running them over, a frantic boy inside struggled to turn down the music. His blond bangs were slicked back and he was wearing blue jeans and a black T-shirt.

"Did he steal that buggy?" Lillian asked alarmed. "And what was that he was drinking?"

David didn't seem worried. As they watched the boy disappearing down the road, he said, in an envious tone, "That's Milo Yoder. It's his *rumschpringe*."

During *rumschpringe*, the community expected a certain amount of misbehavior from a teenager. But all this? Loud music, blue jeans, and whatever the boy was drinking in the brown bottle?

"Wonder where he's going in such a hurry and dressed like that?" she asked, frowning. She thought it tainted the Amish reputation for him to be acting like that.

"I can't wait until my *rumschpringe*!" David said as Milo Yoder's buggy disappeared completely, leaving only a dusty cloud behind him. "I'm gonna go to the movies, wear *Englisch* clothes, watch television in town, listen to loud music . . ." He paused. "And smoke cigarettes."

"Oh, David, I hope you won't smoke." She realized right away that it wasn't her place to speak to him in such a harsh tone, but the thought of David smoking bothered her. Turning to face him, she asked, "Why would you want to do all those things anyway?"

"Because you can do all those things during your *rumschpringe*," he said sheepishly, as if her tone surprised him. He looked down at the ground and kicked the dirt. "Besides, I bet you've done all those things."

Ouch. She certainly had. But that was different. David hadn't been exposed to any of those things, and she didn't want him to be. She wanted him to stay exactly as he was—free of complications and worldly ways. The outside world could snatch his innocence away before he realized what happened.

"Yes, I have done all those things," she answered. "And, it's not all it's cracked up to be either."

Standing on the side of the road, David pushed back his hat and gave her an inquisitive look.

"If there's something you want to ask me, go ahead." She folded her hands in front of her. "I'll tell you whatever you want to know."

"Have you ever drunk beer or smoked cigarettes?" His tone was almost demanding, but she'd started it.

"*Ya*, I have." *And please, don't do either one.*

"And I reckon you've seen lots of movies," he hesitated before he went on. "With all kinds of stuff in them."

"*Ya*, I have."

"Gone to a shopping mall and hung out with your friends?"

"Yep."

"Played an instrument?"

Lillian thought back to her short stint as a flute player while in middle school. Even though she had to give it up when Mom couldn't afford to buy her a flute of her own, she had loved making music. However, she knew the Old Order Amish community forbid instruments. Music was worldly and contrary to the Amish ways and was said to stir up emotions.

"I played the flute for a while," she finally said.

"Drove a car?" He crossed his arms, his tone still demanding. She should have never instigated this conversation.

"Yes," she answered. "But, David . . ." She wanted to tell him what a horrific childhood she'd had and how she wished she could have grown up right here. He wasn't done, though.

"Danced to band music?"

"*Ya.* I've done all those things, David. They may all sound fun and exciting to you, but you don't understand that—"

He was quick to interrupt her. "I'm going to do all those things during my *rumschpringe!*"

"Well, maybe just be choosy and make wise decisions when you go through your *rumschpringe.*" Fearing his exposure to the outside world, her emotions spilled out in an unplanned confession of sorts. "I'm sure all those things sound exciting, David. Driving a car, hanging out with your friends, drinking beer, smoking . . . but let me tell you what else can go along with all that fun-sounding stuff."

David was hanging on her words.

"Have you ever woken up and not had any food to eat? Ever slept in a car overnight because you didn't have a home to sleep in? Has anyone ever pushed you or threatened to beat you up at school? Anyone ever stolen from you? What about a terrible crime; ever witnessed anything like that? Been in a car accident that was so scary you didn't drive for six months?" She paused. "There is just a lot of bad stuff out there. That's all I'm saying. I wish I could have grown up here."

David wasn't saying anything. Maybe she'd said too much.

"I'm sorry. I should have never said all those things," she said with regret. She sat down on the side of the road in the grass. Slowly he followed her, his eyes begging for answers. "But living here seems to come with an invisible protective barrier that keeps you safe from everything out there." She waved her hand aimlessly to indicate a far-off place filled with worldly evils. "I told you before, it's complicated. And where there's all that stuff you think is so cool, there's a whole lot of ugliness too. I just don't want you to go through all that—*rumschpringe* or not."

They sat quietly for a few minutes.

"I won't do all those things, Lillian," he said softly. His big blue eyes were warm and tender, like Samuel's.

"Outside of this peaceful, tranquil, wonderful place is a world very different from yours. It might sound fun and intriguing, but trust me—it can steal from you, rob you of all the wonderful qualities that make you special. I just don't ever want to see that happen."

"It's all right, Lillian. I reckon I don't need to do all those things." It was quiet for a while before David said something Lillian felt sure she would remember for the rest of her life.

With a maturity way beyond his years, and possibly *her* years, he said, "Pop says when God closes doors, other doors will open. I had to think 'bout that for a while—like if I was in a big room with lots of doors." He paused. "I reckon sometimes we might not pick the door God woulda picked for us. But I think the door is like a two-way mirror. You best be happy with whatever ya see, no matter which side of the door you're on." He turned toward her and smiled. A smile she affectionately returned. "I reckon it'd be better to just try to pick the right door in the first place."

He couldn't have been more right.

Samuel noticed right away that the boy's frame of mind seemed much improved after his talk with Lillian. Neither one of them offered up any details, but that was all right. He reckoned they were forming their own special bond.

Lillian headed home after she filled him in about the barn raising on Saturday. He figured all his kin would be there, so maybe they'd find some time to visit with Lillian there, as opposed to the private shindig they had planned. A barn raising was a whole bunch of work, but a festive occasion just the same.

He found it a little worrisome that Lillian and Sadie might be pursuing a friendship, but he knew Lillian needed some womenfolk as friends. Sadie was a good girl; she'd just never been the one for him.

It was later that afternoon that his son shared some troublesome news. "Me and Lillian had a real *gut* talk today," David said. He settled into a rocker on the front porch next to Samuel.

"And what did you two have your heads together about?"

"She's done a whole bunch of stuff in her life. Sounds like she had a pretty hard time growing up."

"*Ya*," Samuel said. "But I think she turned out real fine."

"Hard to believe she's smoked cigarettes, drunk beer, seen crimes and all kinds of bad stuff." David took a swallow of his lemonade, unaware of the can of worms he'd just opened up. "She's even slept in a car and seen people get beat up."

How could she? Had Lillian learned nothing through her studies of the Amish ways? *"Come out from among them, and be ye separate, saith the Lord."* In her studies of the *Ordnung*, did she bypass 2 Corinthians 6:17? Samuel wasn't naïve. He knew the boy would be entitled to a *rumschpringe* in a few years, just as he had been. Along with that would come some misbehaving as he took a peek at the outside world. It wasn't Lillian's place to encourage such behavior, though. Those kinds of things were best not talked about. And it sure wasn't her place to expose his son to behaviors Samuel wanted him to have no part of.

His blood was pumping and bubbling to a boil. David's

next comment sent it rushing through his veins like whitewater rapids.

"I'm real glad she told me all about her times in the *Englisch* world, about all the things she's done. Now I know what to do when my *rumschpringe* comes 'round." He placed his lemonade on the table between them. "I'm gonna go get washed up before we head to Lillian's for Sunday supper. She always makes something extra *gut* on Sunday."

Samuel nodded. They'd been having supper mostly twice a week with Lillian—Wednesdays and Sundays. Tonight, if it was up to him, they wouldn't be going anywhere for supper. He planned to tell Lillian exactly how he felt about exposing his son to her worldly past. It wasn't his way—to get all stirred up about things. It wasn't proper. But she'd crossed the line when she shared her colorful past with his son. Smoking cigarettes, drinking beer? What was she thinking?

15

"ANSWER THE PHONE, MOM," LILLIAN WHISPERED. SOMEhow she and Grandma had let the pantry run dry of flour, so this quick trip to town was a good opportunity to call her mother. She needed to hurry, though. Samuel and David would be heading over for supper soon.

"Hello."

"Hi, Mom."

"Lillian! How are things going?"

"Everything is fine. Did you tell Grandpa you were coming here on Wednesday?" Might as well get to the point.

"Yes, I did. And I'm really going to try, Lillian."

"Mom! What do you mean, you're going to *try*?"

"Well, Lillian, I do have a job. Hopefully it will work out where I can come."

"What made you change your mind? I thought you didn't want to come for a visit?"

"I just . . ." She paused. "I just need to see my parents. And when your grandpa asked me to come, well, it was just hearing his voice, I guess. I know he's sick, and I didn't want to disappoint him. He suggested Wednesday. Where are you calling me from? I've tried to call you on your cell phone several times."

"I don't have my cell phone any more. I'm calling you from a pay phone in town. Mom, Grandpa is counting on you coming. He will be very upset if you don't show up. You were so adamant with me on the phone the other day about not coming. Don't disappoint him, Mom."

"Don't take that tone with me, Lillian. I will do the best I can. I have to get someone to cover for me at work and see if I can get a flight."

"Mother, you should have thought about all that before you told Grandpa you're coming."

"I'm going to do the best I can, Lillian. That's all I can do."

"You're not coming." She wanted to reach through the phone line and—well, that wasn't the Amish way, so she tried to toss the thought.

"I don't know, Lillian. I'll try. I'd like to. Things with Paul aren't going very well either. I'm not sure if it's a good time to leave."

"I have to go, Mom."

"Wait, Lillian. Tell me about your Amish man. How are Grandma and Grandpa?"

"Come to Lancaster County and see for yourself." She slammed the phone down, knowing again that her behavior was not reflective of her newfound faith. Grandpa was going to be heartbroken.

Grandpa was sitting at the kitchen table when Lillian returned. Grandma was placing a loaf of homemade bread on the table. "Sorry it took so long," she said, checking on her beef stew she'd left simmering on the wood-burning oven. "I wanted to call Mom." She turned around and looked at her grandpa. "Grandpa, I'm not sure Mom's going to make it." She thought it best to prepare him.

"She'll be here," he said confidently. "Sarah Jane will be here on Wednesday."

"Jonas, did you hear Lillian?" Exasperated, Grandma evidently doubted the arrival of her daughter on Wednesday as well. "Sarah Jane might not make it."

Grandpa rattled off a round of *Pennsylvania Deitsch* Lillian didn't understand, but Grandma scowled, walked to him, and poked him in the arm.

"We don't talk like that in this *haus*, Jonas." She leaned down closer to him. "Sarah Jane has not been to this house in seventeen years. You needn't go gettin' your hopes up. That's all I'm saying."

Grandma was on the same page as Lillian.

"Lilly, what will you be cookin' for your *mamm* on Wednesday?" Grandpa questioned, obviously pretending he hadn't heard a word either of them said.

"I'll come up with something *gut*, Grandpa."

"Where's Samuel and the boy? I'm hungry," he belted out. Grandma rolled her eyes.

Samuel and David arrived about ten minutes late. Uncharacteristic. They were always on time. Samuel looked tired and bothered about something throughout the entire meal.

"Didn't you like the stew?" Lillian asked, noticing that although

228   BETH WISEMAN

everyone else was about finished, Samuel still had quite a bit in his bowl.

"The stew was fine. Can I talk to you on the porch, Lillian?"

Something was wrong. Everyone at the table shot Samuel a questioning look.

"*Ya,*" she whispered softly. "Do you want some peach pie first?"

"No, *danki,*" he said, standing up.

This isn't good. Why was he so bothered? Everything was fine when she left his house earlier.

"You kids run along," Grandpa said. "David, I've been needin' me a chess partner for a long while. Your grandma won't play."

"Jonas, someone has to keep this house running," Grandma said. She stood up and began to clear the dishes.

"I'll help you in a minute." Lillian stood up to follow Samuel to the door.

"No, no. You go on. I've got it," Grandma replied.

"Let's be headin' into the den, David. A good game of chess will help settle our full bellies." Grandpa shuffled out of the kitchen.

Out on the porch, Samuel didn't waste any time. "I don't know what you were thinkin' when you told my boy all the things you did in your world. I don't want him to know anything about your world. Bad enough he witnessed that *baremlich* scene here with your friend, Rickie. I'm not sure I want you around him." He knew his eyes were ablaze and his tone sharp.

Instantly, her eyes glassed over. She looked shattered. Samuel realized right away he should have eased into the conversation, or at least toned it down a notch.

"What?" she asked. Her legs appeared wobbly before she folded into one of the rockers. Samuel took a seat in the other rocker.

"I don't want David exposed to your world, Lillian." He shook his head, but could hardly look at her.

"But this is my world." Her voice was cracking. This was harder than he'd reckoned it would be.

"But your worldly ways are spilling into our ways, Lillian. What were you thinkin' when you told David about drinking and smoking?" He paused. "And all that other stuff you told him about life in the city? The boy needn't be hearing any such things. It will be right hard enough when he has his *rumschpringe*. He doesn't need any encouragement from you to try all those things."

Her hands were on either side of her cheeks and her eyes were all watered up. His first instinct was to go wrap his arms around her, but that wasn't going to help things. Refocusing on what was best for David, Samuel knew he couldn't let her reaction muddle his thinking.

"But I don't want him to do *any* of those things. The reason I—" Her voice was still cracking, but he didn't want to hear her excuses.

"There is no reason for any of it, Lillian. And, I'm sorry to say, I just would rather you not spend so much time with David."

"Samuel, you don't mean that. You and David have become like my family."

He knew she was crying, so he just avoided looking at her.

Didn't she realize his heart was breaking too? But he had to do what was best for the boy.

"Don't you care about me?" She sounded pitiful. He wasn't sure he could respond without his own voice breaking up.

"*Ya,*" he said softly, forcing himself to look down at the ground and not at her.

"Samuel," she reached for his hand, and it took every bit of his might to pull away from her.

"I'm gonna go, Lillian. And I think it's best if me and David stop comin' for supper." He stood up, but this time his eyes were drawn to hers like a magnet. He had trouble looking away, but he did. If he didn't go now, he'd never be able to.

She was all curled up in the rocker crying hard. Walking away from her would be difficult.

"Samuel, please . . ."

"I'm real sorry, Lillian, that you're hurtin'."

"Just let me explain."

He could barely understand her for the crying. He walked back into the kitchen. As the door slammed behind him, he worried how he'd keep his emotions inside. He just kept telling himself it was the best thing for David.

"David, we need to be goin'," he said as he walked into the den where Jonas and David looked like they'd barely gotten started on their chess game. Irma Rose wasn't around.

"We're just getting started," Jonas said, sounding disappointed.

"*Ya,* Pop. I figured you and Lillian would be talkin' for a while." David smiled, but it quickly faded when he saw the look on his pop's face.

"Come on, boy. We've got things to tend to. Sorry, Jonas." He grabbed his hat off the rack and headed for the door.

Lillian was still curled up in the rocker. It took everything he had to make his legs walk down the porch steps and leave her like that.

"Lillian, what's wrong?" David made his way onto the porch and was standing behind Samuel, his eyes dark with worry.

He turned around in time to see Lillian jump out of the rocker and run into the house.

David didn't move. "Pop, what's goin' on?"

Samuel motioned for David to come along. It was going to be a hard conversation to have with his son. But it was for the best.

"But, Pop, she was just tryin' to tell me not to do all those things," David said later. "I think she was just tryin' to protect me."

He knew David was suffering right along with him and Lillian. "It's not right to talk about such things, David."

"But I want her to be *mei mamm* someday!"

Samuel had suspected the boy harbored the same hopeful image of the future he did: all of them as one big happy family. "Watch your tone, boy," Samuel said, careful not to scorn him too much. He was hurting for sure.

"But, Pop—"

It was tough to see his son's eyes welling up with tears. But someday he'd realize that this was the best thing for him. "On up to bed now," Samuel said, fighting his own emotions. Couldn't let the boy see him watering up.

David ran up the stairs without saying another word. Samuel put his head in his hands. He couldn't shake the image of Lillian crying.

"Lillian, can I come in?"

Lillian attempted to control her crying, to no avail. *"Ya,"* she said to her grandma, through the bedroom door.

How could Samuel do this? Was his friendship so limited that there was no room for mistakes or forgiveness? She thought she was helping David see how bad choices could turn out. Samuel didn't even want to hear her explanation. Obviously, he didn't care about her the way she cared about him. If he could give up on their friendship so easily, then maybe it truly wasn't meant to be.

No. She just didn't believe that. It *was* meant to be. It had to be. He and David were in her life. And she'd prayed so hard about it. Wasn't God listening? How could this be happening?

"There, there," Grandma comforted, taking a seat on the bed.

Lillian wept in her arms. "He didn't even let me explain, Grandma," she said after telling her what happened. "I want David to make good choices when he has his *rumschpringe.* He'll be exposed to so many evils out in the world. I was just trying to prepare him so he'd know what to avoid. I would never encourage him to make any of the mistakes I made." She cried some more while her grandma held her.

"I know you wouldn't lead the boy astray, Lillian. Maybe just give Samuel some time to think things out."

"He was so cold, Grandma. He just left me there, in pieces. It was horrible—like he didn't care about me at all. How could he do that? I don't understand."

Grandma gently pushed her away and cradled her cheeks with

her hands. "Let me try to explain something to you in a way I reckon maybe you can understand. I know you love me and your grandpa. I know you love Samuel and David. But when you have *kinner* of your own, you'll understand a whole different kind of love. It's a love so powerful that you'll cause hurt to yourself if it means protecting a child."

"David doesn't need protection from me. I do love him. I would never, ever do anything to hurt him." She pulled away from her grandma and threw her head on the pillow.

"I know that, dear. I think when Samuel talks to David and thinks this through, in his mind he'll come to know that too." Stroking Lillian's hair, she went on. "Sometimes, we think we're doin' right by our young ones. Maybe sometimes we don't always do so."

As Irma Rose tried her best to comfort Lillian, she couldn't help but wonder why her own daughter had left so abruptly—if it was something she did. There was no handbook for raising children, and she reckoned she'd done the best she could. Her heart went out to Lillian. And to Samuel. He was only trying to do what he thought was best for the boy. Hopefully he'd come to reason that Lillian only had David's best interest at heart.

"Did you call your *mamm*?" she asked when Lillian seemed to be a little better.

"*Ya.*" She sat up on the bed and dabbed at her eyes. "She said she's going to try to come. But I know her, Grandma. She won't come and it will break Grandpa's heart."

And mine. As nervous as she was to see Sarah Jane, it was all

Irma Rose had thought about since Jonas shared the news of
her visit.

———————

Three days since his conversation with Lillian, Samuel wasn't
feeling any better. To worsen things, David was barely talking to
him. Maybe he'd acted too harshly. If he did, it was out of love
and fear for his son. He thought back to his own *rumschpringe* and
cringed, doubtful he'd experienced hardly a tad of what Lillian
must have experienced in the *Englisch* world. Should he fault her
for that? No. But sharing her past with his son was strictly off-
limits. She should have known that.

Lost in regret and confusion, Samuel realized it was nearing
four o'clock. He'd need to stir up some supper for him and
David. Normally they'd be heading to Lillian's on Wednesday.
His heart was heavy as he thought about facing each day without
Lillian in his life.

"Have you talked to Lillian?" he asked, sitting down at the
kitchen table across from his son.

"*Ya.*" David bit into a cookie. It didn't appear he was going to
say anything about it.

"Is she okay?"

The look David fired at him surely deserved a trip to the
woodshed and some discipline, but he let it go.

"No, she's not *okay.* And she fears talking to me—afraid she'll
get me and her in trouble."

Samuel hung his head. "I was just trying to protect you."
Maybe I made a mistake.

"Pop, I'm gonna be seeing the *Englisch* world in a few years. She was just trying to tell me not to make some of the same mistakes she made."

"*Ya.* But such *Englisch* things are best unspoken." He shouldn't have to justify his actions to David.

"Why? If her blunders might help me to not walk a bad path, then why should they not be talked about?" David's tone was bordering on rude, and Samuel didn't like it. But he considered the possibility that maybe his son was right.

"Maybe I should talk to her." Samuel stroked his beard and thought about what he would say. He was having a world of trouble trying to figure out how he was going to reconcile this situation.

"I don't think she wants to talk to you, Pop. I think she's gone from being real upset to real mad." David paused and bit into another cookie. "Besides, she's got worry in her heart about Jonas. She's fearing he's going be real upset when her mother doesn't show up today."

Samuel had been so focused on how much he missed her he'd forgotten that Wednesday was the day Sarah Jane Miller was due to arrive. It was gonna break Jonas and Irma Rose's hearts if she didn't show. And Lillian's. He should be there to wait with her or comfort her if her *mamm* didn't show up. What a fine mess he'd made of things.

"Your grandpa hasn't moved from that rocker on the porch for the past two hours. It's nearin' six o'clock, way past the supper hour," Grandma said. "He needs to accept that Sarah Jane isn't coming."

Lillian could hear the regret in her grandma's voice. Honestly, she wasn't sure who was more upset, Grandma or Grandpa.

"I'm sorry, Grandma. Maybe I should go talk to Grandpa." She stood from the kitchen table and headed toward the door. Grandma just shrugged.

How could everything have fallen apart like this? She missed Samuel so bad it hurt, but she was equally angry at him for snatching away their friendship as if it meant nothing. And now this. She knew her mother wasn't going to show. Just history repeating itself.

She took a seat in the other rocker on the porch. "Grandpa," she said hesitantly. "How long are you going to sit out here?"

He stared down the dirt driveway. "Until Sarah Jane gets here."

Lillian started to ask him how long that would be, but he spoke first.

"So, when are you and Samuel going to mend your ways?"

"I don't know if we are." She didn't want to talk about this right now. There were enough emotional issues swirling in the air.

Grandpa winked. "Sure you are."

"I don't know, Grandpa. He walked away from me like I meant nothing to him."

"*Ach*, Lilly, he was just not thinkin' right at the time. Thought he was doin' the best thing for the boy. He's come to his senses by now, and I'm bettin' he's missing you up a storm about now. You two have spent a lot of time together these past few months."

"Well, I don't miss him." It was a big fat lie, which Grandpa saw right through.

"Sure you don't," he said, drawing out his words. "Might

take a little more time, but you kids will be seeing eye to eye again soon."

She hoped so, but it had been three days. Of course, she'd made her feelings pretty clear to David when she told him how mad she was. *Wonder if David told his dad?*

She didn't feel any better today than she did on Sunday. However, she was really worried about her grandparents.

Mom, this is so like you to do this.

The screen door slammed, and Grandma joined them on the porch. "Lillian, I've left some supper keepin' warm on the oven. You need to eat yourself something."

"She's waiting to eat with her *mamm*, Irma Rose," Jonas said with a forceful tone.

Grandma glanced at Lillian and then back at her husband. "Jonas, you can't stay out here all night."

When he continued to stare down the driveway and didn't respond, Grandma shrugged. "Suit yourself. I'm going in the den to read for a bit." She turned to head back in the kitchen.

Grandpa moved faster than she'd seen since her arrival. He sprang from the rocker so abruptly you'd have thought his behind was on fire. "There she is!" he yelled. "There's my Sarah Jane!"

Lillian could hardly believe her eyes as a car turned onto the driveway. She reached for her grandpa to steady him. He was so much better lately, but he was sure unsteady on his legs. She strained to see better.

"What?" Grandma asked, turning to rejoin them on the porch. Her voice crackled with disbelief. "Is it true? Is it Sarah Jane?" She put her hands to her mouth and Lillian could see her trembling.

As the car neared the house, Lillian strained even harder to see. She smiled.

"It's Mom," she said, running down the steps. "Thank You, God," she whispered on her way to the tan Ford pulling to a stop. She looked back at her grandparents and waved them to come closer.

The car door opened, and Mom stepped out. Lillian didn't think she had ever looked more beautiful. Her black slacks and conservative blue blouse framed her tall and slender figure. Perfectly groomed, as always, her blonde waves rested at her shoulders, teased for some height.

It warmed Lillian's heart the way her mom's face lit up when she saw her. There was no shock at Lillian's apparel, no snide comments. She just smiled.

"You look beautiful, Lillian," she said.

Lillian fell into her arms. "So do you, Mom. I'm so glad you came."

The embrace lasted a long time. Lillian felt like she could have stayed in her mother's arms forever. Memories of all the good things she experienced over the years came flooding over her. Yes, there had been hard times. But her mother deserved credit for the good times too. This being one of them.

Gently, her mother pulled away and eyed her up and down. "You really do look beautiful, Lillian. The Amish look works for you." She kissed her on the cheek before glancing up at her parents on the porch.

Sensing her nervousness, Lillian said, "It'll be fine, Mom. They are so excited." She grabbed her mother's hand and began pulling her toward them.

Grandpa stretched out his arms wide in front of him. Tears poured down his face. She glanced at her grandma, whose hands were folded over her mouth. The rise and fall of her shoulders indicated she was unable to control her sobs of joy.

"Sarah Jane," Grandpa said, weeping. He took her in his arms and held her tight. It was only seconds before Sarah Jane cried out, "Pop, I'm so sorry. Oh, Pop, I'm so sorry for everything. I'm so sorry . . ."

Grandma ran to them, throwing her arms around them both. "Sarah Jane," she cried.

"*Mamm*, I'm sorry. I'm sorry. I didn't know how to come back. I didn't know what to do. I'm sorry." She turned toward her mother and lovingly embraced her.

Lillian stood frozen, tears streaming down her face. It was a joyous moment. Only one thing would have made it perfect.

No sooner had she processed the thought when she turned to see a buggy pulling up the driveway.

"Samuel?" she whispered.

16

"I'LL BE BACK IN A MINUTE," LILLIAN TOLD HER GRAND-parents and mother over her shoulder. Grandpa acknowledged hearing her, but she wasn't sure what he said. She was focused on the approaching buggy. Disappointment flooded over her when she realized it wasn't Samuel.

It was Samuel's brother, Ivan. Maybe he was here to deliver a message from Samuel.

"Hi, Ivan. What brings you out here?" Lillian watched him step out of the buggy.

"Everything all right?" he asked, approaching her.

She wasn't sure what he meant. Was he talking about Samuel?

"What?" she asked.

"I saw a car I didn't recognize pulling in. I worried maybe Jonas was down again. Just stopping to check on you all."

Not what she was hoping to hear. "Everything is fine," she said, forcing a smile. "Actually, my *mamm* is here, so my grand-parents are very excited to see her."

"*Gut* news," he said, crawling back into the buggy. "Just checking."

"Ivan, I was wondering—" She stopped. She didn't know Ivan well at all. To question him about Samuel seemed inappropriate. "Thank you for checking on us." She waved.

Guiding his horse into motion, he tipped his hat and said, "Anytime," as he pulled back down the driveway.

For the next two hours, Lillian listened to her mother confessing to her parents more than was probably necessary. But it seemed to be a cleansing of her soul. She began with her affair with Daniel Foster and subsequent pregnancy and led into how shame and embarrassment kept her from returning to the Old Order district, with the exception of a few visits here and there. Much of what she said Lillian had never heard before or didn't remember. Grandma and Grandpa hung on her every word.

Lillian knew it was difficult for her mother to share her past, and she had never been more proud of her. As Mom released years of pent-up emotion, her face twisted in agony as she recalled certain events. In the dimly lit kitchen, Grandma never let go of Sarah Jane's hand, and Grandpa cried a lot. Lillian sat with her arm around her mother, giving her a gentle squeeze when she struggled to continue.

She concluded with Lillian's confrontation with Daniel.

"Oh, Lillian," Grandma said sadly, shaking her head, "I'm sorry we didn't know what you were goin' through."

"It's all right, Grandma. I have put it behind me. I just needed some answers to be able to move forward."

Not entirely true. It would take a while to recover from the sting of meeting her father.

As everyone attempted to gather themselves after the emotional conversation, her mother asked, "So, Lillian, where is your friend?"

Her heart sank with regrets about Samuel. As she opened her

mouth to try and communicate some sort of response, Grandpa interjected his own thoughts about it.

"Lillian and Samuel are like peanut butter and jelly. They ain't nothin' alike, but they're real good when they're together. They're both mixed-up over some silly nonsense they need to get worked out. My guess is they'll be workin' it out at the barn raising this Saturday." He smiled, which was a welcome sight after all the heartache the past couple of hours. "Nothing like a good barn raising to lift the spirits. Wish I was a younger man not all eaten up by the cancer. I'd be out there on Saturday lending a hand."

"I don't know how things will turn out," Lillian said, despair in her voice. "I miss him a lot, but he's made no attempt to come see me. I'm pretty sure he meant what he said."

"Hogwash! He'll be back here at suppertime every few days before you can shake a stick." Grandpa said. "Then the whole family will be back together again."

Lillian tried to perk up. "I hope so, Grandpa. I really do."

"Pop, maybe you ought to go talk to Lillian," David told his dad. Samuel dimmed the lantern in his bedroom. "And tell her you're sorry."

The boy was right. Plus, Samuel knew he'd been a hard man to live with lately. Hearing David's spirited talk of the *Englisch* ways had left him fearful about his son's future. But his reaction to everything Lillian had said to David was from the hip, without thinking about her intentions. He'd been preaching faith to her, yet his own faith in *her* had temporarily deserted him.

"I'm planning on talkin' to her at the barn raising Saturday.

Ivan stopped by and said he dropped by their place to check on things. Her *mamm* was there. I know they all have lots of catching up to do, so I'm going to let them all be for now."

"Maybe she won't be so mad by Saturday. You hurt her feelings real bad, Pop."

Samuel watched his son's eyebrows jutting inward and his lips scrunching. There was a time when he'd have never allowed David to speak to him in such a manner. But he reckoned he might have made a mistake and it had obviously had great effect on the boy.

"*Ya*, David. I know." He shook his head. "Saturday, I will talk to her."

As Sarah Jane loaded her suitcase into the car, Irma Rose stifled her tears. Jonas had said his good-byes to Sarah Jane upstairs. Irma Rose knew how badly her husband wanted to come downstairs, but he was having one of his bad days. Lillian walked with them to see her mother off, but the child was clearly in another world. Hopefully, she and Samuel would be getting things worked out real soon.

It had been a glorious two days, and Sarah Jane promised to be back for Christmas.

"I'm sorry I can't stay longer." She hugged Lillian first and then Irma Rose. "I would have liked to stick around and go to the barn raising tomorrow. It's been a long time since I've been to one." She looked at Lillian. "I hope that tomorrow you and Samuel will get things worked out. Tell him I'll look forward to meeting him when I'm here for Christmas."

"I don't know if we'll get things worked out or not, Mom."

Irma Rose sure hoped so. Lillian had been a miserable soul the past few days.

"Nothing like the festivities of a good barn raising to set everyone's sights in order," Irma Rose said.

As Sarah Jane gave her a final hug, Irma Rose wished the embrace could last forever. Her daughter's return was a dream come true and a prayer answered. So many issues put to rest. Now it was time to move forward with refreshed spirit and joy. The Lord's blessings were with them.

"I love you, *Mamm*," Sarah Jane whispered in her ear. "I never stopped loving you."

Irma Rose couldn't control her cries of happiness. "Oh, my blessed daughter," she began, "you were our gift from the Good Lord, and you still are. I love you so very much."

As her granddaughter stood watching, Irma Rose struggled to pry herself away from Sarah Jane. It had been so long—and two days just wasn't enough. She would count the days until Christmas when they'd all be together again.

Samuel woke up Saturday with high hopes he would get things fixed with Lillian. It had been a terrible six days since he had seen her. He should've explained his feelings about the situation and not reacted the way he did. She had come a long way since she arrived in Lancaster County, and he should have kept the faith she would never do anything to soil David's upbringing.

"*Guder mariye*, Pop," David said, rubbing his eyes as he walked into the kitchen.

"Good morning to you. I made us some red-beet eggs this morning. We'll need all our energy to help with the barn raising." He shoveled some eggs alongside a piece of toast for his son.

"We'll see Lillian today too."

"*Ya*, we will." And Samuel couldn't wait. He was going to make things right.

"I sure hope things go back to the way they were before you—" The boy clamped his mouth shut, seeming to force back comments that might get him in a heap of trouble.

"I'm sure everything will be *wunderbaar gut*. It'll be a grand day," Samuel said, taking a seat beside his son. "Now, eat your eggs. We need to be there at daybreak and that's sneaking up on us."

There were over fifty buggies parked up near the Zook farm when Samuel and David arrived. John Lapp, an Amish carpenter by profession, was already lining the men out and assigning areas of work. No time to waste. They would need to complete the framing by the noon meal, giving time to eat, and then they'd put on the roof in the afternoon. As long as that much got done, the closing in could be handled by family and friends the following day, if need be.

The last of the buggies pulled in. Samuel reckoned there were over a hundred and fifty people in attendance. The women were gathering in the kitchen to prepare the meal, and the smaller children were scurrying around and playing games. Without a cloud in the sky, it was a fine day for a barn raising. Although it neared the end of August, the summer heat was still upon them. Yes, it was warm. But a slow breeze eased the effects of the sun's brilliant rays.

Samuel watched his son accepting an assignment from John Lapp, then turned and scanned the work area. There was no sign of Lillian. A few of the women were scattered about, but most of them were inside busy with meal preparations. She would have to come outside sooner or later. He hoped it was sooner so he would have a chance to talk to her, explain his harsh reaction.

The men and older boys had been at work about two hours when the first offering of iced tea was made. Several of the women-folk began walking around handing glasses to the workers.

Samuel was ready for a cold glass of tea. More than that, he was ready to see Lillian. He was surprised he hadn't caught a glimpse of her yet. Surely she wouldn't forego the barn raising because of him.

"Why, Samuel, what in the world are you doing here?" Ellen Zook asked, handing him a glass of tea.

Sending her a questioning look, he asked, "Why wouldn't I be here? You know I wouldn't miss a barn raising. I'm mighty pleased to help."

Ellen looked confused. "Well, I guess I was figuring you to be at the Miller place this morning." She paused. "I mean I think the whole district knows you spend a lot of time out there with Irma Rose, Jonas—and their *kinskind*. Word is that you and Lillian might have taken a fancy to each other."

"Isn't Lillian here? I thought she'd be inside helping with the meal?" Maybe she'd decided not to come.

"Uh, Samuel," Ellen began, "I just assumed someone had gotten word to you."

"Word about what?" He didn't like her tone. "Word about what?" he asked again.

"Why, Samuel, I'm sorry to say . . . Irma Rose passed this morning. I just figured you'd be with the family. They said she just went in her sleep and—"

He didn't hear another word she said, as his legs mechanically carried him to the buggy. He yelled at Katie Ann to keep an eye on David while he quickly maneuvered the buggy onto the road. "Let's go, Pete!" he yelled, jolting the horse into a full run.

He and Lillian had talked about death on more than one occasion. One thing Samuel knew for sure: nothing scared her more than death. And as much as Lillian had grown to love Irma Rose and Jonas, he knew she must be over the edge with grief.

"Come on, boy!" he yelled, picking up even more speed.

Lillian was anxious to see Samuel at the barn raising. From the moment she opened her eyes Saturday morning, it was all she could think about. Despite the fact he hadn't come around, maybe, just maybe, he'd had time to reflect on his decision and had a change of heart. Maybe he missed her and realized she'd never, ever do anything to hurt David. She couldn't rewrite her past. Besides, she had changed so much. Didn't that matter?

"You're up earlier than usual," Grandpa commented when she served him some scrapple alongside his eggs. She wrinkled her nose. She had never acquired a taste for this popular Amish meal. She didn't want to eat anything made up of leftover parts of a hog. She was floored the first time she saw Grandma putting parts of hog heads, hearts, liver, and other scraps in the mushy mix of cornmeal and flour. But Grandpa loved it, so she cooked it for him on occasion.

"The barn raising is today," she said. "From what I understand, it all gets started at daybreak. So I don't want to be late.
You're the one who's up early." She smiled.

"Food," he said. "The smell of food gets me movin' in the
morning. Your Grandma, on the other hand, is out like a light."

"Well, I'm glad to see you're feeling better this morning." She
knew the past two days had exhausted him both physically and
mentally. In addition to the heart-wrenching conversations, they'd
all stayed up much later than usual while her mother was there.
Both her grandparents had looked worn-out the night before.

"Maybe you better go give your *mammi* a nudge. You know
how much she likes scrapple, and she'll be all upset if she has to
eat it cold." He dove into the soupy mush. "Um, um . . . mighty
gut," he said.

Thinking how Grandma liked to get her day off to an early
start, Lillian headed up the stairs. She knocked on the door twice,
but there was no answer. "Grandma?"

Knocking again, she yelled a little louder, "Grandma, I made
scrapple. Come get it while it's hot."

Nothing.

She walked down the upstairs hall to the small bathroom.
Gently she pushed the door open. "Grandma?" The door swung
wide, but no Grandma.

She headed back toward her grandparents' room, pondering
whether or not Grandma would have gone outside. No, there
wouldn't be any reason to.

An unfamiliar tingling rushed from her head to her toes, causing her to feel light-headed as she turned the doorknob. Something
wasn't right. Her heart rate increased, and she was suddenly afraid

to enter the room. And yet, unable to turn back, she pushed the door open.

Well, thank the Lord. Grandma was curled up in bed asleep, facing the other way. She hadn't gone missing and wasn't lying in a pool of blood from a bad fall or anything.

"Grandma, wake up. You scared me." She walked toward the bed. "Wake up, sleepyhead. I made scrapple—that nasty mush you and Grandpa like."

As she neared the edge of the bed, the tingling rush shot through her veins again. She stopped. "Grandma?" she said softly. Her feet were rooted to the floor, and she couldn't move. Grandma snored. She always snored. Why was there no snoring?

"Grandma!" Still unable to move, she yelled again, "Grandma, wake up!"

She could hear footsteps coming up the stairs. *Oh God, no. Please, no.* She forced her feet to move and sat down on the edge of the bed. As she reached over and touched her grandma's arm, she knew instantly—Grandma was dead. Her cold, lifeless body was curled into a ball.

Lillian knew Grandpa would be in the room within seconds. Maybe she was wrong. She ran to the other side of the bed so she could see her grandmother's face. The older woman's eyes were closed; she looked peaceful. But clearly she wasn't breathing.

"Grandma." She pushed her gently. Nothing.

"What are ya hollering about up here, Lilly?"

She turned around to see Grandpa standing in the doorway. A tear rolled down her cheek. "Grandpa . . ."

He stood frozen in place. "No, Lilly. She's just sleeping. I'm going first. I got the cancer." Staring at her with a blank look, he asked, "Did you tell her you made scrapple? That'll get her moving."

"Grandpa," she said again, trying to control herself—for once. The man nearing the bed had been married to this woman for almost fifty years. She couldn't even imagine how he must feel. Her own heart was breaking.

His feet edged slowly toward the other side of the bed. "Irma Rose, get on up out of that bed and get you some scrapple."

Lillian couldn't hold it anymore. Crying softly, she attempted to swipe away the tears trailing down her cheeks, in an unsuccessful effort to stay strong for Grandpa. She stood up from the bed and walked to the window to make more room for Grandpa. As she gazed out the window, she heard his sobs from behind her.

"Oh, Irma Rose, not now. It's not time. Sarah Jane will be back for Christmas."

Lillian turned around to see her grandpa lifting the love of his life, limp and lifeless, into his arms. How could this have happened? She wasn't even sick. Grandpa was the one who was sick. Grandpa was the one she'd prayed for, every night, to get well. And he was so much better. Had this happened because she didn't pray enough for Grandma?

She began to go over her nightly prayers, reciting them in her head. Maybe she had given Grandpa more prayer time. But it was because he was sick. This was unfair of God. Had she known her grandma was at risk, she would have prayed harder for her.

First Samuel. Now this. God wasn't listening to her. Otherwise he would have never let this happen.

It was even more heartbreaking to watch Grandpa swaying back and forth, cradling Grandma in his arms.

"Oh, my Irma Rose, my darling beloved," he wept. "Don't leave me on this earth without you. Wake up, Irma Rose."

While her own heart ripped in two, she knew she would need to produce all her strength to see her grandpa through this. She walked to the bed and sat down beside him.

"Grandpa, I think we need to send for someone," she suggested. Tenderly, she stroked his arm.

"Call the Good Lord and tell him to send her back to me, Lilly. Get your cell phone and call heaven. Tell God to send her back to me for a bit longer."

"Grandpa, it was just her time. She's with God now." She wasn't sure where the words were coming from because it *wasn't* Grandma's time.

"*Ach*, no . . . Oh, no." He cried harder, and Lillian didn't think she'd ever seen a more frail creature. Like a lost child, he wept.

"Let her lie in peace," she said softly. "Come on, Grandpa." She tried to pull him away, but he clung tightly. "Grandpa, we are going to have to go into town and let someone know. I think there are, uh, things that we have to do."

She had no idea what they needed to do, and she had no idea where her strength was coming from. Perhaps it was knowing Grandpa's pain was far worse than her own. Seeing him like this was almost as heartbreaking as losing Grandma. She took a deep breath and tried as best she could to gather herself. She hated to leave him alone. Why hadn't she held onto that cell phone? Why hadn't she prayed harder? Why did this have to happen?

She started to cry again.

"Lilly, travel to town to the funeral home. They'll tell you our ways. I want to be alone with my Irma Rose," Grandpa said as he gently laid her back down.

"Okay, Grandpa." She gazed upon the woman who had taught her so much, whom she had grown to love over the past months. Nothing would ever be the same.

Forcing herself to stand up and do as Grandpa asked, she turned to face him when she reached the bedroom door. Still cradling his beloved wife in his arms, his body trembled with grief. He'd cried out to Lillian to do something, to reverse the situation, to beg God for more time. She realized even a man with Grandpa's faith couldn't accept such a loss as merely God's will. It didn't make him any less faithful to God, only human.

As Samuel pulled up at the Miller farm, his heart was heavy. The timing of all this was terrible. *And Irma Rose?* It was shocking. He'd reckoned Jonas would go way before his wife.

He shook his head as he parked the buggy and walked toward the front door. Lillian was going to be a wreck. The girl was as emotional a person as he'd ever known, and he knew she would be falling apart. She should have come to him this morning. He should have been the one to help her with things, to comfort her.

Yet . . . he reckoned if the situation were reversed, he wouldn't have searched her out either. He'd said some pretty strong things to her.

"Hello, Samuel," Lillian said as she opened the screen door and motioned him to come inside. "It's very nice of you to come." Her tone was unusually curt.

"Lillian, you should have sought me out this morning when this happened. I'm so sorry, Lillian." He hugged her—a hug she did not return.

"Grandpa's in the den if you'd like to visit with him. The funeral home has already been here to pick up Grandma. They will be bringing her back on Monday. The funeral will be here on Tuesday. Mr. Jackson said they are familiar with Amish customs and will make sure everything is done accordingly."

She rattled on like a robot, with hardly a hint of expression on her face. But he knew better. Her red, swollen eyes told the tale.

"Lillian," he said softly, reaching for her. "You don't have to be strong for my benefit."

"I'm fine," she said, turning toward the den.

"Grandpa, Samuel is here to pay his respects." She sat down in a chair near her grandpa, and she wouldn't even look at Samuel.

He extended his hand to Jonas, who clasped it with both of his hands. "Thank you for coming, Samuel. The *Englisch* doctor said he thinks Irma Rose's heart just plumb gave out." He squeezed Samuel's hand before letting it go. Hanging his head, he said, "Probably my fault. She'd been working too hard to take care of me. But I reckon it was God's will. I sure will miss my Irma Rose."

Jonas didn't seem to notice, but Samuel caught on to Lillian's attitude right quick at the mention of God's will.

"It's nobody's fault, Jonas. Don't do that to yourself," Samuel said. He glanced at Lillian, trying to make some sort of connection, only to find her keeping a solemn look on her face. She wouldn't even look his way. "I reckon we don't always understand why things happen the way they do."

Jonas' shoulders began to heave up and down, and Samuel could see he was trying to hold back tears. "Sarah Jane was here, Samuel. Irma Rose only had two days with her. She just left last night. She was comin' back for Christmas."

Samuel sat down in a chair on the other side of Jonas, which put him face-to-face with Lillian. "I'm so sorry, Jonas." He reached over and put his hand on his shoulder. "Do you want me to arrange for the coffin carriers?"

"That'd be mighty fine if you'd do that."

"And I'm sure Katie Ann and my sisters will pitch in with the meal, along with a lot of other folks 'round here."

Lillian still wouldn't look his way. "All that's not necessary," she said in an almost hateful tone. "I can arrange the food, and I can—"

"Lillian, let Samuel handle those things," Jonas said.

"Grandpa, we don't need Samuel to handle those things. I can do it," she insisted. She was dead set on hurting him. That was clear. She didn't want him involved in anything to do with her or her family.

"Lilly." Grandpa looked up at her and gave her a look that caused her to sit up straighter. "You know I love you, no?"

"Of course," she answered with questioning eyes.

"I'm gonna say this one time: you get that chip off your shoulder right now. Quit blaming God for this. And get outside and go get things straightened out with Samuel. It's been bad enough, you moping around this house. And now my Irma Rose is gone. I don't have an ounce of tolerance for that attitude of yours."

Before he finished his harsh reprimand, Lillian's eyes were

full of water and she wasted no time jumping up and running toward the kitchen. He heard the screen door slam.

"Don't let her fox you, Samuel. This is killin' her inside, and she's seeing fit to blame the Good Lord. I reckon she's acting the only way she knows how, to be able to help herself cope." He sighed. "And another thing—you know she'd never do a thing to hurt that boy of yours, no?"

Samuel didn't think he could feel any lower. "*Ya*, Jonas. I know that. I made a *baremlich* mistake."

"Then I reckon you need to go out there and tell her that. She's going to need a lot of help getting through this, and I don't have the strength, Samuel. Lilly's come a long way in admonishing her old ways and learning our ways. I don't want to see her fall backward because of this. I know you care about that girl."

"Very much."

"Then get out there and make sure she stays on course with her studies, so she will want to stay with us. Don't let this be settin' her back."

Samuel stood up and headed toward the kitchen. "I'll make things right, Jonas."

Making his way out the back door and onto the porch, Samuel found Lillian sitting in the rocker on the front porch—the same rocker she was curled up in when he left her crushed and heartbroken the previous Sunday. She looked mad as a hatter.

"Leave me alone," Lillian said as Samuel took a seat in the rocker beside her. Grandpa had never talked to her that way, and she didn't need a lecture from Samuel right now either. She would handle this situation as best she could.

"Lillian," he said softly, reaching for her hand. She jerked it away.

"I don't want to talk right now, Samuel." Being angry—at Samuel and at God—was the only thing working for her at the moment.

"We're going to have to talk, Lillian," he said, looking down at the ground. "Because I made a terrible mistake, and I'm here to apologize. I know you love David and that your tellin' him about worldly things was only your way of trying to keep him out of harm's way. I know that, Lillian. And I'm sorry. I should have let you explain . . . should have thought everything through before I said all those things."

It should have been music to her ears, but she couldn't get past everything that had happened. Not right now. Staying mad was all that was keeping her together.

When she didn't respond, he went on. "I know how sad you feel right now, Lillian. We'll get through this together." He reached for her hand again, and again she pulled away. "The pain gets better over time," he added.

A huge part of her wanted to run into his arms and allow him to comfort her. The pain felt like it was eating her from the inside out, nibbling at her heart, a tiny little bit at a time. To be able to function or maintain at all, she would not be able to succumb to his offer. She would handle this on her own.

"Samuel, I can get through this, and I will be just fine." She raised her chin slightly and pulled her lips tight, fearful he might see them quivering. She had never felt more on the edge in her life.

"Lillian, I want to help you. I want to be here for you. I'm so sorry . . . about everything."

In an irrational display of emotion, she bolted from the rocker and put her hands on her hips. "Help me what, Samuel?" She knew she was yelling, and that had not been part of the plan. The plan was to stay void of feeling, to stay angry, so she didn't have to feel the pain ripping at her insides. "Help me to forget that I came from another world? Well, I can't! It is part of my past, and I can't make that go away. Do you want to help me get over Grandma dying? Well, I can't. I loved her. Do you want me to accept this as God's will? Well, I can't do that either."

The tears were falling and she was losing control. Samuel was on his feet, his arms outstretched and waiting to make everything right. Problem was things could never be right again. "I can't accept things as God's will. I just can't." There, she'd said it. Now he wouldn't have a problem walking away from her. Her inability to accept God's will would surely be more than enough for him to not want her around him or his son.

"So, there—you can go now. I will get over this on my own." She took a step backward, only to have him take two steps forward.

"I'm not goin' anywhere, Lillian," he said in a tender but determined tone. He inched closer to her. With no room to continue backward, unless she wanted to fall off the porch, she held her position by trying to stare him down. Although she could feel the tears pouring down her cheeks and suspected she wasn't being very convincing. "I don't need you, Samuel," she cried. "You gave up on our friendship. You gave up on me." She put her hands over her face and wept.

"I made a mistake, Lillian," he said. She felt his hand pull her head to his chest. His other arm molded around her back and drew her closer. "And you can go ahead and be mad at me, mad at God, and mad at the world. I'm not going anywhere."

"But I can't accept this as God's will, Samuel. I can't. I don't know what I'm going to do every day. When I make bread, can fruits and vegetables, wash the clothes, cook, practice my *Pennsylvania Deitsch* . . . All those things Grandma and I did *together*. We spent hours talking." The pain in her heart seemed unbearable, and her stomach was burning. This is what she wanted to avoid. She didn't want to feel this way. It hurt too much. "And what about Grandpa?"

His hand still cradling her head, he held her tightly against him. "It's hard, Lillian, but this is something you have to go through to be able to move on."

"I can't," she cried. "It hurts, Samuel. It hurts too much. I can't."

"*Ya*, you can," he said. "And you will. I'm going to be right here beside you."

"I'm not strong like you are." She shook her head as her nose brushed against his shirt, now wet from her tears.

"You're stronger than you think. And we will get through this together . . . because that's what people who love each other do."

She heard him loud and clear. Her knees buckled.

"I'm tired of fighting it, Lillian." He pulled her closer. Wrapped in the security of his arms, she wept. Then, gently, he eased her away, cupped her cheeks with his hands, and gazed into her eyes. His own eyes were swimming. One blink and he would be shedding tears as well.

"I love you, Lillian."

"Samuel . . ." she whispered.

With slow tenderness, he gently kissed away her tears. The feel of his lips brushing against her cheeks as he continued to cradle her face with his strong hands caused her to cry harder. Samuel loved her. He'd said they would get through this together. Her heart hurt, and nothing was going to change that. But knowing Samuel would be with her softened her feelings about God's will.

When one door closes, another one opens . . . While it was God's will to take Grandma, it was also His will for Samuel to love her. It didn't lessen her grief about Grandma's death, but it gave her hope for the future. Right now, she needed hope to cling to. She needed Samuel.

"Do you love me, Lillian?" he asked, looking hard into her eyes as he tilted her head upward to face him.

"With all my heart, Samuel. I love you with all my heart."

As if knowing her trembling legs struggled to support her, in one swoop he whisked her into his arms. Resting her head in the nook of his shoulder, she'd never known such comfort. She was safe. She was home. And somehow Samuel would help her to make sense of all this.

"We will get through this together," he said again, kissing her on the forehead.

Samuel knew from personal experience that in a time of loss, even the most faithful could doubt God's reasoning for things happening the way they did.

"I know you feel real bad right now. But you're not always gonna feel like this." He paused, clutching her tightly within his arms. With watery eyes, he said, "Me and the boy need you every bit as much as I know you need us. I know it's been hard for you to accept God into your heart as openly as you've accepted me and David into your heart. But He is in there, Lillian . . . in your heart. And He will be there to help get you through your grief."

He gently set her down on the porch and coaxed her to sit on the steps beside him. Turning toward her, he reached for her hand. "When Rachel passed, I was angry at the Lord. I never told a soul about it. Just didn't make sense at the time. It seemed awfully unfair to leave me and the boy alone—no *fraa*, no *mamm*."

He paused and looked away from her, staring down the dirt road. "I even had thoughts about leaving here. Taking the boy and just headin' somewhere else. I felt like my faith wasn't strong enough to stay."

He turned to her and smiled. "But I'm glad I did stay. There's nowhere on God's earth I'd rather be than here, in this district, and now with you."

Samuel had envisioned it in his dreams a thousand times, but nothing could prepare him for the reality of when he leaned in and felt the touch of her lips against his. He could feel her love rush through him. Resting one hand behind her neck, he pulled her closer. One kiss turned into two.

"Everything is going to be fine, Lillian," he finally said, as he brushed a loose strand of hair from her face and kissed her gently one more time.

17

THE FUNERAL WAS ALMOST TWO HOURS LONG AND HELD AT the Miller homestead. As tradition dictated, Grandma wore her wedding dress and white apron for her burial. Her wooden coffin was plain and simple—no ornate carving or fine fabrics. The community offered expressions of respect for Grandma, although admonition for the living was plentiful.

Lillian wished there were flowers and a eulogy for her grandma. However, such *Englisch* traditions were not the Amish way. Instead of singing, they spoke the words of the hymn. Following the service, Grandma was laid to rest in the Amish church district cemetery, in a hand-dug grave. The modest tombstone was identical to the others in the cemetery. As was custom, members of the community gathered to share a meal afterward. Sadie Fisher offered her home for the occasion.

"Thank you, Sadie, for organizing the meal," Lillian told her, catching her away from the crowd of women in the kitchen.

Sadie hesitated, then gave her an unexpected but much needed hug. "You're quite welcome. The entire community thought the world of Irma Rose. And it's best if these things are handled by someone not in the immediate family. How is your *mamm* holdin' up?"

Lillian looked toward the den, where her mother was comforting her grandpa. Mom was barely back in Houston when she
had to turn around and come back for Grandma's funeral. She
was a mess when she arrived, rambling on to Lillian about what
a mess she'd made of her life. For Grandma to die the day after
Mom's visit was quite a blow, but Lillian wondered how much
worse it would have been if they had not been blessed with the
time they had together. Bittersweet for sure.

But Mom pulled herself together, for her dad's sake. He
needed her, and she needed him. Looking at her mom now, it was
clear to Lillian that her mother's utmost priority was taking care
of Grandpa. She hadn't left his side since her arrival.

"My mom is tired. She was up with Grandpa most of the
night. He was sick. I don't know how much of it is from grief
about all this or from his medications. The medicines make him
sick sometimes." She paused. "You know, Mom hadn't seen her
parents in a long time. She had just seen them for two days, and
Grandma died the day after she left, and . . ." She shook her head,
finding it hard to go on.

"It was just a real shock about Irma Rose," Sadie comforted,
gently rubbing Lillian's arm. "We were all just so sorry to hear."

"You're a nice person, Sadie."

She smiled. "*Ya*, I try."

"I mean, I didn't think you were going to like me—because
of Samuel and all."

"*Ach*, I was a tad bitter at first. Samuel's a good catch for marrying. But he was smitten with you from the get-go." She offered
her a pat on the shoulder. "Besides, my letter-writing with the
Texas man is goin' real good."

Sadie wasn't the only one who had opened her heart during this difficult time. Both of Samuel's sisters and sister-in-law had bent over backward to help with arrangements. Samuel's mother, Esther, was warming up to Lillian as well.

Grandma had worked so hard to make sure Lillian had a clear understanding of the *Ordnung*. Despite her constant questioning of the Amish ways—sometimes defiantly—Grandma never gave up on her. With patience and love, she nurtured Lillian toward a way of life she had been searching for. Lillian would be lying to herself if she accepted where she was now as her final spiritual destination, though. She still had work to do. Her inability to accept everything that happened as God's will would require faith—in God and in herself.

Samuel was proud of Lillian. Those who didn't know her well wouldn't recognize the effort it was taking for her to stay strong. He reckoned the extra effort was due to the state her mother and Jonas were in. Samuel could tell the whole ordeal was taking its toll on Jonas. Sarah Jane was glued to her pop's side and was trying hard to take care of him. But she looked like *she* needed taking care of herself. Lillian was filling the job, even though he knew her own heart was hurting in a big way.

"Lillian sure is being strong today," David said, echoing Samuel's thoughts. He took a seat beside Samuel at a wooden picnic table in the yard.

"She's trying to be strong for her *mamm* and *Daadi Jonas*."

"I remember when you tried to be strong for me when *Mamm* died. I knew you were hurting, like I reckon Lillian is hurting too."

"Sometimes we bury our burdens to tend to the needs of others," Samuel responded, remembering back to Rachel's funeral. At that time, he wasn't sure how he would live his life without her. But time had a way of mending the heart. "God so built us to heal ourselves through our love and faith in Him."

Lillian's fingers entwined with Samuel's as they sat at the overlook. It had been three days since Grandma's funeral and her heart was still leaden, as she expected it would be for a long time to come. But as she and Samuel sat quietly at the edge of the overlook, she reflected on everything that had recently happened. Rickie was out of her life. She'd found her father, however painful. She and her mom were in a new place—a good place. She'd been fortunate enough to get to know her Grandma before she died. She still had her grandpa. And Samuel loved her.

Knowing God didn't keep score, she was trying not to either. But there was a certain balance to it all. Maybe she'd started out looking for proof there was a God—proof that she could reach out and touch. Her search was misdirected in the beginning. But when she asked to have a relationship with Him, to know Him, God showed Himself to her many times over.

Completely accepting Grandma's death as God's will was going to take her a little longer. Just accepting her as gone was a painful conclusion for her right now. But through her faith, she hoped to continue to grow toward a complete acceptance of all things.

"It takes time, Lillian," she recalled Grandma saying during one of their talks—one of the many when Lillian questioned such blind acceptance of certain events as being God's will. "First get to know God, put your trust in Him, and He will work miracles in your life. You will learn to accept His will, even if you can't see the reasoning behind it at the time," Grandma had said.

She'd always wished the *Ordnung* was a book she could memorize and just make herself live by. But so much of the *Ordnung* was unwritten, visible only in the minds of the faithful followers, like Grandma. And Grandma had been a good teacher.

Being at the overlook was the perfect place to tell Samuel her news.

"Samuel," she said softly, squeezing his hand. "I have something to tell you."

He squirmed uncomfortably. "Me first," he sputtered. "I have something to tell you first."

Lillian doubted it was as important as her decision to be baptized into the Amish faith, but her news could wait. Whatever was on Samuel's mind had him extremely nervous. He took off his hat, pushed back his hair, put his hat back on, stroked his beard, twisted around in the grass again. What in the world was wrong with him?

"What is it, Samuel?"

When he didn't answer, she rushed on. "Because my news is pretty important." Playfully, she nudged her shoulder against his.

"Maybe you should go first, then," he said hesitantly.

"No, you go ahead." She was curious to know what news had him so worked up.

Turning toward her, he grabbed both her hands in his. He gazed lovingly into her eyes and said, "I love you, Lillian. When Rachel died, I didn't think I would ever love another woman the way I loved her." Struggling with his words, he forced them out with determination. "I wasn't sure I ever wanted to move on. But you changed all that. I fought it and fought it. You are as challenging an *Englisch* person as I've ever met. But one thing is for sure: I love you. David loves you."

Taking a deep breath, he went on. "It took me a long time before I could give myself permission to move on. But I want to move on with you, Lillian. I've wanted to ask you something since we were on the porch the day Irma Rose passed, but the timing wasn't right."

Lillian felt her heart leap. Quite sure all her feelings were visible to him, she tried to contain herself. Was Samuel about to propose?

"I know you haven't made mention of staying here or getting baptized, but I'm asking you to stay here, with me. I want you to marry me, Lillian. Do you think you could be happy here, in our district, with me and David? I'm real confused because you aren't baptized, and I don't know how you feel about that. It'd be impossible for us to wed if you aren't baptized, but I felt the need to tell you what my hopes were."

Thank You, God. She had struggled with her decision to be baptized, prayed hard that she was doing the right thing and for the right reasons. She still had a lot to learn. But she knew that she wanted to learn it here, around those she loved. With confidence, she had spoken to the bishop about her decision. Although a proposal from Samuel was the last thing she expected so soon after he professed his love for her.

As if reading her mind, he said, "I know it might seem soon, Lillian. But once you know who you want to spend the rest of your life with . . . *Ach*, I just couldn't see wasting time. I know we couldn't marry until after your baptism, if that's what you choose to do, and—"

"How's November sound to you?" she asked, opening her eyes wide and blinking back the salty sting of emotion.

"What?" he asked, confused. "That's only three months away, and your baptism would have to be in October. That's in only a couple of months, and—"

"October 19 to be exact." She threw her arms around him. "Oh, Samuel! That was my news. I talked to the bishop about being baptized. I wanted to make the decision to stay for the right reasons. I had hoped you would want to marry me *someday*, but I was staying either way."

As his lips met with hers, he drew her closer. "Lillian, nothing would make me happier than to watch you receive baptism in October and marry you in November."

"Then that's the plan," she said, leaning in for another kiss.

⸺⸺

Lillian was surprised her mother was still around after nearly two weeks. Grandpa had several good days following the funeral, and several bad days. Mom was there for the good and bad. She got up with him at night when he was throwing up, helped him bathe when he needed help, and played chess with him as often as he was able. Seeing them together warmed Lillian's heart. But often she had to walk away to hide her tears. How Grandma would have loved Mom being here.

Something about Mom was different too. While Grandma's death devastated them all, there was something in Mom's demeanor reflective of a significant change. There was a calmness about her Lillian didn't remember seeing—ever. She'd gotten used to having her around too. Surprisingly, she enjoyed having her here. After spending so much time trying to cut the cord from her mother and their turbulent relationship, it was refreshing to be in new territory with her. They were kind and loving to each other. They talked, often late into the night. They shared stories, worries, past mistakes, and hopes for the future. It was the way mothers and daughters should be. In the aftermath of something so sad, something wonderful had happened. And Mom was thrilled about the wedding plans and excited to be involved in the planning.

Samuel and David resumed their places at the supper table almost every night. Much of the food continued to come from Samuel's garden and butchered livestock. Grandpa was able to eat downstairs some of the time, and Mom sat on the bench next to him. Everyone was painfully aware of the empty chair at the end of the table. Mom refused to sit in it, even though Grandpa said he would have more elbow room if she did.

David's summer vacation from school ended, and he wasn't able to help as much with chores around their place. He and Samuel did what they could to help keep both farms manicured, but work was piling up at both farms. Lillian wasn't sure how much earlier they could all get up in the mornings to accomplish all they needed to do. Grandma had certainly made her share of the daily chores look easy. In her absence, Lillian and her mom struggled to match up to Grandma's way of keeping things neat and orderly.

The family talked of Lillian's impending baptism often. Soon she and Samuel would publish their wedding announcement for the first Tuesday in November. Weddings were usually held on Tuesday or Thursday, most commonly the slowest days of the week. November was the wedding month, following the busy fall harvest and before the risk of unfavorable winter weather.

They had avoided the specifics of how all this was going to work since the first time Lillian made mention to Grandpa that perhaps he could live with them at Samuel's place. His gruff response left no doubt he would leave his family farmstead feet first. "I was born here, and I'll die here," he groaned.

But Grandpa's grief was taking a toll on his health. He couldn't take care of himself, and Lillian was not about to leave him alone. She and Samuel had discussed it several times, and each time there was no resolution. As much as they wanted to be together as husband and wife, Grandpa was not capable of taking care of himself.

A few days later, Samuel and Lillian excused themselves from the supper table early. Jonas wasn't sitting as tall as usual, barely touching his ham and potato salad. As they walked hand in hand toward the barn, Samuel knew Lillian had the same thing on her mind that he did.

"Grandpa can't stay alone," she said. "There's no way, Samuel."

"I know." He turned to face her. The sun had yet to give in to the moon, and in the evening light her eyes were full of worry. "I reckon me and David can move here when we're married. I just want us to be a family, Lillian. Jonas is a part of this family."

She sighed. "You love that farm of yours, Samuel."

A lot of heartfelt labor had gone into making his farm a

place to be proud of. The house had been run down and the fields overgrown when Samuel purchased the old property, back before he married Rachel. Now it was as nice a place as any in their district.

But despite his attachment to the farm, his attachment to Lillian was greater. "I love you, and leaving Jonas is not an option."

She buried her head in his chest. "What are we going to do? I love you so much, Samuel. I'll live anywhere, as long as it's with you. I just hate for you to give up your home, and I hate for Grandpa to have to give up the only place he's ever lived. But the only way I see this working is for one of you to let go of your property. It needs to be Grandpa. He can't take care of this place. It's hard on you and David tending to both farms."

"Home is where you make it, Lillian. My home is with you, David, and Jonas."

Kissing her tenderly, he could not imagine his life without her. Despite their challenges, Lillian filled his heart with love in a way he didn't think possible again. David loved her too.

But love of the land, tilling of the soil, and producing—it was the Amish way, and he had done a fine job at it. Letting the land dissolve into a barren oasis of deeply planted dreams was hard to swallow.

As darkness neared, they turned their attention to headlights rounding the turn onto the driveway.

"Are you expecting anyone?"

"No," she said, surprised.

They waited as a large truck slowly made its way down the dirt driveway. By the time the driver parked the truck, Samuel noticed Sarah Jane and David making their way down the porch steps. It was a really large truck with a sign on the side that said *Leeway Moving*.

"What's going on?" Lillian asked.

"It's your farm." He joked. "I have no idea."

"Over there!" Samuel heard Sarah Jane yell. "Park over by the barn."

As Sarah Jane and David met up with them, Lillian asked, "Mom, what is this truck doing here?"

Sarah Jane smiled. "It's a few of my things I couldn't live without. You know, my four-poster bed that I finally purchased from that lovely shop at the Trader's Village in Houston, and some other things I really *need*."

Samuel wondered if an answer to their prayers had just arrived. But he wasn't quite sure.

"Mom, what are you saying?" Lillian's face glistened as the sun faded and the moonlight seemed to focus exclusively on her.

"You should know, Lillian, I will be taking over some of those dresses from upstairs when you leave to be Samuel's wife. So you need to start thinking about sewing yourself some more. Because, if you must know, those dresses you are wearing are *mine*."

She winked at her daughter and headed toward the truck. "I said, park by the barn!" She threw her hands in the air and pointed toward the barn, continuing to instruct the driver.

Lillian was quickly on her mother's heels. "Mom?"

"I'm staying, Lillian," she confirmed. "We'll figure out what to do with all these things later."

"But, Mom—"

Samuel watched as Sarah Jane faced her daughter. "He's my

pop, Lillian. I'm going to take care of him. You need to start your life with your husband in November. I plan to spend the second half of my life making amends for the mistakes I made during the first half."

"But, Mom . . ." Lillian said again.

"By the barn!" Sarah Jane yelled. "We are putting everything in the barn for now!"

The driver got as close to the barn as he could.

While the moving van distracted her Mom, Lillian latched on to Samuel's hand and gave it a squeeze. "Oh, Samuel," she said, gleaming. "Is my mother answering our prayers?"

It seemed an unlikely source, but one that was upon them. "I think so," he answered.

Once Sarah Jane had the movers unloading her necessary belongings in the correct manner into the barn, she walked toward David, who was standing a few feet from Samuel and Lillian.

"David, your pop and my daughter look speechless," she said, giving the boy a hug.

Samuel noticed David's eyes light up. He had a clear reckoning as to what was happening.

"You're going to stay here and live with Jonas while Lillian comes and lives with me and my *daed*?" he asked, seeming a little unsure.

"*Ya*," Sarah Jane answered. "But I'm hoping I'll still have you to help us in the afternoons after Lillian marries your *daed*."

Lillian's eyes were aglow and she seemed pleasantly surprised at her mother's use of the *Deitsch*.

"You bet," David said. "Jonas will be expecting me to play chess after my chores."

"Well you'll have to beat me first," Sarah Jane said.

"Mom, are you sure about this?" Lillian asked her mother. "What about Paul? What about your job? Are you sure?"

Sarah Jane grew solemn and faced her daughter. "I should have come back here, Lillian. I should have trusted the love of my parents." She paused. "And the love of God. Being here reminds me of what it's like to live a lifestyle void of complications. I want to live out the rest of my years this way."

"Mom," Lillian said, embracing her, "does Grandpa know?"

"I sure do."

Samuel followed the voice to see Jonas hobbling down the porch steps.

"You people are the loudest bunch I've ever known. What does a sick ol' man with cancer have to do to be gettin' some rest around here?" He continued to hobble toward Sarah Jane, a smile stretched across his face.

"Pop," she said lovingly, walking toward him, "and I want to stay together."

He tried to hide it, but Samuel could see Jonas's eyes welling up.

"There's nothin' I'd like more in this *wunderbaar* world the Good Lord created," Jonas said, hugging his daughter. "Irma Rose is smiling from heaven."

Samuel looked at Lillian, whose eyes glazed with emotion. "The Good Lord has a way of takin' care of things," he said.

"*Ya*, He does."

Samuel watched as Sarah Jane gently eased her father away and walked toward him and Lillian. "Will it be all right with the two of you if I boot you out in November, after you're married?

It would be too crowded in this house with Lillian." She kissed her daughter on the cheek.

"Oh, I guess I'll have to take her to my place after we're married," he said jokingly.

"Lillian?" her mother asked. "What about you? Think you can go live with this man in marital bliss while I take care of your grandpa?"

"Mom, *danki*," Lillian said, wrapping her arms around her.

"No, Lillian, thank *you*," her mother said softly, but still in earshot of Samuel. "This is where I belong. It's where I've always belonged. I just didn't know how to find my way home."

Sarah Jane turned to Samuel. "A hug for your future mother-in-law?"

Samuel welcomed the hug. Whatever it took to make his Lillian as happy as she was at this moment.

"Bunch of mushy stuff goin' on, I say." Jonas rejoined the three of them after sharing some time with David.

"Now, I have another surprise for all of you. It's a really big surprise," Sarah Jane announced.

Samuel watched as Lillian's mother lovingly wrapped her arms around her daughter again. "And, Lillian, I'm so sure that everything is going to be *gut!*"

Irma Rose would have been so proud, Samuel thought to himself. *But what in the world was Sarah Jane's surprise?*

18

Evidence of fall was abundant. Colorful leaves swirled around in the crisp air as buggies lined the drive at the Miller farm. It was the perfect day for a baptism. Lillian greeted community members from the den. Most of them she knew, and several she had gotten to know well over the past couple months since Grandma died. Particularly Sadie. They'd become quite close. She took Lillian to a quilting party and introduced her to other women in the community. Lillian even asked her new friend to be a *waiter*—the Amish term for bridesmaid—at her upcoming wedding, along with her mother.

Only two more weeks until she would be Lillian Stoltzfus. She glanced at her husband-to-be across the room, also greeting guests. Being in love with Samuel filled her heart with a joy she didn't know possible. It had been hard to accept God into her heart and to accept His will, but with Samuel and David's help, she had put all doubts to rest. For the first time in her life, peacefulness consumed her. The peacefulness of knowing all things of this earth were in His hands.

She was thankful to Him that Grandpa was having one of his good days. Following a rough couple of weeks, he looked strong and handsome. Glancing upward, she whispered, *"Danki."*

Still, not a day went by that she didn't think about Grandma. She missed her in a terrible way and knew this would have been a proud moment for her.

As everyone took their respective places, as they did in worship service, Lillian prepared to leave all worldly things behind and accept her birthright with newfound faith and confidence. However, once everyone settled in, she turned to her left . . . to see her mother preparing for baptism alongside her. Mom had mentioned she had a surprise, but Lillian couldn't have imagined this. What a blessed moment and a wonderful surprise—to choose baptism after all these years. Mom could have just chosen to stay and take care of her father, without committing her life to the *Ordnung*. It was yet another reflection of God in both their lives.

Despite exhaustion from taking care of Grandpa, Mom spent countless hours making sure Lillian was comfortable with the *Ordnung* and helping her with her *Deitsch*. As she took up where Grandma left off, teaching Lillian the Amish ways, Lillian witnessed an incredible transformation, a profound renewal of faith in her mother. A woman injured by life—and with scars to show for it—she seemed to be exactly where she belonged.

Now she merely smiled and squeezed Lillian's hand before returning to her preparations.

With three females and four males seeking baptism, they each sat with one hand over their faces to represent their submission and humility to the church. The deacon ladled water from a bucket into the bishop's hand, and the bishop sprinkled each of their heads three times, in the name of the Father, Son, and Holy Ghost.

The bishop blessed each new male member with a holy kiss,

and his wife blessed each new female church member with a holy kiss. They were then all welcomed as new church members. And as was the Amish way, a bountiful meal followed.

———

Samuel took a stroll out to the barn. His Lillian was a church member and now they would be married in a couple of weeks. He wanted some time to be alone, to thank the Lord for all the blessings bestowed upon him and David.

The old newspapers were still scattered on the dirt floor of the barn. He gathered them up and placed them neatly back in the box. What a long way they had come. It was a struggle, but Lillian had put the past behind her and moved forward with hope and determination. He smiled as he recalled her receiving baptism. She had never looked more beautiful.

"I saw you sneaking out here," he heard her say when she entered the barn. "Most of the kitchen is cleaned up, so I snuck out too."

Samuel put the last newspaper in the box and stacked it atop the other boxes. This was a special day, and he hoped seeing the newspapers didn't bring back any painful memories for her. He walked toward her, and she smiled. Pulling her close, he said, "Have I mentioned how beautiful you look?" He kissed her on the cheek.

"Several times," she said, her face nuzzled into his chest. "I feel so good about everything, Samuel."

"Do you feel any different?" He remembered feeling wonderfully different after his baptism.

She gently pulled away and looked up at him, her eyes aglow

with joy. "I do feel different. In some ways, it's all very surreal. I mean, if anyone had told me a year ago that Mom and I would be as close as we are, or that both of us would be baptized into the Amish faith, I never would have believed it." She paused and twisted her mouth into a frown. "Bad things happen sometimes. It was hard for me to accept those things as God's will in the beginning." She smiled again. "But, *gut* things happen too. It's a balance, I suppose. I shouldn't question His will. I miss Grandma every day. But I'm so grateful for Mom, and I never thought I would be able to say that. I'm so thankful, Samuel. To you. To God." He watched as her eyes glazed over with tears of contentment. "I'm just very happy."

"And soon we'll be married." He pulled her close again.

"I am so ready to be your *fraa*, Samuel. I'm going to be a good wife and a good *mamm* to David."

"Not just a *gut mamm* to David, I hope. I reckon there will be a lot of little Stoltzfus *kinner* running around some day."

"There is nothing I want more."

Samuel kissed her tenderly on the mouth. "I guess we need to go back to the others," he said with regret. He wanted to hold her in his arms forever. Only two more weeks—and then they'd be together for the rest of their lives.

———————

Sarah Jane fumbled with the letter that arrived in the mail. With only two days until Lillian's wedding, she tossed the envelope nervously from hand to hand. It was addressed to Lillian and opening it would be wrong. It would be equally as wrong to toss it into the trash bin, but she was tempted just the same. The return address was from Oklahoma, and she cringed as her eyes met with the name above the address. Daniel Foster. Hearing from him was the last thing either of them needed.

"I'm exhausted just thinking of all the things left to do before the wedding," she heard Lillian say while walking into the kitchen. "Maybe we should have waited until the end of November, since we just had the baptism here a couple of weeks ago." She plopped down on the bench at the kitchen table and brushed back a strand of hair dangling in her face.

"I don't think you or Samuel could have waited a couple more weeks." Crossing her arms, Sarah Jane tucked the letter out of sight.

"Mom, I just didn't know I could feel this happy." She smiled. "How's Grandpa this afternoon?"

"Actually, he's having a good day. He's napping right now. Be warned, though—the doctors changed his medicine again, and you know what that means. We just never know how he'll respond to the change."

"*Ya.* I'm glad he's doing so well today. I pray he will be having a good day on Tuesday."

"I'll pray too," Sarah Jane said, smiling, but with the letter still hidden from Lillian's view. She knew she would have to turn it over, but still she hesitated. Despite her exhaustion, her daughter had never looked happier, and she didn't want to ruin that.

"David is going to mow the yard after school," Lillian said. "I'll finish making the bread and apple butter, and then I know we need to—"

"Lillian," she interrupted.

"*Ya?*"

"This came in the mail today." With reluctance, she handed over the letter. As she feared, Lillian's bright eyes lost some of their glow. Her face was solemn and she just held the envelope and stared at it.

"You don't have to open it," Sarah Jane told her, wishing she wouldn't. "We can just throw it away and pretend it never came." She thought about all the letters from her mother she had tossed into the trash. Her heart ached.

Lillian tilted her head to one side and held the letter up toward the window, as if trying to catch the sun's rays to read through the envelope. "No," she said softly. "I have to open it. I'm not going to let whatever is in this letter upset me. I've put all that behind me."

Sarah Jane took a seat on the bench across from Lillian. "I still say we can just throw it away." She cupped her chin in her hands.

"Mom, we can't do that." Lillian's tone was a tad reprimanding, and Sarah Jane knew she was right.

Lillian's heart was racing. Peeling back the flap of the envelope, she slowly removed the two-page letter, handwritten in blue ink on lined white paper.

Dear Lillian,

What is often at the heart of a man's soul is lost or forgotten by the time you reach my age. Bitterness, divorce, and life have a way of doing that. I know it might seem like I'm feeling sorry for myself, but that is not my intention. Rather, I would like for you to know that at my core, I am not the evil person that my actions have certainly dictated. Since you share my genes, I do not want you to fear the passing down of poisonous heritage. It is my hope that by breaking down the iron walls surrounding my heart, you will see a small glimpse as to who your father is—or once was.

Sarah Jane was a beautiful, vibrant woman. She probably still is. I have no excuse for the way I handled her pregnancy. To say I was young, at the height of my career, and afraid seems like a lame excuse. When you arrived at my shop, I assumed you were there to cause trouble for me somehow. Looking back, I know you just wanted to know who your father is. You remind me so much of your mother. Despite her unworldly ways, she had a zest for life she obviously passed on to you. It's unfortunate that as a young man I took advantage of her spirited nature and robbed her of the life she was intended to live. She had no real understanding of life outside of her community. I suppose all that changed when she fled the only life she had ever known to raise a child on her own.

If you sense remorse in this letter, you are right. Not many days went by when I did not wonder about you. When my wife and I married many years later, we were unable to bear children. I often suspected it was my punishment for abandoning you and your mother.

I understand from friends in Paradise that you were baptized into the Amish faith and will be married soon (not to worry—they do not know you are my daughter). There is no wedding gift I can give you to make up for my behavior years ago, or my behavior most recently. I can only hope that, in some small way, this letter will suffice as my gift to you, for it comes with a heartfelt and sincere apology.

May your new life bring you happiness always.

Regards,
Daniel Foster

Lillian handed her mother the letter. "Maybe this will give you some closure too," she said. With no memories of those hard times Daniel referred to, Lillian assumed perhaps her mother had more to gain from the letter than she did. Based on Mom's expression as she was reading, Lillian was right.

"He really wasn't a bad man," Mom muttered, fighting tears. "But I have struggled these past couple of months to forgive him. This helps." She handed the letter back to Lillian.

"I forgave him a while back, but this helps me too." There was comfort in knowing that her father had wondered about her and that he regretted his actions years ago, as well as his more recent ones. The tone of his letter saddened her, though. He sounded like a lonely man. She would say an extra prayer for him tonight. Maybe she would write him back someday.

Tuesday took forever to arrive. As Samuel and David hurried to get ready, Samuel feared he was going to be late for his own wedding. He had heard rumors that over two hundred people would be attending. What a mighty noon feast they would have after the ceremony and another grand meal in the evening. It was going be right crowded in the Miller house.

He couldn't wait to make Lillian his wife. "David, it's time, boy!" he yelled upstairs. "Are you 'bout done?"

Samuel was as nervous as a man could be. From the moment he laid eyes on Lillian, he'd connected with her in a way that made him fearful—fearful they could never be together. Now she had become a church member and today they would marry. And tonight . . . Well, Samuel couldn't help but think about tonight, their wedding night. The passionate kisses they shared were only a prelude to what he knew would be a *wunderbaar* night.

Sharing their love as husband and wife was a vision he couldn't shake. Nor did he want to. The thought of his beautiful Lillian, held close in his arms . . .

He hollered for David to hurry.

It was customary for the bride and groom to stay with her parents on the wedding night, so as to help with the cleanup the next morning. He packed a small duffel bag for him and one for David, since David would be heading to Ivan's place later in the evening.

"We ain't got time to waste, David," he bellowed up the stairs. "Come on with yourself."

———

"Oh, Lillian," her mom said when she walked downstairs. "You look beautiful."

Dressed in traditional Amish wedding attire, Lillian felt beautiful in her new blue linen dress, black *Kapp*, white kerchief, and apron. She knew this would be the only time she would wear the outfit, until they buried her in it. Sadie had made the dress for her and it fit perfectly.

"*Danki*, Mom." She was nervous, and she didn't think much was going to change that. "Samuel said there are going to be about two hundred people in attendance. That's more than when we held the baptisms here."

"The joining of two hearts for eternity is a blessed event," her mother said. "I'm so proud of you, Lillian. Against so many hardships, you prevailed and turned into a beautiful young woman. And an Amish woman at that." Mom pulled her in for a hug.

"Mom," she said warmly. "I'm proud of you too. I'm proud you're my *mamm*."

Gently her mother eased Lillian away from her. "I have something to give you."

She darted upstairs. When she returned, she handed Lillian an envelope. "It's the money I borrowed from you, Lillian. I had Claire, my friend back in Houston, sell the rest of my things."

"Mom, no," Lillian said, handing the envelope back. "I don't care about this money. I don't need it."

"What am I going to do with it, Lillian? I have everything I have ever wanted or needed." She pushed the envelope back toward Lillian. "Go and buy a wedding present for you and Samuel."

"This would buy a *really* nice wedding present, Mom," she said, counting the money.

"*Ya*, and that's what I want you to do with it."

"Do you miss Paul or your life, Mom?"

"Where did that come from?"

"I don't know. I just wondered." She hesitated. "It's just . . . you've always . . ."

"Had a man in my life?" Mom questioned. "I used to think that completed me, Lillian. I know that's not true. Having God in my life completes me. Besides, I imagine you and Samuel will give me lots of *kinner* to keep me busy. Plus, I have Pop."

"Did I say how proud I am of you, Mom?" She threw her arms around her mother again.

"I think you did. And I am very proud of you. Now, let's get you married. A crowd is gathering outside. Where's the groom?"

It was nearing eight o'clock in the morning when the crowd moved into the house. Lillian glanced around until she finally saw Samuel. Her heart took on a fearful pulse when she realized the time for the ceremony was upon them and Samuel had not appeared. She smiled at him from across the room.

As everyone prepared for the four-hour ceremony, she twisted her hands together. There was no wedding ring and no flowers to carry or flowers in the house. Instead, they placed celery in simple white glasses throughout the house—one of the symbolic foods at Amish weddings. She suddenly had an urge to steal one of the cut stalks and take a nibble. She should have eaten breakfast, but an early-morning bout of nerves had prevented her from indulging in her mother's *dippy eggs* this morning.

Lillian knew the ceremony would be void of the traditional kiss at the end. Of course, there would be no photographers or fancy catering. It was not the wedding she'd dreamed of since she was a child. It was better. The overabundance of love in the room more than made up for any preconceived ideas about what her wedding would be like.

Preparing to take her vows with the man she loved, she looked around the room. As was customary, the women were on one side and the men on the other side. Samuel had never looked more handsome. Grandpa and David stood side by side, each of them with a twinkle in his eye. Mom was beautiful. She had tossed out her makeup and other worldly goods prior to her baptism, and the lines of time and her hardships were evident. However, the radiance in her heart manifested itself across her smiling face, lending her a beauty that makeup could have never matched.

Lillian beamed at several women she had grown fond of over the past couple of months. Struggling to keep her emotions intact, she knew without a doubt that everything was perfect. She was ready to take her place as a daughter of the promise. Her journey of faith, hope, and love guided her to this moment. Now she would begin her life as Samuel's *fraa*.

They sang several songs in German at the beginning of the ceremony. The worship service was in German with a mix of *Pennsylvania Deitsch*. She was surprised how much of the language she now understood. After the preacher presented stories of the Old Testament, he offered marriage advice to her and Samuel.

"The Bible teaches us to treat each other with respect, not to raise our voices at each other, and to always show love," he recited. "Work hard, remember the man is the head of the home, and, Lillian, you are his helpmate."

Fondly, she recalled her learning session with Grandma concerning the preacher's statement. Not so long ago, his words would have caused Lillian to gasp. Instead, she was more than ready to allow Samuel to take his role as head of the home. By his side, she knew their partnership would be one of mutual respect.

Several other pastors spoke to the congregation, and specifically to Samuel and Lillian. It was near eleven o'clock when she and Samuel took their vows in front of their family and friends. With unwavering faith in herself, Samuel, and God, Lillian proclaimed her love to the only man she'd ever loved. "I, Lillian, take you Samuel . . ."

She managed to stifle tears of joy until Samuel professed his love for her. But upon hearing his solemn vow to love her forever, through good times and bad, a tear trickled down her cheek. He gently brushed it away. Had she looked around, she would have noticed there was hardly a dry eye in the house. But all Lillian saw was Samuel.

———

The wedding dinner was bountiful, consisting of the traditional *roasht*, along with mashed potatoes, gravy, creamed celery, buttered noodles, steamed peas with butter, and homemade bread and jam. There were side dishes of applesauce, chowchow, and pepper cabbage, and more pies, cookies, puddings, and dessert than Lillian had ever seen. Plus she was told no wedding would be complete without Amish *wedding nothings*, a deep-fried traditional wedding pastry. It was an amazing display, and on this day she planned to partake of all of it.

"We sit here, at the *eck*," Samuel whispered in her ear as he guided her to the corner of the wedding table.

They had placed tables together in the den to form a large hollow square with one side open. Samuel and Lillian sat at one of the outer corners, known as the bride's corner, or *eck*. Lillian's waiters sat to her left, along with other young unmarried women. Samuel's waiters sat to his right, along with more unmarried women. Young unmarried men sat on the remaining side of the formation.

Much preparation went into rearranging furniture in an attempt to accommodate the guests during the ceremony. However, they served the meal in shifts. Lillian and Samuel were served first, along with their wedding party.

Lillian realized she had worked up an appetite. A fabulous wedding cake sat before her and Samuel. As she waited for the ladies to serve the meal, the temptation to swipe the white icing with her finger was overwhelming. She felt Samuel's hand intertwine with hers beneath the table.

"I love you, Lillian Stoltzfus," he whispered, oblivious to the people scurrying around the room.

"I love you too, Samuel Stoltzfus."

It was a glorious day, and Lillian bowed her head in prayer to thank God for the many blessings He had bestowed upon her and her family.

They sang traditional Amish hymns after the noon meal, followed by folk games in the barn for the children and unmarried young adults. As everyone socialized, mothers put babies down for naps upstairs, men gathered in the barn to smoke cigars and tell jokes. It was an all-day affair filled with fellowship, prayer, and a sense of belonging for Lillian.

"There you are," she said to Samuel, finding him on the porch later that afternoon. "I didn't see you for a while. I missed you."

"Hello, Mrs. Stoltzfus," he said smiling.

"I like the sound of that." She placed her hands on her full stomach. "I can't believe we have to eat again. I'm still full from the noon meal."

"I reckon the ladies are already preparing supper. But before we eat, we get to go play matchmaker for the young people out in the barn."

"Sadie told me about that. We actually get to pick out a boy and a girl and send them in the house holding hands?" She grinned at her husband. It sounded like great fun.

"*Ya*, the matched up boy and girl will go in the house, holding hands, and sit together at suppertime." Samuel arched his eyebrows and whispered, "The married ladies will all be gossiping about who is sitting together, who their parents are, and remarking about what a nice couple they will make."

"What if the kids don't like who we match them up with?"

"Then I guess a wedding won't be in their future," he said, snickering.

"No, I guess not."

She watched as Samuel's face took on a serious expression. "I love you so much, Lillian. I can't wait to show you how much I love you tonight."

———

After matching up the teenagers in the barn for supper, more socializing went on for several more hours. Lillian wasn't sure how she'd managed to eat another meal. It had been a long, exhausting, wonderful day. It was almost nine o'clock when their guests began to leave. Grandpa had a fabulously good day but had been in bed for hours. Mom had been a trooper all day, making sure everything was perfect.

As she sat next to Samuel at the wedding table, Lillian hated for it all to end. But, she reminded herself, it was only the beginning. And she was ready to begin her life as Samuel's wife.

"It's time, Lillian," her mother said as she leaned down and kissed Lillian on the cheek. "Time to start your life as Samuel's *fraa*."

Samuel and Lillian stood up. Hand in hand, they bade farewell to those guests standing nearby. Lillian knew the next morning would start early and members of the district would be on hand to help with the cleanup. The next few weeks would be spent visiting members of the community, as was customary. These post-marriage visits were when she and Samuel would receive a lot of their wedding gifts.

It was to be a busy time after the wedding. But, for tonight, it would just be her and Samuel, his loving arms wrapped around her.

19

THE MID-FEBRUARY TEMPERATURES CAME WITH A BLAST OF arctic air that was keeping most of the community huddled inside with the comfort of woodburning stoves and fireplaces. Luckily, David's trek to school was a short distance from home. After tending to the cows, Samuel had gone to the farmer's market to pick up a few things. Normally, it was a task Lillian handled, but the weather was hardly fit to get out and Samuel insisted on making the trip for her.

Lillian was thrilled to see the delivery truck make it up the drive, and even more excited that her surprise would be in place before Samuel returned. She knew her husband had been goggling over the beautiful handmade table in town since before they were married.

She glanced around her Plain kitchen, void of all the gadgets she was once dependent on. It was amazing how she didn't think about or miss all the modern conveniences she'd grown up with. Everything she needed, she had right here.

With the weather at its worst, Samuel still made a trip to check on Mom and Grandpa daily. His latest report was that Grandpa's medication was continuing to help him tremendously. The two of them were making regular trips to town and playing lots of chess.

Although she had not had an opportunity to talk with Mom, rumor had it that a widower or two in the district were vying for her mother's attention. Sadly, Lillian knew Grandpa wouldn't always be around. Mom said she didn't need a man in her life. But Lillian still hoped that perhaps the right man might come along for her mother, giving her someone to share the second half of her life with.

Lillian was bursting at the seams by the time Samuel's buggy pulled up the drive. He was going to be so surprised—in more ways than one. She pulled a loaf of bread out of the oven and placed it on a cooling rack on the kitchen counter, near a platter of cookies she'd made earlier. She and David feasted on cookies and milk every day when he returned from school. It had become their special time to talk about the day.

Her heart raced as Samuel pushed open the screen door.

"I reckon my toes are never gonna thaw," he said, snow still clinging to his long black coat and speckling his black felt hat. "But it sure smells *gut* in here." He hung his coat and hat on the rack and entered the kitchen.

Lillian clasped her hands together and smiled as she watched her husband's face light up.

"Lillian," he said in awe, his hand skimming the surface of the large table he had been eyeing in town for over a year. He grabbed her in his arms and kissed her tenderly. "But, how—"

"It's a wedding present, from my *mamm*."

He shook his head in disbelief. "I reckon I've been wanting this table for as long as I can remember." His eyes twinkled with boyish appreciation. "This is the best present I've ever received. Someday we will fill it up with little ones."

Lillian smiled. "Samuel," she said softly, with a hint of play-fulness in her tone.

"*Ya?*" He was still enamored with the new table and matching benches.

"Someday has arrived."

All the cold weather in the world couldn't have taken away the warmth in Lillian's heart when she saw the look on her husband's face. "You mean . . . ," he asked, unsure.

She placed his hand on her stomach and smiled. "*Ya.*"

"Oh, Lillian. I love you so much."

"And I love you, Samuel."

Samuel came over to Lillian and held her, then took a seat on one of the benches. Lillian slid in beside him and reached for his hand. "I imagine our family will eat a lot of meals at this table."

Giving her hand a squeeze, Samuel nodded. "*Ya,* our family."

They sat quietly for a while. As the peacefulness and calm she'd so desperately searched for swept over Lillian, she bowed her head and closed her eyes.

Thank You.

Acknowledgments

THANK YOU TO MY FAMILY AND FRIENDS FOR YOUR SUPPORT and encouragement.

To Patrick, for sharing your life with me and believing in me every step of the way. You become more dear to me with each passing day. To my sons, Eric and Cory, you are my most precious gifts from God who inspire me daily. You three are the loves of my life.

Mother, how blessed I am to be your daughter. And what a bonus it is that you are a super, speed-reading, typo-catching queen! And to Daddy, may you rest in peace knowing I write happy endings . . . the way you always thought it should be. Thank you to my Mama, for your unwavering faith in God and me. I know you are smiling from Heaven. To my sister Laurie, who found her true love late in life. May you be blessed with all the happiness you deserve.

To my best friend and lifelong editor, Reneé Bissmeyer. You've read more manuscripts than I care to count, and your unwavering support always keeps me going past chapter six. Thank you for believing in me when I had doubts. We both know there aren't enough pages for me to express what our friendship means to me.

You are my "life editor," as well as my manuscript editor. It is a privilege to dedicate the book to you.

Thank you to Rene Simpson, my dear, dear friend who stepped up to the plate at the very last minute and spent four days at my house editing nonstop until the last revision was complete. And you did it all for "Happy Eggs" and guacamole. You are my hero! Your Samuel awaits. Don't give up.

To my second family at *The Schulenburg Sticker* newspaper, your flexibility with my job during my son's illness, and throughout the publication of this book, far surpasses the employer/ employee relationship. Saying thank you hardly seems enough. A special thank you to my editor at *The Sticker*, Darrell Vyvjala, for teaching me about the wonderful world of editing. You are my mentor and my friend.

Sue and Darrell Buttrey, the miles may seperate us, but you are forever in my heart. Thank you for your dear friendship and support.

Thank you to my good friend and critique partner, Carol Voelkel, for finding time to overhaul the manuscript amidst a challenging job, family, and writing projects of her own. Never stop writing!

Thank you to Mary Sue Seymour for recognizing the potential of the manuscript from the first three chapters. It is a pleasure to work with you and call you my friend. Miracles *do* happen to those who believe.

Many thanks to Barbie Beiler and Anna B. King, who jumped in at the eleventh hour and critiqued the manuscript for accuracy. Your Mennonite and Amish backgrounds provided a wealth of information about the Plain people of Lancaster County.

To the Amish families in Lancaster County who opened their homes and hearts, allowing my endless stream of questions . . . blessings to you all.

A special thank you to Leslie Peterson for her encouragement during the revision process. Your suggestions and edits were delivered with kindness and patience. It was a pleasure to work with you on this project.

A huge thank you to Natalie Hanemann for believing in the book . . . and in me. You alleviated much of my "first-novel fear" by walking me through the process and explaining things as we went along. You, along with the rest of the staff at Thomas Nelson, made this a wonderful experience for me.

And, most of all, to God, for offering me the opportunity to fulfill my dream of writing through words I pray will glorify Him, and for the many other blessings He has bestowed on me.

Reading Group Guide

1. At the beginning of the story, Samuel had some serious qualms about being "unequally yoked" with Lillian, who was an unbeliever. Do you think that Samuel's worries are justified? Have you ever been in a relationship where you felt unequally yoked? Where did you draw the line between sharing the love and Word of God to unbelievers and being yoked or pulled down by an unbeliever?

2. What are some of the ways the Amish community gathers to help one another in *Plain Perfect*? Have you experienced similar support in your own community? What can we take away from the Amish example of community and fellowship? Are there any disadvantages to this close-knit community?

3. Why do you imagine Samuel feels guilt that thoughts of Lillian intermingle with his thoughts of Rachel? If you were in his place, do you think you could love again?

4. Do you think Sarah Jane made the right decision to leave the Amish community when she became pregnant with Lillian? What do you think the repercussions would have been had she stayed? Why do you think Sarah Jane never told Lillian who her father was?

5. Why does Lillian have such a hard time accepting everything as God's will? Are you able to accept the hard times in your life as God's will? What about the blessings and successes in your life—are you able to credit those to God's will as well?

6. David always believed that his pop and Lillian would end up together. How does that relate to what Christ teaches us about the faith of children? Compare his eager faithfulness to Irma Rose's hesitancy. Why do some adults seem to lose that faith?

7. What do you think Sarah Jane was trying to find in all of the men in her life? Is there someone you know that is guilty of the same misdirection—that is, filling up the emptiness in his or her heart with bad relationships or material things such as nicer cars and homes? Would you ever broach this subject with him or her?

8. Is admitting your past mistakes helpful or harmful in the raising of children? Was Samuel out of line in his reaction to hearing that Lillian told David all about her worldly past? Should Lillian have denied her past?

What do you think would have happened if she hadn't told David all about her past and just forbidden him from those worldly temptations? Is there a benefit to letting children make their own mistakes?

9. Food is an important theme throughout the novel—the preparation, the sharing, the eating. Is the Amish approach to food and meals different than an "outsider" view? Are there similarities?

10. Why do you think Lillian chose to bury her worldly things in that hole by the lake? Is there anything you wish you could bury in a hole, eliminating from your past and present? What's stopping you?

11. Why do you think Sarah Jane decided to come back to Lancaster County to visit her parents? What made her stay? Why do you think it took her so long to return?

12. Are there parts of the Amish life you would like to incorporate into your own way of life?

A Man of His Word

KATHLEEN FULLER

A Note from the Author

A Man of His Word is set in the lovely village of Middlefield, Ohio, located in Geauga County in northeast Ohio. About forty minutes east of the city of Cleveland, Middlefield is the fourth largest Amish settlement in the world, making up 12 percent of the county's population. The Amish established themselves here in 1885, when David Miller, in search of cheaper farmland, moved from Holmes County, Ohio, to the Middlefield area.

Middlefield's slogan, "Where Industry Meets Agriculture," neatly describes this pleasant town. Amish buggies share the gently sloping roads with "Yankee" cars and motorcycles. Modest white houses and barns dot the landscape amid large businesses like Middlefield Cheese House and Dillen Products. Shops producing handcrafted Amish goods are as easy to find as the local CVS pharmacy and Wal-Mart.

Many of the Middlefield Amish, like the Lancaster County Amish, are Old Order. While both the Middlefield and Lancaster settlements are divided into districts, each with its own *Ordnung*—an unwritten set of rules members abide by—there are noticeable differences in buggy style, dress, and cultural influence. In Middlefield non-Amish are referred to as Yankees, while in Lancaster they are called *Englischers*. A Lancaster Amishman might drive a gray-colored buggy, while Middlefield buggies are always black. A Middlefield woman's prayer *kapp* at first glance might look the same as a Lancaster *kapp*, yet upon deeper inspection one realizes they are of differing design. There are also varying guidelines for the use of technology. While these superficial differences are evident among all Amish settlements, they do not detract from the main tenets of the Amish faith—a desire to grow closer to God, the importance of family and community, and living a plain and humble lifestyle.

With the help of some extremely generous Amish and Yankee friends, I have tried to portray the Amish in Middlefield as accurately and respectfully as possible. If there are any mistakes or misconceptions in my story, they are of my own making.

I hope you enjoy *A Man of His Word* as much as I enjoyed writing it. If you are ever in the northeast Ohio area, I invite you to visit Middlefield and experience everything this wonderful village has to offer.

Kathleen Fuller

Pennsylvania Dutch Glossary

Ausbund: hymnal
bann: excommunication from the Amish
Biewel: Bible
boppli: baby
braut: bride
bruder: brother
daed: father
dawdi haus: a separate dwelling built for aging parents
danki: thank you
dochder: daughter
dummkopf: dummy
Frau: wife, Mrs.
Fraulein: unmarried woman, Miss
fehlerfrei: perfect
geh: go
grossdochder: granddaughter
gude mariye: good morning
gut: good
Herr: Mr.

kapp: an Amish woman's prayer covering

kind: child

maedel: girl

mei: my

mami: mother

mudder: mother

nee: no

nix: nothing

Ordnung: an unwritten set of rules members abide by

recht: right

reck: coat

rumspringa: the period between ages sixteen and twenty-four,
   loosely translated as "running around time." For Amish
   young adults, *rumspringa* ends when they join the church

schwei: sister-in-law

schwester: sister

schwoger: brother-in-law

sehr: very

seltsam: weird

sohn: son

Wie geht's: How are you?

willkum: welcome

wunderbaar: wonderful

ya: yes

Yankee: a non-Amish person

yank over: to leave the Amish faith

He healeth the broken hearted,
and bindeth up their wounds.

To Maria . . . *Danki.*

Chapter 1

*M*oriah Byler ran her fingers across the soft fabric of the dress hanging on her closet door. Its powder-blue hue, her favorite color, resembled a clear summer sky. Giddiness coursed through her. In three hours she would don this new dress, and before God and her church, she would become Mrs. Levi Miller.

Closing her eyes, she pictured her handsome husband-to-be, his sandy-brown hair falling across his forehead, his chestnut-colored eyes filled with mischief when he was up to something —which was often. She smiled broadly. Was he experiencing the same excitement she felt? Since he had proposed to her a few months ago, she had dreamed about this day, the day she would marry the man she loved, the man God had set apart especially for her. Memories of his proposal flashed through her mind. He had taken her by surprise that day in the barn, first by asking her to marry him, then by boldly kissing her.

Opening her eyes, she touched her cheeks, flushing at the memory. She had always thought she would experience her first kiss after she married. Then again, Levi had always been unpredictable. Although he had tried to kiss her again, she had stopped him.

Kissing led to other things—things that should occur after marriage, as their faith taught. She had seen the disappointment in his eyes, but he had agreed to her wishes. Since then he had also been on his best behavior.

She took one last look at the dress she and her mother had finished a week ago, then frowned. Was that a hole in the sleeve? She removed the dress from the hanger. Sure enough, a part of the shoulder seam had separated. She retrieved a needle and thread and quickly stitched it up. After knotting the thread, she snipped it close to the stitches with a small pair of scissors. *There. Now it's perfect.* The dress and her wedding day would be *fehlerfrei*.

Moriah hung up the dress and walked to her second-story window, peering into her family's backyard. She gave thanks for their two-acre spread, which included a large clapboard barn and storage shed, both painted in the same shade of white as the house. She spied her father and two of her younger brothers, Lukas and Stephen, bringing inside a long wooden table the family had borrowed several days ago. Behind them followed Gabriel, Levi's identical twin brother, carrying a couple of wooden chairs.

As she watched Gabriel, she recalled the close friendship the three of them had shared as children. Some of her favorite memories revolved around watching Levi and Gabriel try to outdo each other in everything. Gabriel always had the better grades and was physically stronger, as he had proved in third grade when he and Levi had taken turns to see who could lift her up. Gabriel had carried her across the yard as if she weighed no more than a kitten while Levi had carried her only a few feet. But Levi soon proved he could best Gabriel in games of speed and agility, and she smiled as she remembered his determination to climb trees faster and higher than anyone in their school.

She and Levi had begun courting at age sixteen, just after *Frau* Miller had passed away. Gabriel quickly distanced himself, as if they had never been friends at all. At first, she thought Gabriel was grieving the loss of his mother, but he continued to treat her coolly, more so with each passing year. She hoped that would change once she was a part of his family. She missed his friendship.

Moriah started to turn away when she heard a *plink*ing sound against the windowpane. Then another. She gazed at the ground to see Levi standing below. Sans hat and coat, he had on a long-sleeved, white shirt with black suspenders attached to his dark trousers. Oh, how handsome he looked! He was bending down to pick up another pebble when she shoved open the window. The chilly November air rushed into the warm bedroom.

"Levi! What are you doing?"

Levi's boyishly wicked smile spread across his face. "Looking at *mei braut.*"

She couldn't help but smile when he called her his bride. "You'll see enough of me at the wedding."

"I can't wait that long." The sunlight glinted off his hair.

Giggling, she said, "You'll have to. I shouldn't even be talking to you."

His shoulders slumped slightly. "Don't you wish we could just run away and get married? Forget all this"—he spread his arms out and gestured to the house and backyard—"and do something different?"

His words shocked the smile from her face. Run away? She knew Yankees sometimes eloped, but she would never consider getting married anywhere but among her family and friends, receiving the full blessing of the church and the Lord. "Levi, why would you even say something like that?"

"I was only kidding," he said, the tone of his voice dropping. Then he straightened his shoulders and grinned again, calming the twinge that had suddenly pinched her heart. He reached for a ladder that had been propped against the house. Her father and several other men from the church had finished reroofing the house last week, and the ladder had been in heavy use. Levi moved the ladder until it clattered against the house, right next to her window.

When he placed his foot on the bottom rung, her jaw dropped. "Levi, you can't come up here."

"Why not?" His hands gripped the side of the ladder and he took a step up. "I have every right to see my bride."

"But not this way." She put her hand to her head. She didn't even have her *kapp* on, nor was her hair brushed and pinned up. He couldn't see her like this, and he definitely couldn't be alone in her bedroom. He knew that. "Levi, if *Daed* sees you—"

He glanced up but kept climbing. "Everyone is inside, Moriah. Don't worry, he won't catch me."

Alarm rose within her. She couldn't be alone with Levi, especially not in her room while both their families were downstairs. Other than a few buggy rides together, they hadn't been by themselves since he had proposed to her, and she had been fine with that. They would spend plenty of time together once they were married. "Levi, *nee!*"

He climbed one more step, then stopped. He was halfway up the ladder now, and it would only take him a few more seconds to reach her bedroom. She froze, wondering what he would do. Meeting his gaze, she saw something in his eyes she had never seen before. Frustration? "You don't want to see me?" he asked, sounding hurt.

She shook her head. "Not right now."

After a fleeting hesitation, he gave her his trademark cocky smirk, and she thought he would respect her wishes. Instead, he continued to climb.

"Levi!" Gabriel's voice startled her. She stepped back from the window, far enough so she wouldn't be seen from the outside, but still within hearing distance of the two brothers.

"What are you doing?" Gabriel asked, his tone hard.

She listened as Levi shimmied back down the ladder, straining to hear his words. "Just having some fun, *bruder*."

"By sneaking into Moriah's bedroom?"

Although she couldn't see Gabriel, she could imagine him standing in front of Levi, his arms crossed, his facial expression set in stone as it often was when he and Levi argued.

"She's *mei braut*, Gabe. Lighten up."

"I'd think you'd have better things to do than goof around on your wedding day."

"That's right," Levi retorted. "*My* wedding day."

Moriah's brow furrowed. What did he mean by that? She leaned forward as much as she dared, but the men's voices grew faint. Peeking outside, she saw them heading toward the barn, still arguing with each other.

Moriah closed the window, wrapping her arms around her body. The cold air had pierced through her cotton nightgown, icing her fingers and toes. What had gotten into Levi? They would be married in such a short time, why would he risk getting both of them into trouble by doing something so reckless? Certainly he wouldn't entertain something that would put not only him, but also her, in the *bann*? While she often found his spontaneity attractive, he had unnerved her this time. Fortunately only Gabriel had spotted him. It would have been much worse if their parents had.

Taking a deep breath, she relaxed and started to dress, putting

Levi's antics out of her mind. He'd done no harm, and she some-how knew Gabriel wouldn't say anything to anyone. A tiny smile played on her lips. One thing she did know, life with Levi would never be boring.

She brushed out her waist-length, blonde hair and wrapped it tightly in a bun before fastening her white prayer *kapp* with two bobby pins. She would later cover the *kapp* with her black bonnet, which would conceal her hair completely. In three hours, the cer-emony would begin, and after slipping on her shoes, she went downstairs to the kitchen to help with the preparations.

The thick scent of stuffed roast chicken baking in the oven mingled with the tangy aroma of coleslaw and potato salad. As she entered the kitchen, she also caught a whiff of spicy cinnamon from the apple pies that had been set on the countertop to cool.

Argumentative voices reached her ears—the deep bass of one of her younger brothers, Tobias, mingled with the melodic yet irritated soprano of Rachel Detweiler, one of his former classmates from school and the daughter of one of her mother's dearest friends.

"You don't know what you're talking about," Rachel snapped. The two had turned the kitchen into a battle zone. The petite nineteen-year-old cast a glance toward Moriah, irritation splashed across her delicate features. "Tell your *dummkopf* brother to stay out of the kitchen. He keeps adding more spices to my cauliflower casserole. *Unnecessary* spices."

"That's because it tastes like wet cardboard smeared with moldy cheese." Tobias, who at five feet ten was a good six inches taller than Rachel, reached around her slim body and shook some salt on the steaming casserole.

"You're going to ruin it!" She swirled around until she faced him, then grappled at the salt shaker he held over her head.

"Too late for that." He put the shaker behind his back and taunted her with a mocking look.

Moriah watched the two of them with amusement. Tobias and Rachel had grown up together, just as Moriah had grown up with Levi and Gabriel. But unlike the easy friendship she'd had with the Miller brothers, Tobias and Rachel could barely abide each other's company. Though Moriah thought that lately it seemed her brother enjoyed teasing Rachel a little *too* much and that Rachel didn't seem as put out by him as she had in the past.

"Are you two at it again?" Emma Byler, Tobias and Moriah's mother, entered the kitchen. She readjusted her apron around her trim waist and scowled at Rachel and her son. "We still have much to do, and I can't have you two bickering the whole time. Behave yourselves."

Tobias set the salt shaker back on the table, a lock of dark blond hair slipping across his forehead. He looked appropriately contrite. "Sorry, *Mami.*"

Rachel apologized as well, but Moriah didn't miss the quick, triumphant look the girl shot at Tobias, as if she'd won their little spat.

"Tobias, you shouldn't be in here anyway," Emma added.

"That's what I said," Rachel muttered.

Emma walked over to her son. "I need you to see if we have enough chairs and tables for everyone. Also, help your *daed* and brothers in the barn. He's making sure there's enough hay and feed for the extra horses."

Tobias nodded and headed out the back door of the kitchen and toward the barn, without giving Rachel a second glance. Moriah thought she detected a slight frown on the young woman's face in response to being ignored, but she could have been imagining it.

Turning, Emma gave Moriah a look of surprise, as if she'd just noticed her standing nearby. "What are you doing down here?"

"Offering to help."

"*Nee*," clucked Emma. "Not on your wedding day. You've done enough this week already. We have everything under control, and there are plenty of people giving a hand. Rachel is finishing up her casserole, and her *mudder* will be here shortly. Now, you go upstairs and relax. You have a big day ahead."

For the first time since Levi had proposed, she felt anxiety seeping into her. Not about marrying Levi, but about the wedding itself. The focus would be on her and Levi, and she wasn't comfortable with that realization. She preferred to be involved, helping with preparations in the background. Somehow she had to keep busy, as she couldn't imagine pacing the floor of her room upstairs for the next couple of hours.

As if sensing her daughter's apprehension, Emma put an arm around Moriah's shoulders and spoke in a soft voice, "Go upstairs and read your *Biewel*. Pray for Levi, for your marriage, and for God to bless you and give you a family. I can think of nothing more worthwhile than spending time with the Lord before your wedding."

Moriah nodded, comforted by her mother's wise suggestion. "*Ya, Mami*. I will do that."

"*Gut*." Emma kissed her daughter on the temple. "I want this day to be *fehlerfrei* for you."

"It will be, *Mami*. I'm sure of it."

Emma playfully shooed Moriah from the room. "Now, *geh!*"

Just then Joseph, Moriah's father, walked into the door. He took off his hat and ran his hand through his dark-brown hair liberally streaked with silver. He placed his black hat back on his head and eyed Moriah with a slight smile. "What are you doing in here?"

"I already told her she wasn't needed," Emma said, moving to stand by her husband. She glanced up at him. "Have you enough chairs?"

"*Ya,*" Joseph said, looking down at his wife. He leaned down and whispered in her ear. Emma smiled and gave him a light-hearted pat on the arm. "*Geh!* I've enough work to do without you messing about in here."

Joseph chuckled and walked out the kitchen door.

Moriah grinned. For as long as she could remember, her parents had been like that—playful, in perfect partnership, and totally in love. If her marriage was half as wonderful as theirs, she would be a blessed woman indeed. Her thoughts filled with Levi and the love they shared, she turned to go back upstairs, but not before she caught Rachel discreetly adding a dash more salt to her casserole.

Gabriel Miller tugged on the neck of his collarless shirt; the growing warmth of the crowded house grated on him. He could bear the heat if he weren't watching his twin brother, Levi, standing only a few feet away, speak his wedding vows to Moriah Byler. Gabe tried to keep his focus on his brother, but he had never seen Moriah look as lovely as she did today. Her simple sky-blue dress accentuated her round, blue eyes that, as she looked at Levi, shone with evident happiness. She was a beautiful bride. But she wasn't his.

Guilt stabbed at him. Once again, he was coveting his brother's woman, and he didn't know how to stop. When Levi and Moriah had started courting, he fought against his attraction to Moriah, begging God to take it away, to make his heart pure. He'd hoped when he joined the church last fall, months before Levi, he could relinquish his sin forever. Yet since then, his feelings hadn't ebbed. Instead, they had only grown stronger.

It was torture, witnessing Levi marry Moriah. He should be happy for his brother. He *wanted* to be happy for his brother. But his intense jealousy clouded any other emotions. Why Levi and not him? Did Levi know what a precious woman she truly was? Gabriel wondered if he did, especially after catching him trying to sneak into her bedroom right before the wedding, an act that showed a lack of respect not only for her but for her family. What had his brother been thinking? But Gabriel knew the answer to that. As usual, Levi hadn't been thinking at all. Just doing whatever he wanted, never mind the consequences to anyone else. Gabe was only two minutes younger than his twin, but many days he felt years older.

His gaze strayed to Moriah again, and another surge of emotions swelled within him. It wasn't just her outer beauty that drew him. Moriah Byler possessed a humble, gentle spirit and an unmatched generosity that plucked at the strings of Gabe's heart. How many times over the years had he witnessed her offer to help an overwhelmed mother with her children, or go out of her way to care for an elderly member of their church? He couldn't bear to see her hurt in any way. All he wanted was her happiness, and if she found that with his brother, then he would have to learn to accept it.

Levi uttered more words, promising to care for her, to be a loving spouse. The same thing all Amish husbands pledge to do. Gabriel shifted in his chair and tugged at the neck of his shirt again. When would the ceremony *end*?

Finally, after three and a half hours had passed, Abel Esh, the gray-haired bishop, gave the couple his blessing. His beard, nearly down to the center of his chest, bobbed up and down as he spoke. Gabe glanced at Levi and Moriah's hands, their fingers intertwined.

As soon as the wedding ended, he shot out of the house into the cold winter air. He breathed in deeply, the crispness prickling his lungs. A pretty good snow had fallen a few days ago, the second in the month of November, but most of it had melted, leaving small piles of white slush and bigger pools of muddy water behind. The bright glare from the overhead sun added to his agony, its light betraying him as it seemed to bestow approval on Levi and Moriah's union.

He stuffed his icy hands deep into the pockets of his black trousers. He'd left his overcoat in Tobias's room, upstairs in the Byler's huge farmhouse, but Gabe wasn't ready to go back inside. Wearing only his thin dress shirt and a black vest, he figured he deserved to shiver in the cold for his sinful thoughts about his brother's wife.

Inside, the women and young boys were readying the front room for the wedding supper. He usually loved the food: the stuffing, creamed celery, fried and baked chicken, rolls, and probably twenty different types of casseroles and pies. Everyone in the community brought a dish to share among the almost two hundred guests in attendance. Even his father, who had become an excellent cook since their mother had passed away four years ago, had brought German potato salad, the twins' favorite. But Gabe doubted he could eat a bite.

A few more men braved the chill and came outside, but they had the good sense to wear their coats. Tobias and a few of his friends held baseball gloves and started a game of ball in the sprawling front yard. Rachel Detweiler appeared, dressed in her Sunday best—a dark, plum-colored dress with a black cape for an overcoat, complete with a stiff, white prayer *kapp*. She was a little thing, but not afraid of the boys, or of the muddy ground serving as their ball field. Slipping her hand in her own well-worn mitt, she intercepted a ball intended for Tobias, then whipped it back to Christian Weaver, who caught it cleanly, taking a step back due to the force of the throw.

"Go inside, Rachel," Tobias yelled at her, clearly annoyed that she had horned in on their game. "You should be in there helping the women get dinner ready."

"Go soak your head, Byler." Rachel looked up at him, one hand on her slender hip while the other slapped her mitt against the side of her thigh. "They've got plenty of help. If I wanna play ball, I'm gonna play ball. I don't care what you say."

Tobias looked at the other guys as if searching for backup, then shrugged his shoulders in defeat. Score one for Rachel Detweiler.

Gabe's lips twitched in an almost smile. Rachel was close to marrying age. It would take a strong fellow to deal with such a spitfire. He briefly questioned if there was a man in Middlefield who would be up to the challenge.

"They're serving the food." John Miller, Gabe's father, sidled up to his son. He put his huge hand on Gabe's shoulder. "You should go inside and eat."

Staring down at the smooth stones of the sidewalk, Gabe replied, "You go ahead. I'll wait until the next shift."

"Your brother is expecting you. Wouldn't be right not to be one of the first people to congratulate him."

Gabe turned and looked into his father's brown eyes, eyes that were similar to his and Levi's, except there were deep crinkles at the corners, new crevices he hadn't noticed before. Although a widower of four years, his father kept his marriage beard, which had reached to the front button of his shirt, with only a few strands of brown nestled within the gray. He had vowed never to remarry; his love for Velda remained as strong as it had been before she had passed away from cancer. Eternal, as he referred to it. They had been together over forty years, having the twins late in life. Their "miracle children," Gabe's mother had often called them. Their family had been an anomaly, a small one in the midst of many large ones.

Taking in the disapproval glinting in his father's eyes, Gabe relented. "I'll be in shortly."

"See that you are, *sohn.*" White puffs emitted from John's mouth as he said the words. He squeezed Gabe's shoulder once more, then turned away, his shoulders stooped from years of hard labor at the blacksmith's anvil.

Steeling himself, Gabe followed his father's footsteps into the house. He could handle this. He was skilled at masking his emotions about Moriah. He'd been doing it for so long. No one knew of his secret love for her.

Only God knew what was festering inside him. He aimed to keep it that way.

Moriah's face ached from smiling so much, but she wouldn't complain. After almost a half an hour accepting congratulations and receiving hugs and good wishes, she felt happiness beyond her expectations.

"Moriah!" A short, stocky young woman walked up to her. She

enveloped Moriah in a tight hug. When the woman released her, she smiled. "You don't remember me, do you?"

Tilting her head to the side, Moriah searched her memory, frowning. She couldn't recall ever seeing her before. "*Nee*, I'm sorry, I do not."

The young woman laughed, her cheeks plump and ruddy, her hazel eyes filled with merriment. "I'm not surprised, since we haven't been together since we were very young. I'm Katharine. Katharine Yoder."

Moriah's eyes widened. "*Mei* cousin!" She hugged her again. "I can't believe you're here! *Mami* said you wouldn't make it."

"And my *mudder* said she wouldn't miss her niece's wedding for the world."

"How was your trip from Paradise?"

"Long, but *gut*. We arrived yesterday. I haven't been out of Lancaster County since I was a small child, and I'm surprised at how different things are here compared to back home. You don't have as many tourists hanging about, and your buggies are a different color and shape." She reached up and touched her *kapp*. "Even your *kapps* are a slightly different style then what we wear." Katharine laid her hand on Moriah's arm and laughed. "But it is all still lovely. You are a beautiful bride, Moriah."

Moriah blushed at the compliment. While beauty was vanity, she did appreciate her cousin's kind words. They had been pen pals for almost fifteen years, since Katharine and her family had moved to Lancaster when the girls were both five years old. It warmed her heart to see her after all this time. "*Danki*, Katharine. Still, though there are some differences, we are all Amish, *ya*?"

"*Ya*. And family too." She took Moriah's hand and gave it a squeeze. "I'm so happy for you."

Katharine slipped away to visit with other family members, and Moriah spotted Levi a few steps away. Her new husband was in his element greeting the wedding guests. Filled to the brim with charm, he loved talking with people, and they seemed to gravitate toward him.

"*Danki*," he said to his uncle Eli, who had just given them his blessing. Levi clapped the man on the back. "Me and Moriah appreciate you coming."

"Wouldn't have missed it. We always knew you two'd get hitched someday." He shook his head. "Makes a man feel old, it sure does, all these young folks getting married."

"*Ach*, age is just a number," Levi said. "You're fit as a fiddle, that's all that counts."

Eli grinned. "S'pose so." He looked at Moriah. "You take care of this boy, you hear? Needs a good woman to keep him in his place, dontcha know."

With a grin, Moriah said, "*Ya*. That I know."

Levi placed his palm at the small of her back. "I think I'm in good hands, Eli."

The warmth from his hand seeped through the fabric of her dress, causing a frisson of delight to course through her. She loved this man so much, more than she ever thought possible. Although her faith believed in eschewing pride for humility, she was proud to be his wife. She was Mrs. Levi Miller, from now until forever.

Suddenly the sound of a man clearing his throat reached her ears. She turned away from her husband to see his twin, Gabriel, standing before them. Eli must have discreetly disappeared, for there was no sign of him nearby.

"Congratulations, *bruder*." Gabe extended his hand to Levi, who grasped it immediately and shook it with enthusiasm.

"Thanks, Gabe." Levi gently pushed Moriah forward. "Why don't you welcome your *schwei* into the family, your new sister-in-law?"

Moriah faced Gabe, the mirror image of her husband. His black hat was pulled low on his head, covering much of his sandy brown hair. Like Levi, he had broad shoulders and a barrel-like chest that tapered to a narrow waist. His cheeks were smooth, indicative of a single man. When their gaze met, she thought she saw something flicker in his brown eyes, eyes that were so similar to Levi's. Regret? She wasn't sure.

Yet while Levi always had a playful spark in his eyes, Gabriel's reflected his somber demeanor. He kept his feelings wrapped up tight, which made the brief dash of emotion in his expression even more puzzling. But as quickly as it had appeared, it left, and his stoic mask returned, firmly in place.

"*Daed* and I are looking forward to you and Levi visiting us soon."

"It won't be long before we will," she said. "Saturday for sure. We'll be staying with my parents until then."

Gabe nodded, then glanced away. "Saturday it is."

"Is that the best you can do?" Levi shook his head, grinning. "Give her a hug, Gabe. She's family now."

Gabriel hesitated, but finally he extended his arms to her and gave her a slight embrace. "*Willkum*," he said, then quickly released her, as if her touch burned him. He turned on his heel and made his way to a table with an empty seat next to his father.

Moriah tried to hide a frown. Why was he so reluctant to be near her? "Something wrong with Gabriel?" she asked.

Levi smirked, then gave her a knowing look. "No, nothing's wrong with him. Gabe's just being Gabe."

"I suppose." She cast Gabriel another glance, but he was involved in a conversation with a young woman who had sat down next to him. As far as Moriah knew, Gabriel hadn't actively courted anyone, and she always wondered about that, since there were many available, and interested, young women in their community. Maybe that one had piqued his interest.

"You know how my brother is," Levi continued. "Hard to figure out what's going on in that head of his. Heck, I'm his twin and half the time I don't know what he's thinking." He leaned in close, his breath warm in her ear. "I can promise you this— he's just fine with you joining the family. Everyone is, can't you tell?"

Levi was right. The last person to object to Moriah would be Gabriel. He had plenty of time to get used to the idea of his brother's marriage, since he'd been the first person they told they were getting married. He'd found out by accident, walking in on them when they were in the Miller's barn minutes after Levi had proposed. If Gabriel thought their union a bad idea, he'd had more than enough time to speak up.

But why was she concerned about what Gabe thought in the first place? She didn't need his permission or approval to marry his brother. Still, she wished their relationship could have been the way it was when they were younger. While Gabriel was more reserved and pensive than Levi, he could be just as charming and witty as his brother when he wanted to.

Levi glanced around the room. "Looks like everyone's happy," he said in a satisfied tone.

She looked up at him, forgetting about Gabriel. "Are you happy, Levi?" A tiny knot of apprehension formed inside her belly. All she wanted was his happiness.

He gave her a wink. "Of course I am. I'm married to you, aren't I?"

Moriah let out a relaxing breath. A tiny flutter swirled around in her belly as she gave him a loving smile. She was the luckiest woman in the world.

Turning her attention back to her guests, she saw them digging into their meals. Her stomach growled as the smell of the wedding dinner filtered through the air. When *Mami* brought out another huge basket of yeasty rolls, steaming hot from the oven, she couldn't resist any longer. "I'm starving," she whispered to Levi.

"You and me both. Let's eat."

With Levi taking the lead, Moriah followed him to one of the head tables, where her younger sister Elisabeth brought them two heaping plates and two large glasses of lemonade. Elisabeth leaned forward and whispered in Moriah's ear.

"Tomorrow morning, I want details." She wiggled her eyebrows.

Heat crept up Moriah's face. "Details?" she said, feigning ignorance. She loved her romance-crazed sister, but she could be nosy—and inappropriate—at times.

"You know what I mean." Moving back, Elisabeth winked at her sister, then handed a glass of lemonade to the next guest at the table.

"What did Elisabeth say?" Levi asked.

"Nothing." She hoped her husband didn't notice her blushing. Her sister might want "details," but she wouldn't get them. Moriah wasn't about to discuss her wedding night with Elisabeth. Five years separated them, but despite the age gap, they had shared nearly everything with each other. However, her wedding night with Levi was private, and it would stay that way.

The calm she'd experienced moments before evaporated, replaced by a new worry that tapped on her nerves. Would she disappoint him? She couldn't bear the thought of that.

Beside her, Levi talked with guests, grinning and laughing, unaware of the sudden turmoil churning inside her. Moriah stared at her food, her appetite gone.

Suddenly she felt Levi reach for her hand under the table and give it a squeeze, as if he had sensed the chaos in her mind. She tilted her head toward him and smiled. He grinned in return.

A semblance of peace washed over her, and for that she was grateful. With the smallest of gestures, Levi had calmed her down. She was thankful to the Almighty for Levi's love. He would be a fine husband and father. She knew of a couple of women in the community whose husbands treated them badly, and she pitied them. But with Levi, she wouldn't have that worry. He was kind, trustworthy, and loyal. They would be there for each other, through the good times and the bad.

Chapter 2

*T*obias Byler could pinpoint the precise moment he had noticed Rachel Detweiler had become a woman. Last year, at a Sunday night singing in late May. She had just turned nineteen. Before that night he had thought of her as the biggest thorn in his side, a bratty, boyish-looking girl who acted way too big for her britches. Fiercely competitive, she often nagged him into sporting contests—usually fishing, volleyball, or softball. Lately she'd also become an expert corntoss player, tossing the corn bag easily into the hole of the wooden platform. He hated that she won their matches on a regular basis, and she never missed an opportunity to rub it in his face.

But that night six months ago, when he saw her at the singing, his attitude had changed. She was still a pest, but now he thought her a beautiful one. The plain, light-green dress she had worn that night, one that left everything to the imagination, accented her womanly figure. Until then he had never noticed how smooth her cheeks were, or how her bright blue eyes were framed by long, silky, light-brown lashes. He'd also never noticed how sweet her smile was, but that was probably due to her genuinely smiling at everyone but him. Usually he received a smirk or a haughty frown. Yet that spring night at the Yoder's, he would have done anything to have her grin at him the same way she had smiled at Christian Weaver.

Of course she didn't, and Christian had taken her home in his buggy after the singing. The two of them had never become an item, though. That had surprised everyone, including Tobias. Probably Christian too, even though he'd never said anything about it. Since then Rachel had allowed nearly every young man in the community to take her home after social events, save for him. Ordinarily this would have given her a loose reputation, except all the fellows knew Rachel wasn't interested in them like that. She was their pal, friendly to everyone, with one exception: him.

Of course, just because he thought Rachel was pretty didn't mean he liked her. How could he like a girl who kept showing him up in front of his friends? He had no choice but to put up with it. His father had always taught him to be a gentleman, to respect women and to treat them well. Not all the men in the community did that, but Tobias honored his father's wise edict. He hoped to emulate his parents' wonderful marriage.

But not—*definitely* not—with Rachel Detweiler. For some reason being friends with Rachel, much less having any other kind of relationship, was like searching for a rainbow in the middle of a thunderstorm. While wearing a blindfold. In other words, *impossible.*

Right now he was annoyed with her for joining their game. She had taken off her cloak, clearly warmed from the combination of the strong sunlight and the exertion of playing during his sister's wedding dinner. He and his friends had discarded their black overcoats as well, and Christian had already rolled up his sleeves. At least they were on opposite teams.

He picked up his old wooden bat, one his father had made

many years ago. Despite the nicks and chips accumulated from years of use, it still had a nice sweet spot. The handle had been worn down so that it matched his grip perfectly. He'd hit many a home run with this simple stick of wood, and he intended to take another trip around the makeshift bases today.

Stepping up to the flat rock that served as home plate, he stared her down. Rachel was rolling the grimy ball around in her right hand, not caring that her palm had turned black from the sticky mud or that her dress was smudged with it. He'd never admit it out loud, but she was a good pitcher too, which made him hot under the collar. No way would he let her strike him out. Not again.

"You don't scare me," she said, giving him a cool glare. "You couldn't hit the broad side of a barn."

Considering they'd moved their game from the Byler's front yard to the field behind the house, where the barn was in plain view, he now had the prime opportunity to make her eat her words. But before he could get set up in the batter's box, a fastball whizzed past him.

"Strike!"

Tobias glared at his younger brother Stephen, questioning the wisdom of having a thirteen-year-old referee their game. However, since Stephen was a stickler for rules, he had been everyone's unanimous choice for umpire.

"I wasn't ready," Tobias groused.

"You're in the box, you're ready." Always serious, Stephen pulled his black hat low over his brow and bent at the waist behind the home plate rock. "Play ball."

Tobias adjusted his grip on the bat. This time he wouldn't miss. He swung at the next pitch.

"Stee-rike two!"

Rachel smirked.

Ach, he hated when she did that. But he was just warming up. Now he would hit the broad side of *his* barn, and he couldn't wait to rub it in *her* face for once. When the third pitch flew by, he connected with a crack of the bat.

But instead of hitting the whitewashed wood structure a hundred yards away, the ball plowed right into Rachel's shin. Tobias watched in horror as she crumpled into a heap on the grassy ground, clutching her leg, her forehead touching the top of her knee.

"What'd you do that for?" Stephen hollered.

Tobias ignored him and threw down the bat. He sprinted toward Rachel, reaching her before anyone else. He knelt down beside her. "Are you all *recht*?"

She looked up at him with watery eyes, her teeth biting down on her plump bottom lip. He noticed her cheeks were rosy from the cold and exertion, and now probably from the intense pain. Without giving him answer, she folded herself into a tight ball and put her head down.

Tobias felt as if he'd taken a boot in the gut. He looked up at his friends—Christian, David Yoder, Isaac Stutzer, and his two younger brothers, Lukas and Stephen. Their expressions were filled with concern and . . . blame. More blame than concern, truth be told.

"I didn't do it on purpose," Tobias exclaimed.

"No one said you did." Christian hunkered down and put his arm around Rachel's small shoulders in a friendly, but somewhat intimate, gesture. "Rachel, can you stand?"

When she lifted her head, Tobias felt like he had been knocked in the stomach again. Tears streamed down her cheeks, but she didn't utter a sound, only nodded in response to Christian's question. She was trying to be tough; everyone could tell that. With Christian's help, she rose to her feet, gingerly putting pressure on her injured leg.

Tobias went to her other side and offered to prop her up. "Let me help you in the house."

"You've done enough." Her voice sounded hoarse. And angry. He caught the black expression on her face. Surely she didn't think he meant to hit her? He'd never stoop so low.

Christian intervened, pulling her closer to him. "Tobias, go tell your *mudder* we need a cold cloth. Lukas, let's get her to the kitchen. Mrs. Detweiler can take a look at her leg there."

Scrambling back to the house, Tobias burst through the back door, nearly running over a woman who was picking up a big pot from the top of the stove. "Where's *Mami*?"

"Land sakes, boy, watch what you're doing." Ida Yoder tightened her grip on the cast-iron pot. "She's busy in the front room, taking care of the guests. What do you need?"

"A cold cloth," he mumbled.

"Then get it yourself." Ida huffed and carried the stuffing out of the kitchen. "There's a cooler of ice in the barn."

Tobias ran back outside, passing by Christian, David, and Rachel, who were slowly making their way to the house. He dashed into the barn and found the cooler. He pulled his handkerchief out of the pocket of his good trousers, thankful it was clean. Laying it over his hand, he filled it with cold cubes before folding it into a pouch. He sped back to the kitchen, arriving just as Christian eased Rachel down on one of the chairs.

"*Mami's* busy," Tobias explained, holding the freezing handkerchief in his hand, but he barely felt it as he focused his attention on Rachel. "All of the women are."

Rachel leaned back in the chair, her eyes screwed shut. "Just give me the ice," she groaned through gritted teeth.

Silently Tobias handed her the cloth. She bent over and lifted up her mud-spotted dress, resting the hem above her knee. His mouth went dry as he scanned her shapely leg, a sight he rarely witnessed. All Amish women wore their dresses to at least shin length, if not longer. He found himself staring at the view, until he spotted her injury. Despite her dark stockings, he could see the hard bump swelling on her shin. No wonder she was in such pain. He sucked in his breath through his teeth. "Rachel . . . I'm sorry."

"Don't talk to me!" Strands of her wispy blonde hair had escaped from her prayer *kapp*, lying against her cheek near her eyes. Before he could stop himself, he touched one of the feather-soft locks. Quickly she jerked her head up, gaping at him as if he'd lost his mind. He glanced around and saw his friends staring at him with the same shocked expression.

Snatching his hand back, Tobias cleared his throat. "Think I'll see if I can find your *mudder*." His voice cracked on the last word, and he ran out of the kitchen as if his pants were on fire.

Stupid, stupid. What had he been thinking, touching her like that? In front of his friends? Wouldn't be long before word got out that Tobias Byler not only slammed a baseball into Rachel Detweiler, but he's sweet on her too.

Threading his way through the mass of people in the front room, he caught sight of his sister, Moriah, and her husband, Levi. They'd finished their meal and were now visiting with friends. Although she'd seemed nervous before the ceremony, now she wore a smile. At least someone was happy today. He'd never been so embarrassed in his life.

Blades of searing heat shot through Rachel's shin, making her stomach churn. She gritted her teeth, refusing to let anyone, especially Tobias and the other boys, see her in pain. The ice did little to relieve the burning sensation. Tobias had said he would look for her *mudder*, but she wondered if he would keep his word. By the way he'd scuttled out of the room, she suspected his promise was just an excuse to leave the kitchen . . . and her.

Whatever. She was glad he was gone.

Christian knelt in front of her, concern etched on his lightly freckled, boyish face. Kind, considerate Christian. Tall, with dark brown hair and a five o'clock shadow that never seemed to go away. He'd always been like a big brother to her, convincing the other boys to let her play with them, never bothered when she beat him in a race or threw a better fastball.

Unlike Tobias, who took everything she did as a personal slight.

Christian fixed his gaze on her. "I should see what's taking Tobias so long. You gonna be all right?"

Rachel nodded, even though her shin continued to throb. The other guys had already abandoned her now that the excitement was over, saying something about apple pie as they'd left the kitchen. But Christian had stayed. "I'm fine. Don't worry about me," she said. "I'll survive."

He chucked her under the chin with a light tap of his fist. "I never do. You're the toughest person I know—male or female." Rising to his full height of six feet, he gave her a sweet smile, then left.

Moving her leg, Rachel gulped at the pulsating pain radiating from the lump. She gingerly touched the skin and felt warmth seep through her black tights. Tobias had hit her hard. If she'd been paying better attention, she would have jumped over it, and he probably would have had at least a triple, considering his speed. But she'd been so focused on striking him out, she hadn't thought about him actually hitting the ball.

She'd never admit it to anyone, but she considered him the most talented athlete in the settlement. And although she'd spent a good portion of their childhood defeating him in most of their games, he'd matured physically in the last year, and she doubted she could keep up with him much longer.

But Tobias Byler acted like he was oblivious to everything, so maybe he wouldn't notice that he could beat her. After all, either he didn't notice or he ignored the attention of several of the girls in the community.

She was sure his blasé attitude was insincere. There was no way he couldn't be aware of the female attention he received at the singings and frolics this past year. She'd heard the girls giggling over him time and time again, swooning about his mischievous blue eyes and crooked smile.

Sure, she might admit he was nice looking. But how could he not be, blessed with that mass of dark-golden hair that couldn't be restrained even under a hat. His forearms were finely muscled from hours and hours spent in his father's woodworking shop, sanding and carving rough cut wood into elegant pieces of furniture . . . Her cheeks suddenly heated, and a funny tickle started in her stomach. Probably a reaction from the injury. A part of her believed Tobias hit her on purpose; she knew he disliked her that much. True, she brought it on herself most of the time, but he was so infuriating, with his cocky attitude that he seemed to save mainly for her. Someone had to put him in his place. This time, however, she should have kept her mouth shut.

A lock of her hair dangled in her face again, and she remembered Tobias brushing it back. Why had he done that? That was the type of gesture a man made to a woman he was smitten with, or even a woman he loved. Didn't make sense, because he practically hated her. But he smoothed her hair nevertheless. He was a boy—no, a man, she had to at least admit that—filled with contradictions. If she lived to be a hundred years old, she'd never understand him.

Christian returned with her mother in tow. He had already explained to her what had happened during the game. After taking one glance at her leg, Sarah Detweiler told her daughter to go home.

"I'm fine, *Mudder*, really. I can stay."

"*Nee*, you need to put your leg up. That will help the swelling go down. Christian, would you mind taking her?"

"Not at all," he replied.

"But—"

"Don't argue with me." Sarah gave her a stern look, one Rachel had seen a million times before. "Aaron's home, he can keep an eye on you."

"More like I'll keep an eye on him."

"What was that?"

"Nothing." Rachel didn't want to get into an argument with her mother, especially in front of Christian, and particularly not about her brother, who was in the throes of his *rumspringa*, running around and giving the family fits. "I'll go."

"I'll get my coat and bring the buggy around," he said.

Sarah nodded her approval. "*Danki*, Christian."

When he left, Rachel looked at her mother, not missing the exasperated glint in her eyes. She steeled herself for her next comment, which was sure to come.

"Rachel, your dress." Sarah sighed as she scanned her daughter's attire. "We'll never get the stains out of it."

"I'm sorry, *Mudder*."

"There was no reason for you to be outside with the boys, Rachel. Not when there is so much work to be done in here."

Glancing away for a moment, Rachel said, "I asked several women if they had anything for me to do. They said no. So I went outside."

Her mother leaned over slightly, her lips drifting into a frown. "We've had this discussion before. You are no longer a child, Rachel. You need to think about your future, about your responsibilities as a woman and soon, Lord willing, as a wife. No man is interested in a tomboy."

Rachel fought the urge to roll her eyes. Her mother had been saying such things since Rachel had turned thirteen, and they disagreed about it frequently. But she kept her annoyance at bay, trying to show her mother respect. *"Ya, Mudder."*

Apparently satisfied she'd gotten her point across, Sarah switched topics, softening her voice a tad. "Such a nice young man, that Christian."

"He's very nice."

"Didn't he bring you home from a singing one time?"

Surprised her mother remembered that, Rachel replied, "He did."

"I've always thought you two would make a good match." Sarah raised a light-brown brow. "But I only saw him that one time. Why hasn't he come around more often?"

Rachel leaned back against the chair and shrugged. "I don't really like him that way."

"But why don't you? He would make a good husband. He is kind and smart. Most of all, he is already a member of the church."

Rachel started to speak, but thought better of it. Her mother would never understand. She liked Christian, but when it came to romantic notions about him, she felt nothing. Weren't you supposed to at least feel *something* for the man who courted you?

But maybe she was looking at relationships from the wrong angle. Truly, there was nothing wrong with Christian. Nice looking, a complete gentleman, and as her mother had already pointed out, a member of the church, as she was. When she viewed him objectively, she saw a good Amish man, strong in his faith and devoted to his family.

Sarah took the damp, cold handkerchief—Tobias's handkerchief, Rachel couldn't help but notice—out of her daughter's hands. She crossed the kitchen and shook out the partially melted ice cubes into the large metal sink. "All right, then. If you don't like Christian, then I'm sure there are several other young men who could spark your interest. What about Tobias?"

Rachel scrunched her nose. "*Nee. Nee, nee, nee.* You see what he did to me."

"That was an accident," Sarah said, glancing over her shoulder.

"Maybe."

"I'm sure he feels terrible about it." Sarah turned around and folded the handkerchief into a small, neat square, then laid it next to the sink.

"That's the problem, *Mudder*. I don't think Tobias feels anything. About anything. He just floats through life, without a care in the world, thinking all he needs is his charm and good looks."

"Oh, so you think he's charming?" her mother said teasingly.

"I didn't say that." She swiveled in her chair so she could face her mother directly. "I never said he was charming."

"But you have to admit he's good-looking."

"I'm not admitting anything!" Now it was Rachel's turn to be exasperated. She turned back around, the pain in her leg growing more intense. She heard the soft ruffle of her mother's skirt as she neared.

Sarah put her hand on Rachel's shoulder. "There's no reason to get upset about this. I keep forgetting you don't like to be teased. Much like your *bruder*, Aaron."

"I am nothing like Aaron."

"*Ach*, I think you are more alike than either of you are willing to admit." She walked around Rachel's chair until she stood in front of her. She touched her cheek. "Just know that your *daed* and I love you. You are our only *dochder*, and we want what's best for you."

"Which is to get married."

Her mother smiled, her grayish eyes twinkling. "*Ya*, Rachel. You are of age now to at least be thinking about your future, which should include a husband."

Rachel expelled a heavy breath. She had no argument, because her mother was right. Deep down, she wanted to get married and have a family. Not necessarily right away, but eventually. At the moment she was happy and successful enough in her job as a waitress at Mary Yoder's Amish Kitchen. There really wasn't any urgency to find a suitable mate, even though her mother obviously felt otherwise.

The kitchen door slammed shut. Both women turned to see Christian walk into the room. "Ready?" he asked, looking at Rachel.

She hadn't expected him back so soon. He must have hitched up his buggy in record time.

"I can carry you, if you want," he added, looking directly at her.

Rachel couldn't believe he'd asked her that, especially in front of her mother, who would eagerly blow any hint of prospective romance for her daughter into epic proportions. But then she caught the teasing spark in his eyes, and she relaxed. "*Nee,* I can manage to walk to the buggy, thank you very much."

Sarah helped Rachel to her feet. "Your *daed* will be home soon to check on you. I will stay late and help Emma with the cleanup, but tell Aaron I'll bring him a plate home for supper." She gave Christian one of her trademark sweet smiles. "I know I'm leaving you in *gut* hands."

Rachel's cheeks burned. Could she be more obvious?

Fortunately Christian hadn't caught her meaning, or if he had, he graciously chose not to say anything. As her mother opened the door to the front room of the house, Rachel heard voices intermingling, then muffling when the door closed again.

Rachel fought the urge to breathe out a sigh of relief. She loved her mother, but that didn't mean she wasn't occasionally embarrassed by her. Taking a step forward, she winced as pain shot up her leg.

"Here, let me help you." Christian came up beside her and wrapped his arm around her waist.

She leaned against him only slightly, not wanting to appear as pitiful as she felt. He helped her into the buggy, placed a heavy quilt on her lap to keep her warm, then jumped in beside her. Within moments they were heading for her house a few miles down the road.

Several cars whizzed by as their buggy slowly made its way down the asphalt street. It shook as each vehicle zipped alongside them. Christian's horse, with its blinders on, remained unfazed, used to dealing with traffic. Rachel wrapped her black cloak more tightly around her, warding off the chilly, late afternoon air. A few clouds had appeared in the sky, with one large fluffy one blocking the sun, taking away its soothing warmth.

"You're awful quiet," Christian said suddenly, breaking the silence that had been between them since they'd left the Bylers. "Something bothering you?"

"*Nee*, not really." Not anything she wanted to talk about anyway. "My leg hurts, that's all. I do appreciate you taking me home."

"Don't mind at all." He pulled up on the reins a bit, slowing down his horse. "Gives me time to ask you something."

Turning her head, she looked at him, her curiosity piqued. "What?"

"I wondered if you'd mind me courting you."

Rachel's jaw dropped. "Did *Mudder* say something to you?" she blurted out, then wished she could take it back. Christian had been nowhere near the kitchen when she and her mother had their conversation.

He glanced at her, confused. "No, she didn't say a word to me. Should she have?"

"*Nee*," she said, slinking down in the seat.

Christian cast her a sideways glance. "*Gut*. Because I really don't want to talk about your *mudder* now. I want to talk about us. Or the possibility of there being an *us*."

One thing she could say about Christian is that he was to the point. He deserved her directness in return. "I'm surprised, Christian. This seems rather sudden."

341

"I guess it does in a way. But I thought I made it pretty clear last May that I liked you."

"I like you too." It wasn't a lie, she really did like him. She just wasn't sure she *liked* him.

"That's good to hear." He grinned at her, taking his eyes off the road for only a few seconds.

"As a friend," she quickly added, worried she'd inadvertently given him the wrong message.

His smile diminished somewhat. But he remained undeterred. "I understand that. But I think our friendship could grow into something else. Especially if we spent more time together." He gazed her again, his eyes latching onto hers. "Alone."

Suddenly the painful lump in her leg had become the least of her problems. Christian was serious, and from the determined look on his face, it didn't appear he'd give up easily. Uncertainty filled her. "Christian . . . I don't know . . ."

"Why won't you give us a chance, Rachel? We've known each other a long time. Our families are good friends. You're not seeing anyone else, and neither am I."

They were at the top of a gently sloping hill. The trees lining both sides of the road had shed their dead leaves, the naked, spindly branches pointing skyward. They passed by a white Amish house with the black buggy parked beneath a pristine carport, flanked by two fancy brick Yankee homes. Rachel spied her house in the near distance. Christian looked toward it and slowed his horse up even more. "Is it because you like Tobias?" he asked.

"What?" Rachel let out a strained laugh. "How could you even think such a thing? Tobias Byler is the last man I'd be interested in."

"Just checking. I thought maybe you two had something

private going on, especially after he touched your hair back there in the kitchen."

"I have no idea why he did that," she said, her face heating from the memory. She looked straight ahead, hoping Christian was doing the same so he wouldn't see the flush blooming on her cheeks. "Probably because he's *seltsam*."

Christian chuckled. "Okay, you proved your point, especially if you think he's weird. Tobias is definitely out of the picture." Then he sobered quickly. "Look, all I'm asking is that you give us a chance. If it doesn't work out, then no harm done. We both move on, and we'll stay friends."

She averted her gaze and looked at the countryside. The jagged tops of cut, dried cornstalks jutted out from a nearby field, presenting a raw and desolate landscape. Maybe she wasn't being fair. Maybe there had never been any sparks between her and Christian because she hadn't been open to the possibility. Maybe he and her mother had been right all along. Still, she wasn't completely sure.

Despite his efforts to prolong their ride, they arrived at her driveway. He turned onto a narrow dirt road and drove straight back to her house. He halted his horse, jumped out of his seat, and met her on the other side. Holding out his hand, he helped her out of the buggy, offering to assist her inside.

"I think I can manage," she said, limping toward her front door. "It doesn't hurt as much anymore."

"*Gut.* Glad to hear it." He paused for a moment, then reached down and lightly cupped her shoulders with his hands. "Promise me you'll think about what I said, Rachel."

She could feel the warmth from his palms through her cloak. Lifting her face, she gazed up at him. His black, wide-brimmed hat sat low on his head, nearly covering his eyes and shading the rest of his face. But she could still see his beseeching expression, and hear the pleading in his voice.

"I promise," she heard herself say softly.

His face split into a wide grin. "*Gut. Sehr gut.* You've made me one happy man."

Unable to resist his joy, she smiled back. Perhaps there was a chance for them after all.

Chapter 3

The movement beside her woke Moriah out of her light sleep. Her eyes opened and tried to adjust to the darkness as she sensed her husband getting up from their bed.

"Levi?" She heard the scratchiness of her voice as she sat up.

"Shh."

She couldn't see him in the engulfing blackness of the room. In the four months since their wedding she was still getting used to living in a different house, especially sharing a room with Levi. Leaning on her side, she picked up a small battery-operated flashlight and flicked it on. A chill cloaked the room, a byproduct of the typically cold February weather. Scanning the room, she spotted Levi by the closet, taking out one of his blue shirts. "What time is it?" she asked

"Time for you to go back to sleep." He slipped on the shirt, then pulled his suspenders over his shoulders.

"Where are you going?"

"Same place I've been going for the past month, Moriah."

"Gates Mills? I thought you were finished with that job."

Levi shook his head as he reached for his boots. He didn't

bother to sit down, instead choosing to hop on one leg, then the other, as he put them on.

She thought he'd said he would be finished working at that horse ranch this week. Or maybe that was just wishful thinking on her part. She threw off her covers, gooseflesh rising as the coldness of the room seeped into her skin. "I'll start some coffee."

"*Nee.*" He held up his hand, but he didn't come near her. Instead he reached for his black hat, which hung on a peg next to the closet. "I'll get some on the road."

Already out of bed, she wrapped one arm around her body, shivering in her white cotton nightgown. The light from the flashlight illuminated the distance between them. Although it was only a few feet, lately it seemed like miles separated them. And at times it did, as the affluent community of Gates Mills was farther than the twelve-mile limit a horse and buggy could manage. But physical distance wasn't their only problem. An emotional chasm had grown between them, and she had no idea why.

"When will you be back?"

He shrugged. "Not exactly sure." Finally, he looked directly at her. "Don't hold supper for me."

Unable to stand being apart from him anymore, she closed the space between them. "Tomorrow is our four-month anniversary."

"Already?" He put his hat on his head, but averted his gaze. "Time flies, don't it?" He went past her to walk through the doorway of their room.

"Levi?" she called out.

He stopped, then slowly turned around. "*Ya?*"

"I'm making a special supper for you tomorrow night. To celebrate. All your favorites. Liver and onions, green bean casserole, sweet cornbread, and cinnamon pumpkin pie. I even got your *daed's* German potato salad recipe."

"Sounds *gut*. Moriah, I got to go. My ride's probably already here. I'll see you later on tonight."

"Okay. I love—" But he was gone before she could finish the sentence.

She turned the flashlight toward the small clock near on the bed table. 5:45. Levi had given her the porcelain clock on their wedding night. Pure white, with a picture of a cherub painted in washes of pale blue and light pink on the base. It was fancy and looked expensive, but he had said he wanted to give her something special, something she could look at every day and remember him by. The clock wasn't really her taste, as she preferred simple, unadorned things, but she cherished the gift because it was from him, and he had seemed so pleased to give it to her.

Grabbing a quilt off the end of the bed, she wrapped it around her shoulders and looked out the window. She and Levi had moved into his family's house after they had married, and from the view from their bedroom—Levi's old room—she saw two figures moving in the shadows. One was Levi; the other had to be Gabe. The men talked for a few moments, then Levi walked off to the end of the driveway, where a white van arrived to taxi him to Gates Mills. He climbed in, and she watched until the van's red taillights disappeared in the darkness.

For over a month now, they had followed this pattern. Usually he left before she awakened and returned after she had fallen asleep. She had been so tired lately, and even when she tried to wait up for him, she usually didn't succeed. The only day he didn't leave was on Sunday, but even then it was as if he were gone. He picked at his food, seemed distracted during their conversations, and went to bed before her on Sunday nights, saying he was exhausted from working so hard during the week.

Tugging the quilt closer to her body, she wondered if this was normal, if the blissful bloom of the first weeks of marriage usually withered so quickly. She could barely remember the last time he kissed her, held her, shared the joys of marriage with her. Open displays of affection between a man and a woman weren't the norm among their people, but she hadn't thought that extended to the privacy of their home. Even her parents had shown their love for each other with tender words or a brief clasping of hands.

She must be doing something wrong. She had overheard some of the older women say that a husband's happiness often depended on his wife's competency. Maybe he didn't like her cooking, although he had never complained about it before. Or her housekeeping skills were lacking, even though not a speck of dust could be found in the house. Or perhaps she had disappointed him in more intimate ways.

Biting down on her lip, she chased away the thoughts. The wretched job in Gates Mills was the problem, not her . . . she hoped.

Turning from the window, she was tempted to crawl underneath the warm covers. Sleep beckoned her, but she had too much to do. Gabriel and his *daed* would open their blacksmith shop soon, and she needed to prepare coffee and breakfast for them. Gabriel and John had voluntarily relocated to the *dawdi haus*, a small three-room cottage situated a few feet behind the shop. Typically, a *dawdi haus* was built to house aging Amish grandparents, but the houses and shop had been in John Miller's family for years. He had inherited them when his father had passed, and he had gifted the main house to Levi and Moriah as a wedding present. Ever since, he and Gabriel had spent most of their time either in the small cottage or in the shop. They had never once asked her to fix their meals. But she enjoyed doing it, and wouldn't think of leaving them to cook for themselves. They were her family, and it was her responsibility, and joy, to take care of them.

Dressing quickly, she made her way downstairs to the first level of the house, leaving the flashlight behind. She knew the way in the dark, and when she reached the kitchen, she turned on the tall gas lamp in the corner and started on her morning chores, distracting herself from her troubling thoughts about Levi and their marriage.

"You're going to Gates Mills *again*?" Gabe watched Levi grab two leather bags of horseshoes and tools and hoist them over his shoulder. Despite the early hour, Gabe had been in the shop for half an hour already. After Gabe retrieved his tools, he followed Levi outside, his irritation with his twin rising.

Levi headed to the end of the driveway, where he'd arranged for a taxi service to pick him up. Although their Old Order community forbade their members from driving an automobile, the *Ordnung*—the unwritten rules their Amish community followed —allowed them to pay a driver to take them longer distances. Some communities had different rules for their members concerning travel by car and other "modern" conveniences, and while his church allowed its members to ask Yankees to take them long distances, members weren't permitted to own cars themselves.

The bags were heavy, but Levi easily hauled them as if they were filled with feathers instead of metal. "They have a lot of horses," Levi said, not bothering to turn around and look at Gabe.

Gabe continued to dog Levi's heels. His brother had been gone every day save Sundays for the past month, working on that fancy horse farm in Gates Mills, a ritzy suburb of Cleveland. Levi had started shoeing their horses when the farm's owner, Mr. Johnston, had come to Middlefield to check out their blacksmith and farrier business. Their shop was so simple it didn't have an official name, but the Millers' reputations as excellent smiths and shoers had extended beyond their settlement. Now Levi spent more time away than in the shop.

Gabe pushed his hat off his forehead. "I need you here, Levi. The Stutzers placed a big order that they need by the end of next week. *Daed* and I can't do it by ourselves."

"I gave the Johnstons my word, Gabe." Levi finally looked at him. "Besides, they pay more than the Stutzers ever could. Mr. Johnston's also asked me to break one of his fillies. Said he'd triple my going rate."

Gabe couldn't believe what he was hearing. "You would take money over helping out a neighbor?"

"I've got a wife to provide for, remember?"

Gabe winced. Salt rubbed into a raw wound. He didn't need his brother to remind him about his marriage to Moriah. All he had to do was look at the short growth of beard on Levi's chin, the Amish man's wedding ring, to remember who his twin had married. He'd distracted himself with work and tried to avoid Moriah, but he couldn't get her out of his head and heart.

Absently Gabe rubbed his own smooth cheek and forced himself not to think about Moriah. He looked at Levi, unable to understand the man's eagerness to work for outlanders, especially ones who lived over an hour away. The blacksmith shop made enough to provide for all of them. They didn't need any extra income. What they needed to do was help out a fellow member of the church.

"My ride's here." Levi's boots crunched in the icy snow as he stepped toward the street.

"What about the Stutzers?"

"I'll try to be home early. I can pitch in then." A large white van pulled up beside him. Without another word, Levi climbed into the vehicle and shoved the sliding door shut.

Resentment churned inside Gabe as he watched the van crest the hill. His brother had been acting strangely the past couple weeks. He briefly wondered if there was trouble at home. If there was, it was none of his business. And if there wasn't, he didn't want to know about their perfect marriage either.

"Forgive me, Lord," he whispered, his breath hanging in puffs in the frigid air. "Forgive me for my sin." He had repeated that prayer so many times that he wondered if God heard it anymore. He forced himself to focus on the problem at hand—how to fill the Stutzer's order without Levi's help. Tomorrow would be too late. And lately *Daed* had been unsteady on his feet, something that unsettled him even more than Levi's peculiar behavior. The other day he'd almost fallen near the blazing forge, which would have seriously injured him. His father had shaken off Gabe's concern, saying he must have tripped over something. But Gabe knew better. He hadn't missed the sudden appearance in their kitchen of several types of herbal tea used to cure illness and increase strength.

Shivering, Gabe headed back to the warmth of the shop and lit the forge. There was no way to get around it—he would have to hire some help. The names of several employment candidates popped into his mind, and then he thought of Aaron Detweiler. The boy had been in a peck of trouble over the past few months, having left the family fold for his *rumspringa* as soon as he turned sixteen, only to get involved with drugs. He'd returned to the Detweiler's four months ago, after spending a few months in the Geauga County jail. Aaron wasn't the first Amish teen to find living outside the community perilous, and he wouldn't be the last. But at least he was trying to turn things around. As far as Gabe knew, he wasn't working anywhere steady other than his family's farm.

Gabe's own *rumspringa* had been uneventful, as he had chosen to join the church at eighteen and had no desire to experience the Yankee world. Levi, however, had snuck out a few times at night to hang out with non-Amish teens, unbeknownst to their father. Gabe doubted even Moriah knew about that secret part of Levi's life. But he had joined the church as well, and put those worldly dabblings behind him.

It was decided then. As soon as *Daed* came to the shop, Gabe would visit the Detweilers and offer Aaron a job. If and when Levi decided to become dependable again, there would be enough work for all four of them. Everyone needed a chance to redeem themselves. Gabe thought it a blessing he could offer Aaron that chance.

The scent of fresh-brewed coffee, combined with the peppery aroma of breakfast sausage and scrambled eggs, filled the air. Moriah covered the eggs with helpings of savory Swiss cheese she had picked up from the Middlefield Cheese House, then divided them over four slices of bread. She added a patty of sausage on top and finished the breakfast sandwiches with four more pieces of buttered bread. She wrapped them in foil, filled a thermos with steaming coffee, and packed it all in a large wicker basket. In her mind she was already planning their lunch meal—a platter of hearty slices of meatloaf, brown gravy, mashed potatoes with plenty of butter and milk, and apple crisp for dessert.

While she delighted in preparing and serving Gabriel and John their meals, her feelings were often pricked by Gabe's reception. John, of course, was always grateful, and always praised her cooking talents. But Gabriel often said little more than thank you. Although Levi had seemed distant as of late, Gabriel acted indifferent toward her, even more so since her marriage. She had hoped their relationship would improve, but it hadn't. But she determined that his attitude wouldn't keep her from taking care of them. As two single men, they needed some pampering every once in a while.

She donned her coat, then walked the short distance to the blacksmith shop. Like the main house and the *dawdi haus*, it was painted crisp white, with a black roof and plain wooden door. Outside, she could hear the echo of metal clanging against metal. She hung the food-laden wicker basket on the crook of her arm and opened the door with her free hand.

Heat immediately blasted her body, engulfing her in warmth, a welcome contrast to the coldness of the outdoors. The tin ring of a bell sounded as she shut the door, and both Gabriel and John looked up. John gave her a smile, while Gabriel acknowledged her with a small nod.

"I hope that's what I think it is," John said, as he put aside a fat metal file and walked toward her. He took a few steps, then touched the side of a table, as though trying to gain his balance.

She hadn't noticed John being so unsteady before, but then again, she didn't spend much time in the shop. Moriah set the basket of food on a nearby table. While John peeked inside, Gabriel stayed at the anvil, pounding away at a red, glowing piece of metal. John rarely worked the anvil anymore, preferring to let his brawny sons do the hard labor. She didn't blame him—he'd spent many years putting in long and exhausting hours as a blacksmith. He'd earned the well-deserved rest.

She caught sight of Gabriel again. His shirt sleeves were rolled up to his elbow. The muscles flexed beneath his skin as he slammed the hammer down. Quickly she glanced away, feeling a twinge of guilt for staring at her brother-in-law. "What did you bring us today, *dochder*?" John asked, rubbing his callused hands together.

Glad for the diversion, Moriah named off the items as she withdrew them from the basket and laid them on the table. "Sausage and egg sandwiches and a thermos of coffee."

"*Gut, sehr gut.* Everything smells delicious, Moriah. *Danki.*"

Her lips formed into a smile, genuinely happy that her father-in-law was pleased with her offering.

"Gabriel, come and eat," John said as he picked up a sandwich. He peeled back the foil and inhaled, closing his eyes and grinning. "Manna from heaven."

"In a minute." The sizzling sound of hot metal meeting cold water filled the air, and for a moment Gabriel was completely obscured by a cloud of steam. He withdrew the cooled piece of iron, balanced it on the anvil, and walked toward her and John. His gaze remained cast downward, as it usually was whenever he and Moriah shared the same company.

"You have to try one of these. They're still hot." John handed Gabriel a sandwich. Gabriel accepted the sandwich, then unwrapped it and took a bite. He nodded his approval, but his face remained unreadable.

Moriah took out two coffee mugs from the basket. She unscrewed the lid off the thermos and poured John and Gabriel each a cup of coffee. She handed Gabriel his first.

His gaze flicked to her as he took the cup from her hand, but he took two steps back and looked at the floor again. Downing the sandwich, he balled up the foil and took a swig of the coffee before putting the mug back on the table. "Got to get back to work."

"Gabriel, you can take a break." John took a big bite of sausage, cheese, and egg. "We'll get the work done, *sohn.*"

As Moriah listened to John, her stomach suddenly felt like it had been turned upside down. Perspiration beaded her forehead as she inhaled the mixed scents of black coffee, sausage, and coal burning. The aromas made her gag. She reached out to grab the table as the room started to swirl.

"Moriah, you all right?"

John's voice sounded far away. Where had the table disappeared to? Suddenly she couldn't see anything.

She sensed something behind her just as she tilted backward. Something solid. Closing her eyes, she fought for consciousness.

The instant Gabe saw Moriah sway, he rushed to her. He'd just managed to move behind her when she fell against him and started sliding to the floor. Grabbing her shoulders, he drew her closer to his chest, calling out her name.

"Moriah?"

Her head lolled for a moment and she mumbled something incoherent.

John reached for a nearby chair and dragged it to Gabe. "Let her sit down, Gabriel."

Gabe eased her into the chair as his arm cradled her shoulders. Her complexion had paled, and her normally peach-toned lips were nearly white. Bending his legs at the knees, he crouched down beside her, one arm still across her shoulders.

"I'll get a cold rag," John said, and he shuffled over to the sink on the other side of the shop.

Gabe heard the trickling of water in the sink as he scanned Moriah's features. Her eyes were closed, but she was still conscious. "Moriah? Can you hear me?"

She nodded, her eyes opening. Some of the color seeped back to her face now that she was seated. "What happened?" she asked in a breathy, surprised voice.

"You passed out . . . I think." He searched her face again. "Are you all right?"

"I don't know." She licked her lips, which were still stark white.

His gaze went involuntarily to her mouth. Under other circumstances, he might have enjoyed being so close to her, only to emotionally flog himself later, but now all he could think about was her welfare. "Do you need something to drink?"

"She needs this." John handed her a wet rag. The faded red cloth was filled with stains. "Wipe her face with it," he instructed. "Don't worry, *sohn*. That rag might look filthy, but it's clean."

Carefully Gabe dabbed the damp cloth against her smooth forehead, then slid the rag over the plumpest part of her cheeks. She closed her eyes again, leaning even further against him.

"Did you eat something this morning?" John asked.

Opening her eyes, she shook her head. "I wasn't very hungry."

Gabe glanced up at his father, whose expression had suddenly become inscrutable. John took one of the sandwiches and handed it to her. "Here, take a bite of this. I'll go get you some water."

She shook her head. "I don't—"

"No arguments, Moriah. Eat it." John turned and trekked back to the sink, where they kept a small supply of clean glasses and coffee cups.

Moriah brought the sandwich to her mouth and took a small bite. She chewed for a moment, then swallowed. Clearly she was forcing the food down.

Concern filled Gabe. She didn't look well at all. "Moriah, are you sick?"

"No . . ." Her eyes suddenly widened. The paleness of her cheeks gave way to a rosy red as she refused to look at him.

And at that moment Gabe *knew*. She was carrying his brother's child.

A jumble of emotions passed through Moriah. Embarrassment that she'd almost fainted in the shop. Appreciation for the way John had taken charge and made her eat something. With a bit of food in her stomach, she felt less queasy. She hadn't eaten anything that morning because the thought of consuming even one bite of food made her stomach turn. But now she knew that to ignore her body's hunger signals would be even worse.

She also felt something else, something completely unexpected. As Gabe still stayed beside her, crouching on the ground, looking at her with genuine concern, she felt safe. Protected. Cared for, and in a way she'd never felt before, not even with Levi. How could she feel that way in her brother-in-law's presence, but not her husband's?

Perhaps it was the hormones from the baby. If today's near fainting spell didn't prove she was pregnant, she didn't know what would, other than a pregnancy test of course. But she didn't need to take a test to know there was a new life growing inside her. She had suspected it for a while, since she'd missed her last monthly cycle. She brought the partially eaten sandwich up to her mouth to hide the smile twitching on her lips.

"I think you're coming out of it." John handed her a cup of water, then propped his hip against the table. The overhead lights in the shop, powered by the white propane tank in the backyard, illuminated the salt and pepper colors in his hair and beard. "You shouldn't skip breakfast, young lady. Didn't your *mudder* always tell you that?" The twinkle in his brown eyes indicated he was only half scolding her.

"*Ya.* Don't worry, I won't miss a meal again."

He nodded, apparently satisfied with her answer.

She glanced at Gabe, who was still crouched by the chair. An odd expression spread across his face, and this time he was looking at her. Although he seemed to look right through her, as if he had something else on his mind. Something that bothered him, from what she could tell. "I'm okay now," she said, sensing that he needed the reassurance.

"What? Oh." He jumped to his feet. "I'm glad." He stepped away from her to stand behind John, reverting back to his habit of not looking directly at her.

Sighing inwardly, she wondered if she would ever understand

her brother-in-law. She took another small bite of the sandwich, then felt refreshed enough to stand up.

"Are you sure you're all right?" John asked, stepping toward her. Gabe had already returned back to the forge.

She felt normal, as if she hadn't been overcome with dizziness only moments ago. "I'm fine," she said sincerely. "I'd planned to visit my family today, and I feel well enough to do so."

"Are you sure?" John didn't look convinced.

The reverberating sound of Gabe's hammer against the anvil filtered through her ears. "I'm sure. Thanks for taking care of me. I appreciate it." She smiled. "If I start to feel strange again, I'll turn around and come home."

"You'd better." The twinkle was gone from his eyes, and she knew he was serious.

"I will." She turned to say good-bye to Gabe, to thank him for keeping her from hitting the floor. But he was engrossed in his work and didn't even look up when she moved toward the door.

Had she imagined his earlier concern? If his current indifference was any indication, she had.

She left the shop, confused by Gabe's bewildering treatment of her. Maybe he was unhappy that she had displaced him from his house. Both she and Levi had insisted he stay in the main house with them, but he had been all too eager to move into the *dawdi haus* with John. Maybe his curt behavior didn't have anything to do with his living arrangements. Maybe he just wanted to get away from her.

Tamping down the hurt, she returned to her kitchen and cleaned up, forcing Gabe from her thoughts. Instead she focused on the baby. *Mine and Levi's.* She couldn't wait to tell him about the pregnancy. A baby would bring them closer together, she was sure of it. As she finished up her chores, she praised God for the blessing growing inside her.

A short while later she arrived at her mother's house, still not feeling any ill effects from her earlier fainting spell. The sun had risen fully, but was obscured by a flat, grayish sky that cast a cloudy pall over everything. On the other side of the black asphalt driveway stood her father's woodshop, where he and her brothers made the handcrafted furniture the tourists always seemed to crave. Normally she could hear them working, but the shop doors were closed tight against the winter cold.

"*Mami?*" she called out when she entered her parents' home through the front door. An odd sensation came over her as she scanned the living room. Now that she and Levi had settled into their own place, she found it strange coming back here, even though she had spent so many hours in this sparsely furnished but cozy and welcoming room, sitting on the comfortable brown sofa near the coal fireplace, reading a book or talking with her siblings. She had spent her entire life in this house, but now it was no longer home, despite everything being so familiar to her.

"In here, Moriah." Her mother's voice came from the kitchen at the back of the house.

Moriah walked through the living and dining rooms, breathing in the scent of freshly baked bread. Baking day. The scent, instead of making her nauseous, beckoned her. She followed the delicious aroma into the kitchen.

"You must have read my mind, daughter." Emma brushed the back of a flour-covered hand over her damp forehead. Although it might be thirty degrees outside, the radiating heat from the stove made the kitchen toasty. "I just started a fresh batch of sticky buns. I could use your help."

"What would you like me to do?"

"You can start by rolling out that dough."

Moriah went to the sink and washed up before sitting down at the table. She then dipped her hands into the canister of flour and grabbed the glob of dough and a wood rolling pin. Immediately she set to work.

Her mother removed two finished pans of buns from the oven and began spreading them with cream cheese frosting. "I considered keeping Elisabeth and Ruth home today from school to help, but thought better of it. Besides, Ruthie would howl if I even hinted at not allowing her to go to school."

Imagining her twelve-year-old sister, Ruth, throwing a tantrum wasn't too difficult. But fifteen-year-old Elisabeth, who was in the eighth grade at the Amish-run school, wouldn't have minded missing a day or two. Or more, for that matter. She hated school and couldn't wait for her last year to end.

Moriah felt a bit relieved that she wasn't here. Elisabeth would try to pump her for more personal information about her relationship with Levi, which she'd done the day after their wedding night. Moriah had ignored her probing questions until Elisabeth had finally given up. Her sister then launched into a detailed report about her latest crush, whom she swore she was madly in love with. Moriah highly doubted that, as Elisabeth's targets of affection were usually discarded on a weekly basis.

"How are things at home?" Emma asked, smearing a knife full of frosting onto the second batch of hot rolls. "Levi doing well?"

"He's fine, *Mami.*" To reassure her doting mother, she repeated,

"Everything is fine." The words *I'm pregnant* danced on the tip of her tongue, but she kept the knowledge to herself. No need to worry her mother. Also, she wasn't ready to tell anyone about the baby. Not until she told Levi first.

"I hear his shop is very successful. They've gotten quite a few Yankee customers."

"*Ya*. Levi's working with one now, in Gates Mills."

Emma turned and looked at her daughter. "Really? I didn't know John let his boys make house calls to outlanders."

"He hasn't before. But Levi insisted, and Mr. Johnston seems like a nice man." Moriah had met him the day he'd come to check out the Millers' shop.

Emma's brows furrowed. "How often is he gone?"

Moriah paused before answering. She didn't want to cause her any worry—or hear a lecture about Levi spending too much time in the "devil's playground." Besides, he would be finished with that job soon.

She was pondering a suitable answer when Tobias suddenly burst into the kitchen from the back door. He paused and gave the air a long, satisfied sniff, then bellowed with enthusiasm, "Sticky buns. Talk about good timing." His hand shot out for a freshly iced bun, but Emma snatched them away.

"These are for your *daed* and your brothers. You can have yours when you come back."

"Back from where?" His blond eyebrow arched from beneath his hat.

"The Detweilers'. Sarah left one of her pie plates here, and I keep forgetting to give it back to her."

Tobias looked pained. "Why can't Lukas or Stephen take it?"

"Because you came in first. That makes you the lucky one."

Emma smiled and tapped the brim of his hat with her finger. Her lighthearted nature warmed the Byler home, creating a comfortable atmosphere of laughter and playful teasing. She handed him a glass pie plate. "Here you go. Oh, and take this batch of sticky buns with you and give it to Sarah."

"Now you're just torturing me," Tobias said with exaggerated drama. "I can't eat these, *and* I have to smell them all the way to the Detweilers'?"

"I'm sure you'll manage."

He turned and looked at Moriah, acknowledging her for the first time. "Hey, sis, why don't you take these to the—"

"Oh no you don't." Emma shooed him out the door. "I won't have you pawning your responsibilities off on your sister. Now go!"

Moriah laughed at the helpless expression on her brother's face as he disappeared outside. She knew he wouldn't refuse *Mami* any request, but he had a good time ruffling her feathers before capitulating.

"That boy," Emma said, shaking her head as she plopped down at the table. "He'll be the death of me, I'm sure of it. Why can't he just say 'yes, ma'am' like my other two sons and get on with it?"

"Because then you'd think there was something wrong with him." Moriah grinned as she turned the dough and continued rolling. She was glad she'd decided to visit her family today. It lifted her spirits, making her concern over her relationship with Levi seem far away.

Emma sighed. "You're right. I just wish he'd find a nice girl to court. But he's too busy playing games and having fun."

"Now that's not quite true, *Mami*. You know he works hard in the shop and around here."

"*Ya*, that he does. But he certainly has plenty of free time. More than your father had at that age." She brushed a few specks of flour off the table. "I thought maybe he liked that sweet Rachel Detweiler, but she's been seen with Christian Weaver quite a bit."

"Rachel and Tobias can't stand each other, *Mami*."

"There's a fine line between passion and hate, Moriah." Emma sighed and leaned her elbow on the table, putting her chin in her hand. "Doesn't matter what Tobias thinks about Rachel, she's pretty close with Christian now. Sarah suspects they'll be wed this fall."

"She does?"

"*Ya*. She's planting plenty of extra celery in the garden this spring. You know, Tobias needs to pay attention to what Christian's doing. He needs to put childish things behind him and start thinking about his future. Like you did when you married Levi. Although that young man dragged his feet for so long we didn't think he would ever get around to asking you."

Moriah hid her frown. Her mother's words stung a little, digging deeper into Moriah's insecurity.

Emma must have noticed, because she quickly added, "Doesn't matter anyway. You two are married now. And happy, *ya?*"

"*Ya*. We're happy, *Mami*."

With a grin Emma said, "*Gut, gut*. Then my prayers have been answered, praise God."

Her pricked emotions assuaged, Moriah couldn't resist the chance to rib her mother. "Maybe you should pray for patience with Tobias."

"Believe me, I do. Every single day of my life."

Chapter 4

*T*obias couldn't believe his bad timing. The last thing he wanted to do was go to the Detweilers'. He hadn't seen much of Rachel since he zinged her leg with the baseball last November, and that suited him just fine. She'd been keeping company with Christian, even sitting next to him during the singings. Neither of them had been at the last frolic, and Tobias remembered someone mentioning that they had spent the day in Ashtabula, shopping with Christian's family.

Tobias gripped the reins tighter, barely hearing the clopping of the horse's hooves against the slushy roads. Guess things were pretty serious between Christian and Rachel. Not that he cared. She could marry whomever she wanted, and he liked Christian. Although he wondered how a calm, soft-spoken guy like Christian could handle Rachel's crazy moods. Especially when she was angry, those gorgeous eyes of hers sparking, that pert mouth emitting a diatribe that would burn even the most seasoned man's ears. A spitfire, that's what she was. She could be so passionate—

He jerked on the reins. Where the heck did that come from? *Passion* and *Rachel* in the same thought? Heat crept up on his neck, and his coat was suddenly too warm, even though it was thirty-something degrees out.

Maybe his *mami* was right. He should find some nice girl to court, someone to marry and have a family with. Several of his buddies had already chosen their wives, and Christian seemed well on his way to doing so. Perhaps if he had his own girl to focus on, he would quit thinking about Rachel Detweiler all the time.

But then again, women tended to complicate things. His life was fine the way it was—good job, fun friends, nice home, a great family. He was young, only nineteen. Plenty of time for him to get married—if he even wanted to.

A few moments later he pulled up to her house and turned in the driveway. He brought the buggy to a stop, then hitched up his horse. If he was lucky, Rachel would be at Mary Yoder's restaurant, serving her customers some of the authentic Amish cooking that drew tourists and locals looking for home-style meals or tempting baked goods. But nothing could beat his mother's sticky buns. He would just leave them with Mrs. Detweiler, then rush home to finish the load of work waiting for him. He hated working late. Why his mother hadn't sent Moriah to run this errand was beyond him. Not like his sister had anything else to do.

On the Detweilers' front porch, he knocked on the white oak door, his knuckles hurting from the cold. While he waited, he breathed out white puffs into the chilly air. He had just formed his mouth into a perfect O to see if he could make a circle with his breath when the door opened.

Rachel planted her hands on her hips. "What are you doing?"

His lips froze in the O shape as he stared at her. Wow, she looked pretty in her midcalf-length dress and white *kapp*. Light purple was a good color for her. It brought out the blue in her eyes, eyes that were suddenly looking at him as if he had totally lost all his marbles. For the second time in ten minutes, he felt a rush of heat surge over his face. "Sticky buns," he said, thrusting the plate at her.

The plate wobbled in his hand, nearly tipping over until she reached out and grabbed it. When she did, their fingers touched for the briefest of moments. Tobias wanted to slap some sense into himself. No wonder she thought he had lost it—he was starting to think the same thing.

"Thanks," she said, still giving him a wary eye. "I'll give these to—"

"Who's at the door?" Sarah Detweiler appeared behind her daughter. "Oh, Tobias, hello. What brings you by?"

"Sticky buns," he repeated, then fought the urge to roll his eyes. Apparently those were the only two words in his vocabulary this morning.

"From Emma?" Sarah took the buns from Rachel. "They smell marvelous. How about you come inside and we can share them together? I just put a pot of coffee on to perk."

Rachel's eyes grew wide, and Tobias could tell that the last thing she wanted to do was share sticky buns with him. That helped him make up his mind. "I'd be obliged, ma'am," he said, walking past Rachel and removing his hat. He hung it on a peg near the door, then slipped off his snow-covered boots. He turned and gave Rachel a big, smug smile.

She responded with a glare.

"Goodness, Rachel!" Sarah said. "Shut the door; you're letting in all the cold air."

Rachel dutifully closed the door. She started to head to the kitchen when Sarah stopped her. "Why don't you and Tobias get settled in the living room? I'll bring out the buns and coffee. How do you take yours, Tobias?"

"Black," he said, grinning even wider as he saw Rachel's frown. "If you please."

"Rachel?"

"None for me," she mumbled, then scooted past Tobias into the front room, which served as the Detweilers' visiting area. She plopped down on the most comfortable looking chair and crossed her arms, her mouth in full pout mode. He followed her into the room and could almost feel the daggers shooting from her eyes. Her resentment cast a pall over the neat, plainly furnished room.

Tobias caught the warning glance Sarah gave her daughter before heading to the kitchen at the back of the house. He lowered himself in the chair directly across from her, his eyes never leaving hers.

"Don't you have work to do?" she asked, tilting her head and looking at him dead on, as if she could wish him away if she glared at him hard enough.

"Don't you? Thought you'd be at the restaurant."

"I'm off today. You still haven't answered my question."

"I just can't resist my mother's sticky buns." He smirked.

"Then you should go home and eat them there." She met his gaze, unflinching.

"But I wouldn't want to disappoint your mother."

"I'll explain why you left."

"Then you'll look like a fool, because I'm not leaving." He put his hands behind his head and leaned back in the chair, reveling in the fury he saw building inside her. Good Lord, she was fun to rile up. The spark that leapt to her eyes affected him, like touching a lit match to a stick of dynamite.

Rachel suddenly jumped from her seat. "You are the most *infuriating* person I have ever met."

"Wow. That's a big word," he said drolly. "You been reading the dictionary in your spare time?"

"Ooh," she said, going to him. She poked him in the chest. "You are *seltsam*, Tobias Byler!"

He grasped her hand midpoke, not even caring that she had called him weird. Instead of letting go of it, he held on. His own hands were rough, scarred, and gouged from working with wood since he was a child. Her hands, in contrast, were small and soft, with slender fingers that he had a sudden urge to intertwine with his own. Their gazes instantly met, and for the life of him he couldn't move away from her, even if he wanted to. Which he didn't.

"Nothing better on a cold winter morning than coffee and sticky buns," Sarah's voice sounded in the hallway, as if she were warning them of her approach.

They both jumped apart, Rachel snatching her hand out of his grip and flinging herself into the chair. Tobias looked at Sarah as she entered the room and placed the tray on the coffee table. While she settled herself on the sofa, he gave Rachel a quick glance, and was surprised to see the blush blooming on her cheeks, making her look even prettier than before.

Sarah looked up and directed her attention to Rachel, a frown forming on her lips. "Are you feeling all right, daughter? You look flushed."

Her mother's comment seemed to only intensify the reddening of Rachel's face. "I'm fine."

Suddenly, his pleasure at putting her on edge disappeared, replaced by a tiny bit of shame, and a large dose of confusion. Since when did he have the urge to hold her hand, especially since everyone knew she and Christian were courting?

The parlor, which had been so welcoming and comfortable minutes before, now seemed stuffy and claustrophobic. He scrambled up from his chair, assailed by an uncontrollable urge to get out of there. When he started to speak, the words came out in a foggy croak, so he cleared his throat and tried again. "I gotta go, *Frau* Detweiler."

Surprise crossed Sarah's features, her blue eyes so similar to Rachel's. "So soon? You haven't even had your coffee yet. Surely you can stay for just a little while."

"I know, but I just remembered I promised *Daed* I would do something for him." He grappled for a more thorough explanation, but his mind went blank. "Something important" was all he could come up with. He nodded toward the tray. "I'm sorry to put you to so much trouble. *Danki.* I appreciate the hospitality." Spinning on his sock-clad heel, he dashed to the front door, yanked on his boots, and grabbed his hat, then flew down the steps to his buggy. He slapped the reins on the horse's flanks.

As the horse and buggy sprinted home, he felt a tingle in his hand. The hand that had held Rachel's. He glanced down at it, remembering how much he liked the feel of Rachel's skin against his.

Dummkopf. He should have never accepted *Frau* Detweiler's invitation. Now she probably thought he'd lost his mind. With a hard shake of his head, he tried to clear the scene from his mind. If Rachel's mother thought he was crazy, she wasn't the only one.

"What on earth has gotten into that boy?"

Rachel shrugged, but she didn't look at her mother.

"Did you two have a fight? Rachel, look at me." Sarah moved closer to her daughter. "Did he say something to you?"

"*Nee, Mudder,*" she replied, hoping her mother didn't notice that Rachel's face was perilously close to exploding with embarrassment. As if that wasn't bad enough, she was dealing with some other emotion she couldn't define. A tickling, yet tingling sensation that started as soon as Tobias had touched her hand. "He's just *seltsam.*"

Sarah frowned, the parentheses-shaped lines around her mouth deepening. "That's not a nice thing to say, Rachel Anne. It doesn't matter how you feel about someone, when they are a guest in your home, you are to treat them with kindness and respect. Part of the duties of a good wife is to make her home a welcoming place. Not just for family, but for the community. Tobias is a part of this community, whether you like it or not."

Properly chastised, Rachel leaned back in the chair. "Sorry."

With a nod, Sarah picked up the untouched tray from the coffee table. "Besides, it doesn't hurt to keep your prospects open."

Rachel popped up from her chair. "What do you mean?"

"In case things don't work out with Christian."

"Things are fine with Christian." At least she thought they were. True, their relationship was building slowly . . . very slowly. Probably at a slower pace than she had expected. But that wasn't necessarily a bad thing. She and Christian both needed to be sure about their feelings for each other before they became serious. They were suitably matched—they had a deep connection to their families and faith, they enjoyed reading, and . . . well, she knew there were more things they had in common, she just couldn't think about them right now. One thing she did know for sure, Christian was better for her than Tobias could ever be.

"Don't be surprised if he changes his mind," Sarah said.

"Tobias?"

"*Christian*," Sarah said as she walked out the door. "Men can be fickle, you know."

Rachel fell back in her chair. She didn't know about men and their inconsistencies. In fact, she knew very little about men at all. True, she had brothers, but they were all several years older than her, except for Aaron. While her friends in school had spent their younger teen years crushing on one boy or another—with Tobias as the object of their affections at some point—she had focused on schoolwork and grades. Her diligence paid off, she had made straight As all through her school career. While she was proud of that accomplishment, her singular devotion to her studies—and her relentless competitive streak—had come at the expense of some of her friendships. Then she took that same ambition and applied it to her job at Mary Yoder's Kitchen, not paying much attention to the social opportunities she might be missing.

For the first time she regretted not being a little less ambitious and a little more pacifying. Then she might have gained an insight or two on how men ticked. Or maybe not. Maybe this had nothing to do with her, and everything to do with Christian.

Was he having second thoughts about their relationship? The good Lord knew she had more than a few.

Rising from her chair, she straightened up a small pile of Family Life magazines on the end table and began fluffing the already full sofa pillows. She should have a talk with Christian. A serious talk, not the superficial conversations they normally had. She should find out what his intentions truly were. When she agreed to date him, she had done so with an open mind and—she hoped—an open heart. But every time they were together, it seemed they treated each other more as friends than romantic interests. Her mother had probably picked up on that as well.

"Rachel?"

Rachel turned around to see her mother poke her head in the doorway of the parlor. "*Ya?*"

"When you're finished in here, I need you to clean the upstairs bedrooms."

"Aaron's too?"

"*Ya.* You do such a wonderful job, even better than I do." Sarah smiled. "Your husband will be very lucky indeed to have such a good housekeeper."

Rachel managed a half smile and wondered if her mother had lost her mind. *Mami* was clearly obsessed with Rachel's future marriage—when or if it ever happened.

But her mother's compliment about her cleaning skills warmed her; Rachel abhorred untidiness and had always kept her room in order. Still, she didn't relish straightening up Aaron's room. She wondered if he was even out of bed, despite it being midmorning. Since his return from jail, her parents had been dealing with him as if he were made of thin glass. They said it was because he was still in drug recovery, but Rachel was keenly aware of the difference between the way they treated her and her older brothers, though her brothers now were married and out of the house.

The bulk of the chores often fell to her, even more so after Aaron had fallen in with a bad crowd during his *rumspringa*. He had been belligerent, lazy, and argumentative, especially with their parents, something she had never done. While she had experimented with a few forbidden things during her own *rumspringa*, such as borrowing one of those little music players and trying on one of her Yankee friend's makeup, she didn't have the rebellious streak her brother possessed. Since his return, he had stayed holed up in his room for the most part, and she hadn't talked to him much. If anyone asked her to describe her brother, she doubted she could do it, other than give just a physical description. She didn't know him anymore.

Yet she still had to clean his room.

As she passed by the front door on the way to the stairs, she heard someone knocking. Glad for the reprieve, however slight, she turned around and answered it, surprised to see Gabriel Miller standing at the front door.

"Good morning, Rachel."

"Good morning, Gabe. What can I do for you?"

"Is Aaron around?"

"Why don't you come in?" she offered, remembering her mother's words about hospitality. "I haven't seen him this morning, but I'll check upstairs."

"*Danki.*"

"Would you like to sit down in the parlor? I could bring you a cup of coffee. We have some sticky buns too."

"No, I'm fine. But thank you. I'll just wait here."

Rachel dashed up the stairs and stopped in front of her brother's room. The door was shut, so she knocked. Even though she didn't strike the door very hard, it opened in response. She expected to see him asleep in bed, but his bed was already made, their grandmother's black-and-white quilt neatly pulled over it. She stepped inside and saw him sitting in a chair beside the only window, staring out into the barren, snow-covered field behind the house. Unsure of her brother's mood, she looked around the room. Nothing amiss. A small chest of drawers sat next to the tiny closet. A round, braided rug, made by their mother from pieces of leftover, faded rags, covered the middle of the wood-planked floor.

"Gabe Miller's here to see you," she said in a soft voice.

Slowly he turned around and faced her, his expression blank, as it had been since he'd returned from jail. Without verbally responding, he pushed back his chair and walked passed her to exit the room. Not even a single thank-you for her trudging up the stairs to fetch him.

A passage from Romans entered her mind as she battled the resentment rising within her. "Do not let the sun go down on your anger." Easy for Paul to say.

As she thought more on the passage, her ire cooled. She really did need to work on managing her anger. It seemed she'd been more and more volatile lately and didn't fully understand why.

Well, might as well clean Aaron's room while I'm here. Examining the small space, she searched for what needed to be cleaned and straightened. After five minutes she realized, surprisingly, that there was nothing for her to do. He had done it all.

"I need someone four days a week." Gabe and Aaron stood on the Detweilers' front porch, Aaron in a simple broadcloth shirt, pants, and socks. Gabe figured the boy must be freezing, but if he was, he didn't say anything. Instead he silently listened to Gabe's offer, nodding in understanding every once in a while.

"Mostly you'll be cleaning up around the shop, oiling the

tools, and helping me out at the forge when necessary." Gabe thought about adding the duty of keeping his father away from the forge, but he wouldn't humiliate his *daed* like that. He would keep an eye on him himself. "The pay is pretty good, but not as much as you'd get at one of the factories around here. I know for sure that Dillen's pays more. I gotta be honest about that."

"Not worried about the pay."

Gabe stroked his chin as he sized up the seventeen-year-old. He had a thin frame, but that was to be expected from his recent drug use and time spent in jail. Blond fuzz covered his scalp. When he first came home, he looked something like what the Yankees called a skinhead, but at least he wasn't completely bald anymore. The kid's face was, however, completely unreadable. Blank was the best description he could come up with.

"You've heard my offer," Gabe said. "And my terms. What say you? Will you take the job?"

Aaron nodded slowly. "*Ya.*"

Gabe grinned. "Be there at seven sharp tomorrow morning. Levi and I usually start at six, but we won't need you until seven."

"I can start this afternoon, if you want."

Gabe considered his offer for a moment. "All right. Do you need a ride?"

"*Nee.* I'll walk."

"Then let's say in a couple hours. I can show you around the place, tell you how we run things." He held out his hand and Aaron clasped it in a gentleman's agreement. He scanned the young man's lack of winter attire. "You better get inside before you freeze," he said.

"I'm fine," Aaron replied with a shrug. He turned and went inside.

Satisfied, Gabe descended the steps, unhitched his horse, and headed home. He'd closed down the shop for an early lunch while he went to talk to Aaron. His father hadn't minded or questioned him; he just went back to the house and said he would have some tea and read for a while. The old man looked tired, and Gabe wasn't in any hurry to have him back in the shop again.

As he made his way back to his house, he passed by the Byler's and recognized Levi and Moriah's buggy in the driveway. Her beautiful face immediately came to mind, and he remembered her near fainting spell earlier that morning. The past four months had been difficult, knowing that she lived only a few feet away from him in the main house.

And now she carried Levi's child. Another blow, even though he had known it would eventually happen. He slapped the reins against the horse's flanks. The sooner he accepted that Moriah was lost to him, the easier life would be. Every night he prayed the same prayer to the Almighty—to free him from this prison of sin and covetousness. His prayers were still unanswered.

God rewards the faithful in His time, not man's. Gabe knew this, and clung to it. God would answer his prayer eventually and release him of this burden, of that he was sure. In the meantime, He was molding Gabe into a new vessel, one worthy and strong enough to serve Him. As a worker of iron, he was well acquainted with the heat and pressure and power necessary to change raw material into something useful.

He just wished the process wasn't so painful.

Chapter 5

*B*utterflies danced a jig inside Moriah's belly as she prepared supper, although she wasn't exactly sure if it was caused by nerves or nausea. First thing this morning, she'd had to run to the bathroom. Levi had already left for Gates Mills, saving her from having to explain to him why she was throwing up. He would find out why tonight, during their anniversary dinner. She had spent the previous day cleaning the house from top to bottom, hoping Levi would notice her efforts. Unfortunately, he hadn't, or at least he hadn't said he'd noticed.

She placed her hand over her stomach and stirred the simmering liver, spooning the brown gravy over the meat and onions. Liver had never been one of her favorites, and she wasn't sure she would be able to eat a bite. But Levi loved it, and she wanted this meal to be special.

Remembering her promise to John about not skipping meals, she decided she'd eat at least a small portion with Levi tonight. The aroma of yeast rolls and a fresh-baked apple pie filled the kitchen. She knew he liked pumpkin pie better, but she'd forgotten she had used all of the canned pumpkin at Christmastime. Even though February was drawing to a close, the food cellar still held plenty of apples from the fall harvest. She had even sliced a few hearty wedges of cheddar cheese to accompany the pie. She hoped Levi would be pleased.

She placed the rolls in a basket and wrapped a tea towel over them to keep them warm. When the liver and onions finished simmering, she turned off the burner and placed a lid on top of the pot. Glancing at the battery-run clock on the wall, she saw she'd finished just in time. Levi would be home any minute. When he had been late last night, he had promised to be home in time for supper tonight. Anticipation filled her as she went to the sitting room and sat on the sofa by the large picture window, waiting for the familiar white van to arrive. She imagined what his reaction to her news would be. An image of his handsome face lit up with joy came to mind. Surely he would be as happy as she was about the baby. Of that she had no doubt.

"*Moriah . . . Moriah.*"

The sound of her husband's voice penetrated her mind. Moriah opened her eyes, surprised to find herself in a darkened room. A strong hand touched her shoulder, shaking her gently. Then soft, glowing light flooded her eyes.

She squinted, trying to figure out where she was, then realized she had fallen asleep on the sofa in the sitting room. Moving to an upright position, she focused on the man turning away from the gas-powered lamp he had just lit. Through sleepy eyes, she smiled as she looked at his back. He hadn't even had a chance to take off his coat and hat. He must have had to work late, but she was glad he was finally home. Now she could tell him about their precious baby.

But when he turned around, her anticipation dimmed. Although many people had difficulty telling the twin brothers apart, she never did. "Gabriel?"

His expression solemn, he came and sat down next to her on the couch. A strange thing for him to do, since normally he kept his distance from her.

"Moriah, are you awake?" he asked, his voice quiet, but with a slight edge to it. "Fully awake?"

She rubbed her eyes to rid them of sleep, then looked at him. "*Ya*, Gabriel. I'm up." Only then did she see the distress in his brown eyes. "What is it? What's wrong?"

He turned from her and looked at the wall for a moment before slowly rubbing the back of his neck. Then he took off his hat and set it on the end table next to the sofa.

The longer he took to answer, the faster the panic built inside her. Finally, she couldn't take it anymore. "Gabriel, what is going on?"

Without a word he reached into his pocket and withdrew a folded piece of paper. He handed it to her. "Levi sent this," he said tightly.

Her gaze dropped to the note. She stared at it, not wanting to accept it from him. Her throat tightened at the thought of reading it, sensing it contained something she didn't want to know. She raised her head to see Gabriel's expression, but his eyes darted from hers, as if he couldn't bear to look at her directly. His reaction only fueled the anxiety rising inside her. He pushed the note toward her again. This time she took the paper and unfolded it. She first noticed a business heading stamped at the top: *Johnston's Farms*. Had something happened to Levi at the horse farm?

Moriah,

This is a hard letter for me to write. You have to know up front that I never meant to hurt you. In my own way, I did love you.

Tears sprang to her eyes, blurring the small, uniform lines in front of her. Not hurt her? Did love her? What kind of words were those? She blinked, and round circles of moisture dotted the page. She forced herself to read on.

I am leaving you and the Amish. I haven't felt right about being Amish for a long time, but I thought I didn't have any choice. Everyone in my family joined the church, and it would have broken my mother's heart if I hadn't joined. But Mami is gone, and I want to be free.

I don't want to follow rules all the time. I don't want to be stuck in four-hour church services or banging on a forge until I die. I've found my place with the Yankees. There's no drudgery, no self-denial. Only total freedom to be who I am.

I hope you can understand why I had to do this, Moriah. And I hope someday you will forgive me. I think we'll both be better off.

Levi Miller

Moriah let the letter slip through her fingers and drop to the floor. Slowly she rose from the couch and wrapped her arms around her body. She'd let the fire go out in the stove. She had to get more wood and light the stove. Maybe then she would feel warm again.

Gabe wasn't sure what he expected when Moriah read his brother's note, but the silent way she left the room wasn't it. Alarmed, he jumped up from the sofa and followed her. As he entered the kitchen, the faint scent of rolls mingled with liver and onions hung in the air. One glance at the kitchen table and his heart broke even more.

She'd obviously taken pains to make the setting perfect. She had covered the table with a white linen cloth, the one his mother had reserved for special occasions. A small gas lamp bathed the room in soft light. A basket of rolls, the red tea towel covering the bread in an attempt to keep it warm, sat next to a sunken apple pie that looked like it had been out for hours.

His gaze jerked from the table when he saw Moriah walking out the back door, without a coat or wrap on. Although spring was only a month away, the damp night chilled the bones. "Moriah," he called, following her out the door. "Where are you going?"

"Stove's out," she said, her voice monotone and barely audible. "I shouldn't have fallen asleep."

He came up behind her as she bent to pick up several split pieces of wood. "Go inside, Moriah," he said. "I'll get the wood."

In the darkness of the night he couldn't see her expression, but he could see the shadow of her movement as she nodded her head. She went back inside, her steps slow, as if she were in shock. Gabe realized she probably was.

He snatched up enough wood to make a decent-sized fire, then dashed back inside where Moriah stood in the middle of the kitchen, staring at the withered pie on the table. "I should have made pumpkin," she mumbled. "He likes pumpkin better than apple."

Concern filled him as he shoved the wood in the opening of the stove. He moved beside her and led her to a chair. "Sit down, and don't move. I'll get the fire started." He started back to the stove but added for good measure, "Don't move."

He lit the stove. Soon the kitchen would be warm. Hopefully

that would help; she appeared so cold. He could see her body trembling, her fingertips a bluish hue. Remembering the quilt he saw lying over the back of the couch in the front room, he went to fetch it. Within moments he came back and put it around her shoulders, then sat down next to her.

He was glad to see she had gathered the quilt closer to her body. At least she wasn't completely catatonic. "Do you want some coffee? Tea maybe?"

"Coffee," she said, then looked up at him, her eyes not so empty now.

As he moved around the kitchen, easily locating what he needed—she hadn't rearranged anything since moving into the house—he thought about his brother. That Levi would leave the church, leave his *wife* . . . Gabe could barely comprehend it. That he would do such a thing by an impersonal letter added even more fuel to the angry fire stoking inside him.

Levi had sent Gabe a letter as well, through the driver that had taken him to Gates Mills for the past couple months. In the short note, he had said he was leaving the church and the community—to do *what*, Gabe didn't know—and told him not to try to contact him. Right now Gabe didn't care if he never saw his brother again. The coward had left it up to him to deliver the news not only to Moriah but also to their father.

As the coffee perked on the stove, he dropped his head in his hands. How could he tell *Daed* what Levi had done? Did his brother not realize their father's increasingly fragile state? Was he so selfish that he didn't care if their father died from the heartbreak of knowing his son had chosen the world over God?

"Gabriel?"

He looked up at the sound of Moriah's voice. Her features

seemed less pale, less haunted. But the pain was still evident in her eyes, in the downward turn of her mouth. He hated seeing her suffer this way.

She stood up from her chair and walked over to him. Placing her hand on his arm, she said, "Let it go, Gabriel. Let your anger for Levi go."

How did she know what he was thinking? He followed her gaze to his hands, which were clenched so tightly the knuckles where white. When she looked at his face, he relaxed his hands.

The coffee pot finished percolating. Gabe started to reach past Moriah's shoulder for a cup from the cabinet when she stopped him. "I'll get it."

"*Nee*, Moriah. Let me do it."

She shook her head. "I can't just sit here. Do you want some?"

He nodded, not wanting to argue with her, then went to sit down as she took two white ceramic mugs from the cabinet and poured coffee into them. She spooned a little sugar into Gabe's, then poured cream into hers before sitting back down at the table and handing him his cup. Surrounding the mug with her hands, she stared into the caramel-colored liquid.

"How do you do it?" he asked after a few moments of silence.

She glanced up. "Do what?"

"Stay so calm." A few moments ago she'd seemed ready to fall apart. Now she was a pillar of strength. How she managed to regain her equanimity he had no idea.

"I'm not calm," she said. The tremble in her lower lip as she spoke revealed the truth behind her words. "I don't know what I feel right now, but it's definitely not calm." She looked back at her coffee, but didn't make a move to drink it. "Does your *daed* know?"

He shook his head. "I didn't want to wake him."

"What time is it?"

"Twelve thirty."

With a sigh, she said, "I must have been asleep for hours. I was waiting for Levi . . ." Her hands tightened around the mug. "Why is he doing this?" Her voice sounded thin.

"I don't know." Gabe stood up from his chair and started pacing the room, his coffee untouched as well. "It doesn't make any sense."

"Did he say anything to you about leaving?"

"*Nee.* Not a word."

"Did he . . ." She paused, her gaze averted. "Did he say he was . . . unhappy?"

Gabe immediately caught her meaning and sat back down. "*Nee*, not ever. Moriah, I'm sure that whatever crazy thing is going on inside my brother's head, it has nothing to do with you." But as he said it, he saw a tear roll down her cheek.

"He doesn't love me. Not anymore." She wiped her face with the back of her hand, still not looking at him. "I wonder if he ever did."

"Moriah," Gabe said, lowering his voice. How he wished he could take away the pain, the humiliation she so clearly felt. "This isn't your fault."

Her head snapped her head up. "But what if it is? What if he left because I wasn't a good wife? What if I pushed him to do this?"

He couldn't imagine her being anything but the perfect wife. "I don't believe that."

"Just look at this supper," she said, her voice rising an octave. "The rolls are burned."

"Moriah, they're fine—"

"And I know he likes pumpkin pie more than apple, but I didn't have any pumpkin. I should have bought some; I should have prepared better. A good wife would have put her husband's needs first, right?"

Her words were coming out faster now, and the worry that had filled him when she first read Levi's letter returned. "Pie is not a need, Moriah. He would have been fine eating apple, trust me."

She stood from her chair, letting the quilt fall to the floor. She kept talking as if he hadn't said anything. "I must have done something wrong, something horrible for him to leave me. I wasn't good enough. I wasn't pretty enough, or desirable enough, or . . ."

Gabe couldn't take listening to her tear herself down. He leapt from his chair and went to her, putting his hands on her shoulders. "Stop it, Moriah. Stop saying things that aren't true!"

Her eyes filled with moisture, and she reached up and grabbed his shirt. "I should have made pumpkin, Gabriel. I should have made pumpkin . . ." She fell against his chest and sobbed.

Instinctively his arms went around her. He could easily rest his chin on her head, and he wanted to do just that, to press her against his chest and never let her go. He squeezed his eyes shut.

He knew he should step away, but he stroked her back, even pressed his cheek against her *kapp*, breathing in the sweet smell of her. While Levi would cast her away, Gabe would treasure her forever.

But she wasn't his to treasure. With a huge effort, he lifted his head, stilled his hand, and stepped away from her. His shirt was damp with her tears and pain. When she looked up at him, her eyes brimming with tears, it took every ounce of his resolve not to draw her against him once more.

"I was going to tell him something tonight," she whispered,

her cheeks and lips shiny with moisture. "I was going to give him the best news in the world."

Gabe sucked in a breath. He didn't have to hear the words; he already knew what she was about to say.

"We're having a baby." Somehow she managed a watery smile. "I'm pregnant with Levi's child." She laid her palm flat against her stomach. "This baby was going to fix everything between us, Gabriel. Draw us closer together, make us a real family." Once again she leaned against him, pressing her cheek against his shirt. "Now what am I going to do?"

Gabe continued to hold her, convincing himself he was only offering her comfort, even though with every fiber of his being he longed to offer her more. Most of all he wanted to take on her pain as his own. But he couldn't. He could only give her solace, and weak solace at that. "I don't know, Moriah," he said, reveling in her nearness while wallowing in his own guilt. "I don't know."

"Gabriel . . . Gabe, *sohn*, wake up."

Gabe's eyes flew open at the sound of his father's voice and the touch of the old man's hand on his shoulder. He straightened to an upright position as the kitchen came into focus. A dull ache spread across his shoulder blades. Glancing around, he realized he'd fallen asleep at the table. Arching his back, he looked up into his father's concerned eyes. "What time is it?" he asked, his voice still heavy with sleep.

"Past seven thirty. When you didn't show up at the shop, I got worried. Aaron had to come get me to unlock the door."

Gabe rubbed the back of his neck. "I'm sorry, *Daed*." He

surveyed the kitchen once again. The fire had burned out in the stove, and a chill hung in the air. He spied two nearly full cups of cold coffee on the table. Then the prior evening's events replayed in his mind.

Soon after Moriah had told him about the baby, he had managed to convince her to go upstairs and sleep. Despite the fatigue that had seeped into her features, she had resisted. Finally, she agreed to rest for the baby's sake. He had planned to stay up, to be there if she needed him. Sometime during the night he must have fallen asleep on the table.

The impact of her pregnancy continued to swirl around in his brain. A baby. Moriah was pregnant, and her husband gone. His heart squeezed in his chest at the thought of the pain she must be going through. There was no option of divorce in their faith. Levi would be her husband until death, whether he was here or not.

"Gabe? Are you gonna tell me what's going on here or am I gonna have to drag it out of you?"

His father's voice yanked him out of his musings. Gabe looked at the old man, dread spinning in his gut. He didn't want to tell him about Levi, but he had no choice. He couldn't prolong it; his father would find out soon enough anyway. Unless . . .

Unless Levi came back.

Once his brother knew about the baby, he'd have to return. He'd put away self-centeredness for the sake of his wife and child. They would work out their problems and be the family God intended them to be. Then his father wouldn't have to know anything about his son's betrayal.

Gabe popped up from his chair, his decision made. "I need you to do me a favor, *Daed.*"

A bewildered expression crossed the older man's face. "Sure, *sohn*. Anything. But I still want to know what's going on."

"You will, soon enough." He went outside and grabbed a few chunks of wood, then started the fire in the stove. The wood crackled as the fire burned through the bark. He dumped the stale contents of the coffeepot in the sink, then started a fresh brew. Moriah would probably want a cup once she awakened.

"Gabriel?" John questioned, sitting down at the table. "Are you going to tell me what you need me to do or not?"

"Sorry. Can you stay with Moriah? She's upstairs, asleep. She's not feeling well."

John raised his bushy brows in surprise. "Where's Levi?"

Gabe hesitated for a moment before answering. "Gates Mills," he said.

John frowned. "He didn't come home last night?"

"He had some extra work to do." Gabe checked the stove again, even though the fire was at the perfect temperature. He hated lying to his father, and he couldn't look at him while false-hoods flew out of his mouth. But it was necessary, at least for the moment. "Levi will be back later tonight." *Lord willing.*

That simple explanation seemed to pacify John. "Good. I have half a mind to tell that boy to quit working for those Yankees. We need him here. It isn't as if we're desperate for money. The Lord has seen fit to provide us with everything we need."

"*Ya*, He has." Eager to end the conversation before his father asked more questions, Gabe searched the kitchen for his hat and coat, then remembered he left them up front. He took a deep breath to steady his nerves, inhaling the rich scent of coffee brew-ing. "I'll be gone for part of the day, *Daed*. Please stay here and keep an eye on Moriah. I'll close the shop, but Aaron can do a few things in there. If I'm not back by the time he's finished, go ahead and send him home."

"That's a fine boy you hired," John said. "I can tell he's going to be a *gut* worker. Hard to believe he spent time in jail."

Gabe nodded, only half-listening to what John was saying. "I'll see you this afternoon."

After grabbing his coat and hat, he rushed to the shop. Aaron was already at work sweeping the floor, even though it didn't need it. He had swept it thoroughly the day before.

"Aaron," Gabe called.

Aaron looked up, then set the broom aside before shoving his hands in his pockets and lumbering over to Gabe. "What can I do for you?"

His standard question. Since starting work two days ago, Aaron Detweiler hadn't said much and mostly kept to himself, but he always asked Gabe and John what he could do for them. Gabe had confidence that he was leaving the shop in good hands. "I've got some errands to do, and I'll be gone most of the day. *Daed's* inside the main house, but I don't want him working out here today. I'm closing up the shop, but I hope you'll do a few things for me." Aaron nodded and listened carefully to Gabe's instructions. "When you're done, just let *Daed* know before you go home."

Aaron nodded again but remained silent.

"*Danki.*" Gabe hurried out the door and hustled to the end of the driveway. He sprinted along the road to the telephone box situated in between his property and the Fishers', his neighbors. The church's *Ordnung* allowed the Millers to use cell phones for their business, but they hadn't made the switch yet. Four families, including his, shared this telephone for business or emergency purposes only. Today constituted an emergency. He called Guy Thompson, a fellow he knew who ran a taxi service for many of the Amish. As the hollow-sounding ring repeated in Gabe's ears, he prayed Guy was home.

"Thompson," a man with a low, gruff voice answered on the fourth ring.

Gabe offered a quick, silent prayer of thanks. "Guy, this is Gabriel Miller."

"Hey, Gabe. How are you?"

"Doing all right," Gabe said, but that was far from the truth. Inside the dense wool of his gloves, his palms broke out into a sweat while his stomach churned. Confronting his brother was the last thing he wanted to do, and he knew he needed God's help to keep his temper when he saw him. He fought to keep his tone steady. He didn't need Guy asking any questions. "I need a ride. Are you available today?"

"Sure am. Where you wanna go?"

"Gates Mills," Gabe said, letting out a frosty breath. "I need to see my brother."

Moriah's eyes ached as she struggled to open them. Somehow she had managed to fall asleep, but she didn't know when or how. She had only agreed to go upstairs to placate Gabe, who had insisted she get some rest. Thank the Lord he had been there last night. What would she have done without him? Uncharacteristically, he had been kind to her, giving her comfort, trying to reassure her that everything would be all right, even though she could see in his eyes how deeply Levi's betrayal had affected him. When he told her she had to sleep for her baby's sake, she finally, albeit reluctantly, agreed.

But when she'd begun to climb the stairs, the tears came again. Over and over she had asked herself how Levi could do this—to her, to their families, to himself, to their community. Didn't he realize what it meant for him to leave their faith? He had agreed to live by the tenets of their church for the rest of his life when he had been baptized. How could he break that vow? And why would he break their marriage vow?

She couldn't shake the thought that somehow his leaving had to be her fault. What she had done to fail him. What she could have done differently.

She'd cried until she had fallen asleep.

Now, with bright winter sunshine streaming through her window, she forced herself to wake up. Breathing in the air of a new day, her sorrow multiplied as she looked around her bedroom. The room she had shared with Levi for the past four months. Every bit of her surroundings reminded her of him. She spied the open closet door, taking in the dark outline of his black Sunday suit. He had looked so handsome in his stark-white shirt and black vest. Her gaze fell on his spare pair of work boots, one boot lying sideways as if it had been cast asunder.

She sat up and threw off the covers. The emptiness of this room, the dreams that would be unfulfilled, they all assaulted her.

She glanced down and saw that she wore the same dress she'd had on yesterday. Shoving away her thoughts, she rose from the bed and trudged to the closet, swallowing the lump in her throat. As she reached toward her dresses, she tried to ignore Levi's shirts, particularly the one she'd sewn and given to him on their one-month anniversary. She had commemorated each monthly anniversary with something special. Last night was to be the most special of all.

Blinking back tears, she grabbed the first dress she touched and carried it to her bed, tossing it on top of her scattered bedclothes. Within minutes she had stripped off her wrinkled dress and was in her underclothes, her exposed skin pebbling in the cold air. She hadn't bothered to start the small propane heater in the bedroom last night, and she felt the chill seep into her. But instead of dressing, she shut the closet door and stared at her reflection in the mirror hanging on the back.

Her hand went to her flat stomach. Soon the new life inside her would grow, stretching out her belly more than she would think possible. She remembered when her youngest sister, Ruthie, had been born. Her mother had been so swollen Moriah thought she would pop. She wondered if her baby would do the same thing to her.

Her teeth started to chatter, but she didn't care. The cold numbed her, both outside and in. She could stand here forever, not feeling a thing. No pain. No regrets. No heartache.

Nothing.

"Moriah?"

The faraway sound of her father-in-law's gravelly voice travelled up the stairs.

"Honey, are you awake?"

Her body began to shake violently as the cold set into her bones. She noted that John's voice was steady, and she realized Gabe hadn't told him about Levi. She briefly wondered why, but figured he had his own reasons. She wouldn't say anything either, not wanting to be the one to break the bad news to him. She also didn't want to raise his suspicions, so she quickly dressed, then pinned up her hair with shaky hands before fastening her *kapp*. Slipping on her shoes, she went downstairs, hoping her father-in-law wouldn't notice the redness in her eyes.

John stood at the bottom of the staircase, one gnarled hand

resting on the simple banister. "*Gude mariye*," he said, his kind gaze giving her a once over. "Gabe said you were feeling poorly last night. Are you doing any better this morning?"

"I'm f-fine," she said, unable to keep her teeth from chattering.

His good-natured expression changed to one of concern. He reached out and touched her forehead with the rough pads of his fingers. "Goodness, you're freezing." John put his arm around her shoulders and shook his head. "Chilled to the bone. Didn't you have the heat on last night?"

"I forgot," she said as he led her to the kitchen. "Guess I was too tired last night."

"You must have been. Well, we'll warm you right up."

They walked into the kitchen, and her cold body welcomed the heat emanating from the stove. The aroma of fresh coffee comforted her as she sat down at the table.

John walked over to the stove and picked up the percolator. "Gabriel made some coffee before he left. Thought you might want some. Would you like a cup?"

Bless Gabriel. Moriah wrapped her arms around her body. How stupid of her to stand upstairs and freeze. That's all she needed to do—catch a cold and get sick. She had more than herself to think about now.

"Or would you rather have some tea?" John turned and looked at her. "My own special brew. Will fix whatever ails you." He smiled.

Not knowing what John's "special brew" consisted of, or if it would be safe for her baby, she shook her head. "Coffee will be fine."

John poured her a cup of coffee. "Sugar? Cream?"

"Black," she said, even though she hated the taste of black

coffee. But she didn't want to put him to any trouble. Knowing Gabriel, he had probably asked his father to stay with her. Yet another reason to be grateful for her brother-in-law. She needed the distraction of John's company.

Her father-in-law placed the mug in front of her, then set his own mug in front of him before he sat down.

"Where's Gabriel?" Moriah said, breathing in the scent of the strong beverage. Her stomach performed an unexpected summersault. Maybe she should have had the tea instead.

"I don't know. Said he had to go somewhere, and he'd be gone most of the day. He left Aaron in charge of the shop."

Moriah nodded, bringing the drink up to her lips. She surmised Gabriel had gone to see Levi, to convince him to come back to the community. A glimmer of hope flickered inside her. Levi's return would be the best thing for everyone, but where would they go from there? Levi didn't love her. He didn't want her. How could she deal with that?

She would have to accept it with patience and humility.

Her father-in-law leaned forward, his smile slipping somewhat. "Moriah, are you sure you're all right? You've turned awful pale all of a sudden."

Her belly bubbled and gurgled, and nausea rose up in her throat. Perspiration beaded on her upper lip. The coffee suddenly smelled putrid and rank. She shoved away from the table, her hand covering her mouth.

"Moriah?"

Flying to the bathroom, she slammed the door behind her, kneeled over the toilet, and threw up.

"You should really try some of my tea," John said from the other side of the door. "Does wonders to settle the stomach."

Chapter 6

*O*h my, these dogs are howling." Gladys Johansson plopped her ample behind on the low concrete-topped brick wall directly across from Mary Yoder's restaurant. The plump waitress slipped off one of her tennis shoes and rubbed her chubby foot. Wisps of her dyed-red hair swayed in the cold breeze, revealing her silvery roots. "Yep, I'm gonna have me a good soak in the foot tub tonight. Just me, my bubbles, and some trashy reality television. The perfect way to spend an evening."

Rachel grinned as she sat next to her Yankee coworker. Mary Yoder's Amish Kitchen was owned by Yankees but employed both the Amish and outlanders. It was only two in the afternoon, but Gladys obviously planned to begin her evening as soon as possible.

Their morning shift had just ended, and Rachel was waiting for Christian to pick her up. He had made the offer after the singing last Sunday evening and she had accepted. Two days had passed since then, and she was kind of looking forward to seeing him.

Gladys shoved her foot back in her shoe, wiggling her heel back and forth until it was completely encased in white leather, then bent over and tied the laces. After one last stretch, she stood, then slung her black purse over her shoulder and turned to Rachel. "Sure you don't want me to give you a ride home, honey? It'll only take a few minutes. I'll just bring my car around and off we'll go."

Rachel tugged her navy blue *reck* closer to her body, the wool blend soft and warm. Despite the cloudless sky, the sun offered little heat. February in Ohio could be brutal. "No thanks, Gladys. Christian is coming to pick me up."

"The fellow who's had breakfast here a few times? The one who always sits at one of your tables?"

"No, that's Tobias. And he only sits at my table so I can *serve* him. He lives to aggravate me."

Gladys tilted her head. "Hmm. I thought he sat there because he was sweet on you."

"Hardly. We can't stand each other."

"Oops. My mistake." Gladys smiled and headed toward the restaurant's huge parking lot. It wasn't unusual for Mary Yoder's to serve tour bus travelers, so there was plenty of room for parking. "You lovebirds have a wonderful time."

Rachel waved good-bye to her coworker, then tucked an errant strand of hair into her *kapp* as she waited for Christian to pick her up. A few minutes later his buggy pulled into the parking lot. He steered his horse alongside her, then waited for her to climb in on the passenger's side. When she was settled, he handed her a lap blanket. "This will help you warm up."

She smiled as they pulled away. He really was the perfect gentleman. As he made a right turn onto North State Street, she glanced at his unassuming profile. Inside the buggy, only inches separated them. Since they were courting, she thought they should be sitting closer to each other. She scooted to the left until the skirt of her gray dress touched his black pants, expecting him to notice her bold move.

But Christian kept his gaze straight ahead as he guided his horse along the road. The black winter covering of the buggy buffered them from the harshest parts of the wind and cold. Traffic whizzed by, some cars giving them a wide berth and others coming perilously close. It made sense that he would have to keep his concentration on the road, but she had hoped for at least some kind of reaction. Even a small glance would have been encouraging.

She tried a different tack to gain his attention. A man's heart could definitely be reached through his stomach; that's one thing she'd known since she was a child. Her dad and brothers were never stingy with the compliments when it came to eating the foods they loved, which in the Detweiler home were plentiful. She took the small white sack she had brought from the restaurant and opened it up. Immediately the buggy filled with the nutty, sweet scent of homemade pecan pie.

"Smells good," Christian said without turning to look at her.

"I brought you a piece of the pecan pie I made at the restaurant. It's fresh from the oven." She gave him what she thought might be a pretty, charming, appealing, and desirable smile. The kind that didn't hide any secrets. Hopefully he would notice it soon, since it hurt to contort her mouth in such a foreign way.

He gave the pie a cursory glance before staring straight at the road again. "I'm allergic."

Her smile slid from her face. "You're what?"

"Allergic to nuts. I thought you knew that. All kinds of nuts—hickory, walnuts, and especially pecans. Make me swell up so much I can't breathe."

Rachel stared down at the piece of still-warm pie encased

in a foggy, clear plastic box. She'd had no idea he was allergic to nuts.

"Nice thought, though." He gave her a quick smile.

She smiled halfheartedly back and returned the pie to the bag. Even though he couldn't enjoy the treat, he seemed to have appreciated the gesture.

Suddenly he scooted over to his left, creating another space between them. "Don't mean to crowd you," he said.

Rachel's shoulders slumped. This wasn't working out at all like she had planned.

They rode the rest of the way to her house in silence. *Boring* silence. She had no idea courting could be this dull. Christian was a nice guy, but not much of a conversationalist.

When he pulled up to her driveway, he got out of the buggy and met her on the passenger side. When she stepped on the ground, he asked, "Can I take you to the frolic this Sunday night?"

"*Ya*." Although she thought she should be more excited about it. Why weren't her emotions cooperating?

He grinned. "I'll see you then." Turning around, he started to climb back in the buggy, but stopped and faced her again. Before she knew it, he leaned forward and kissed her on the cheek, then turned and left.

Rachel watched him go, even more confused than before. Her fingers pressed against her face where his lips had touched. Her first kiss. Granted, it was a peck on the cheek, but that was more than any boy had done before. His unexpected show of affection surprised her, but that was her only reaction. Frowning, she kicked a pebble on the driveway and walked toward her front door.

Shouldn't she have felt something else when he kissed her?

Instead, she felt nothing, other than bewilderment over what she should do about Christian, if anything. She couldn't shake the feeling that something wasn't right between them. Her lack of response to his kiss only reinforced it. Maybe things would change once they spent more time together. Even though she had known Christian all her life, he mostly kept to himself, and rarely revealed much to her. In many ways he was like her brother Aaron. A mystery wrapped up in an enigma. She didn't truly "know" him, not like she thought she should. She wondered if she ever would.

Gabe repeatedly clenched his fists until his knuckles ached as he stood in front of the truck-stop counter. Guy had picked him up over two hours ago, but he'd also picked up three other men and dropped them off in Ashtabula to work on a construction project. Now they were at a truck stop for gas and coffee, and Guy was flirting with the woman at the cash register. She was far too young for Guy, who was well into middle age and had the soft gut and silvery hair to prove it. Gabe tried to keep from tapping his foot as Guy paid for his gas and beverage, flashing his yellowish grin.

The girl was clearly bored with the attention. "Thanks. Have a good day." She handed him his receipt, the tiny silver ball underneath her bottom lip glinting under the fluorescent lighting. Then she pulled her cell phone out of her pocket and started texting.

"I sure will, sweetheart," Guy said, baring his teeth again, oblivious to her ignoring him. "I'll see you tomorrow."

She nodded, her gaze not moving from the small screen of her lime-colored phone. Her fingers, the nails coated in black polish, flew fast and furious on the tiny keyboard.

"Yep. That one's mine," Guy said, as they walked out of the store. He gave Gabe a contrite look. "Sorry, Gabe. Shouldn't be talking like that in front of you."

"Shouldn't be talking like that at all," Gabe mumbled.

"What?" Guy asked over the cacophonic sound of passing cars and semitrucks.

"Nothing," Gabe said, deciding he needed to keep his mouth shut. He didn't want to say or do anything to jeopardize his ride to Gates Mills. It would cost him a pretty penny to get there, as Guy would have to hang around to bring him back. But if he could convince Levi to come home, it would be worth it.

They climbed into Guy's minivan, and Guy turned the key. Country music blared from the speakers. Gabe tuned it out. He glanced at the illuminated clock on the dashboard. Nearly two o'clock. The day was wasting away. He clenched his fists again.

Guy snapped off the radio. "Something bothering you, Gabe?"

Gabe relaxed his hands and placed his palms on his thighs. "No. I'm fine."

With a shrug, Guy grabbed his Styrofoam coffee cup with one hand while his other hand lay limply over the steering wheel as he maneuvered his way onto Interstate 90. "You seem kind of keyed up, that's all."

"Nothing's wrong." He turned and looked out the window. The bare branches of trees lining the interstate spiked into the cloudless sky. Black slush coated the freeway while a thin layer of pale white snow glistened on the grassy land. His mind whirled as he thought about what he would say to his brother. What he could do to convince him to return home.

Then his mind shifted to Moriah, as it always did. What if Levi refused to come home? What would she do then?

The hour-long drive seemed to drag. Guy had turned the radio back on and spent the rest of the trip singing off-key. Gabe normally didn't mind Yankee music, even though he heard it only on rare occasions. Radios and any type of music players were forbidden by the *Ordnung*. Yet when he did hear it, he kind of enjoyed it. The songs were a welcome change from the monotone singing at church services.

But not today. The music sounded like buzzing bees in his ears. He ground his teeth as Guy exited the freeway and headed toward the Johnston's horse ranch. When the impressive metal gates rose into view, Gabe pointed. "Turn here."

"Yep." Guy spun the steering wheel and passed under an arch with the letter *J* curved around the top of the gates. Gabe grudgingly admired the extraordinary scroll work.

Guy drove up the long driveway toward a huge brick house with a circular driveway of red-stone pavers. A fountain made of sand-colored stone stood in the center, holding an urn-shaped centerpiece emblazoned with a huge lion's head.

Gabe had been here only once before and, as before, was struck by the size of the house and the property. Gates Mills was an exclusive community, and Johnston's Farms was just on the outskirts of the village. He knew the Johnstons had only one child, a daughter. Why would they need a house that big for only three people? The imposing dwelling looked large enough to house two large Amish families.

Guy let out a low whistle. "Nice. Very nice." He turned to Gabe. "Want me to drop you off here?"

"No. I need to go to the horse barn." He pointed to part of the brick driveway that led to the back of the property. They followed it until the neat pavers turned into a windy but well-kept dirt road. A four-wheeler with two riders whizzed by, seemingly heading for the same destination. As the minivan neared an extravagant, bright-red barn with a white roof, Gabe held up his hand and signaled Guy to stop. "Drop me here."

Guy applied the brakes. "When do you want me to pick you up?"

"Give me an hour."

"Sure enough."

"Thanks," Gabe said as he opened the door.

"Hey," Guy called as Gabe stepped to the ground. "Good luck with whatever this is you're doing. Seems really important."

"It is, Guy. It is." He shut the door and watched for a moment as Guy backed up and turned around, then headed for the main road. Gabe swiveled around, his shoe crushing and sliding against the slushy, dirty snow. He took in the two-story structure in front of him. Even Gabe could tell it was top of the line. He imagined the extraordinary horseflesh occupying the stalls inside. Behind the barn was a wide pasture, bordered by a thick white oak fence. Although the field was covered with snow, when spring came there would be enough grass for at least twenty horses to eat their fill.

The rumbling sound of the four-wheeler filled the air again. Gabe jerked his head around and saw the shiny red machine with its two riders coming toward him. The vehicle stopped a few feet behind him, and both riders got off, their faces hidden by their black helmets. Gabe fully turned just as they both took off their headgear.

His mouth dropped open as he looked at his twin brother, wearing a new black-leather jacket and blue jeans. He had shaved his beard and his hair was cut short over his ears, with a big hank of brown bangs hanging over his forehead. The other rider, a woman with long, free-flowing red hair and brightly painted red lips had her arms around Levi's waist, as if he were her personal property. Laughter filled the air as they looked at each other, oblivious to anyone else around them.

A wave of nausea threatened to cut Gabe at the knees as he watched the two of them cavorting around. He thought of Moriah, miserable and pregnant, not understanding what had happened to her husband and her marriage. Meanwhile Levi was having the time of his life with another woman.

Gabe couldn't stand to watch anymore. He stormed toward his brother, shoving aside the anger threatening to bubble to the surface.

Levi's and the woman's laughter abruptly stopped as they noticed Gabe approaching. Levi's eyes narrowed into angry slits. "What are you doing here? I told you not to come."

The woman standing beside him moved even closer, until her body was pressed up against his. She flipped her unbound hair over her shoulders. Even in the dull light of the gray sky Gabe could see how beautiful and shiny it was. As he breathed in, he could smell the heady scent of her perfume. "Who is this?" she asked, peering at him. Then her eyes widened. "You have a twin?"

"Yes." Levi spoke in a low, guarded tone.

She gaped at Gabe, then looked at Levi. "You never told me."

"The subject never came up."

Gabe cringed inside. "I need to talk to you. Alone." He spoke in Pennsylvania Dutch and gave the woman a pointed look. Clearly she had a major part to play in his brother leaving his wife.

"Excuse me?" The woman turned to Levi. "What did he say?"

Levi scowled. "He wants to speak to me. Alone."

She lifted the corner of her upper lip in an indignant smirk. "Does he know who he's talking to?"

Just as Gabe was opening his mouth to say that he knew exactly who he was talking to, Levi intervened. He pressed his cheek against her forehead and said, "Go on in the house, honey. I'll be there in a bit."

"But—"

"It's fine. Let me talk to him."

She looked at Gabe again, her green eyes assessing him coolly. "Okay." Even though they stood in the cold, she didn't suggest that Levi and Gabe go inside the barn, or even in the house, to have their conversation. Instead she turned, tilted up her head, and kissed Levi fully on the lips.

The sickening lump in Gabe's belly expanded as he witnessed his still-married brother kiss her back with enthusiasm. When they were done, the woman walked past Gabe, tossed him a look of conquest, then headed back into the expansive house, her helmet tucked underneath one arm.

Levi looked directly at Gabe. His face suddenly flushed, and he stepped back and looked away, wiping his mouth with the back of his hand as he did.

At least his brother had the decency to appear embarrassed. "Who is she?" Gabe asked, fighting to keep his tone even.

"A friend," Levi said after a long pause.

"You looked more than friendly to me."

Levi turned his gaze back on his brother. "I know why you're here, Gabriel, and it won't do any good. I'm not coming back."

Gabe stepped toward him, shoving his hands into the pockets of his coat to keep from clocking Levi across the face. "You have to."

"*Nee*, I don't. You can't make me. No one can. Not you, not the bishop or ministers. When you go back, you tell them not to bother visiting here, because nothing they say will make me change my mind." Levi walked over to the four-wheeler and set the helmet on the seat. Then he turned around, his expression determined. "This is my home now."

"This?" Gabe yanked his hands out of his pocket and thrust out his arms wide. "This is where you *work*, Levi. You are an employee here, nothing more."

"That, *bruder*, is where you are mistaken."

"Your home is in Middlefield. With your *wife*. Remember her?"

"Of course I do," Levi said hotly. "But I took care of it when I wrote her that letter."

"A letter? You think a letter will absolve you from everything? Your marriage vows, your church vows?" His breath hung in frosty clouds as he paused, still struggling to remain calm but finding it harder with each passing minute.

Levi stormed toward him, anger sparking in his eyes. "*That* is why I'm not going back."

"What? You don't want to hear the truth?"

"I don't want to hear *your* version of the truth. You don't get it, Gabe. You've been sheltered—we all have. All we do is follow rules. Don't wear this. Don't talk like that. No electricity. No music. No *life*." He took a step back. "I can't do it anymore. I want to live. I want to be free to be myself, my real self. I can't do that and be Amish too."

"And what are you free to do, Levi? Get your hair cut? Wear Yankee clothes? Cheat on your wife?"

Levi turned his head. "It's not like that."

"That's what it looked like to me."

Whipping his head around, Levi said, "There you go again, judging me. My perfect brother. Never commits a sin." Levi's eyes narrowed. "Except in his heart."

Gabe froze. Surely his brother didn't suspect . . .

"You have no right to say anything to me, not when you've been lusting after Moriah for years. You thought I didn't know, but you weren't very good at hiding it." He crossed his arms. "I thought you'd be glad I was gone. Then you could have her for yourself. In fact, why don't you? This is what you've always wanted, isn't it? It just kills you that she chose me over you."

Years of resentment and bottled anger suddenly burst. With one hand, he grabbed Levi by the collar of his new, slick jacket and made a fist with the other, ready to plow it into his brother's face.

But Levi didn't cower. He didn't flinch. He stared Gabe straight in the eye and said, "Go ahead. Hit me. Show me what I've known all along—you're no better than I am."

Gabe paused, his fist raised in midair. If he hit his brother now—and Lord knew he wanted to more than anything in the world—he would prove Levi right. Violence of any kind was not permitted by the *Ordnung*. How could he hit his brother, then turn around and tell him what to do afterward?

Slowly he lowered his fist and released Levi's jacket. His brother stepped back and adjusted his collar, his gaze not leaving Gabe's. Finally, Gabe looked away, the anger and energy flowing out of him.

"You're not denying you love her," Levi said.

Gabe let out a long breath. Why bother admitting what his brother already knew? "Moriah's pregnant," he said flatly. "She told me yesterday."

Levi suddenly paled. "I . . . I had no idea."

"No one did. She was going to tell you last night. Instead, she got your letter."

Running a hand through his newly short hair, Levi began to pace. "What am I gonna do?" Over and over he mumbled as he stalked back and forth, arguing with himself in low tones.

In Gabe's mind, there was only one answer, and he didn't understand his brother's struggle. "It's an easy decision, Levi. Come home. If not for your own sake, then for your child's."

"You don't understand." Levi stopped and gave Gabe a haunted look. "Taylor's pregnant too."

"Taylor? Who's Taylor?"

"The woman you just met. Taylor Johnston."

Gabe's heart fell to his knees. "You didn't."

"I couldn't help it. She's special—"

"So is your wife," Gabe gritted out.

He stared at the snowy ground. "Look, I love Taylor."

"Seems to me you love what she can give you." Gabe gestured to Levi's clothes. "Did she buy those for you? Did she tell you to cut your hair, shave your beard?"

"So what if she did? She didn't make me do anything I wasn't ready to do." Levi looked directly at him. "I love her, Gabe. More than I ever loved Moriah."

Shaking his head, Gabe asked, "How is that possible? You've known her for a couple months. You've known Moriah for years."

"But I never loved her. Not like this. I should have never married Moriah. I should have known it wouldn't work when . . ." He stared off into the distance.

"When what?"

Levi leveled his gaze at his brother. "You remember when I went to Indiana last spring?"

"*Ya.*"

"I never told anyone this, but I . . . met someone else."

"A Yankee?"

"*Nee*, she was Amish. I had planned to stop courting Moriah, but when this girl found out about her, she didn't want anything more to do with me."

"Sounds like a smart *maedel*."

Levi leaned against the seat of the four-wheeler. "She is."

"I suppose Moriah didn't know anything about this other *maedel*."

He gazed down at the ground. "*Nee*. She didn't. But it didn't matter, because I came back home and proposed. I thought if I married her, when I was fully committed, I would never look at another woman again. I really wanted things to work out with her."

"Levi, I don't understand why they can't."

"Don't you see? It isn't Moriah; it's me. Ever since we got married I've been feeling smothered."

"But you said you loved her—"

"That was before I knew what love really was!" He jammed his hands into his pockets and looked down on the ground. "Moriah was convenient, Gabe. She was always there, always available. She's a nice girl, a *wunderbaar* woman, but she's suffocating me. The only time I can breathe is when I'm here with Taylor." He looked up.

"Taylor has given me everything I've dreamed of, things I didn't even know I wanted. All this?" He gestured to the barn, the house, the land. "It will be mine someday. That's more than I'll ever have working my fingers to the bone in the shop."

"Do you really love all this excess, Levi? Is this all about money?"

Levi shook his head. "*Nee.* It's not about the money. Like I said, I love Taylor."

"But Moriah is pregnant! How can you abandon her like this?" Gabe walked up to him. "Levi . . . I don't understand. How can you leave your child behind?"

Suddenly Levi's shoulders slumped. His tortured eyes met Gabe's. "I have to, Gabe. I can't go back. Not ever. My life is here now. And that's how I want it to be." He nodded, as if trying to convince himself that his words were true. "Her family and the rest of the community will take care of her and the baby."

Shock coursed through Gabe. He barely recognized his brother any more. "You'd let someone else raise your baby?"

Levi swallowed, hesitating before he responded. "In this case, *ya. Ya,* I would."

"You have a responsibility to Moriah first, Levi. If you're willing to give up one of your children, then let Taylor find someone else."

"Her father would tear me apart."

"We could protect you. If you confess your sin, the whole community will stand behind you."

Levi let out a bitter laugh. "There you go again, branding me with your righteousness. I won't confess anything, because I have nothing to confess. Even if her father had nothing to do with it, I'd still want Taylor. It's best for everyone."

"Except Moriah. You know the *Ordnung* doesn't permit divorce, under any circumstances. She'll never be able to remarry."

"You think she'd be better off trapped in a loveless marriage?"

"I want her happy. She'd be happy to have her husband back."

"I doubt it."

Gabe was getting nowhere with his hardheaded twin. His brother was rationalizing his choices, twisting everything to satisfy his own selfishness.

Stepping toward Gabe, Levi said, "You could take care of her. I know you love her, Gabriel. You can have her now, if you want to."

Gabe couldn't believe what he was hearing. "Levi, she is married to you! She will always be married to you. I'm not an adulterer."

"Except in your heart."

His nostrils flared. "You have no right to accuse me of anything."

Levi paused. "You're right. But you would be a better friend to her than I would be a husband. We both know that."

"What about *Daed*? Have you thought about him? How he will feel once he knows you've left us?"

His brother looked out over the snowy landscape. "He'll understand," he said in a low voice.

"You know he won't."

"He'll have to. And he'll move on, just like he did after our *mami* died."

"Levi, what if—"

"Are you even listening to me?" Levi sprang up from the seat of the four-wheeler, getting directly into Gabe's face. "I'm not. Coming. Back. Not ever. The sooner you and everyone else understand that, the faster we can all move on." He snatched his helmet off the four-wheeler, his expression dark and angry. "We've got nothing more to talk about, Gabe." Stalking past his brother, he headed for the house, never once looking back.

A wave of frustration flowed over Gabe as he stared at Levi's back, threatening to pull him under. Nothing he said made any impact on his brother. Then his anger diminished, replaced by deep sadness as he realized that Levi fully intended to leave the Amish, and nothing would change his mind. Levi hadn't even asked about the state of their *daed*'s health. He'd already written off his family, fully embracing a woman and a life he barely knew.

Chapter 7

*M*oriah tapped her fingers against the kitchen table, the sound a steady, monotonous tattoo that broke the silence of the empty house. John had left a short while ago after she'd convinced him she'd be all right until Levi came home. She had gone along with the ruse, unable to tell him about her husband's letter. He had seemed so weary by the end of the day, she knew he needed to lie down and rest in his own room, in his own comfortable bed.

She stilled her fingers, antsy but annoyed with the noise. Rising from her chair, she peered out of the kitchen window into the dark, cold night. The sun had disappeared beyond the horizon an hour ago. Gabriel should have been home by now.

Her stomach twisted itself into another knot. Not only because of the nausea of the pregnancy, but because her mind was completely occupied with Levi. Had Gabriel been able to persuade him to return? Maybe Levi had been drinking when he wrote the letter, so he wasn't in his right state of mind. But she dismissed that outright—his words had been clear, his writing steady. Besides, she had never known her husband to touch alcohol. Letting out a sigh, she crossed her arms over her chest to ward off the sudden chill that had infiltrated her body.

Where was Gabriel? More importantly, would he have Levi with him?

All she wanted was for her husband to be here, to tell her the letter was a mistake, to reassure her that everything would be all right between them from now on.

But something deep inside chipped at her, causing fresh wounds, telling her that her hopes were fruitless. Nothing would be the same again.

A sharp knock sounded behind her. Whirling around, Moriah ran to the door and flung it open. She took one look at the man standing in the doorway and for a fraction of a second, her heart soared. Levi had returned!

But it wasn't Levi gazing at her. It was Gabriel, his eyes filled with sorrow and regret. Her hopes had played tricks with her eyes, and her heart.

She stepped back until her waist banged the countertop. Reaching behind her, she gripped the cold Formica, forcing herself not to sway. She'd fallen apart in front of Gabriel the night before; she refused to do it again.

"I'm sorry, Moriah." His voice was thick, as if his vocal cords had tightened up. "I tried talking to him. I really did."

The droop of his shoulders spoke more than his words ever could. She realized he had taken the burden of his brother's betrayal on himself and had tried to make everything right. But he couldn't, and it was tearing him apart. She could see that, plain as day. Forgetting about herself for the moment, she gestured for him to come inside.

"Cold night tonight," she said lamely, shutting the door behind them. "Come warm yourself."

He took off his hat, walked into the kitchen, and dropped into the nearest chair. Moriah followed him. Looking into his ragged face, she said, "It's all right, Gabriel. Thank you for trying."

Gabriel ran his hand through his hair as he tossed his hat on the table. With a sigh he looked at her. "He's not coming back, Moriah."

"I know." She sat across the table from him, a numbing cold infiltrating her body, as if she'd been submerged in a tub of ice. "What did he say?"

Gabriel stared down at his fingers. He curled them inward to his palms, making two fists. "He doesn't want to be Amish anymore. Too many rules."

From his vague explanation to the way he avoided looking directly at her, she suspected he wasn't telling her the whole truth. "That's it?"

"*Ya.* That's it."

His words sliced through her. "Did you tell him about the baby?"

A long moment passed before he answered, compassion in his eyes. "*Ya.*"

She swallowed. "I see." She had to look away from him, unable to face the pity she saw in his gaze.

"I can't believe he did this to you," Gabriel muttered. "I could . . . I swear, Moriah, I could—"

With a gasp, she glanced up to see his full mouth stretched in a straight line. His hands were still clenched so tightly she thought his knuckles would snap. "What did you do?" she whispered, afraid to hear the answer.

His hands relaxed. "*Nix.* I did nothing."

She breathed out a sigh of relief. "Praise God."

"How can you say that? He deserves the worst for what he's doing to you."

"Gabriel," she said softly, reaching for his hand. "Just because he turned his back on our beliefs doesn't mean you should."

His eyes met hers, anger still sparking in them. "How can you not—"

"Hate him?" She looked away. A part of her did, but she had to overcome it. She had to be strong for their baby's sake. Tending the bitter weed of hate would only cause it to grow and overtake every aspect of her life. That wouldn't be fair to the child blossoming inside her. "God will see me through this. He will see us all through it . . . even Levi." Her eyes moistened, and she looked at him through misty vision.

He disengaged his hand from hers, and for a split moment, she missed its comforting warmth.

"I have to tell *Daed*," he said. "I don't know what this will do to him."

"Wait until morning," Moriah said. "He was very tired."

"I'm worried." Gabriel sat up and rubbed the back of his neck. "He's not as strong as he used to be, but he still wants to work in the shop. I'm afraid he'll hurt himself. But how can I tell him to quit?" He let out a bitter, flat chuckle. "It's not like I can just fire my father."

They were silent for a long time, lost in their own thoughts, dealing with their own emotions.

Then Moriah finally said, "I'll move back home tomorrow."

Gabriel's gaze shot to her. "You don't have to do that. You can stay here. *Daed* and I don't mind."

"*Nee*, I cannot. This isn't my home anymore."

"Moriah, it will always be your home. You can stay here as long as you like."

She shook her head. "Gabriel, I have to leave. You know that. You and your father can move back into the house. I'll be fine with my family. Once I tell them what happened, they'll understand." She closed her eyes, humiliation rising through her at the thought of telling her parents that her husband had left her, and for no other reason than he didn't want to be Amish anymore.

Pushing away from the table, she said, "I'll pack my things in the morning. Would you mind taking me back home?"

He stood and stepped toward her. "Moriah, I mean it. You don't have to leave."

Her bottom lip began to quiver. Why couldn't she be strong? Pressing her teeth down for a split second to quell the movement, she then said, "I want to go home. I need my family right now. So does my child."

He opened his mouth as if to protest once more, but then clamped it shut. "I understand. I'll take you home whenever you're ready."

"*Danki*. And thanks for trying to convince Levi to come back. I know it had to be a hard thing to do."

"Harder than I thought." He looked at her for a moment. "I don't think you should be alone tonight. Mind if I bunk in downstairs? I can sleep on the couch."

A tiny thread of relief wound its way through her. He must have read her mind, as she dreaded being alone in the big house. Too many memories, too much loneliness. "I don't mind. In fact, I'd appreciate it."

Tobias nursed the last dregs of his coffee in the nearly abandoned dining room of Mary Yoder's. There were only three other customers left in the restaurant—a tiny, elderly couple eating two crumbly pieces of apple pie and a rotund man, who looked only a few years older than Tobias, busily slurping the last watery droplets of his iced tea.

He didn't know what he was doing here. Mary Yoder's served good Amish food, but his mother's was ten times better. Besides, he'd already had dinner and dessert at home a couple hours ago before hitching up his horse and ending up at the restaurant. For some reason he'd felt restless tonight, and spending the evening at home alone didn't appeal. Everyone had plans for tonight—his parents were visiting an elderly neighbor, Elisabeth and Ruth were spending time with some of their girlfriends, and Stephen and Lukas were making some extra money helping their cousin clean out a barn in West Farmington.

He'd thought about doing some extra work in the woodshop, but he'd spent the entire day in there. All work and no play made Tobias dull indeed. At least he thought so. Although he did have a good time working today, except for cutting his fingertip on one of the saw blades. But he'd cut his fingers and hands so many times over the years. One more slice on his skin didn't make a difference.

Tapping his foot on the carpeted floor, he sucked down the last drink of coffee and signaled one of the bus girls for the check. She was about the age of his sister Elisabeth, who couldn't wait to finish school and start working outside the home. No doubt so she'd have ample opportunity to flirt with guys. He'd noticed how boy-crazy she'd gotten in the past couple months. He suspected his mother would have her hands full once Elisabeth turned sixteen.

The bus girl nodded at Tobias and went to get his server. When Rachel appeared, he hid a smile. As she had when he arrived, she looked less than pleased to see him. With determined steps she walked to the table, crossed her arms as she usually did when she was around him, and looked down the length of her cute little nose. "What do you want now?"

He leaned back in the chair, his restless spirit inexplicably easing. He pointed to his coffee cup. "I'm done."

"About time." She pulled out a computer-printed ticket from inside her apron, as if she'd been waiting all day to give it to him. "Here." She put it down on the table. "You can pay up front." She took the cup from the table and walked away.

He looked at the amount on the ticket, then stood. Digging out his leather wallet from his trousers, he felt two pennies in his pocket. He knew leaving such a cheap tip would get a rise out of Rachel, and he couldn't resist the opportunity. Retrieving the coins, he dropped them on the table, then walked out of the dining area and into the gift shop.

He passed Amish crafts of all kinds and noticed a couple of wooden train sets his brother Lukas had made a few months ago, hoping to sell them for an extra bit of pocket money. There were also candles, books, and stuffed animals available for purchase. He approached the empty bakery counter where the cash registers were located. The manager, a Yankee woman, took his ticket and rang up the total. "$1.25," she said.

He gave her two dollars, then took out another five from his wallet. "Could you give this to my server, please? Just don't tell her it came from me. If you could add it to the rest of her tips, I'd appreciate it."

The manager tilted her head and gave him a strange look, but nodded. "I'll be happy to do that. Are you sure you don't want to just put this on your table, though?"

"Positive." He stuffed his wallet back in his pocket and adjusted his hat. "Thanks for the coffee. You all have a good evening."

"You do the same."

Tobias grinned as he left the restaurant. *Ya*, Rachel would be steamed when she saw the measly tip he left her. He almost wished he could witness the volcanic explosion of temper when she picked up the two cents. As he entered the parking lot and headed for his buggy, he thought about the spark that would light up her blue eyes, the lovely rosy glow that would spread across her creamy cheeks, the—

"Tobias Byler!"

He halted in his tracks at the zinging sound of Rachel's voice behind him. Turning around, he watched with amusement as she stomped forward, fury pulsating from her like an old wood stove belching heat.

Boy, he'd gotten her good.

"What is *this*?" she said, holding out the pennies in her hand. "Do you think this is funny? I work hard for my tips. Very hard." She threw the coins at him.

He held up his hands in a weak defense as the pennies ricocheted harmlessly off his pants leg. "You gave me *one* cup of coffee," he said blandly. "That's it. Big deal."

"You . . . *you* . . ." Her body started to tremble as she sputtered.

Was she that angry? Suddenly realizing that it was below thirty degrees and all she had on was her short-sleeved dress and apron, he whipped off his coat. "Here, put this on. You're freezing."

She stared at the jacket as if it had thorns poking out of it. "No, thanks."

"Then go inside and warm up."

"Not until I get my real tip. The tip you owe me."

"Rachel, don't be stupid," he said, still holding his *reck* out to her. Her teeth were chattering. Why did she have to be so stubborn? "Get inside where it's warm."

She held out one shaking hand. "M-my m-money."

"I'll give it to you—if you put on my coat."

Her eyes grew wide at his insistent request. In fact he was a bit surprised by it himself. But he couldn't stand to see her shivering out here, and he knew she wouldn't leave until she got her money. At least she would be a little warmer while he fished out his wallet.

Without a word she took the jacket and wrapped it loosely around her shoulders. The dark blue, woolen fabric practically engulfed her.

"Rachel! What are you doing outside?"

"Oh no," she whispered.

Tobias looked up to see Rachel's boss holding open the front door of the restaurant. Quickly Rachel spun around and ran back inside, taking his coat with her.

A blast of cold night air hit him as the glass door shut behind Rachel. Great. Now *he* was shivering out here in the cold.

For Pete's sake, this was crazy. He couldn't drive all the way home without his coat. Although the winter curtain on his buggy would keep some of the frigid air at bay, it would be a miserable ride. He plodded back to the restaurant, opening the front door for the elderly couple as they exited.

"Aren't those Amish just the nicest people?" the petite woman said.

"*Hmmph,*" the man grunted as he leaned on his cane. Together they hobbled over to their car.

The cloying scent of about a million varieties of candles hit Tobias's nose as he walked back into the restaurant. Women really loved those things—his mother lit them all the time. He scanned the gift shop area and saw there was no one behind the counter or in the front of the building. What should he do? Go back and ask for the manager? Or just walk through the empty restaurant and call out for Rachel? After weighing his options, he decided to search for himself.

The third time he said her name, the manager appeared through the door separating the kitchen from the dining room. "We're closed, sir. Was there something else you needed?"

He felt heat creep up his neck. Somehow every time he tried to one-up Rachel he always ended up looking like a fool. "I came to get my coat, ma'am."

"Did you leave it in the dining room?" The blonde-haired woman walked farther into the large room and began looking at the tables and chairs.

"No, I didn't. Rachel has it."

She frowned. "Were you the one she was talking to outside?"

He nodded.

"I'll go get her." The manager started toward the kitchen, then stopped and turned around, annoyance coloring her expression. "I don't know what kind of game you teenagers are playing, but this is a place of business and Rachel is an employee. I want you to remember that in the future. I'm sure you would like your friend to keep her job."

422

"Yes, ma'am. I'm sorry."

A few moments later Rachel appeared from the kitchen, carrying his *reck*. "Here," she said, thrusting it at him. When he took it from her she headed back to the kitchen, but he stopped her.

"Hang on," he said, pulling out his wallet again, feeling bad that she could have been fired over his little, and obviously not very funny, joke. He took out a five-dollar bill and handed it to her. This was becoming the most expensive cup of coffee he'd ever had.

She looked at the money with disdain. "Now you're being insulting. No one gives a five-dollar tip for a cup of coffee."

Yeesh, I cannot win with this woman. Either I give her too little or too much. "Would you just take it? Before your boss comes out here and you lose your job and I get another lecture."

"Fine." She took the bill out of his hand. "You know there are lots of other places that serve coffee."

"*Ya*, there are," he responded as she placed her hand on the metal doors that led to the kitchen. Then for some unknown reason he blurted out, "How are you getting home?"

"My cousin Melvin is picking me up," she said, then started toward the kitchen again.

"Not Christian?"

She spun around and faced him. "If you must know, he and his parents left for Holmes County today. They're spending a long weekend with his mom's sister down in Charm. His uncle broke his arm, and he needs some help with the chores."

"Rachel?"

The manager came out of the kitchen and approached her. She held a small yellow Post-it note in her hand. "Your cousin just called." Handing Rachel the note, she turned around and left.

Tobias watched Rachel's expression as she read the note. From the look on her face, he could tell it was bad news. "Melvin can't pick me up. He's got an emergency. A couple of his cows have gotten loose."

"That's not *gut*. I wouldn't want to be searching for a cow in the dark."

"Me neither." She tapped the note against her chin, her light brows furrowed. "I'm sure someone here can drive me home."

"I could take you."

She gave him a dubious look.

He really needed to figure out a way to tape his mouth shut. Why he was offering to subject himself to her company in the small quarters of his buggy? She was already furious with him for stiffing her. The smart thing to do would be to let her fend for herself. Except he didn't like the idea that she might not be able to find a ride home.

To his further surprise she seemed to be considering his offer. She wrinkled her cute nose. "Are you sure?"

He nodded. "No problem." At least he hoped there wouldn't be. With Rachel Detweiler, he never knew for sure.

She expelled a deep breath. "All right," she said slowly, with an expression that suggested she'd just agreed to walk off the plank of a very tall ship. "Not like I have much of a choice anyway."

"Gee, thanks." He had half a mind to tell her to forget about it if she was going to act that way.

She ignored his response. "It'll take me about half an hour to finish up. You can wait up front." With that, she disappeared into the kitchen.

Her gratitude was underwhelming. And irritating. "Why, thank you for offering, Tobias," he muttered in a high falsetto, mimicking her voice. "I appreciate you coming to my rescue. Thank goodness you were here tonight. I don't know what I would have done without you."

He turned around to make his way to the front of the store, only to run smack-dab into the manager. Somehow she'd snuck up on him.

The woman was about half his height, but intimidating never-theless. She peered at him with disapproval over her red, wire-rimmed glasses. Tobias didn't have to be a genius to figure out that she'd overheard him mocking Rachel.

"I'll just wait up front," he said, lowering his hat over his eyebrows and quickly walking past her.

"Good idea," she called out after him.

Tobias hoped Rachel would hurry. After tonight, he'd prob-ably never show his face in Mary Yoder's again.

As she took off her work apron and put on her *reck,* Rachel thought about Tobias's offer. Although she would never admit it out loud, and never to Tobias, she was grateful to him for taking her home. But he'd really annoyed her with that two-cent tip. She took her job seriously, working hard to serve her customers, a fact that hadn't gone unnoticed by her boss—and usually showed in her tips. For Tobias to come in, only order a coffee, then leave her a two-cent tip . . . well, obviously it infuriated her, and she'd made a pretty big idiot of herself in front of him, something he'd probably expected. Somehow she had to figure out a way to keep him from getting under her skin.

But if he wanted to make her miserable, then why did he offer her his coat when they were outside? Not only did he offer it, he'd insisted she wear it. Then he asked if he could take her home. She thought he'd rather see her walk along the side of the road in the darkness, shivering, as he pulled his buggy past her, all cozy inside. Instead he wanted to make sure she was warm and that she got home safely.

She'd never figure that man out.

She found her boss and apologized again for running out of the restaurant.

"You're going home with him?" she asked quietly from the back of the gift shop. They could see Tobias near the front of the store by a book rack, reading the back cover of one of the several Amish novels available for purchase.

"He's *taking* me home. My other ride couldn't make it. Don't worry, I've known him forever. He's harmless. Irritating, but harmless. I'll see you tomorrow. Have a good evening."

"You too."

Rachel came up behind him as he put the book back on the rack. "Do people really read that stuff?" He gestured to the books with his thumb.

"*Ya.* We sell a lot of those. Along with the cookbooks."

"The cookbooks I can see. Everybody has to eat. But novels?" He shrugged. "Never was much for reading myself."

"I remember," she said, thinking back to their days in school. Tobias passed his classes, but barely. More often than not he was busy goofing around with all the other boys, driving the poor school teacher to exasperation. The young woman, *Fraulein* Lucy, had only been a few years older than the oldest student, and had her hands full with a couple of the boys, Tobias included. Rachel thought she had probably dropped to her knees and thanked the Lord for several hours the day they had all graduated.

"Are you ready?" he asked, walking toward the exit.

"Yes." She followed him as he opened the solid glass door. But instead of passing through it ahead of her, he paused and opened it wider. "After you," he said.

She smirked at him as she strolled through, but secretly she was impressed. The gesture was something Christian would have done, but was unexpected from Tobias. Neither had she expected him to hold the buggy door open for her, which he also did. Tonight he was full of surprises.

Soon they were on their way home. Although the night was cold, it was beautiful out. The inky black sky resembled rich velvet studded with sparkling diamonds. The stars weren't exactly clear through the window in the curtain covering the front of the buggy, but she could still see their twinkle. Suddenly a shiver ran through her and her body shook involuntarily.

"Cold?" he asked.

"*Nee*," she said, but she was lying. She crossed her ankles and pressed her legs together as she bent forward slightly, hugging her arms. Her coat didn't seem warm enough tonight.

"Here," he said, reaching behind her and withdrawing a thick quilt. Then he handed her the reins. "Hold this."

She arched a brow as he tucked the quilt around her waist, letting the heavy blanket fall over her legs and trail to the floor. Instantly she felt warmer. He took the reins from her and steered the buggy to the right, turning on Nauvoo Road, right behind the Middlefield Cheese Factory.

"Why are you being so nice to me?" she asked, bewildered by his unexpected behavior.

"*Mei mami* raised me right." He turned and grinned.

She could barely see his smile, except for the gleam of his

white teeth. They weren't perfectly straight, like Christian's. The two top front ones overlapped slightly, and his bottom teeth were a little crooked. Yet she hardly noticed as he continued to grin at her.

How could she, when her heart was thumping a million miles an hour.

She jerked her gaze from his and stared straight ahead, trying to figure out why she was having a hard time catching her breath. This was Tobias, for heaven's sake. The thorn in her side, the pain in her behind . . . The most handsome man she'd ever seen.

"Besides," he added, breaking into her disturbing, but not all that unpleasant, thoughts. "I can never resist a damsel in distress."

With that remark, any schmoopy thoughts she currently had for him disintegrated like ashes in the wind. "I am *not* a damsel in distress. I just needed a ride."

"And a blanket to wrap around you," he added. "And a pretty *wunderbaar* guy to take you home."

"You are so full of yourself, you know that?"

"Not at all. Now you . . . that's a different story."

She looked at him. "Excuse me?"

"You know what I'm talking about."

"No, I don't." She flung the quilt off her lap. "Stop this buggy. I'll walk."

"Don't be dumb," he said, the teasing hint in his voice disappearing.

"I mean it. If you don't stop, I'll jump out."

"For the love of—" He yanked up on the reins. "This is what I'm talking about, Rachel. You're the most difficult woman I've ever—"

Bright, fast-moving lights suddenly appeared out of the

darkness. They headed toward the buggy. Rachel lifted her hand to shield her eyes from the blinding light.

"Rachel!" Tobias yelled as the lights came upon them.

The roar of an engine sounded in her ears as the car clipped the side of the buggy, causing it to flip over. Her scream pierced the air.

The buggy turned over, breaking loose from the horse's hitch. Her body was thrown against the top of the buggy as it hit the ground. Her eyes slammed shut. Something cupped the back of her head. Then everything came to a stop.

A heavy body lay partly on top of her. Heavy and warm and solid. She opened her eyes. In the darkness of the upside-down buggy she could barely make Tobias out. But she felt him. His hand remained at the back of her head, his other arm stayed pinned protectively behind her back. Most of his body rested against the length of hers.

Their breathing intermingled in the small space, coming in short, gasping spurts. This was the first buggy accident she'd been in, and thank God they hadn't been killed. But Rachel wasn't completely positive she had to catch her breath solely from the accident.

"Are you okay?" he said softly, his mouth close to her ear.

A shiver traveled through her, but she wasn't the least bit cold at all, not while she was cradled in Tobias Byler's strong embrace, feeling his warmth against her. "I-I think so."

"You're trembling."

Her mouth suddenly dry, she swallowed. "I know. I-I can't seem t-to stop."

Her eyes now adjusted to the darkness, she could see him move his head. Their eyes met, the lightness of his blue irises visible to her. She could read something in those gorgeous eyes. Something that made her shiver even more.

Her *kapp* had dislodged during the accident, and a lock of her hair was askew. She drew in a sharp breath when he slowly pushed it back from her face, his fingers lingering on her cheek, his embrace tightening.

Without thinking she kissed him.

It was barely a brush on the lips and lasted less than half a second, but it was a kiss nevertheless.

"Hey! Anyone in there?"

A beam of light shone on the buggy. Rachel saw the shock on his face, knowing it mirrored her own.

"Are you two all right?" A man knelt down beside the overturned buggy. "What happened?"

Tobias climbed out of the buggy's opening, then turned and looked at Rachel with a strange expression, as if he didn't recognize her. He extended his hand to help her out, and when she came to a standing position, he cleared his throat and said, "Got hit by a car."

"What about you, hon? You okay?"

Rachel squinted at the kind man holding the flashlight. She tried to straighten her *kapp*, which was practically dangling from the side of her head, but she was fumbling so much she just made it worse. "I think so," she finally answered, shoving in a pin and hoping the *kapp* would stay put. But she was anything but fine.

"My horse," Tobias exclaimed, spinning around. His gaze darted around in a panic. He faced the helpful stranger again. "Have you seen my horse?"

"Down the road a bit," the man answered. "Seems to be all right though. Scared, I imagine. Looks like you took quite a spill."

Rachel turned and looked at the buggy, taking in the wheels. One of them was twisted, probably ruined. The full impact of what happened suddenly hit her. She'd known several people from her community and neighboring ones who had been killed in car-and-buggy accidents. That she and Tobias were still alive, much less with not a scratch on them, was a miracle.

"We should call the police," the stranger said. "They'll want you to file a report."

"There's no need to do that," Tobias said. "I'll get my horse, and I'll come back in the morning for the buggy."

"But, son, this was a hit and run. The person that did this needs to be caught and prosecuted."

"That's not our way," he replied.

He tugged on his black knit skull cap, seemingly perplexed by Tobias's response. "Well, all right. If you're sure."

"I'm sure."

"How about if I give you two a ride home?"

Rachel met Tobias's gaze. They were at least two miles from her house, and over three miles from his. It would be a cold walk, but she didn't relish the idea of letting a complete stranger drive her home.

"We'll be fine," Tobias said, saving her from having to answer. "Thank you for your kindness. It's appreciated."

A confused look crossed the man's face. "I feel bad leaving you two out here in the cold. I can drive down the road to a phone and call someone for you. I accidentally left my cell phone at home."

"We'll be okay. We must go now. I need to find my horse." In dismissal, Tobias tilted his head at Rachel and started walking.

Rachel looked at the kind gentleman. "Thank you for

stopping. We both appreciate it. Tobias . . . he's just worried about his horse."

"I can understand that. I'm glad you're both okay."

"Me too. And thanks again."

When the man walked back to his car, she turned to follow Tobias, who was already heading down the road.

Tobias suddenly started up short. "Wait a minute," he said to Rachel, then dashed back to the buggy.

Rachel watched the red taillights from the car disappear into the darkness. She crossed her arms in a vain attempt to keep warm.

Tobias ran up to her, carrying the quilt. Without a word he wrapped it around her shoulders, then started walking again. Although the moon wasn't completely full, it cast enough silvery light for them to find their way.

A flurry of emotions swirled inside her as she tried to process what had just happened between them. She'd kissed Tobias Byler. Not only that, but she had felt *something* when she did it. A warm, fuzzy feeling. A good feeling. No, not just good. *Wunderbaar.*

She'd never felt that way about Christian. Guilt overpowered her. She shouldn't be feeling about Tobias this way. Or thinking about him this way. Or wishing they hadn't been discovered so soon. Her thoughts and loyalties should only lie with Christian.

But they didn't.

She was the lowest of the low.

Burdened by her guilt and falling farther behind as Tobias hurried his steps, she heard the whinny of his horse up ahead. The animal stood a few feet from the road, beside an open field. Tobias ran and caught him by the bridle. She heard him talk in soft, hushed tones to the horse, calming the animal until he came to a complete stop.

The buggy hitch was still attached to the harness. Tobias quickly detached it and left it in the field. Another piece of equipment he would have to get in the morning.

Rachel had finally caught up to him when he turned and faced her. There were a few houses on the road, interspersed among wide open fields. The glow of a single streetlamp mixed with the moonlight, but she couldn't see his expression. She wasn't sure she wanted to.

Why, oh why, had she kissed him?

"We can ride home," he said matter-of-factly, as if nothing had happened between them.

"There's no saddle."

"I've ridden him bareback before. Don't worry, he's a good horse. Smart too. He'll lead us back to your place." He held out his hand to her.

She looked at it, hesitating. Her shoulders had started to hurt, undoubtedly from the spill in the buggy, and her toes were numb with cold. To refuse his offer would be stupid. Slipping her hand in his, she allowed him to help her on the horse. When she was situated, he slung his body up in one smooth motion, then positioned himself behind her.

She could feel the heat seeping from his chest to her back, even through the quilt. His nearness embarrassed her, but thrilled her at the same time.

"Hand me the reins," he said, his tone as assured and confident as it normally was.

She did as he asked, and they were on their way. Sometime during the ride he wrapped his arm around her waist. When she turned her head to look at him, he said, "Don't want you to fall off. We've had enough accidents tonight."

"I'm sorry about your buggy," Rachel said, though she knew he wasn't just talking about his buggy.

"Just glad we weren't hurt," he said.

It didn't take long for them to reach her house. Before he could get off his horse, she slid down the animal's back and handed him the quilt.

Looking up at Tobias, she knew she had to fix this. "I'm dating Christian," she said, a little too loudly, as if the volume of her tone could hammer that point home for both of them.

"I know," he said solemnly, laying the quilt in front of him over his horse's back.

"Just wanted to make that clear."

He nodded, looking down at her. "He's my friend. I don't want to hurt him."

"*Gut.* I'm glad we understand each other."

Tobias paused for a moment, as if he wanted to say something. Then he nickered to his horse and steered the animal around before making his way down the driveway.

Rachel watched him go, her heart heavy with guilt over the kiss. He must think her an idiot. Worse yet, a betrayer. Yet guilt and shame weren't the only emotions pulsing through her. Something had awakened inside her tonight after she kissed Tobias. She wasn't sure what it was, but she knew she would never be the same again.

Chapter 8

*M*oriah awakened before sunrise, double-checking her suitcase to make sure she had packed up all her belongings the night before. She looked at the clock Levi had given her on the nightstand, but she didn't care about the time. For a few moments she contemplated taking the clock with her. But what would be the point? It would only serve as a reminder of her failed marriage. Turning, she left the clock behind as she exited her and Levi's bedroom for the final time.

She entered the kitchen and set her suitcase against the wall next to the back door. As she glanced around the kitchen, taking in the old-fashioned wood stove, gray Formica countertops, and the unadorned window over the metal sink, she fought back tears. She had spent so many hours in here, preparing meals, studying recipes, trying to make sure every bit of food she made would satisfy her husband. Yet it was all for naught. This was no longer her kitchen. No longer her home.

The door opened and she turned around. Gabriel walked in, a few pieces of wood in his arms. He laid them down next to the stove and removed his hat. "I didn't expect you to be up."

"I couldn't sleep."

"Neither could I." He held her gaze for a moment, then put his black hat on one of the three pegs next to the door. "I'll make some coffee."

"*Nee.* I can do it."

Gabriel held up his hand. "Are you hungry? I make a mean plate of scrambled eggs."

The thought of food made her stomach flip over, but she nodded. He seemed so eager to prepare breakfast for her that she couldn't bear to turn him down, even though she knew he was doing it out of guilt over Levi. She remembered other times he had taken on his brother's burden. More than once when they were in school, the teacher would confuse the twins. Often it was Levi getting into trouble, but Gabriel didn't protest if he was the one being punished. Since Levi wasn't here to make things right, she had no doubt Gabriel would try to.

Gabriel squatted in front of the stove and threw a couple handfuls of crumpled up newspaper into the firebox. He added two small pieces of dried cordwood, then struck a match and lit the fire. "This will be going in no time."

Moriah nodded, then sat down at the table. She held her head in her hands. When she felt Gabriel's hand on her shoulder, she jerked up.

"Moriah?"

The worried expression on his face touched her. "I'm all right." She sat up straighter and tried to force a smile. She wasn't successful.

"Can I get you anything? Are you cold?" He knelt down beside her. "What can I do to help you, Moriah?"

She couldn't speak for a moment. While she appreciated

Gabriel's concern, she couldn't help but question it. He'd kept her at arm's length for so long. Now he was treating her with such compassion, such tenderness. She didn't know how to react.

John suddenly came in through the back door, his expression a mask of concern. "There you are," he said, looking at Gabriel as he shut the door behind him. "You weren't at the house when I woke up, and it didn't look like your bed had been slept in. Had me worried for a minute." His gaze went to Moriah, then back to Gabriel, who was now standing. His bushy brows furrowed. "Want to tell me what's going on here? Where's Levi?"

Gabriel expelled a long breath. "Sit down, *Daed.*"

Shaking his head, John said, "Now I'm really worried. If you have something to say, just say it."

Moriah watched as Gabriel quickly told his father about Levi. John sank down in the chair and never said a word. Silent tears streamed down his wizened cheeks. Gabriel walked over and put his arm around his shoulders.

Sorrow filled her as she witnessed Gabriel trying to comfort his father. He knelt down, and John wept on his shoulder. For the hundredth time she wondered why Levi would do this. How could he hurt all of them so deeply? She wiped at the tears dangling on her eyelashes, not wanting Gabriel to see her crying also. He couldn't comfort them both, even though she knew he'd try.

John sat back in his chair and swiped at his face with the back of his hands. "I don't know why Levi did this, but we can't lean on our own understanding. God is in control." He looked at Gabriel, then at Moriah. "He will see us through this. I trust in that, and I hope you do too." He held out his hands. "We need to pray for Levi."

Moriah hesitated to take John's outstretched hand. Pray for Levi?

"Levi made his decision, *Daed*."

She looked up to see that Gabriel hadn't moved either.

"*Ya*, but we don't know what has influenced that decision." John kept his hands out, palms facing up. "We can pray against whatever has come between him and his faith and family. We can also pray that he comes back."

Drawing the slightest bit of hope from her father-in-law's words, she slipped her hand into his roughened one. After a bit more hesitation, Gabriel finally did the same. Moriah closed her eyes and listened with a heavy heart as a father prayed, through fresh tears, for his wayward son.

The next morning, after spending her first night back at home, Moriah laid on her bed, staring at the ceiling but not really seeing anything. She rolled over and tucked her covers under her chin. She didn't want to get up. Elisabeth, who she shared a room with, was already dressed and downstairs. Fortunately her sister had the good sense not to ask any questions about what had happened with Levi. But eventually she'd want to know. Everyone would.

With a sigh she realized that it was Sunday. A church Sunday. Services were held every other week, and the whole community would be there. They'd know Levi was missing, and the questions would fly. Part of her wished she had stayed with Gabriel and John. At least then Gabriel would have run interference, sparing her the pain of having to explain to everyone that her husband had left her.

But that would make her just like Levi, wouldn't it? Refusing to take responsibility, fleeing from the consequences. She wouldn't do that. She wouldn't put more of a burden on Gabriel. He had put up with enough.

A soft knock sounded on her bedroom door. "Moriah?" The sweet sound of her youngest sister Ruthie's voice penetrated through the wood.

"*Ya?*"

"*Mami* wants to know if you're coming down for breakfast. She made your favorite. Buttermilk pancakes. She even made some strawberry syrup to go with them."

Moriah's stomach growled, but she had no appetite. She thought to tell Ruthie no, but knew she had to eat for the baby. "Will you tell her I'll be right down?"

"*Ya.*"

She listened to Ruthie's retreating footsteps, gathering her courage to go downstairs. When Gabriel had dropped her off late yesterday morning, only Ruthie and her mother had been home. Her brothers were still in the woodshop with their *daed*, and Elisabeth was visiting a friend. After exchanging a few words with her mother, Moriah had gone upstairs, and stayed up there until her mother and father had come to talk to her. She didn't want to face a barrage of questions from her siblings.

At that point she explained everything to them. Her mother had cried, but her father had remained silent and stone-faced. Moriah had never seen his countenance so stoic. Her father had always been an easygoing person, quick to laugh like her brother Tobias, but pensive when need be, like her brothers Lukas and Stephen. After a few moments he stood up and walked out of the room, never saying a word.

"Don't worry about your *daed*," her mother had said, wiping her tears with her handkerchief. "He needs some time."

"*Mami*, I'm so sorry."

"Oh, Moriah, sweetheart." Her mother grabbed her hand and squeezed it tightly. "You don't have to apologize. This isn't your fault."

"Isn't it? He wouldn't have left me if I had been the wife he needed."

Emma Byler frowned. "No more talk like that, daughter. The blame is squarely on Levi's shoulders, not yours. You understand? Blaming yourself doesn't do any good."

"I know," she whispered. "I just can't help feeling so . . . awful."

"My sweet *kind*." A tear escaped out of her mother's red-rimmed eyes. "I hate to see you going through this. I'm glad you came home. We'll help you through this. All of us will."

Now, lying in her bed, thinking about that conversation with her mother, she knew she had to lean on her family almost as much as she had to lean on God. Just because her life was a mess didn't mean she could avoid them, or anyone else. Church attendance had always been mandatory, and she would be expected to be at the service with her family. She'd always loved attending church services in the past. She loved spending that special time with the community, and the hymns and sermons fed her soul. But today, she wanted to stay in bed. She didn't want to go, but she knew she'd be expected.

Rising from her bed, she put on her Sunday dress, fastened her *kapp*, slipped on her shoes, and headed downstairs to the kitchen. The hum of her family engaged in quiet conversation reached her ears before she made it to the kitchen.

But when she entered the room, all activity stopped. Everyone except her mother and Elisabeth were already seated at the table.

Moriah turned her gaze on each one of her siblings. Tobias had an uncharacteristically sullen expression on his face, along with a dark bruise on his forehead. She briefly wondered how he'd been injured. Lukas, the only black-haired member of the family, looked at her with a mixture of pity and concern. He'd turned eighteen last month, but had an old soul. Thirteen-year-old Stephen kept his focus on the plate in front of him, even though it was empty. Ruthie gave her a look of encouragement that far surpassed her tender age of twelve. Elisabeth finally turned around, carrying a basket of fresh-baked biscuits. She went straight to Moriah and held them out to her. "Want a biscuit, *schwester?*"

With a smile, Moriah took one. "*Danki,* Lis."

"No problem. Welcome back. It'll be nice to have another set of hands around here. I'm tired of washing the dishes all the time."

"Hey," Ruthie said, scowling. "I wash them too, you know."

"When you don't have your nose planted inside a book. Which is never."

"All right, all right, girls," Moriah's father said, holding up his hand, palm facing outward. "Let's stop arguing and sit down for prayer."

"Yes, *Daed,*" Ruthie and Elisabeth said simultaneously. Moriah didn't miss the taunting looks that passed between them.

When everyone was seated, the family joined hands. "Dear heavenly Father," Joseph said. "We thank Thee for bringing us together and for the abundant meal You've given us. We also thank Thee for bringing Moriah to us today, Father. Let her know that she is deeply loved, not only by You, but by all of us. Amen."

Her eyes burning, Moriah opened them and looked at her family, who had immediately started tucking into their meal. For the first time since she'd read Levi's letter, she didn't feel utter despair. This was where she was meant to be. With her family. Her father hadn't needed to petition God to show her how much she was loved. She felt it all around her.

Gabe watched the barn entrance for Moriah. He wouldn't blame her if she had decided to stay home. By now it had spread through half the community that Levi Miller had left his wife and the church. The hard wooden bench felt less comfortable than ever, and he shifted in his seat as he looked at his father surrounded by several men, including the bishop and two ministers. He knew they were offering words of comfort, but he also knew that words were meaningless. Thousands of words, even delivered with good intentions, wouldn't heal the fissure that had formed in his father's heart.

Over the past twenty-four hours, Gabe had watched his father weaken physically. If he thought his father would even consider it, he would've taken him to the doctor, but he knew *Daed* would have none of it. A firm believer in alternative medicine, John Miller would put his faith in the healing power of God and in the other natural remedies he preferred, especially the teas he insisted on drinking.

Gabe watched as his *daed* sat on the edge of the bench in the front of the cavernous room, his shoulders in a permanent hunch, his long white beard touching the center of his chest as Amos Helmuth, one of the ministers, sat next to him, speaking to him in low tones.

The chill in the air began to fade as warm bodies filled the barn. The men took their seats on the left side of the barn, while the women found their places on the right side. The scent of fresh hay filtered through the air. Gabe took one last look at the barn entrance before sitting down in the back of the church. Not only did he not see Moriah, he didn't see the rest of the Byler family either. Had they decided to skip church? He wouldn't blame them if they had. Levi's decision had shamed both of their families.

Abel Esh, the bishop, stood at the front of the room and opened the *Ausbund*, the Amish hymn book. The hymn leader signaled for the congregation to begin singing. Every voice chimed together in an a capella chant, the haunting monotone echoing off the wooden slats of the barn.

They were nearly finished with the first hymn when out of the corner of his eye, Gabe saw Joseph Byler take a seat on the opposite end of his bench, flanked on both sides by his sons Tobias, Lukas, and Stephen. None of them looked at him, instead directing their attention to the ministers up front. On the other side of the room, Gabe caught sight of Moriah, seated between her mother and her sister Ruthie. He didn't see Elisabeth, but she often sat with her friends.

Suddenly Moriah turned, meeting his gaze, as if she knew he was looking straight at her.

His heart soared at the calm he saw in her eyes, a serenity he hadn't seen since before Levi had left. He had wanted her to stay in the large house, not only out of guilt for what his brother had done to her, but also because he wanted her near. She was so fragile, so vulnerable, and with good reason. His brother had been right about one thing—Gabe wanted to look after her. But she had insisted on moving back home, and he could see now that it was the right decision.

The hymns continued, one after the other, but Gabe did little singing. He surreptitiously kept his gaze on Moriah throughout the first hour of the three-hour service, unable to keep from looking at her, wishing she would acknowledge him, but also hoping she wouldn't. She seemed completely involved in the singing, and other than that one time at the beginning of the service, she kept her attention focused on the bishop.

After the singing ended, Abel stood and began his sermon. The words passed through Gabe's ears, his mind not registering anything but the plights of his brother, Moriah, and his *daed* weighing heavily on his soul. He vowed to keep close watch on his father, and considered hiring another part-time employee, at least until *Daed* had a chance to recover from Levi's departure. He couldn't risk anything happening to his *daed*. Not when he'd already lost his brother. He couldn't lose the only immediate family he had left.

When the service finally reached its conclusion, the congregation rose to sing another hymn. After the dismissal, he turned to look for Moriah, but she was already headed to the Eshes' house, probably intending to assist with lunch preparations. He wouldn't have blamed her if she hadn't stayed, but he wasn't surprised that she would offer to help. Throughout this ordeal, she had continually surprised him with her inner strength.

He suddenly heard the hushed tones of his father and Joseph Byler behind him. Turning, he saw his *daed* speaking to Joseph and the bishop. Gabe could see his father's eyes were glistening with tears. "*Danki* for listening to me, Joseph. I ask you to forgive my son. I beg you to forgive my Levi for what he has done to your daughter and your family."

Gabe quickly went to his father's side. "*Daed*," he said in a low voice.

Joseph stilled them both by putting his hand on John's shoulder. "Don't take your son's burden on yourself."

"But I have already. Can't you see? His burden is mine. It always will be."

Gabe looked at Joseph, who remained silent for a moment. Finally, he dropped his hand from John and spoke. "We'll pray for Levi to realize his folly and return. When he does, we will welcome him home."

"*Danki*, Joseph," John said quietly. He stared at the ground as Joseph turned and walked away.

The bishop drew Gabe to the side. "Your *daed* is in a bad way, Gabriel."

With a nod Gabe said, "He's taking this hard."

"Of course he is. None of us blame him for that. But perhaps it would be best if you took him home. The ministers and I will come by this afternoon and see how he's doing." Abel looked squarely at Gabe. "How both of you are doing."

Giving his father a quick glance, Gabe suddenly felt as tired as his *daed* looked. He didn't want to be here, fighting to keep his composure while worrying about John. "*Ya*. I will take him home."

Fortunately, John readily agreed to leave the Eshes'. "Not much in the mood for socializing," he said wearily.

"Me either." They walked to their buggy. Before John got in, he looked at Gabe. "Will we ever see him again, Gabriel? Will I ever see my son again?"

More than anything Gabe wanted to tell his father that Levi would return, that everything would be back the way it was. But he couldn't because nothing would be the same for any of them again. Yet he refused to take away his *daed*'s hope. The old man needed something to cling to, even if it was a lie. "I don't know," he finally managed. "I don't know."

Moriah watched John and Gabriel as they headed for their buggy. *Poor, poor John.* Her heart went out to her father-in-law. Yesterday as they'd prayed together, his strength and faith had given her hope. But today the man was obviously consumed with grief over what Levi had done. And there was Gabriel, right by his side, offering his support. He had not only been Moriah's rock that first night, but he continued to be his father's as well.

She turned around and started to go inside to help with lunch. But something stopped her, causing her to look at her father-in-law and brother-in-law again. While everyone was gathering for the afternoon meal, John and Gabriel were alone. And despite what Levi had done, she was still part of their family. Even though she was suffering with her own pain, she didn't want to leave them alone. She had to find a way to help somehow.

She went inside and found her mother with the other women in the kitchen. Making her way over to her mother, she whispered her intentions in Emma's ear. *Mami* looked surprised, but she nodded, then went to find the bishop's wife.

Moriah hurried back outside just in time to see Gabriel step up to get inside the buggy. She called out his name and rushed toward him.

He stopped and looked at her, his visage grim.

"Is he all right?" she asked.

"I have no idea." He lowered his voice, adding, "He's taking this very hard."

"I know."

"Gabriel?" John called to his son.

Both Gabriel and Moriah peeked inside the buggy. When John's gaze met hers, he smiled. "Such a sweet *maedel*," he said. "You didn't deserve this. I'm so sorry for what Levi has done."

"We should be going," Gabriel said as he climbed inside. He seemed to be in a hurry, but then he paused. "Will you be all right?"

Moriah nodded, but wondered if she'd ever be all right again.

Seemingly satisfied with her response, Gabriel touched the reins to the flanks of the horse and pulled out of the Eshes' drive.

Moriah watched as they left, her heart not only bleeding for herself but also for Gabriel and John.

Gabe and John rode home in silence. Once they reached the house, he helped his father into the bedroom he had shared with his wife for over forty years. The modest space still held reminders of their mother—a quilt she had made as a child draped over the back of the rocking chair she had used to rock Gabe and Levi to sleep. An old Bible passed down through her family lay on the nightstand next to the bed, on the side where she used to sleep.

A nearly unbearable sense of sadness engulfed him. He'd never missed his mother more than now. He had grieved deeply for her after she died, but Levi had been there to share that grief. Both of them had been close to her, Levi even more so.

She would have known what to do about *Daed*. Gabe had no idea how to handle his father's pain. Even after his wife had died,

John Miller had been strong. Now, with Gabe's arm supporting him, guiding him to his bed, he was a broken man.

"*Daed*, why don't you lie down for a little while? I'll bring you some lunch in a bit."

John sat down on the edge of the bed, but he shook his head. "I'm not hungry." He looked up at Gabe. "I was right in asking Joseph for forgiveness."

"That's what Levi needs to do."

"He can't. Not now."

"You mean he won't."

Squaring his shoulders as if he had a sudden burst of strength, John said, "I know what I mean, *sohn*. Levi is lost. He's strayed away from God. I don't know what led him down this path, but I do know that he has to seek out the Lord and ask His forgiveness. Only when he's given himself fully to God will he be able to come back." He bent over and took off his boots, then stretched out on the bed, closing his eyes. "You're right. I am tired."

"I'll leave you alone." Gabe turned to go. "Come downstairs when you're ready." He slowly shut the door behind him and made his way to the first floor of the house. As soon as his foot landed on the bottom stair, he heard a knock on the front door. He opened it and saw Moriah standing on the porch. His eyes widened with surprise. "What are you doing here?"

"We brought you lunch."

Gabe looked beyond her and saw *Frau* Byler coming up the porch steps, carrying a large picnic basket. Joseph was tending to their horse. He looked back at Moriah, who gave him a small smile that warmed his heart.

"We thought you and John might be hungry."

"Come on in." He opened the door wide and gestured for the

two women to step inside. He then went out to help Joseph with his horse and buggy. When the men returned, they were welcomed by a feast of sliced ham, bread, pickles, potato salad, rolls, banana bread, and two different kinds of cookies. Gabe was thankful for the bounty, and for the generosity of the Bylers.

"*Daed*'s upstairs," Gabe stated as he went to the sink and washed his hands. "He said he wasn't hungry, but I know he'd want to be down here to thank you for bringing such a *wunderbaar* meal."

"Don't worry about bothering him," Emma said as she filled their glasses with iced tea. "He should rest. We have plenty and this will all keep 'til later.

They took their chairs, and Gabe sat across from Moriah. After prayer they started to eat, but it became evident that no one had much of an appetite. Moriah just picked at her food, and her mother soon noticed.

"You have to eat, Moriah," she said, her voice soft and gentle. "Even when you aren't hungry, your baby is."

Nodding, Moriah ate a spoonful of potato salad. A long, awkward stretch of silence soon followed. Gabe's attention kept swaying to her. He wished there was something he could do to fix the situation. But he couldn't do anything. And he hated that helpless feeling most of all.

As they made their way home from church, Rachel and her mother rode in silence. Sarah stared straight ahead as she guided the horse and buggy down the road. Her black bonnet obscured her face, keeping Rachel from discerning her thoughts, although she suspected she already knew what Sarah was thinking about. She was thinking about it too.

The entire community had been abuzz this morning at church. Soon everyone knew that Levi Miller had left his wife and the Amish. Rachel could barely believe it. She didn't know Levi well, but she had thought he and Moriah had a good marriage. They were still newlyweds—how could there be trouble in the relationship already? Yet having marriage problems was one thing. Leaving the church was an entirely different story.

She'd known a few people who had "yanked over" by leaving their faith, mostly rebellious teens and young adults who had gotten a taste of the Yankee world and started to chafe underneath the *Ordnung*. Usually those who left hadn't been baptized and were allowed to come back to the community and socialize with their family and friends. She knew of only one woman who had moved away after she had joined the church. Rachel had heard she had fallen in love with a Yankee, but she didn't know if that was a rumor or not, because the woman had never returned. When she left, she was immediately put in the *bann*. Maybe the shunning had kept her away, not an outlander. Rachel could only guess at the true reasons.

Leaving the church had never been an option in Rachel's mind. She had always known she would become Amish when she was old enough to make the decision about baptism. The trappings of the world had never appealed to her, and she had never had the desire to break the *Ordnung*. Why would anyone want to, when their faith offered them so much?

Back at home, Rachel and her mother prepared a cold lunch. Aaron hadn't attended church that morning—he had still been in his room when they'd arrived home. Again, her father, Emmanuel, along with her mother didn't say anything when he came downstairs without a word. Rachel couldn't figure out why he was allowed to do whatever he wanted to do.

"I'm going to visit Emma," Sarah had announced when they finished with dinner. "She needs our support. Rachel, please wash the dishes. I'd like you to come with me."

Rachel had just popped the last bit of her ham and Swiss cheese sandwich in her mouth and she froze midchew. Alarm shot through her at the thought of going to the Bylers. She had managed to avoid Tobias at the service that morning, only seeing him briefly before church had started. Thank goodness they hadn't crossed paths. That would have been embarrassing. Either he hadn't seen her in the service or he was ignoring her, and she would bet a week's tips he'd disregarded her on purpose. The last thing she wanted to do was run into him again, especially after what had happened between them two nights ago.

"Can't I just stay here?" she had pleaded, hoping her mother would change her mind. "I have some reading I want to catch up on."

"Rachel, I'm surprised. You would put a book ahead of the Byler's troubles?"

"Bible reading," Rachel clarified, a twinge of guilt pricking at her as she said the lie. If her mother let her off the hook, then she felt duty-bound to crack open the family Bible. She found the High German translation hard to read, but she had some serious confessing to do about her newfound feelings for Tobias.

"As impressed as I am by your devotion, I think that can wait until later. Emma, Joseph, and Moriah left right after the service and I want to see if they're all right. I should think you would care about their welfare as well," Sarah said again, rising from her chair and adjusting her crisp, white apron.

"I do. But—"

"But what?" Sarah paused, lifting one brow.

Rachel couldn't explain her real reason for not wanting to go the Bylers, so she dropped the issue. "Never mind. Just give me a few minutes to finish the dishes."

"*Danki*, Rachel."

As Rachel took her *daed*'s plate, he said, "Don't forget Aaron's too."

Rachel pinched her lips together as she accepted her *daed*'s dish, then went to collect Aaron's. Part of his sandwich still remained on the white plate. "Are you finished?"

"*Ya*." He got up, pushed his chair back where it belonged, then left the room without a word of thanks. Their father departed shortly after, saying he had some work to do in the barn.

That was two hours ago. Now it was late afternoon, and as they approached the Byler's, Rachel's insides started to churn. She hoped Tobias wasn't home. If she was lucky he'd be out visiting one of his cousins or something. But she doubted he would be out having fun, not after what happened to Moriah. She gripped the side of the buggy seat as her mother turned into the driveway.

"Please tether the horse," Sarah said as she parked the buggy. "I'll meet you inside."

Rachel did as she was asked, then procrastinated by stroking the horse's velvety soft nose. She wasn't in a hurry to go in the house and see Tobias again. The weather had warmed several degrees since the other day, and the sun was out in full force. At least she could be thankful for that. When she couldn't stall any longer, she turned to go inside, but paused for a moment when she spied the wrecked buggy parked behind *Herr* Byler's workshop. The vehicle was completely mangled, and she said a quick prayer of thanks that neither one of them had been hurt. She spun around on the heel of her black shoe, only to run smack-dab into Tobias's chest.

"Whoa," he said, as his arms went around her shoulders to steady her.

She just had to pick that moment to breathe, to inhale the scent of his clean Sunday shirt, which was now inches from her nose. For the briefest of moments she reveled in his nearness, until common sense took over and she stepped back.

"Sorry about that," she said, her hand touching her *kapp* as she tried to steady her nerves.

"It's all right."

The despondent tone of his voice caught her attention. She looked up to see his glum expression.

"What are you doing here?" he asked flatly.

"We came to see how your *daed* and *mami* were doing." And because she couldn't stop herself, she added, "Don't worry, I didn't come to see you."

He ran his hand through his hair, revealing a yellowish bruise on his forehead. A reminder of the accident. As if either one of them needed another one. "*Gut*. That makes me happy."

But he didn't sound anything close to being happy. "What do you mean by that?"

Shoving past her, he headed to his damaged buggy. "Never mind."

Turning around, she followed him. "That's not an answer. I want to know what you meant."

He knelt beside the buggy's broken axle. "You know, Rachel, the world doesn't revolve around you."

"I never said it did."

"You don't have to."

"Excuse me?"

Remaining in his crouched position, he looked up at her, any remnant of his trademark gloating and teasing gone from his crystalline blue eyes. "Go inside. I'm not in the mood for your drama."

She crossed her arms. "I am not dramatic."

He glanced at her folded arms, then went back to inspecting the axle.

Changing her stance, she moved toward him. "This is about the other night, isn't it? You're blaming me for what happened."

"Not your fault we got hit by a car." He jerked on the axle, checking its stability. It immediately came loose. He groaned.

"I'm not talking about the accident." Why was she even bringing this up? She'd told herself that she didn't want to see Tobias, but here she was, not only seeing him, but also trying to engage him in a conversation they really shouldn't be having in the first place. What was wrong with her? "I think you know what I mean."

He stopped his inspection and rested his forehead against the lower side of the buggy. The motion pushed his hat farther back on his head. "That's not your fault either," he said quietly.

"*Ya*, it is. I should have never kissed you. I must have knocked my head really hard to do something as crazy and stupid as that." She looked away. "Not like it was good or anything."

Slowly he rose from the ground and looked at her, eyes filled with fury. She'd never seen him so mad before.

"You're a mean, miserable woman, Rachel Detweiler. I don't know how—or even why—Christian puts up with you." He brushed her aside and stormed off, but not before turning around and adding, "And for the record, I'd kiss a stinkin' pig before I'd kiss you again."

Ouch.

Her eyes pricked as she watched him walk into the woodshop and shut the door in her face. He'd called her mean? He was the cruelest man on earth. She didn't care if she never saw him again. In fact, she'd prefer it.

The sound of a screen door slamming made her turn around. Tobias's younger sister, Elisabeth, approached. Like Tobias, she had blue eyes and blonde hair, along with one of the tiniest waists Rachel had ever seen. When she neared, Rachel could see her eyes were red rimmed from crying.

Rachel met her halfway. "Are you all right?"

Elisabeth nodded. "I'm fine. Just upset over what happened to Moriah. We all are. It's been so hard on her. *Mami* and *Daed* aren't taking it too well either."

Her words caused Rachel's heart to stop. How could she have been so dense? No wonder Tobias was angry with her. She'd been so caught up in thinking about that kiss, so self-centered and defensive, she had forgotten the reason she and her mother had even stopped to visit. His sister's husband had just left her, and instead of trying to offer him comfort, she'd picked another fight.

He was right. She was a miserable person.

"My parents are with Moriah at the Millers," Elisabeth said. "But your *mami* is helping us make some cookies. She said it will keep our mind off of everything. Even Lukas and Stephen are helping, and they hate to cook."

"That's *gut*," Rachel said absently, glancing over her shoulder at the woodshop.

"I've been sent to get you."

Rachel focused on the woodshop for another second, then turned to Elisabeth. "Tell my *mudder* I'll be right there."

The young woman nodded. "I will. Oh, and if you see Tobias, tell him we're making his favorite—oatmeal chocolate chip."

Rachel nodded at Elisabeth and watched her hurry back to the house. But she couldn't follow her inside, not just yet. Not before talking to Tobias one more time and apologizing for being so insensitive. She walked to the woodshop door and placed her hand on the knob, only to hesitate turning it.

Maybe she should leave things be. Tobias was mad at her, but he would get over it. Besides, what did she care if he was angry? He'd been mad at her off and on for years.

But this time was different. He was hurting over his sister, and she'd only made things worse. She had to apologize, at the very least. Taking a deep breath, she opened the door.

He stood in the middle of the shop, sifting his hand through the small pile of wood shavings that lay on a long, tall, tool-nicked table. An unfinished cradle perched next to him, amid millions of tiny flecks of sawdust. The scent of freshly cut wood enveloped her as she breathed in.

"What do you want?" he asked, not looking up.

Rachel looked at his fingers as he continued to push around the shavings. Long, strong fingers attached to a large, calloused hand. The hand of an artist. She'd seen his work before and had grudgingly admitted he had a gift with wood. Always knowing that he had yet another talent had chafed her in the past, but thinking about it now only brought her admiration. Instead of maligning his talent, she should have been appreciating it. Just one more indication of what a rotten person she was when it came to him.

Finally, he glanced at her, his expression lifeless. "What?"

The sawdust made her itch, and she rubbed her nose with her palm. Then she quickly thrust her hands behind her back. "I, um, well, I want to apologize. To you."

He shrugged, then went back to messing with the shavings. "Fine. You apologized. Now leave."

Once again his response triggered a tiny spark inside her, but she pushed it down. He had been right; this wasn't about her. It was about him and his family, a family he obviously deeply cared about. And she needed to show him that she understood.

She didn't stop walking until she was right next to him. "Tobias, I'm really sorry. Especially about your sister. That's a terrible thing to happen to her."

Turning, his gaze met hers, its steeliness softening. "I appreciate that, Rachel. Been hard on her."

"Hard on everyone, I'm sure."

He nodded, his lips flattening in to a thin line. "All my life I've been taught that fighting is wrong, that hitting another person, no matter what, is forbidden. But right now I could hurt Levi Miller with my bare hands for what he's done to Moriah."

"No one would blame you if you did."

"Yes, they would." He let out a flat chuckle. "You know they would." With a flick of his hand he swept the wood shavings off the table. They floated and shimmered to the floor.

She couldn't argue with him, because what he was saying was true. "So what are you going to do?"

"Nothing. There's nothing I can do. Moriah moved back home yesterday. I guess things will go back to the way they were before she was married."

Yet they both knew things would never be the same. Not for his sister . . . and not for them. Their kiss had changed that.

They stood together in silence for a moment, Tobias staring at the mess on the shop floor in front of him. "Guess I better clean it up."

"I'll do it." Rachel quickly went to the back of the shop and found the broom. Without looking at Tobias, she started sweeping the shavings into a small pile.

He let out a breath. "I'm sorry for what I said, Rachel. You know. About kissing the pig. That was uncalled for."

"I deserved it." She glanced around the shop. "Where's the dustpan?"

"Hang on." He disappeared into the back of the shop, then came out with a large metal dustpan. Lowering into a crouch, he placed it on the floor and she swept the debris into it. "No one deserves to be insulted like that," he continued. "I should watch my mouth."

At his mention of the word *mouth*, they both looked at each other. She saw his gaze focus on her lips, then dart away. "Finished?" he finally asked, staring down at the floor.

"*Ya.*"

He picked up the dustpan and deposited the shavings into a metal trash can, then leaned it against the can before taking the broom from her grasp. "*Danki.*"

"Don't mention it. By the way, I just saw your sister before I came in here. Everyone else is inside baking cookies. Elisabeth said they're making your favorite—oatmeal chocolate chip."

"Those are her favorite." Tobias's lips quirked in a half smile. "She thinks everyone should like what she does. That way she always gets what she wants."

"Really? That's an interesting way to look at things."

"Annoying, but that's Elisabeth."

"So what is your favorite cookie?"

"Peanut butter. With little chunks of peanuts sticking out. Actually anything with nuts is good."

Rachel regarded him for a moment. "What do you think of pecan pie?"

"Love it. Why?"

"Just wondering."

"Well, I doubt there's pie in the house, but the cookies should be good. Believe me, I've never met a cookie I didn't like."

"We should probably go get some then. I promised Elisabeth I'd come inside. I'm sure *Mami's* wondering where I ran off to."

"Yeah, we should go. It's a little chilly in here anyway."

As they walked out of the shop, Rachel glanced at the buggy again. "Can it be fixed?"

Tobias nodded. "My cousin works on buggies. He's coming out tomorrow after work to take a look at it. The axle's broken and the wheels are bent, but the rest of it's in good shape. Shouldn't be too much trouble to fix."

"That's good."

They headed toward the house, but Rachel suddenly stopped in her tracks.

He turned around. "What is it?"

They had just put their differences aside for once, and now she was on the verge of throwing everything off-kilter. But she couldn't go inside without knowing if he truly meant what he said a few moments ago. "Tobias . . . do you really think I'm a horrible person?"

His head tilted to the right, regret coloring his features. "Rachel, I'm sorry. My mouth again. Keeps saying things it shouldn't."

"Even when it's the truth?"

He scrubbed his face with the palm of his hand before regarding her again. "You asked me, so I'm gonna be honest. You're always angry with me, Rachel. Most times I feel like anything I do or say will make you mad at me. I'll admit, sometimes I egg you on. But other times, well, it's hard to be around you."

His admission cut deeply, even as she realized his words were true. She was resentful of him, and she didn't understand why. Not completely anyway.

"Hey, let's drop it." Tobias smiled and waved his hand toward the house. "No need for all of us to be depressed. We better get some cookies before everyone else eats them all."

Rachel sighed. Leave it to a man to think of his stomach above all else. But in all honesty she knew Tobias was creating a diversion, and she was grateful for it. He had enough to deal with right now. He had made his observation, and neither of them were interested in pursuing the conversation any further.

Yet she knew she'd be thinking about what he said for a very long time.

Chapter 9

*T*he first few days after Moriah returned home, her family had given her the space she needed. They treated her nearly the same as they had before she married. Her parents didn't ask many questions, which she appreciated. Her brothers were a bit kinder than before, and her sisters were less inquisitive, especially Elisabeth. They all knew about the baby, but naturally their excitement was tempered by the circumstances.

When Moriah accepted that she couldn't spend the rest of her life in her bedroom, mourning what she had lost, she busied herself in a flurry of activity. She helped her family with their chores and practically took over all the cooking duties for her mother. She brought lunch out to her father, Tobias, and Luke in the woodshop, and occasionally she helped with customer orders. A few young wives in the church had new babies, and she sewed several outfits for each one. Since she'd always wanted to learn to knit, she bought an instruction book, needles, and several skeins of pale yellow yarn. By the end of the day, she was usually exhausted.

After three weeks of busyness, she still felt lost and confused. At night, the hardest time for her, sleep was always elusive. She tried mentally repeating Scripture, but that didn't help. Instead, she laid in her single bed, tossing and turning, thinking about Levi, mulling over regrets, asking God why this had happened to her. She was still no closer to an answer. Her future looked bleak and lonely. She could never remarry. Her child would never know his or her father. Or even have a father. Yes, her family had rallied around her, and they would always be there for her. But they couldn't fill the emptiness she felt when she saw other couples, or stop the sadness she felt knowing she would never have another child.

At times she couldn't bear to even look at her own family because doing so brought pain and regret. For years the Bylers had spent every Thursday evening engrossed in a family activity—playing a board game, reading the Bible or other stories aloud, or singing hymns together. But even during those family evenings, she felt like an outsider. She would never have the experience of sitting next to her husband, sharing the Bible with their children, as her parents did. Her siblings would all marry and have families of their own. They wouldn't be looked on by the rest of the community with pity or, even worse, as an outcast. Her dreams of a large family and a loving husband were shattered.

So she did the only thing she could do. She survived and put her focus on her baby. She was powerless to bring Levi back; he had made his decision and there was nothing she could do about it. And while she knew the pain of his rejection and the loneliness filling her soul wouldn't heal quickly, she had to at least try to have as normal a life as possible, for the sake of her child. Her babe would never feel abandoned or betrayed. She would make sure of it.

When the third week of April arrived, Moriah was busier than ever. The Bylers were hosting church that Sunday, and her family members were deep in the throes of preparations. Their house had a large basement where the service would be held. The furniture and wood floors needed to be dusted, cleaned, and polished. Even though there would be a potluck meal after the service, the Bylers still needed to provide a good portion of the food. Moriah had the task of preparing the apple crumb pies.

That Wednesday morning she finished rolling out the last pie crust on the kitchen table, then placed it in a metal pie pan. With her fingers she crimped the edges, then stepped back from the table. Twelve crusts, ready to be filled, then baked later on in the afternoon when her mother came back from the market and her sisters were home from school. Elisabeth and Ruthie would make the crumb topping out of flour, cinnamon, sugar, and butter and sprinkle it on the homemade apple pie filling Moriah had prepared the day before.

As she washed her hands under the cold water, a yawn escaped. Her mother said fatigue was normal in the beginning of pregnancy, but Moriah knew that wasn't the only reason for her exhaustion.

She dried her hands and went to the linen closet, where she found a basket filled with old, clean rags. Selecting a large one, she set to the task of dusting every exposed space in the house. She had just started on one of the end tables when she heard a knock on the door.

"Just a minute." She tucked the rag in the pocket of her white apron and answered the door. Her eyes widened. "Gabriel?"

"Hi." He glanced down for a moment, shifting from one foot to the other. Then he looked back up. "I was driving by, and I thought I'd see if your horses needed any shoes."

"Our horses are fine, but that's thoughtful of you to stop by."

"Oh," he said, shoving his hands in his pockets. "All right then."

When he didn't turn around and leave, she asked, "Is there anything else I can do for you, Gabriel?"

"*Nee.* Nothing else." He paused, looking more unsure than she had ever seen him. "Well, I was also wondering how you're doing."

Ah, so that was his real reason for stopping by. He came to check on her. She was both surprised and touched. "I'm doing all right," she said with a small smile. "As well as expected, I guess."

"*Gut.* Glad to hear it." He rocked back and forth on his heels.

A gust of wind swirled around them, cutting through her dress and chilling her skin. He didn't seem in any hurry to leave, so she asked, "Would you like to come in for a minute?"

He hesitated, then nodded. "If you don't mind."

"*Nee.* I don't mind at all. I'm glad to see you." Gabriel's expression relaxed. He seemed relieved by her welcome. Although she saw him and his *daed* at church, their paths never crossed any other time. She didn't realize until this moment how much she had missed them both.

Once inside, he slipped off his black hat, then ran his hand through his brown hair. "Cold spring day."

"*Ya.* Would you like something to drink? I've got coffee, and there are a few cookies left over from lunch."

"*Danki*, but I'm fine. Had a big meal with *Daed*. *Frau* Stoltzfus brought over a couple casseroles last night." His head dipped down a tiny bit as he looked at her directly. "Everything okay with the baby?"

She smiled. He'd asked the question so tentatively, yet with genuine concern. "So far everything is going well."

"Do you know when he's due?"

"She—or he—is due in November."

His lips curved into a small smile. "A harvest baby. That sounds nice." He rubbed his smooth chin for a moment. "Have you heard anything from Levi?"

Without warning, the sting of tears sprang to her eyes. She didn't think she had any left. "*Nee*," she said softly. "Have you?"

His expression became downcast as he shook his head. Then he glanced at her and winced. "I'm sorry, Moriah. I shouldn't have asked you about him. I didn't mean to upset you."

"It's okay." She brought her fingers to her eyes and rubbed them, trying to send the threatening tears away. When she looked at him, spots danced in front of her eyes, then quickly faded as his kind face came into clear view.

"I better go." He put his hat back on and opened the door. Before he walked out, he turned around and faced her again. "I know I don't have the right to offer, but if you ever need anything, Moriah, just ask."

"*Danki*, Gabriel. I appreciate that." As she watched him step out onto the porch, she added, "Say hello to your *daed* for me."

"I will." He hurried to his buggy, untethered the horse, and jumped in the driver's seat. Moments later he pulled away.

Slowly she shut the door, her thoughts confused. She shouldn't be that surprised by Gabriel's visit, since they were still technically family because of the baby. But he didn't have to stop by and check up on her, or even ask about the baby. He knew that her family would take good care of them both. Still, she was glad he did.

"I'm fine, Moriah." Ruth crossed her arms over her chest as she lay in her bed, propped up by several soft pillows. "I don habe a code."

Moriah placed a bed tray laden with warm turkey noodle soup, orange juice, and two cherry-flavored cough drops. Normally their *mami* had forbidden food in the bedrooms, but she always made an exception for a sick child. "*Ya*, Ruthie, I'm afraid you do."

"I shood habe gone to school today," she said, ignoring Moriah's words and the tray in front of her.

"You should eat your soup. That will help you feel better. Besides, you love turkey noodle soup."

"Not hungry." Ruth turned her head and stared out her small bedroom window. She was the only child that had her own room, a tiny area up in the attic. It would get almost unbearably hot in the summer and frigid cold in the winter, but Ruth loved having a space to call her very own. Except for today. Nothing would make her happy. Not only wasn't she feeling well, but she hated to miss school.

Moriah sat down next to her and tucked a strand of Ruth's dishwater-blonde hair behind her small ear. Her sister had her hair pinned up, but she wasn't wearing her *kapp*. "Ruthie, please eat a little bit of the soup. And have a sip of the orange juice as well. As soon as you feel better you can go back to school."

Ruth didn't respond right away. When she finally faced Moriah, she sighed. "Okay," she said, sounding like she had cotton balls stuffed up her nose. "Thig mebbe I can go to school tomorrow?"

"We'll see. It's up to *Mami*, of course."

"But you wood send me, woodn't you?"

With a smile, Moriah rose from Ruth's bed. "If you were better, I would." She had never met a child so enthralled with school. School had been a necessary part of life, and Moriah had done well in her studies. But she had never cultivated a love for education like her youngest sibling did. After this school year, Ruth would only have two more years left, and Moriah could only imagine how hard it will be on her sister to leave school for good after the eighth grade.

Bringing the spoon up to her mouth, Ruth blew on the pale brown liquid. One thin noodle hung limply over the side of the utensil. "You don habe to stay," she said, then sipped her soup.

"Let me know when you're done then."

Ruth nodded. "I'll probly read a book after that."

"And hopefully get some sleep."

Her sister smiled, her brown eyes red-rimmed from watering. "I will. I promise."

Giving her a nod, Moriah then turned around and went downstairs to the kitchen. When she inhaled the scent of the turkey noodle soup, her belly growled. The nausea had subsided over the past couple weeks. It was the first week of May, and she was almost three months along. Grateful that her morning sickness had been short-lived, she picked up a small white bowl from inside a cabinet and walked over to the soup pot simmering on the stove. Just as she was spooning the steaming soup, she heard the sound of a car pulling in the driveway. Assuming it was one of her *daed*'s customers, she sat down at the table. Folding her hands and closing her eyes, she started to say grace. Before she finished the prayer, someone burst through the front door.

"Moriah! Moriah!"

The voice sounded like Gabriel. What was he doing? She jumped up from her chair and almost ran into him as he dashed into the kitchen. A knot suddenly formed in her throat. Something was horribly wrong. One look at Gabriel's stricken face told her as much. "What happened? What's wrong?"

"There isn't much time, Moriah. We have to leave. Now."

"Leave? What are you talking about?"

Gabriel took her by the arm. "I'll tell you in the car—"

"Car? Where are we going?"

Facing her, he held on to her shoulders. "Moriah, it's Levi."

Hope replaced the dread inside her for a split instant. "You saw Levi? Has he come back?"

"*Nee,*" he said, guiding her to the door. "He's in the hospital."

Gabe hated hospitals. He hated the chemical smell, the unnatural glow of fluorescent lighting, the unending and repetitive questions people asked you while refusing to answer your own. But more than anything he hated the pain and the sadness that permeated the brick building. The last time he'd been in a hospital, his mother was being treated for cancer. Hospitals held nothing but bad memories for him.

And now he was in the middle of another horrible nightmare. He'd received a phone call from the call box early that morning. The caller had identified herself as a "hospital representative." He had no idea how they'd found his number, but he hadn't cared once they told him what had happened to Levi. A three-car accident on Interstate 90. That was all he knew, because that was all they would tell him.

Now, three hours later, he, his *daed,* and Moriah were sitting in the emergency room's visitor area at University Hospital, waiting to hear about Levi. Technically he was still in the *bann,* but nothing would have kept them away from him, not when they weren't sure how injured he truly was. The church used the *bann* as a corrective measure, as a means for bringing the erring person into repentance and back to the Amish. And even though Gabe, his father, and Moriah were expected to limit their interactions with Levi, they'd all agreed seeing him now was worth any chastising they might receive.

Gabe glanced at his father's ashen face as he sat next to Moriah. He could only imagine the memories this place held for him. First his wife. Now his son.

Then he looked at Moriah. Her eyes were dry, her expression stoic. But she had shredded the tissue in her hands to bits. This couldn't be good for her or the baby. Hadn't she suffered enough? Not only had her husband left her, but now she had to wait and see if he was dead or alive.

Gabe closed his eyes at the morbid thought. Levi couldn't die. That was impossible. Regardless of what his brother had done, Gabe still loved him. He couldn't bear to lose him.

Jumping up from his seat, he said, "I'm going to find out what's taking so long. We should have heard something by now."

"*Nee*," John said, holding up his hand. "Give them time to do their job, Gabriel. I'm sure they'll tell us what's happened to Levi when they can."

Gabe was amazed at his father's composure. Then he remembered the pillar of strength he'd been during his mother's illness. Other than his reaction to Levi's leaving, he never showed much emotional weakness. Gabriel admired him for that and wished he had a fraction of the inner strength both his father and Moriah possessed.

While he heeded his father and didn't approach the woman at the front desk, he couldn't sit still and wait either. Instead he walked over to the window and stared outside into the parking lot. Not a horse or buggy in sight. Just lots of cars. Lots and lots of cars.

Suddenly he became aware that he was being watched. He turned and saw a young woman staring at him. He looked out the window again, ignoring her. He was used to being stared at, especially when he ventured outside of Middlefield. The Yankees there were used to the Amish way of life, but this woman likely had never even seen an Amish man before.

"Mrs. Miller?"

He spun around at the sound of Moriah's name. A trim man wearing a white coat stood at the doorway of the waiting room, a stethoscope around his neck. Gabe assumed he was the doctor.

Moriah rose from her chair. "Yes?"

"Can I speak with you privately?"

Although the room wasn't crowded, there were a few people sitting in the chairs, watching TV, thumbing through magazines, or dozing off. Dread pooled in Gabe's belly as he crossed the room to stand next to Moriah. From the doctor's bleak expression, he could tell the news wouldn't be good.

"This is my h-husband's brother," Moriah said. Gabe didn't miss how she stumbled over the word. "And his father. Whatever you have to say to me, you should also say to them."

The doctor nodded, then gestured for them to follow him into the hallway, a few feet down from the receptionist. The area allowed more privacy than the waiting room.

"The car accident your husband was in was extremely serious, Mrs. Miller. He's suffered massive internal injuries, along with a concussion. I'm not going to sugarcoat this for you." He paused and looked at each of them, then returned his attention to Moriah. "We're concerned about the amount of blood he's lost. We're giving him transfusions, but he's lost a great deal."

"What does that mean?" Moriah asked.

"It means that his situation is very, very grave. He needs to have surgery to repair the damage to his organs. You must sign a consent form in order for us to proceed. The faster we get him into surgery, the better his chances are of recovery."

Gabe's blood turned to ice. Chance of recovery? No, he couldn't have heard the doctor correctly.

"The nurse will be out with the paperwork. Will you sign the form, Mrs. Miller?"

Moriah nodded.

As the doctor turned to walk away, a tall, distinguished man in a black suit barged into the emergency room area. "Where is my daughter?" he bellowed, dashing up to the glassed-in receptionist area.

The red-haired woman seated behind the counter slid open the glass window. "May I help you?" she asked, her voice calm and detached.

"I want to know where my daughter is! I demand to see her right now!"

The ruckus caught Gabe's attention. When he took a good look at the older gentleman, his mouth dropped open. Robert Johnston, owner of Johnston's Farms.

"Sir, if you'll kindly have a seat—"

"I will not have a seat! I get this phone call that my daughter's been in some sort of accident, but you people won't tell me anything, and you expect me to have a seat?"

"What's your daughter's name, sir?"

"Taylor Johnston."

"I'll see what I can find out." The receptionist shut the glass window.

Robert Johnston started to pace in front of the waiting room entrance. Gabe glanced down at Moriah, who was staring at the man. He didn't know if she had made the connection yet or not. His father, on the other hand, did. John's worried gaze met Gabe's.

"Mrs. Miller? Here are the forms the doctor needs to you to sign."

Gabe hadn't even heard the nurse approach. He looked to see her handing Moriah a clipboard and a pen. Moriah barely scanned the documents, then signed her name and handed them back to the nurse.

"Thank you. Mr. Miller is being prepped for surgery, which is on the second floor. Just take the elevator down the hall, then turn left. There will be a receptionist in the waiting room area, just tell her who you're waiting for." The nurse placed her hand on Moriah's forearm. "We're doing all we can for your husband, Mrs. Miller."

"Thank you," Moriah whispered.

To his left, Gabe heard the glass window sliding open again. "Mr. Johnston?"

Mr. Johnston stopped pacing and strode up to the counter. "What have you found out?"

"Your daughter is going to be fine."

The man slumped against the window. "Thank God."

"The nurse said you could see her. I'll let you in."

The faint sound of a buzzer filled the air as a set of brown double doors opened near the entrance of the emergency room. Mr. Johnston disappeared through the doors, and they softly closed behind him.

"Gabriel," John said.

Turning, Gabe answered, "*Ya?*"

"We need to go upstairs. Moriah, are you ready?"

She nodded again. The color had seeped from her face, fear and confusion present in her blue eyes.

He followed her and his *daed* to the elevator. Once they arrived at the surgery waiting room, he told Moriah and his father to go sit down. "I'll let the woman know we're here."

After he gave the receptionist the information she needed, he turned to see his *daed* and Moriah seated next to each other, holding hands, both obviously deep in prayer. As he waited for them to finish, he walked over to a pale-blue wall. The décor of the room, from the comfortable chairs to the peaceful paintings of country scenery, were meant to invoke serenity, but inside Gabe felt anything but calm. He struggled to wrap his mind around what had happened. A car accident. Obviously Levi had been with Taylor. She would be okay, but Levi was struggling for his life. Of course he was glad that she hadn't been seriously injured . . . He needed to push her out of his mind. He had to think about Levi. He had to pray for his brother. Taking off his hat, he leaned his head against the wall, closed his eyes, and started to pray.

Moments later he felt the light touch of a hand on his arm. Opening his eyes, he looked down to see Moriah standing beside him.

"Are you okay?" Her luminous eyes, less haunted than when they had been in the emergency room, gazed up at him. Worry lines still etched her features, but she took the time to ask about his well-being. How could anyone expect him not to love such a caring woman?

"*Ya,*" he managed, slipping his black hat back on his head. "How are you doing?"

She shrugged. He noticed she hadn't moved her hand. He hoped she never would.

"Levi will make it, Gabriel," she said, her voice hitching slightly on the last word. "I have faith that he will."

Unable to stop himself, Gabe covered her hand with his own, drawing strength and comfort from her touch. "Then I have faith he will too."

Moriah touched her hand to her forehead, as if applying pressure would relieve the throbbing inside her head. Five hours had passed since they had first arrived at the hospital, and Levi was still in surgery. There had been no word about his condition, but she clung to her hope that he would pull through. She had spoken very little to Gabe and his father. All three of them had been mired in their own thoughts. She had never realized a hospital could be such a lonely place, even when you were surrounded by people. Even when you were with your family.

Finally, a doctor entered the waiting room, one she had never seen before. He wore a green short-sleeved shirt, green drawstring pants, and a white, brimless cap on his head. Striding to the reception area, he said a few words to the dark-skinned woman seated behind the desk who pointed toward Moriah. The doctor nodded, then walked over to her.

"Mrs. Miller? I'm Dr. Whitman. I'm the surgeon who operated on your husband."

Her chest tightened as she stood. "How is he?"

"I'm happy to say he's doing as well as can be expected. We believe the surgery to be a success. It was touch and go there for a while, but he's a strong young man."

Gabriel and John stood on each side of her. As the relief shot through her body, she felt limp, like a rag doll. "Can we see him now?" Gabriel asked as he put his arm around her shoulders.

Dr. Whitman shook his head. "He's in recovery right now. It will be a couple hours before we release him to intensive care. After two or three days we hope to transfer him to a regular floor. Once he's fully recovered, he'll be able to go home."

"Praise the Lord," John whispered. "Praise the Lord."

With a smile the doctor said, "This is the kind of news we enjoy giving. Feel free to go down to the cafeteria and grab some supper. Mr. Miller won't be in his room until around seven."

John reached out for the doctor's hand. "Thank you so much, Dr. Whitman." His voice was raspy with emotion. "Thank you, thank you."

"You're welcome. I'll go back and check on him. We can go over his progress in the morning." He nodded and left the waiting room.

Still feeling weak, Moriah leaned against Gabriel, grateful for his strong support. Levi made it. She vowed not to leave his side until he was well enough to come home. Their home. Surely he would realize that he didn't belong in the Yankees' world. He belonged with his family. With her and their child.

"I don't ever want to see this room again," John said, wiping his eyes with the back of his hand. He grinned. "Let's go get something to eat. Suddenly, I'm starving!"

Gabriel smiled in response. "Me too." Then he removed his arm from her shoulders and looked at her.

"You were right," he said softly. "He's gonna be okay."

"Thanks to God," Moriah said. "All thanks be to God."

Chapter 10

*M*oriah felt the touch of a hand on her shoulder. Her eyes flickered open. She shifted her body in the green vinyl-backed chair and lazily looked up. Gabriel was standing next to her, gazing down with concern. When she fully awakened, she jolted upright, remembering where she was. Levi's intensive care room. "Is he awake?"

"*Nee.*" Gabriel dropped his hand. "The nurse said he was up a little while ago."

"Why didn't they wake me?" she said, dismayed.

"He wasn't conscious for very long. Besides, they knew you needed the rest. I'm glad they let you sleep."

She rose from her chair and smoothed her white apron. The fabric was wrinkled, as was her light-green dress. The rest of her was probably a mess too. "What time is it?"

"Almost five a.m. There's a visitors' waiting room down the hall. *Daed* is asleep on the couch in there. I wanted to check and see how you were doing. And Levi."

Moriah looked down at her husband as he lay on the hospital bed. Wires, endless wires were attached to his body, which in turn were connected to blinking, illuminated machines and dangling bags of fluid and blood. He lay flat on his back, a white sheet draped over his lower body. She touched her mouth with her fingertips, trying to stem the tirade of sorrow and pity that coursed through her. His face was almost unrecognizable from the swelling around his eyes and mouth. A bandage encircled his head, covering his brow. The nurses had assured her that he wasn't in pain; the medication pump ensured that. But she didn't see how.

No one had any concrete details about the accident, but she didn't really care right now. Her complete focus was on being there for her husband. If she had failed him before, she refused to fail him now, especially when he needed her so much.

"Are you hungry?" Gabriel asked. "We can go downstairs and get some breakfast."

"I don't want to leave him."

"Moriah, he couldn't be in better hands. Nothing will happen to him." He moved to stand alongside her. "You've been in here all night. You need to take a break."

She watched Levi for a moment, not moving until she detected the slight rise and fall of his chest. Gabriel was right, of course. The nurses and doctors wouldn't let anything happen to Levi. Turning, she nodded. "Let me freshen up first."

"I'll meet you in the waiting room." Gabriel took one more look at his brother, then left.

Levi's arms lay limply against his sides. She slipped her hand in his and squeezed. "I'll be right back," she whispered, then reluctantly let go. Exiting his small room, she made her way to the restroom, which was just around the corner. Once she was inside the single washroom, she closed the door, then locked it.

Facing the mirror, she sighed at her reflection. Her *kapp* was askew, and there were dark circles under eyes. The inside of her mouth felt pasty, and her shoulders ached. Reaching up, she pulled the bobby pins from her *kapp* and placed it on the side of the sink. She smoothed her hair the best she could, then replaced her *kapp*, tucking the ribbons inside the front bodice of her dress. After splashing her cheeks with cold water, she felt a little better, and more fully awake.

After breakfast she would call her mother and let her know how Levi was faring. Her father had a cell phone in the woodshop, which he used only for business purposes. However, Moriah doubted he would mind if she called. She'd also see if maybe Elisabeth or one of her brothers could hire a taxi and bring her a fresh change of clothes. With Ruth being sick, she didn't want her mother to have to make the trip, and she had no idea how long she would be at the hospital with Levi. Not that the time mattered to her. She wasn't leaving him until he was able to come home. Everything that had happened between them—his rejection of her and his faith—none of that mattered now. Not only had she already forgiven him, she would forget. They had a second chance now, a new opportunity to work on their marriage, and soon a new baby to love and cherish. Glancing at the mirror one last time, she smiled. For the first time in what seemed like forever, she had something to look forward to.

Gabe rocked back and forth on his heels and slipped his hands in his pockets as he waited for Moriah. He considered waking his father, then decided against it. Neither of them had slept much in the waiting room. It wouldn't hurt to let his *daed* get more rest. He'd bring him a muffin and coffee from the cafeteria when they came back.

The hallway was empty, save for the one stocky nurse wearing bright-pink pants and a multicolored top who passed by. He thought about how exhausted Moriah had looked when he had awakened her, and naturally, he was concerned. But he knew she was relieved that Levi would be okay; they were all happy about that.

But what did Moriah think would happen after his brother healed? Gabe wondered if he would come back to Middlefield. His girlfriend, Taylor, hadn't shown up to ask about him. Granted she had been in the accident, but from the emergency room receptionist's account, she was going to be okay. If she loved him, wouldn't she be there for him? Like Moriah was now?

He sighed and leaned against the wall. If anything this should show Levi where his responsibility, and his life, truly was. In Middlefield, with the Amish, with his family. Gabe believed his brother and Moriah could work things out, especially knowing Moriah's forgiving and tender nature. Hopefully his brother wouldn't be so stupid this time.

The outer doors to the intensive care unit opened, and Moriah stepped out. Gabe's breath hitched, as it always did when he saw her. She had straightened up her *kapp*, and her cheeks held a rosy glow, one he hadn't seen since before Levi left. Heavens, she was beautiful, even after all she'd been through.

He suddenly had second thoughts about not asking his *daed* to join them. Being alone with Moriah, even in a public place, wasn't a great idea right now.

But he restrained his reaction and the feelings accompanying it. He buried them deep down, further than he ever had before, keeping his injured brother at the forefront of his mind. "Ready?" he asked, glad for the noncommittal tone of his voice.

"*Ya.* I am hungry. Or should I say *mei boppli* is. I'm eating for two after all." She gave him a sweet smile.

And, despite everything he tried to do to prevent it, he smiled back.

"That hit the spot."

Moriah watched as Gabriel leaned back in his chair, his hands clasped over his flat stomach, covering the bottom part of the straps of his suspenders.

"I should hope so," she said good-naturedly, eyeing the remnants of the huge meal he'd consumed—scrambled eggs, bacon, sausage links, fried potatoes, a biscuit, and two cups of coffee. Her breakfast of maple-and-brown-sugar oatmeal paled in comparison.

"Sure you don't want anything else?" he said. "The food here isn't half-bad. Not like your cooking, of course."

She blushed. "*Danki.* I enjoy cooking."

"I enjoy eating what you cook." He straightened, suddenly appearing flustered. "I mean, I enjoyed what you used to cook . . . before Levi—oh forget it, you know what I mean."

"I do." She smiled. "I'm looking forward to cooking for you all again."

"I hope that's exactly what happens."

"You hope?" Moriah looked at him, uncertainty puncturing her bubble of hope. "You don't think he's coming back?"

He held up his hand. "*Nee, nee.* That's not what I meant. Only that it will take time for him to heal."

She paused before responding, looking at him for a long moment. While his words said one thing, the doubt flickering in his eyes said another. But she wouldn't let Gabriel's reservations about Levi distract her from making sure that her husband and her marriage were fully restored. "We should get back," she said, pushing away from the table.

"*Ya.*"

"I need to call *Mami* first. She'll want to know how Levi is faring. I also need some clothes, and Levi will probably want some of his things too once he's feeling better."

"I tell you what," Gabriel said, rising from his chair. He picked up the small Styrofoam container that held a blueberry muffin for John. "Don't worry about calling your *mudder*. I'll take a taxi back to Middlefield and visit her myself. Let me know what you need and what I should bring for Levi, and I'll make sure it's done."

"You don't have to do that—"

"Moriah, I don't mind. I have to head back and check on the shop anyway. I left Aaron in charge. I'm sure everything's fine, but he hasn't worked for us very long, so I need to check up on him."

"All right," she said as they walked out of the cafeteria together. A sense of eagerness enveloped her at the thought of seeing Levi again. Maybe he would be awake by the time they got back. If not, then surely he would be sometime today. She wanted to be there when it happened.

They exited the elevator on the second floor and walked down the hallway to the intensive care unit. When they stopped by the waiting room, it was empty. "*Daed* must be with Levi," Gabriel said. Turning the corner, he pressed a large silver disk, which opened the ICU's double doors. They stepped into the unit and walked to Levi's room.

Moriah's breath caught when she looked through the glass that formed one wall of Levi's room. John was seated beside Levi, holding his hand . . . and Levi's eyes were open. Tears clouded her vision, and she barely saw John motion for her and Gabriel to come in.

Once inside, John gestured for Moriah to sit in his chair. She did so, then stared at her husband. She almost couldn't believe he was finally awake. Filled with gratitude, she couldn't speak.

"Hi," he said, his voice barely audible.

"Oh, Levi." She took his hand and held it. He didn't squeeze back, but she didn't care. The tears fell down her cheeks.

"Moriah . . . please." He looked at her, his eyes barely open due to the bruising. "Don't."

"I'm sorry." She briskly wiped at her cheeks and smiled.

"That's better." He turned his gaze from hers and looked at Gabriel. "Glad you're here."

Moriah glanced over her shoulder at Gabriel, who was swallowing hard. He moved to the opposite side of the bed so that they surrounded Levi.

"Don't try to talk too much," she said to him. "There's plenty of time for that."

Levi shook his head slightly, and she could see it took a lot of effort for him to do so. "Moriah, I want you to know . . . I'm sorry."

She grasped his hand in both of hers, then kissed his scratched up knuckles. "It's all right, Levi."

"*Nee*, it's not. I don't deserve you. I never did."

"Don't say things like that."

He closed his eyes and didn't respond.

A moment later John said, "I think he's fallen asleep again." He put his hand on Moriah's shoulder. "We should let him rest."

She nodded, then rose from her chair. Taking one last look at her husband, she said, "Don't worry, Levi. I'll be back." Then she turned and John led her out of the room.

Gabe lingered behind. He shook his head as he watched Moriah leave. Despite everything Levi had put her through, she was still tender with him, reassuring him that she would come back. Gabe marveled at her once again.

"Gabe?"

He looked down at Levi, surprised to see him awake again and his gaze intense. That had to be a good sign. "*Ya, bruder?*"

"Promise me something." Levi licked his dry lips.

Bending down closer so he could hear his brother's weak voice, he said, "Anything, Levi. Whatever you want me to do."

Levi's eyes drooped. "Take care of her . . . Take care of Moriah."

Gabe started to respond but saw that Levi had drifted off to sleep once again. Of course he would take care of Moriah. He would as much as she would allow—or as much as Levi would allow after he came back home.

Turning, he left Levi and went to the waiting room, not wanting to disturb his brother. Moriah and his father were seated on the couch, their expressions more peaceful than he had seen in a long time. He expelled a long breath. Everything would be okay. He truly believed that.

"Have a seat, *sohn*," John said, gesturing to the chair opposite the cushioned sofa. "How's Levi?"

Gabe lowered himself into the plush, light-green upholstered seat. "He fell asleep again."

"Not surprised. He's been through a lot, but he's on the mend now." Reaching toward Moriah, John patted her hand, and she smiled in return.

Closing his eyes, Gabe settled back in the chair. It was pretty comfortable, and he suddenly became drowsy. He'd catch a short nap, then make arrangements to go back to Middlefield. He wondered how Aaron was doing at the shop. Hopefully they hadn't had too much business.

"Mrs. Miller?"

Gabe's eyes flew open at the sound of a male voice. He looked up through sleepy eyes to see a doctor, this one unfamiliar to him. The troubled expression on the man's face made Gabe bolt upright.

"Yes?" Moriah said, rising from the couch.

She also looked sleepy, and Gabe assumed she had taken a nap while he had been asleep. He glanced up at the clock on the wall. A little over an hour had passed since he'd left Levi.

The doctor walked into the room. He seemed younger than the surgeon who had operated on Levi. Adjusting his rimless glasses on the bridge of his nose, he cleared his throat. "I'm sorry, Mrs. Miller."

"Sorry?" Moriah's voice cracked. "Sorry for what?"

"We did all we could."

A metallic taste coated Gabe's mouth. What was he talking about?

"We're not sure what happened, but we suspect a clot went to his lung." The doctor paused to give her time to absorb what he'd said. "This isn't something we can predict, or plan for. Sometimes it just happens. I'm truly sorry for your loss."

"My loss?" Moriah raised her hands to her lips. "He's gone? Levi's gone?"

"Moriah," John's voice, filled with grief, reached Gabe's ears.

"*Nee, nee.* He can't be gone. He was fine; that other doctor said so. I just saw him!" She turned an accusing glare at Gabe. "You said he was asleep!"

His legs started to shake. "He was when I left." He faced the doctor, the full meaning of the situation hitting him like a steel rod to his gut. "He was fine when I left."

"Mr. Miller, it happened so suddenly, only moments ago. I don't know what else to tell you. Your brother is gone."

His body felt numb. Levi, dead? It wasn't possible. Yet one look at the doctor's expression confirmed the truth.

"*Nee,*" Moriah moaned. She walked to the glass window and put her hand on it. Sobs wracked her body. "He can't be gone. Not when I finally have him back."

Gabe, consumed with his own pain, came up behind her and wrapped his arms around her. She turned and leaned her head against his shoulder, her tears wetting his shirt, her body shaking against his. Unable to control his own grief, he pulled her tightly against him, and they both cried in each other's arms.

Chapter 11

"Gabe, you don't have to do this." Tobias put his hand on Gabe's shoulder. "The fellas and I will handle it."

"I know you will. Let me help you anyway."

Tobias shrugged, sorrow reflected in his blue eyes. He handed Gabe a shovel, then stepped back.

Gabe choked back his tears as he thrust his shovel into the nearby pile of dirt that had been dug out of the ground the day before. He tossed the first heap of soil onto his brother's grave.

The funeral service had ended a short time ago, and everyone but four of Levi's friends, who had served as pallbearers along with Tobias and Luke, had left for the house. The six men had stayed behind to bury Levi. The Byler family was at his house, preparing refreshments for anyone who wanted to pay their respects. John and Moriah had gone back with them, but Gabe had chosen to stay and help finish the burial.

The men worked quickly—too quickly for Gabe's liking. When the last shovelful of dirt was tamped down across Levi's grave, Gabe experienced pain so wrenching it threatened to double him over. He knelt beside the fresh soil. His brother, his twin—gone forever.

Regrets flooded over him. He had given up on Levi too easily. He should have gone out to Gates Mills more often, worked harder to convince him to come home. Instead he had written him off, letting his anger over his treatment of Moriah supercede everything else.

Now there was nothing he could do. There was no turning back time, no making up for mistakes. Levi was gone, and a part of Gabe had gone with him.

"We're heading back to your house," Tobias said, hunkering down next to Gabe. "Take your time. I'll tell them you'll be along in a bit."

He turned to Moriah's brother and nodded. "*Danki*," he said, his voice sounding gravelly and strange.

Alone at the graveside, Gabe looked at the small, square head-stones on all the graves in the cemetery. Each one was the same size and shape, plain and unadorned. Just like Levi's would be. Details of the accident had slowly surfaced in the aftermath of Levi's death, and over the past three days, their family had been able to piece together what had happened. Taylor had been driving her fancy sports car, with Levi in the passenger seat. They had been side-swiped by a semitruck and sent careening across the berm into oncoming traffic, with Levi receiving the bulk of the injuries. While the surgery had initially been a success, he had indeed died from a blood clot.

Gabe dug his hands into the earth and squeezed. At least when Levi had been with the Yankees, there was always the slim hope they would see him again. Now that hope was gone. Yet even through his grief, he couldn't be angry with God. Levi had made his choices, just as Gabe had made the decision to write off his brother. He couldn't blame God for the mistakes they had both made. He could only try to find a way to heal from them.

The one thing he could take comfort from was that during the breakfast he had shared with Moriah in the hospital, Levi had spoken to their father and asked him for forgiveness, explaining he wanted to come back to the church. Although Levi hadn't repented publicly in the church, under the circumstances the bishop and ministers had accepted that as repentance. Levi would be with his people from now on.

He let the dirt sift through his fingers as he stared at the small, plain, square concrete marker that poked out of the ground. Through the blur of his tears he remembered the last words Levi said to him. "I promise, *bruder*," Gabe croaked. "I promise I will spend the rest of my life taking care of Moriah." He stood, then slowly made his way to his buggy and climbed inside. Taking one last look at Levi's final resting place, he chirruped to his horse and headed back home.

Moriah instantly came to his mind, and he wondered how he could possibly keep the promise he had made. She had just lost her husband—twice. No one would expect her to turn around and accept someone else, especially her former brother-in-law.

But he had given his brother his word, and he would honor it. He had always stood by a promise, and firmly believed that a man should stand by what he says. Gabe would see to it that Moriah and her child would be cared for. He would do everything in his power to make that happen.

He pulled into the front of his house, and took in the numerous buggies that filled the driveway and spilled out onto the yard. He'd have to park close to his neighbor's house, but he didn't care. He took comfort in the support the community offered Moriah and his father. They would need it. They would all need it.

"*Danki.* Thanks for coming." Moriah said. She'd repeated those words so many times they reverberated in her head. Her body and mind both felt numb. Eventually she would appreciate the outpouring of support from everyone, but right now she just wanted to be alone.

"You've been on your feet all day." Her mother came up beside her and put her arm around her shoulders. "I know you're exhausted, so don't try to tell me that you're not. Have you eaten anything?"

"*Nee.*"

The low hum of the conversation dropped as the front door opened. Gabe entered, his complexion gray, his eyes red. He was the last to arrive, and she suspected he had spent some time alone at Levi's grave. She'd heard the twin bond was stronger than that between other siblings. If Gabe's visage was any indication, it was true.

Their gazes met as he made his way across the room. He thanked several people along the way as they gave him their sympathies, but he kept moving toward Moriah and didn't stop until he was right in front of her.

"I'll go check on the sandwiches," Emma said, stepping to the side. "Sarah said she was going to make some more. She could probably use the help. And please, try to eat something."

"I will."

When Emma disappeared, Gabe asked, "How are you holding up?"

Moriah shrugged. "Best I can. You?"

"Same thing. Have you seen *Daed*?"

"He's in the *dawdi haus* with some of his friends. The company started to overwhelm him, I think."

"I should go see how he is." But Gabe didn't move. Instead, he looked at her, biting his bottom lip. "I don't want to leave you alone, but I need to check on *Daed*."

She offered him a weak smile. "Gabriel, this house is full of people. I'm hardly alone."

He looked sheepish. "Right. Didn't think about that." He gave her one last look, then turned and headed to see his father.

Moriah scanned the room, taking in all the friends and family who were giving their support. But despite their presence, despite reassuring Gabriel that he wasn't deserting her, she had been wrong. She'd never felt more alone in her life.

Gabe sat in the old handhewn rocker his grandfather had made over fifty years ago, watching the glowing coals of the woodstove. The sun had set hours ago, but he couldn't sleep. He had decided to stay in the *dawdi haus* with his father, who'd retired soon after their company had left. He remained partly to keep an eye on *Daed*, and partly because he couldn't bear to stay alone in the main house.

Now he rocked in the chair, trying to settle the turmoil inside him. Memories of his brother continually surfaced in his mind. He remembered the tire swing their father had hung on the huge oak tree in their backyard. Every fall he and Levi would rake the leaves into a big pile and then compete to see who could swing higher before letting go and landing in the soft, musty leaves. He could still see the look of triumph on Levi's face every time he won. The memory brought a fresh wave of pain, added another layer of regret.

How was he supposed to survive this?

The sound of his father's shuffling footsteps caused him to sit up straight. He wiped his wet eyes with his hand as John entered the room.

"You shouldn't be sitting here in the dark, Gabriel." He turned on the gas lamp.

"And you should be resting." Gabe shot up from his chair and went to his father, who waved him off.

"I've been resting." John lowered himself onto the couch, then patted the seat next to him. "Let's talk. We haven't done that in quite awhile."

Gabe sat next to him, then leaned forward and rested his elbows on his knees, letting his loosely clasped hands dangle between them. He tilted his head and looked at his father. "You surprise me," he admitted.

"How so?"

"The way you're handling all of this. I remember when Levi left . . . how hard it was on you."

"This is hard too, Gabriel. Very hard. My son died. I won't see him until I get to heaven, God willing. But even though it breaks my heart, I can find some peace in that." He looked at Gabe intently. "When Levi left, he turned his back on the church. That burden was almost too great to bear."

"But you did."

"I only seemed to. You can't live stewing in grief forever. I learned that when your *mami* died. A person's got to move on, live his life following God's lead. But that didn't mean I didn't spend every night on my knees praying for my boy."

Gabe stared down at the polished wood floor. "I should have done that. I should have done more."

John patted him on the back. "Don't let regrets tear you up inside, Gabriel. Levi wouldn't want that."

Lifting his head, Gabe said, "No, he wouldn't."

"Keep remembering that Levi came back to God. I have no doubt he would have come back to us too."

"How can you be so sure he came back to God?"

"Because of what he said. He asked my forgiveness—our forgiveness. He had already been forgiven by the Lord. I truly believe that."

To his surprise, Gabe did find comfort in his father's words. To know that his brother had made things right with the Lord brought a semblance of peace to his soul.

"There's something else troubling you," John said.

Gabe's head jerked in his father's direction. "How did you know?"

"Most of the time you're hard to read, but tonight you're an open book. Levi said something to you. Is that what's bothering you?"

"*Ya.*" Gabe sat back and settled himself more firmly on the couch. "He asked me to take care of Moriah and the baby. But I don't understand why."

"Probably because he knows you're the best man for her."

Gabe sat forward, gaping at John. "What do you mean?"

"I know you love her. I suspect Levi knew that too. And for some reason you've chosen to keep that a secret from her."

"She was in love with my brother, *Daed.* And I thought he loved her. I didn't want to cause any trouble for them."

"But what about you? Did you plan to spend the rest of your life pining for your brother's wife?"

"Of course not! I would have found someone else . . . eventually." But he knew the words were a lie. He had never wanted to be with anyone else. "That doesn't matter now. I promised Levi I'd be there for Moriah, but I don't know how that's possible."

"Why not?"

His father must have lost his mind. "*Daed*, she's newly widowed. She was married to my brother, who is my identical twin. I'll just be a reminder of what she's lost."

"Then you'll just have to convince her otherwise." John yawned. "Pray about it, Gabriel. With God, anything is possible. Even what seems impossible." He stood. "I'm more worn out than I thought. I'm going to bed, and I suggest you do the same."

Gabe nodded. He waited a little while longer after John left before heading to his room. He stripped down to his long johns and climbed into bed, sliding between the cold sheets. Both his father and his brother had known about his feelings for Moriah. So much for keeping them hidden. Suddenly, a thought occurred to him, causing him to sit upright.

Did Moriah know?

He panicked for a moment, then calmed down. She couldn't possibly know how he felt. If she did he would have known, or at least sensed it. She would have kept her distance from him, something he continually failed to do.

Lying back down, he decided to take his *daed*'s advice and pray about it. He couldn't fulfill his promise to Levi without some divine intervention.

Chapter 12

*M*oriah perused the bolts of soft pastel fabric neatly lined up in rows in her cousin's fabric store. She had decided to make a baby quilt, even though she had done little quilting before. Her sewing consisted of making clothing, mostly her own and baby clothes.

After selecting a combination of pale blue, green, and yellow, she picked up a couple spools of thread and a packet of needles, then went to the front of the store to check out. The store was empty this afternoon, and her cousin Mary was sitting behind the cutting table engrossed in a book.

"Find what you need?" Mary set her book down and picked up a pair of shears from a box near the table.

Moriah set the bolts of fabric down. "*Ya*. I need a yard of each."

"Okay." Mary took the fabric and started to measure it out, talking as she worked. "How have you been doing?"

"I'm all right. Keep myself busy."

"I've been meaning to get over to see you," Mary said, not looking up. She slid the sharp scissors down the width of the blue

494

fabric, separating it from the bolt. "I'm sorry, but things have been real hectic here lately." A flush appeared on her face as she glanced at Moriah. "Except for today. For some reason it's really slow. Could be because it's a nice summer day. June is always one of the best months, I think."

Moriah nodded. "That's all right. You can stop by anytime." She'd had few visitors since Levi's death almost a month ago. At first that had been fine with her; she had appreciated the time alone. But now she wished for some company other than her immediate family. And of course Gabriel. He had been paying visits to her on a regular basis. She assured him everything was all right with the baby, but he still insisted on visiting every other day. She wasn't sure what to make of that.

"*Danki,*" Mary said, putting the last yard of cloth in a white plastic bag. "I will."

Once outside, she put her bag in the buggy and began to step inside when a sharp pain zigzagged across her abdomen. Instinctively she put her hand on her stomach, and the spasm soon subsided. The door to the shop behind her opened, and Mary came rushing to her side.

"Are you all right? I saw you through the window. What happened?"

Moriah straightened, expecting to feel another spiky twinge and was relieved when she didn't. "I don't know," she said. "I just had this sudden pain, and now it's gone."

Mary's expression relaxed. "I wouldn't worry about it too much. I got those with my children every once in a while. But if it keeps happening, make sure you let someone know. Are you using a midwife?"

"*Ya.*"

"Next time you see her you might want to mention it. Now, go on home, have some tea, and unwind."

"*Danki.* I'll do that."

As she headed home, Moriah tried to stem her worry. Despite her cousin's reassurances, she couldn't help but be concerned. Her baby was everything to her. She couldn't bear if something happened to her child. Not when she had lost everything else.

Rachel plopped down on her bed and opened one of the new books she'd purchased from the gift shop at the restaurant. She didn't read many novels, but this one looked kind of interesting and featured Amish characters. And a romance. "Might as well get some romance somewhere," she mumbled as she turned to the first chapter. "It's not like I've got any in my life." If she was lucky, she might also learn a thing or two.

Very little time elapsed before she put the book down. Her mind had wandered too much, and she'd ended up reading the second page three times, only to realize she still didn't know what it was about. Shoving the book aside, she flipped over and lay on her stomach, resting her chin on top of her clasped hands. An unsettled feeling came over her.

Christian had been gone about two months now. The Monday after the buggy incident with Tobias, he'd called the restaurant using a neighbor's phone and told her he decided to stay in Charm for a couple more weeks and work on his aunt's farm. He wasn't any more specific than that about his return. Even though he had written her a couple of very brief letters, she felt their relationship was spinning in circles again. How were they ever going to get to know each other better if they spent all of their time apart?

She hated to admit that a part of her was glad he hadn't come back right away. She wasn't sure how she was going to face him after kissing Tobias.

But it was only one teeny, tiny kiss, and that's all it would ever be. Never mind that it was a kiss she still relived in her mind, nearly every night in her dreams.

A glance at the clock told her it was 1:00 p.m. Yesterday she and her mother had tended both the flower and the vegetable garden, and the lawn didn't need mowing or edging either. The day was too nice to spend inside. Scrambling off her bed, she fixed her *kapp* and straightened the white ribbons. She had to find something productive to do or she'd go crazy.

As she made her way downstairs, a thought occurred to her. She would visit Moriah Miller. She hadn't seen her since Levi had passed away a few weeks ago. What a tragedy. The circumstances surrounding his death had been so sad; her heart had gone out to Moriah.

A stab of guilt pricked at her. She should have visited Moriah long before now. Although their mothers were close friends, she and Moriah had never been. During visits to the Bylers', Rachel often played outside with Tobias and his brothers, while Moriah had preferred to be inside with her mother.

The thought that Tobias might be there, and that she might run into him, crossed her mind, but she shoved it out of the way. She wasn't going there to see him; she was lending her support to Moriah. But if she did happen to catch a glimpse of him . . .

Good grief, she was hopeless.

She rushed downstairs and headed for the kitchen. Warm summer sunlight streamed through the open window, illuminating the kitchen. Rachel enjoyed the warmer months of the year. They used the gas lamps and woodstoves less, and the windows were wide open, letting in fresh air. Her mother sat at the kitchen table, sorting through index cards of recipes.

"Where are you off to?" Sarah asked, examining a dog-eared card.

"I thought I'd visit Moriah Miller today."

Sarah put the card down and smiled. "I think that's a wonderful idea. I know Emma's been worried about her." She clucked her tongue. "Poor thing. She's such a sweet girl, and has been through so much."

Rachel nodded. "I won't be gone long, just a couple of hours."

Sarah picked up another card. "Let her know my prayers are with her."

"I will."

Half an hour later Rachel pulled her buggy into the Bylers' driveway. As she maneuvered her horse to the parking area next to the woodshop, she saw Emma leaving her house.

"Hello, Rachel!" Emma walked down the porch steps and met Rachel at her buggy. "What brings you by?"

"I came to visit Moriah. Is she home?"

"Oh, you just missed her. She's at the Millers'." Her expression sobered. "She said something about cleaning their house and making some meals for Gabriel and John. I tried to talk her out of it."

"Why?"

"She's been working hard lately, especially since Levi's death." Emma crossed her thin arms over her chest and sighed. "I don't want to see anything happen to her or the *boppli*."

"I'll be glad to help her, *Frau* Byler."

"That would be wonderful, Rachel. I'm sure she wouldn't mind if you stop over there for a bit. In fact, I think she'd be delighted."

"*Danki*. I'll do that."

A little while later she arrived at the Millers', eager to help Moriah. After tethering her horse, she caught sight of her brother emptying a barrel of trash into a small dumpster behind the shop. If she had seen him infrequently before he had started working for Gabriel, now she saw him even less. He left before she awakened, and always went to the job on foot, which was a good three-mile walk. So far he'd managed to keep the job for a couple months, something he never would have been able to do when he was using drugs.

Still, despite this positive aspect of his life, she felt more disconnected from him than ever. He was more reticent lately. Before his arrest, he and their father had shouting matches, with Aaron's anger verging on physical violence. Yet since his return he had been a model son, albeit a nearly silent one. She'd considered talking to him once, not just words in passing but a real conversation. But Aaron was even less approachable now than he'd been when he first came home, and she wasn't sure what she should say to him. So she didn't say anything.

As if he sensed someone watching him, Aaron glanced at her over his shoulder. He gave her an imperceptible nod, as if she were no more familiar than a stranger, and went back in the shop.

His emotional distance stung. Suddenly, an overwhelming sense of rejection consumed her. Everyone wanted to keep their distance from her—her brother, Christian, even Tobias had been cursorily polite to her the few times she had seen him. What was wrong with her? "Rachel? Is that you?"

At the sound of Moriah's voice, she swallowed her pain. Angling her body a quarter turn, she saw Moriah standing on the front porch several feet from the shop. Mustering up what she hoped was a decent smile, Rachel waved to her. "Hi!" she said, a little too brightly.

Moriah didn't seem to notice. "Are you here to see your brother?"

"*Nee*. Actually, I came to see you."

Moriah's face lit up. "Then come on in. I just made some tea."

"Sounds great." Rachel gave her a real smile this time, Moriah's warm welcome chasing away some of the despair she'd felt a moment earlier.

Moriah held the door open for her, and Rachel walked in. "Come on back to the kitchen. We can visit in there."

Rachel had never been inside the Millers' house before. There had never really been an opportunity, as Gabriel and Levi's parents had been much older than her own folks, and she hadn't spoken too much to the twins while they were growing up. She took in the tidy front room, with its sparse furnishings and small wood fireplace. She noticed the Millers still had a woodstove. Her own family had purchased a propane stove a couple years ago, when the church leaders had agreed to allow some propane-powered appliances in the home.

Following Moriah to the back of the house, she inhaled the scent of chicken stew cooking on the stove. "Smells wonderful," Rachel said.

"Would you like some?"

"*Nee*, I'm not really hungry. But *danki* for offering."

"I thought I'd surprise Gabriel and John when they come in

from work. I'm sure they're getting tired of casseroles all the time."
Moriah retrieved two mugs from a kitchen cabinet, then lifted the
tea kettle off the woodstove and poured the hot amber liquid into
the cups.

"That's thoughtful of you. I'm sure they'll appreciate it."

Rachel accepted her mug of tea but didn't drink it right away.
Instead she sat down at the kitchen table and observed Moriah,
who was rolling out biscuit dough on the floured countertop. The
rolling pin suddenly slipped out of her hands, hit the floor, and
rolled underneath the table.

"I got it." Rachel bent down and retrieved the rolling pin. As
she went to the sink to wash it, she saw Moriah rub her temple
with her fingertips. "Are you okay?"

Moriah nodded and handed Rachel a clean, dry towel. "*Ya.*
I'm fine. *Danki* for washing that."

"You're welcome." Rachel saw dark circles of fatigue underneath Moriah's eyes. Now she understood why Emma was
concerned. "How about if I finish up the biscuits?"

"*Nee,* I can do them." She took the rolling pin from Rachel and
applied the wood cylinder to the dough. "I'm almost done
anyway."

"Is there anything else I can do to help?"

Moriah shook her head, then turned and gestured toward the
kitchen table. "Please, enjoy your tea."

Rachel hesitated, but then finally sat down. She sipped the
lemon-flavored tea, which had cooled to the perfect temperature.
But before long an odd uneasiness came over her. In the past,
though their conversations were infrequent, she and Moriah would
talk about their siblings or funny things that happened to them
during their families' visits together. Yet so much had happened

this past year, especially to Moriah, that for the first time, she didn't know what to say.

Moriah seemed engrossed in cutting out biscuits and averse to accepting help. She also didn't seem interested in making conversation. Rachel watched as Moriah wiped her brow with the back of her hand, her fatigue even more noticeable now. She should offer to help again, but it was common knowledge that Rachel wasn't a very good cook—unlike Moriah, who could make a delicious meal out of the most sparse of ingredients.

Moriah had also experienced things Rachel hadn't—marriage, pregnancy, and unfortunately, the death of her husband. Should she bring up any of those subjects? One thing she didn't want to do was discuss Tobias, especially with his sister.

After a few more minutes of silence, Moriah turned. "How is your tea?"

"Delicious." Rachel could detect the sadness in Moriah's eyes, coupled with loneliness. Rachel couldn't imagine the turmoil churning inside the young woman. She also felt powerless to help her.

Moriah gave her a small smile, then turned to place the last biscuit on a metal cookie sheet. She opened the hot oven and put the biscuits inside. As she closed the oven door she said, "From what I gather your brother has been a big help to Gabriel and John in the shop. He's a really hard worker."

Rachel frowned slightly. Not exactly who she wanted to talk about, but at this point she was glad to talk about anything. She lifted her tea and took a sip then set it down again. "He seems to have straightened himself out."

"I don't know what they would do without him," Moriah added. "Since Levi . . ." A shadow passed over her face, but she quickly smiled again to cover it before turning around to wash her hands in the sink. "I have noticed that he doesn't say much, though. He seems to like to keep to himself."

"No kidding," Rachel muttered. Then she looked at Moriah. "Don't get me wrong. I'm glad you're all happy with him. I just hope he doesn't go back to his old ways."

"Why do you think he would?"

Rachel shrugged, cupping her hands around her mug.

"Do you think he will fail?"

Rachel's eyes widened. "I hope not. But Aaron was a drug addict and he spent time in jail. I'm just saying that it's easy to fall back into old habits. But I didn't say I wanted him to fail."

"I'm sorry, Rachel. I didn't mean to upset you."

With a sigh, Rachel said, "No, I'm sorry. I shouldn't be so sensitive. And I shouldn't have said that about Aaron. I know he's been trying really hard to change his life." She shook the coffee mug, swirling the liquid inside. "To tell you the truth, I don't know what's going on with him. We haven't talked much since he came home. Actually, we haven't talked at all. Sorry, I don't mean to complain."

Moriah stretched her arm across the table and covered Rachel's hand with her own. "That's all right, I don't mind hearing about it. Trust me, we all have our problems."

Guilt churned within Rachel. Her own problems were petty compared to how Moriah had suffered.

Moriah squeezed her hand. "I'll pray for you, Rachel. And for Aaron."

Rachel glanced down at their hands. When was the last time she had prayed for her brother? She couldn't remember. And perhaps that was part of the problem. Lately she had focused all of her prayers on her own concerns—her doubts about Christian, her mixed-up feelings about Tobias. She silently vowed to put Aaron at the top of her prayer list from now on.

"*Danki,*" Rachel said. "I appreciate you praying for him."

"I'm glad to do it. I haven't been praying much at all lately, and you've reminded me how important it is to keep up that personal communion with God." She removed her hand and sat back in the chair. "I'm really glad you came today."

"Me too." Rachel grinned, then sniffed the air. Her stomach growled. "Maybe I'll have some of that chicken stew after all."

With a long pair of tongs, Gabe removed a red-hot horseshoe from the burning forge and set it aside to cool. Some smiths plunged their hot shoes into cold water, but that made the iron brittle and would require a horse to be shoed more often. John had preferred to let his shoes cool on their own, and Gabe had always followed suit. He only cooled off metal by dunking when he made decorative ironwork. His forehead dripping from the heat of the forge and scorching metal, he wiped the sweat off his brow with the back of his gloved hand, knowing he had probably smeared black soot all over his forehead.

While the metal cooled, Gabe tallied how many more shoes he had to make before the day was up. Nineteen. Tomorrow he needed to spend the day applying those shoes to several horses. While he was busy cleaning out hooves and filing the shoes so they would fit snugly, Aaron would work on making a simple iron sconce. Since his father had decided to add fancy ironwork, such as sconces and lantern hangers, to their inventory last year, he and Gabe had taught Aaron how to make a couple of plain styles. He turned out to be a quick study.

Turning around to grab another metal bar, he saw Aaron across the shop, struggling to pick up a heavy load of rods. As was the young man's way, he never asked for help, but this time Gabe could see he really needed it. Putting his iron down, Gabe passed by John, who was filing the rough edges of one of the shoes, and went to assist Aaron.

"Thanks," Aaron said in his trademark quiet tone once they'd moved the rods.

"No problem. Don't be afraid to ask for help, Aaron. You don't have to carry the load yourself."

Aaron nodded in return, but didn't say anything, merely went back to work. Gabe watched him for a moment, wondering what was going on inside the kid's head. He'd been a mystery ever since he'd hired him. But he couldn't complain about Aaron's work ethic at all—sometimes he worked harder than Levi ever had. Then again, they had all been working extra hard since Levi's death. Keeping busy helped stave off a bit of the grief.

One thing he could say for Aaron, he was a thorough employee. He'd been able to find the file that was missing off the pegboard, although he didn't tell Gabe where he'd found it. He just put it back on its peg and went back to work. Gabe didn't care, as long as he had his tool back.

Suddenly the sound of a loud crash caused Gabe to spin around. John, who had moved over by the forge, was reaching out to steady himself. Gabe watched in horror as his father's hand landed on the super-heated side of the forge. The rancid smell of burning flesh permeated the air.

"*Daed!*" Gabe ran over to John, who was holding his burned hand against his chest. Although he didn't utter a sound, agony contorted his features.

He looked at the red flesh of his *daed*'s hand, which was now bubbling with blisters. "You've got to see a doctor."

John sucked in his breath. "I . . . don't need . . . a . . . doctor." John started to sway, and Gabe put a supporting arm around his shoulders. "Just . . . take . . . me inside."

"*Nee*—"

"Don't argue! Help . . . me inside!"

Surprised at his father's sudden burst of energy and convinced by the stubborn look in his eyes, Gabe did as he was told. He led John into the kitchen, where he was surprised to see Moriah talking to Rachel Detweiler.

"Good heavens, what happened?" Moriah said, jumping out of her chair when they entered the room.

"He burned his hand on the forge," Gabriel said, easing his father into another chair at the table. John's complexion had suddenly turned gray, adding to Gabe's worry. "I want to take him to the hospital, but he refuses to go."

"Don't . . . need . . . to," John said, still holding his hand against his chest.

"Now's not the time to be mulish," Gabe said, losing his patience. "It'll only take me a second to call for a ride—"

"He's right, Gabriel." Moriah brought over a clean towel and laid it on the table. Gently she took John's wrist and positioned it on the towel, taking care not to let his burned palm touch the terry cloth fabric. "It will take too long to get him to the emergency room. We need to take care of it here."

"I know . . . what to do . . . anyway," John said, his breathing becoming steadier. He looked at Moriah. "Up in the cabinet . . . second to the right . . . there's salve."

"Rachel," Moriah said. "Help him hold his hand. Be careful

not to touch the burn. There doesn't seem to be any damage on the back, so he can lightly rest it against the towel. Just make sure his hand doesn't move."

With a nod Rachel did as Moriah requested.

Gabe watched with fascination—and a bit of awe—as his father directed the women in tending his burn. True to his word, he knew exactly what to do and instructed Moriah on how to wrap his hand with gauze from the first aid kit he always kept on hand, even when he and Levi were growing up. Moriah seemed to know where everything was in the kit. Gabe surmised she had probably found it and kept it stocked while she and Levi were married.

"That's better," John said, once his hand was securely wrapped. Some of the color had returned to his face. "Now, I need a cup of tea. The nighttime blend, Moriah. And make it strong."

"Do you want a pain reliever?" She rinsed out the kettle and filled it with fresh water.

He shook his head. "The salve is doing the trick."

Gabe plopped down at the table, the tension draining from his neck as he realized his father was going to be all right. "I still wish you would have let me take you to the doctor."

"And miss being nursed by the two prettiest ladies around?" John cracked a smile, albeit a faint one. "*Nee*. Not a chance."

Gabe grinned back. His father's smiles had been so rare lately, ever since Levi had died. It was nice to see him lighthearted, even if he was in pain. "What were you doing by the forge?"

John sobered. "I thought I'd help you with the shoes. I know how many you have to finish off today. Didn't count on tripping over my own two feet." He glanced down at his bandaged hand, his expression filling with melancholy once again.

Not wanting to add to his father's frustration and guilt, Gabe patted him on the back. "I appreciate the help, *Daed*. And you're right, I do have a lot of shoes to make today."

"Then you should get back to it, don't you think?"

"You don't need me anymore?"

John looked up and shook his head, not quite as somber as before. "I've got these two, remember?"

Gabe looked at Rachel, who smiled at him. He didn't know her very well, but he would have to tell her later how much he appreciated her helping his father.

Moriah poured John his cup of tea, then went over to Gabe. "We'll make sure he's okay," she said. "If there's a problem, I'll come get you."

"I don't want you do go to any trouble—"

"It's no trouble," she said, smiling at him.

Dear God in heaven, what a beautiful smile she had. "I didn't realize you were here. Or Rachel."

"I thought you and John might like something different to eat, so I stopped by to make some chicken stew. There's enough for at least two days. I also thought I'd straighten up a little bit around here."

Her generosity touched him. He knew it had to be difficult for her to be here, surrounded by painful memories. Yet she had set aside her own grief to help them out. Although he wished more than anything her motives were driven by something other than a sense of duty to her late husband's family, he knew it wasn't true. "It smells wonderful," he said, breathing in deeply. And it did. She was an excellent cook. "But you don't have to go to all this trouble."

"I don't mind. We're family, remember?"

How could he forget? "Right. Family." Just not the kind of family he wished they could be. As he gazed at her, he noticed a smudge of flour on her temples. He fought the urge to wipe it away. "You look tired," he said softly. "Don't worry about the house. I plan to clean it up this weekend. Besides, you know us bachelors. A little dust doesn't get us too riled up."

Her grin grew wider. "Don't worry about me. Or the house. Just get back to work. Rachel and I will take care of everything here." She stepped toward him and shepherded him toward the door, giving him no recourse but to leave.

A few moments later he entered the shop, the faint acrid scent of his father's burned hand still hanging in the air. He glanced at the forge and gave a quick prayer of thanks that his *daed*'s injury hadn't been worse. Gearing himself up for the rest of the afternoon's hard labor, he looked around the shop for Aaron. When he didn't see the young man, he headed for the back room. The cashbox was open, and Aaron was shoving something into his pocket.

What was he doing with the money? Instantly suspicious, Gabe asked, "What's going on here?"

Aaron slammed down the metal lid of the box. "You had a customer a few minutes ago. Came and picked up two of the sconces."

"What was his name?"

Aaron's complexion reddened. "I forgot. He needed change, and I had enough in my pocket. I was just paying myself back."

"Why didn't you get the cashbox and give him change from that?"

A guilty look crossed his face. "I—I didn't think about it at the time. He seemed in a hurry."

Gabe regarded him for a moment. He hadn't heard a car pull up in front of the shop while he had been inside with his *daed*, nor had he heard a car pull away. Granted, he hadn't shown Aaron how to use the cashbox either, although that was pretty simple and didn't need any training. He could visualize Aaron digging in his pocket for change while trying to appease an impatient customer. Most of their customers, including outlanders, were fine, polite people. But every once in a while they'd get a rude one, and Gabe would respond as humbly as he could, as was the Amish way.

Gabe took the box from Aaron and opened the lid. "How much do you need?"

"I already got it." Aaron stared down at the floor.

Shutting the box with a click, Gabe then opened the drawer of his father's battered desk and put the box back in its usual place. "We need to get back to work. *Daed* will be out of commission for a while, so I need you to help me with the shoes."

Aaron looked up with surprise. "What do you need me to do?"

For the rest of the afternoon Gabe and Aaron worked at completing the horseshoe order. They finished well after sundown. Gabe offered to drive Aaron home, but the younger man refused, saying he'd rather walk. Although the walk wasn't all that far, he figured Aaron had to be exhausted. Still, he declined Gabe's second offer to take him home and left the shop carrying a small, blue cooler that served as his lunchbox, a lone form disappearing into the darkness.

Dog-tired, Gabe dragged himself across the yard and into the kitchen, his stomach growling like a pack of wolves with a fresh kill. A small bubble of happiness burst inside when he saw a plate of food, covered with foil, warming on top of the woodstove. The scent of chicken stew, apples, and spices filled his nostrils and made his stomach growl. He tore off the foil, picked up the plate, then sat down and shoveled the food into his mouth. Once he finished eating, he would check on his father. Right now he had to tame the beast in his belly.

Just as he put the last mouthful of apple brown Betty into his mouth, Moriah walked into the room. He was surprised to see she was still here. She looked as equally surprised to see him in the kitchen.

"I see you found supper," she said, walking to the table. She picked up his dishes and took them over to the sink.

"You don't have to do that." Gabe tried to take a glass from her hand, but she moved it out of his reach.

"Nonsense. I'll just give them a quick wash before I leave."

He picked up a dishtowel off the rack that hung near the sink. "Then I'll dry."

"*Danki*. I hate the drying part." She handed him a wet dish.

"How's *Daed* doing?"

"He's sleeping in his old room. He wanted to go back to the *dawdi haus*, but I wouldn't let him."

"Good idea."

"He seemed fine, though."

"Because of your *gut* care."

"Well, not just me. Rachel helped out too. He's a tough one, I'll say that for him."

"*Ya*. He's tough all right. He's been through a lot." Taking the fork Moriah offered him, he added, "We all have."

She nodded and remained silent for a few moments, the only sound in the kitchen the clinking of the dishes in the sink. After Gabe had wiped the last dish, she turned to him. "I haven't thanked you properly for checking up on me the past couple of weeks. But like I told your *daed*, it's not necessary."

"I know I don't have to." He turned and faced her. "Moriah, don't you understand? I want to."

Chapter 13

$\mathcal{S}$peech abandoned Moriah when she heard Gabriel's words. He wanted to check up on her? Why would he want to do that? She could understand him dropping by once or twice, but he had come to see her at least three times a week since Levi had died. A faint tingling sensation rushed through her as he continued to hold her gaze, his chestnut-colored eyes filled with an emotion she couldn't comprehend. Then it disappeared.

Gabriel cleared his throat as he turned away from her. "Uh, well, that didn't take long," he said, putting away the last dish. "Chores go by a lot faster when there are four hands working instead of two."

"That they do." She watched his profile for a moment, but exhaustion had been dogging her for the past hour or so. She didn't have the strength to try to figure him out. Instead, she turned around and surveyed the kitchen, making sure everything was neat and tidy. She and Rachel had ignored his plea to not to clean anything, and between the two of them, the Millers now had a spotless house, an accomplishment that deeply satisfied her. Rachel had been a great help, and Moriah was very glad she had stopped by to visit. She truly liked the young woman, and hoped they could become closer friends.

When she was satisfied that everything the kitchen was in tip-top shape, she said, "There's coffee cake for tomorrow's breakfast; it's wrapped in foil in the pantry. And there are some sandwiches for lunch. I put the chicken stew in the cooler; you can reheat that for supper tomorrow."

"Wow." Gabriel's brows lifted as he grinned. "*Danki*, Moriah. Sounds like you were busy today."

"I like staying busy. It . . . helps."

His eyes met hers for a brief moment, and they both looked away. "I know. I've taken on more jobs than ever since Levi . . . since he passed. Although I wonder if that was a mistake. *Daed* might not have hurt his hand if he hadn't felt he had to help me out."

"Not everything is your fault, Gabriel."

He frowned. "I know that."

"Sometimes I wonder if you do. Is that why you've been coming by so often? Out of a sense of guilt? Or do you just feel obligated?" She was too tired to worry about the edge in her voice. She didn't want to be someone's obligation, especially not Gabriel's. Obviously he had more than enough to do. He didn't need to waste time driving out to see her.

"*Nee*." His smile faded and his forehead furrowed with con-sternation. "Look, I just told you I wanted to see you. But if you don't want me coming around . . . I don't want to be a bother, Moriah."

Remorse pricked at her, and she closed her eyes for a moment. She shouldn't have spoken to him that way. He'd been nothing but kind to her, and this was how she repaid him, by hurting his feelings. "I'm sorry. I really do appreciate you thinking of me. It's nice to know someone cares."

His eyes suddenly softened, and she found herself transfixed by them. "I do care," he said.

"Because we're family. And friends. At least I'd like to think we are."

"We are. But that's not the only reason—"

Before he could finish his sentence, she was assaulted by a stab of pain similar to the one she had experienced that morning. She bent over and tried to catch her breath.

"Moriah?" Gabriel immediately came to her side, his arm around her shoulders, his body bent in a similar shape to hers. "What's wrong?"

"I don't know." The pain subsided, disappearing almost as quickly as it came. When she didn't feel anything else, she slowly straightened.

"What, is it a cramp or something?"

"Maybe."

"Here, sit down." He guided her over to a chair and held it out for her. "Do you need to put your feet up?"

"My feet are fine." Actually, she felt completely fine now, at least physically. But the alarm she'd felt earlier that day multiplied tenfold. However, she wouldn't let Gabriel know. He looked worried enough as it was.

"Has this been happening a lot?"

"Only one other time." She didn't feel the need to tell him when.

He knelt down beside her. "Do you want a glass of water? Maybe some crackers or something? You shouldn't have worked so hard today."

She found his hovering slightly amusing. And a little surprising. He'd been so aloof during the time she and Levi had been together. And even though they'd grieved together at the hospital and funeral, their subsequent visits had been awkward—at least she thought so, with Gabe saying very little when he stopped by. But she was carrying his niece or nephew; of course he'd be concerned.

"I didn't work that hard," she said, trying to reassure him. "And the pain is gone." All of a sudden she felt another sensation, one she had never felt before. Excited and without thinking about it, she grabbed his hand and placed it on her belly. "Can you feel that?"

His hand twitched and he grinned. "Wow."

She nodded, thrilled with the movement she felt inside her. Then she looked down at her hand covering his, and another familiar feeling intruded on the happy moment. Sorrow. Levi should be here, feeling his baby's light movements. He should be sharing this moment with her, not Gabriel.

But she hid her emotions for Gabriel's sake. His face shone with joy. She wouldn't destroy that for him. They both had so little to rejoice about, and had lost so much—she a husband, him a brother. She had become adept at burying her feelings, shoving them deep down inside until she thought they were completely gone, but even then they often appeared when she least expected it, like now. Yet she suppressed them again, not only for his sake, but also for her own.

"*Danki.*"

His soft voice interrupted her thoughts.

"For what?"

"For sharing this with me." He slipped his hand out from beneath hers and stood up. "That was pretty special."

She smiled, amazed at how affected he seemed to be. "I'm glad you were here to share it. Although I wish . . ."

"I know." His expression dimmed. "I wish he was here too."

Not wanting to dwell on their mutual sadness, she rose from her seat. "I really have to get home. I'm sure *Mami* is starting to worry about me." She smoothed the front of her apron.

"I'm taking you home."

"That's not necessary."

"*Ya*, it's necessary. What if you have another pain? Plus it's dark and you could get into an accident."

"I've driven in the dark before," she said, a little impatiently. What did he think she was, some frail flower whose stem would snap off in a light breeze? Her parents and siblings seemed to think so. Even Rachel had earlier in the day. But anyone can drop a rolling pin. That didn't mean she wasn't capable of doing anything for herself. "I'm not helpless."

"I'm not saying you are. Remember what happened to Tobias a couple months ago? I won't let you risk yourself or the baby because some Yankee doesn't know how to drive a car."

She recalled the buggy accident, remembering how lucky Tobias and Rachel had been, considering her brother had sustained only a bump on the head. They could have been seriously hurt . . . or worse. She couldn't bear the thought of anything happening to her baby. "All right. You've convinced me."

"*Gut.* I'm glad you've come to your senses." He winked at her, a gesture similar to what Levi used to do when he would tease her, yet somehow completely different. Then again, why wouldn't it be? Even though they looked nearly exactly alike, as she was so often reminded, Gabriel was nothing like his brother.

Gabriel grabbed his summer hat, made of tightly woven straw, and plopped it on his head. He opened the door for her, and they walked into the balmy night air. He opened the buggy door on the passenger side and helped her in, then untied his horse and jumped beside Moriah on the seat. Within minutes they started toward her house.

Once the buggy was in motion, she leaned back in the seat. Fatigue instantly overcame her, and she closed her eyes. Only for a moment. She just needed a minute of rest.

"Moriah."

Feeling the pressure of someone touching her shoulder, her eyes flew open.

"We're here," Gabriel said.

"Already?" She tried to stifle a yawn, but didn't quite succeed.

"*Ya*, sleepyhead."

"How long have I been asleep?"

"Since I pulled out of the driveway." He smiled.

"Really?" She opened the buggy door, and he was at her side before she could step on the ground. "*Danki*," she said, then yawned again. "Sorry. I don't know why I'm so tired."

"My guess is you're working too hard."

She ignored his words. "Come on inside. I'll get *Daed* or one of my brothers to drive you back home."

"*Nee*. I'll walk. It's not that far."

"It's too dark to walk."

He stuck his hand in his coat pocket and pulled out a flashlight. "I always come prepared."

She grinned. "Why am I not surprised?"

"Go on in the house. I'll put up your horse."

"Are you sure?"

"*Ya*. Just promise me one thing?"

"What's that?"

"You'll tell the midwife about these pains you're having."

"Don't worry. I will."

"Oh, and one other thing." He looked at her intently and took a step forward. "Consider this fair warning. I'll be checking in on you—whether you like it or not. And don't think it's because I have to. Remember, I want to." He gazed at her for a moment, then nodded. With that he stepped away and led the horse toward the barn.

She had half a mind to go after him and tell him not to bother, but she was too tired. Although he kept insisting he wanted to see her, she wished he wouldn't, and somehow she had to convince him not to. The last thing she wanted to be was a burden on him. He already had plenty of those to bear.

"I can't see that anything's wrong." Rebekkah Fisher, Moriah's midwife, lifted her hands from Moriah's slightly protruding abdomen. Her mother had insisted on fetching her when Moriah told her about the pains she'd been having. "How often have you felt the pain?"

"Just a few times. Twice the other day, in the morning when I was at Mary's fabric store, and in the evening at the Millers'. Then once yesterday. I haven't had any today."

Rebekkah rubbed one of her chubby fingers across her lips. "Hmm. You're perfectly healthy, except you look tired. Are you getting enough rest?"

Moriah sat up in her bed and nodded, cringing inwardly for being untruthful. She clasped her hands together and put them in her lap. She hadn't had a good night's sleep in a very long time, despite her fatigue. Working hard during the day hadn't made sleeping any easier.

Rebekkah eyed her skeptically. "I guess I'll have to take your word for it. Are you napping at all?"

"*Nee.*"

"Then I'm prescribing at least one nap a day. If you can't sleep, then just lie down and relax. Thirty minutes every day. I also want you to lie down if you feel any pain."

"I'll make sure she does," Emma chimed in, moving to stand next to the midwife. She looked at her daughter. "I'm not one to say I told you so—"

"Since when?"

Emma smirked. "Very funny, *dochder*. Hopefully you'll listen to your midwife. You haven't listened to me very well. I've only had six children, you know."

"I know." Moriah rose from her bed. "*Danki* to you both for caring. I really appreciate it. But I'm okay, really." She went to her closet and pulled out one of her long white aprons, then slipped it over her head, making sure she didn't disturb her *kapp*.

"I'm glad you're feeling *gut*." Rebekkah gathered her black leather satchel and slung the strap over her plump shoulder. She gave Moriah a stern look. "I'll be back in a couple of weeks for another checkup. However, if the pains become worse or more frequent, let me know. God forbid, but it could be something serious, and we'll have to take care of it right away. In the meantime, get some rest."

"I will."

"Would you like to stay for some coffee?" Emma offered.

"I'd love to, but I have another appointment."

"All right then. Let me see you out."

When Emma and Rebekkah disappeared downstairs, Moriah

went over to the window and looked outside. The sun was trying its best to pierce through the stubborn cloud cover, casting thin beams of light before disappearing completely behind a blanket of gray. Rain threatened, filling the air with sticky humidity. She glanced down at the ground below and looked at the vegetable garden situated in front of the house. Along with her mother and sisters she had planted several rows of tomatoes, corn, cucumbers, carrots, sweet peppers, and green beans. Yesterday she had pulled every weed out of the soft dirt. Today she would turn her attention to the flower beds that bordered the house, and planned to work outside as long as the rain held off.

Outside Rebekkah steered her buggy out of the Byler's driveway. Just has she left, another buggy drove up, slowed, and turned in. She immediately recognized the driver.

Gabriel.

Her hand went to her *kapp*, making sure it was secure and no loose strands of hair had released from it. She also glanced down at her dress and made sure her apron was straight.

Suddenly she stopped her movements. Why did she care what she looked like in front of Gabriel? Especially when she needed to tell him she didn't want him stopping by anymore.

She exhaled a long breath as she saw him get out of the buggy and head toward the house, taking long, confident strides. From the vantage point of her bedroom, his face was obscured by his straw hat, but she could make out his broad shoulders, his muscled arms straining against the sleeves of his shirt. Her belly started swirling, and she placed a hand against it. Something other than the baby had caused the sensation. She chalked it up to nerves, even though she'd never been nervous around Gabriel. Confused, yes. But not anxious. Yet she'd never been in this situation with him before.

"Moriah!" Emma called from downstairs. "You have a visitor."

She took another deep breath, then went downstairs and entered the front room. He was standing by the sofa next to the window. Quickly he removed his hat and held it in his hands. "Hi, Moriah," he said softly.

Again, the tickle appeared in her belly.

"Would you care for something to drink?" Emma walked into the room. "I've just made some lemonade. It's refreshing on such a sticky day."

"*Nee*," Moriah said.

"*Ya*," Gabriel said at the same time. He glanced at Moriah, wariness creeping into his eyes.

Emma looked at both of them, then said, "One lemonade it is. Please, Gabriel. Feel free to sit down." She shot Moriah a perplexed look before retreating into the kitchen.

Gabriel didn't move. "Do you want me to sit down?"

"Gabriel, I . . . listen, I don't mind if you stay. But I was serious about you not needing to come by so often."

"I know."

His answer surprised her. "Then why did you come?"

"Because I told you I would."

"Moriah!" Emma's voice sounded from the kitchen. "Tell Gabriel I made fresh apple cake! Come in here and I'll cut you both a piece."

"Apple cake?" His eyebrow lifted. "Now, how can I resist an offer like that?"

As Gabe followed Moriah to the Bylers' kitchen, he inhaled the sweet cinnamon scent of Emma's apple cake. And while he was more than happy to partake of the delicious dessert, having the opportunity to spend more time with Moriah was a thousand times more satisfying.

"*Willkum*," Emma said, gesturing to an empty seat at the table. "I'm glad you could stay."

He glanced at Moriah and wondered if she would add anything to her mother's statement. She didn't, so he waited as her mother slid a fork beneath a plump slice of the cake and lifted it from the baking pan. A fat layer of white frosting topped the piece that Emma placed on a dish.

He accepted it with a smile, but he kept his emotions in check. He found it easier to do than in the past, mostly because they didn't torture him as much. He'd come to a decision about Moriah. Even though she seemed resistant, he would continue to check in on her, to make sure she was all right. He would also find opportunities to spend time with her, like they did the other night and were currently doing. They had been good friends in the past, and he wanted to renew that friendship. And who knew, maybe the friendship would turn into something more, and he could fulfill his brother's dying wish to care for Moriah.

Which was also Gabe's deepest desire.

"So how is your *daed* doing, Gabe?" Moriah asked.

"His recovery is slow, but he's going to be okay. I still think he should see a doctor, but he won't listen to me."

"Recovery?" Emma asked.

"Didn't Moriah tell you? He burned his hand on the forge yesterday. She took great care of him."

"Rachel Detweiler was there too," Moriah interjected. "And we didn't do much, just bandaged his hand. Then we poured tea for him and made some apple brown betty. That's his favorite dessert."

"Good thing she was there. *Daed* can be stubborn, and I don't do well with medical stuff. I faint at the sight of blood."

She turned to him, surprise registering on her face. "You do not. I know this for a fact."

He looked at her. "How?"

"First grade. I cut my finger on one of those sharp rocks in the school yard. You took a handkerchief out of your pocket and wrapped it around my finger to stop the bleeding while Levi ran and got the teacher."

"I didn't know about this," Emma said. "Dear me, I hope it was clean."

"Don't worry, *Mami*, it was." She directed her attention back to Gabe. "You didn't pass out then, and I doubt you'd pass out now."

"I'm surprised you remembered that," he said. He had forgotten all about the incident.

"How could I forget? The teacher didn't have any bandages, so I had to spend the rest of the day with a huge white finger. You must have wrapped that thing around it about five times." She laughed. "Even then you were a nice guy."

Gabe smiled. She'd never complimented him before, not in any meaningful way. To hear her words and to see her laugh were like a warm balm on his heart.

"I think I'll take the rest of the cake out to the men." Emma rose from her chair. "Those four have the biggest appetites I've ever seen. Gabriel, can I get you anything else?"

"*Nee*," he said. "I'm fine. The cake is delicious, *Frau Byler*."

"*Danki*, Gabriel. I'm glad you're enjoying it. Moriah, I'm going to Mary's fabric store after I give this to your father and brothers. Do you need anything?"

"*Nee.* I was just there the other day."

After Emma left, Gabe looked at Moriah, who had grown serious again. She picked at her cake, lifting a bit of frosting on the tine of her fork. "You're not hungry?" he asked.

"Not too much."

"Was that Rebekkah Fisher I saw leaving a little while ago?" Moriah nodded.

A tiny thread of panic wound through him. "Did she say everything was okay?"

She looked up at him. "*Ya.* The baby is fine. Rebekkah wants me to get more rest."

Gabe shoved a bite of the cake in his mouth. "Sounds like good advice," he said after he swallowed.

"I get plenty of sleep."

"I don't think so."

Her head popped up, and from the surprised expression on her face, he regretted being so blunt. But he couldn't figure out why she wasn't telling the truth. "Moriah, anyone can see you're tired."

She set her fork down and looked at him squarely, a spark of irritation in her eyes. "What about you, Gabriel? How are *you* sleeping at night?"

Her question rendered him speechless for a moment. He hadn't expected her to be so straightforward in return. "Not so well. Which is why I understand, Moriah."

"You understand?" Her eyes grew moist, and her voice shook. "You understand what's it's like to lose your husband, not once, but twice? To know that he'll never be here to share in the birth of his child?"

His chest tightened. "You know I don't. But I loved him too, Moriah. He could make me so angry sometimes, especially when he . . . when he left. But that doesn't mean I don't wish almost every minute of the day that he was back. That I don't live with regrets. That I don't want more than anything to do things over. A lot of things." He closed his eyes, blocking his own tears. He'd never verbalized the thoughts that had jumbled through his mind on so many sleepless nights since Levi's death.

"Me too," she said, reaching for his hand. Tears dripped down her face. "I can't help but wonder why God took him away from me." She looked at him. "From us."

"I've asked that question so many times." Her touch eased the pain in his heart. "We can't understand God's ways. We can only trust that His plans are for *gut*."

"I don't know how any *gut* can come from this." She withdrew her hand from him and stood, then picked up their plates and put them next to the sink. He could see her wiping her tears with the back of her hands, and when she turned around, her eyes were dry. "*Danki* for coming by, Gabriel."

Dismissed. But he wasn't about to leave so easily. He walked over to her. "Don't push me away, Moriah. Let me help you."

"I don't need your help." She looked up at him. "If you're worried about not being able to see the baby, you don't have to be. You and John will always have a place in my child's life."

"I'm glad to know that, but that's not why I'm here. Moriah, I would be here even if there was no baby. I'm here because I want to be. I'm here because I care."

"But why?" Her lower lip started to tremble. "Why do you care?"

"Because I—"

A knock sounded on the front door. Inwardly he groaned. He had been about to reveal his heart, to tell her why he cared so much. Now she was moving away from him, and he no longer had the chance.

He followed her as she went to the front door and answered it. "Hello," she said to the visitor as he came up behind her.

His eyes grew wide with shock as he saw the woman standing on the Bylers' front porch. Taylor Johnston. Levi's lover.

Chapter 14

*J*oseph, I promise you, there is something going on between the two of them."

Tobias stuffed the last bite of apple cake in his mouth and tried not to eavesdrop on his parents. It was difficult not to, as his mother wasn't exactly whispering. If he didn't have to finish sanding the dresser drawers, he would have gone to the other side of the shop and let them have their privacy. But he wanted to get these drawers stained before the day's end, and he wouldn't be able to do that if he didn't get busy sanding.

The grit of the sandpaper against the rough wood made a good amount of noise, but he could still hear his parents' discussion.

"I think you're overreacting, Em," Joseph said.

"I'm not overreacting. You weren't in there when they were talking. You didn't see the way he looks at her. I can't believe I didn't notice before."

"Maybe because there's nothing to notice."

"Joseph, I know what I saw. That young man's got feelings for Moriah. No wonder he's been dropping by so often."

"You said he was just being courteous, and you liked his thoughtfulness."

"That's what I thought. Now I'm not so sure. What should we do?"

"I don't see as we have to do anything."

"I just don't know if she's ready for this. After everything she's been through and with her being pregnant, she's very vulnerable right now."

"This is Gabe Miller we're talking about here. He's a good man. Always has been."

"That's what we thought about Levi. And look how that turned out."

"Gabe and Levi are different people. You know that. Good boys, both of them, but different."

Tobias flipped over the drawer and started sanding the wood on the underside. The movement must have alerted his parents, because they lowered their voices, much to his relief. The less he knew about Moriah's situation with Gabe, the better off he would be. She was his sister and he cared about her, but that stuff was off limits, in his opinion.

Though she could do worse than Gabe. A lot worse. He had a good reputation and was well liked by nearly everyone in the community. But as his mother pointed out, Levi had been as well, and what he had done to Moriah was inexcusable. Who was to say Gabe wouldn't do the same thing?

With a shake of his head, he returned his attention to the job at hand. He had more important things to think about than Moriah and Gabe. Like getting this dresser done. And like thinking about Rachel Detweiler. Confound it, he couldn't get that girl out of his mind. Especially the kiss she'd given him the night of the buggy crash. Her lips had been so soft, the kiss so whisper light, his senses reeled just thinking about it. He could tell she felt guilty over it, as she had made a point to remind him that she was Christian Weaver's girlfriend. But she wasn't the only one feeling guilty about that night. Even though she'd been the one who kissed him, he had been thinking about doing the same thing. She'd just beat him to it.

He'd mentally kicked himself more than a few times for betraying Christian. What kind of person was he to like another guy's girl? And why did that girl have to be Rachel Detweiler? He'd spent most of his life disliking her. Now all he could think about was kissing her again.

"You keep sanding the wood like that you're going to rub a hole in it."

Tobias looked up to see his father's stern expression. His mother was gone and he hadn't even heard her leave. "Sorry, *Daed*. Guess I got distracted."

"Pay attention next time." Joseph took another look at the dresser, then walked away.

Blowing the large buildup of wood dust off the bookshelf, he turned it on its side and began sanding the top, forcing himself to focus. Even when Rachel wasn't anywhere near him, she still made him forget his head.

Moriah opened the door and stared into the green eyes of a stranger. She didn't recognize the Yankee woman who stood before her.

The visitor's gaze turned from Moriah to Gabriel, and Moriah watched the green eyes widen, then the woman's body begin to sway back and forth as if she were about to faint.

"Levi?" she said.

Confused, Moriah wondered how she knew Levi. But quickly, the woman's expression changed from shock to disappointment. "His brother," she said.

Moriah spun around. So Gabriel knew this woman too? "What's going on?"

"I knew your late husband," she said. "May I come in?"

Gabriel took a step forward until he was standing next to Moriah. "I don't know if that's a *gut* idea, Ms. Johnston."

Johnston? "As in Johnston's Farms?" Moriah regarded her again. The woman's platform heels made her several inches taller than Moriah. Her luxuriant red hair hung in loose waves around her shoulders. She had vibrant green eyes and full, red-painted lips. Perfect skin and a flawless figure, as her tight, white, short-sleeved shirt and blue jeans showed. Moriah felt dwarfed by her presence, and didn't doubt for a minute that she came from a family of great wealth.

"Yes. My father owns Johnston's Farms. Where Levi used to work." She held out her hand to Moriah. "I'm Taylor Johnston. "

Still confused, she glanced at Gabriel briefly before inviting her inside. His expression remained guarded, and Moriah wondered what he had against this woman. "Please, sit down. Can I get you anything? Lemonade? Water?"

She shook her head. "I'm fine. I won't take up too much of your time." She cast a look at Gabriel, then turned her attention to Moriah again. "Can we speak in private?"

Moriah looked at Gabriel. Apparently he wasn't thrilled with the idea, but Taylor seemed unnerved by his presence. "Gabriel, do you mind?"

He hesitated, saying, "It might be better if I stay."

Moriah still felt unnerved by their unfinished conversation moments earlier, so she said, "I'll be fine, Gabriel. *Danki*."

He sighed. "Let me just grab my hat. I left it in the kitchen."

While he was gone, Moriah motioned for Taylor to sit on the couch. "Are you sure I can't get you anything?"

"I'm sure." Taylor scanned the room. "So this is where Levi used to live?"

"*Nee*. This is my parents' house."

"Oh. I just assumed . . . when I stopped at the blacksmith shop, Mr. Miller said I could find you here. I thought you were still living in the same house."

"I moved back here after Levi . . . left."

Taylor's cheeks reddened. "I see."

Gabriel emerged from the kitchen. He looked at Moriah once more, the emotion she'd seen during their encounter in the kitchen still vivid in his expression. She had asked him why he cared about her, and when she saw the intensity of his gaze, the darkening of his brown eyes, she felt new emotions stir within her, which both thrilled and terrified her. Clearly she'd had a momentary lapse of reason, more than likely due to fatigue. Still, even though she could rationalize her feelings, she didn't want to explore them any further. She refused to hope for anything other than a healthy baby.

"All right," he said. "I'll be back by in a couple of days."

It was on the tip of her tongue to protest his visits yet again, but she wouldn't argue in front of Taylor. Instead she barely nodded, a gesture that caused Gabriel to emit a small smile. She'd have to set him straight the next time.

He nodded toward Taylor, then left. Moriah thought she saw Taylor visibly relax once Gabriel was gone, and Moriah knew she was relieved to see him leave too.

"How do you know my brother-in-law?" Moriah asked.

"We met once," Taylor responded, staring down at her hands. "He came out to the farm."

"Oh."

She looked up. "I'm so very, very sorry."

"Thank you. Levi's death has been hard on all of us."

Taylor picked at her index finger with her thumb. "No, I mean I'm sorry for what I did to you and Levi."

Everything seemed to slow down around Moriah, as if her life had been permanently yoked to a leaden, unmovable force. "What did you do?" Her voice sounded feeble in her ears.

"You mean you don't know?" Taylor's cheeks reddened even deeper. "That your husband and I had an affair?"

Moriah gasped. Taylor's words wrenched her heart. "An affair?"

"It was my fault. Since the accident I've had to face some ugly truths about myself. One of those is that I don't care who I hurt, as long as I get what I want." She paused and looked at Moriah. "What I wanted was your husband. He resisted at first, but I can be persuasive. Very persuasive."

Closing her eyes against the fresh new wave of pain assaulting her, Moriah said, "Why are you telling me this?"

"I honestly thought you knew."

"How would I know?" She opened her eyes. "My husband left me. He didn't explain anything in his letter, only that he was leaving me and his faith. And he didn't want to be Amish anymore."

"Didn't you wonder what made him come to that decision?"

She twisted the ends of the ties of her prayer *kapp*. "We believe marriage is for life. What God has brought together, no man—or woman—can break apart." She rose from her chair, not wanting to hear anything this woman had to say. Not only had Taylor Johnston taken Levi, for some reason she wanted to push the knife further into Moriah's back. "I think you should leave. Now."

Taylor looked up at her. "Are you pregnant?"

Moriah gripped the ribbons on her *kapp* even more tightly. "*Ya.*"

"With Levi's baby?"

Moriah's eyes narrowed. "*Ya.*"

All along she had thought he left because of something she'd done, and because of his dissatisfaction with the Amish church. Now she knew the real reason. She had disappointed him so deeply on an intimate level he had taken up with another woman. Would there be no end to her pain? To her humiliation? "Please," she whispered, perilously close to tears. "Just go."

"I will, after I tell you why I'm here. Levi and I had been fighting a lot lately, and I could tell he wasn't happy living with me and my father. Then he found out I wasn't pregnant—"

"What?"

"I told him I was pregnant." Taylor stared down at the floor for a moment, then jerked her head up. "Like I said, I've done a lot of soul searching. I was the one driving in the accident, and even though the police said it wasn't my fault, Levi and I had been arguing right before the truck hit us." She licked her lips. "He'd learned that I'd lied to him about being pregnant. We hadn't been together that long, and I didn't like the idea of losing him. So I told him I was pregnant so he would stick around." She paused and looked down again. "And he told me right before the accident that he was coming back to you."

Moriah breathed in sharply. "Why should I believe you?"

"Normally you shouldn't." She sighed. "But you deserve to know the truth. He said he made a terrible mistake by leaving."

Picking up her huge red leather handbag, she stood. "I just wanted you to know he still loved you . . . and still wanted to be Amish. He said leaving you and his faith had been a mistake."

A blend of caustic emotions ran through Moriah. Hearing about Levi's planned return did little to assuage her pain and grief. Still, she understood Taylor's gesture. The woman didn't have to come here and tell the news in person, yet she did. "*Danki*," Moriah managed.

"Don't thank me. I don't deserve it. What I deserve is your hatred."

"That is not our way."

"I've heard that, but I didn't really believe it. Not until now, and now I know he was right." Taylor's green eyes shimmered with tears. "I really am sorry," she said in a thick whisper.

"I know."

Taylor walked past her and out the door. Moriah didn't move—she just stood there in the center of the living room, listening to Taylor's car engine start and pull away. Only when the sound disappeared did she sit down on the couch. Her movements were still slow as she tried to process what Taylor had said.

Someone knocked on the front door, but she didn't move to answer it. She didn't want to see anyone else. She couldn't take another blow.

Gabe knocked on the wooden screen door again, more firmly this time. Maybe Moriah was in the back of the house or upstairs where she couldn't hear him, which was why she wasn't answering the door.

Halfway down her street, Gabe had realized it was a mistake

to leave Moriah alone with Taylor. He'd hurriedly turned his buggy around. What had he been thinking? He should have stood his ground, or at least stayed in another room. But Moriah had been insistent that he leave. Her tone of voice had been polite, but he saw it in her eyes. She wanted him to go. He supposed his nicked ego had led him to agree to her request. When he pulled in her driveway, he was glad to see Taylor had left.

He knocked for a third time. Drops of water plinked against the roof of the Bylers' porch as a rumble of thunder sounded in the distance. His horse would appreciate the cool shower.

Where was she? Worry shot through him. Lifting his hand to rap on the front door one more time, she finally opened it.

"What do you want?" she said dully.

Gabe discerned instantly that whatever Taylor had said to Moriah had upset her. He'd been afraid of that. Clearly she had been crying. Her eyes were swollen, her nose rosy as if she had been blowing it. "I came to see if you're okay."

"I'm fine." She moved to shut the door.

He laid his palm on the frame, preventing the screen door from closing. "I can see you're not."

"Leave me alone, Gabriel." She sounded on the verge of sobbing.

No way was he going to leave now. He pushed against the door with his hand, gently, but with enough force to show her he wasn't going anywhere. "What did Taylor say to you?"

Moriah looked at him, her eyes consumed with defeat, then turned and walked away.

A knot formed in his gut as he followed her inside. The air felt heavy, sticky, as the sky darkened and rain pelted harder outside. Sweat broke out on his forehead. He took off his hat and laid it on the table. Her back was still to him, and despite the hot July temperature, she hugged her shoulders. "Moriah, I can't help you if you won't talk to me."

Whirling around, she said, "Did you know? Did you know about her and Levi?" Before he could answer she added, "Never mind. I can tell by your face that you did."

"I'm sorry, Moriah." Gabe took a step toward her. If only he could pull her in his arms. He could soothe her, explain why he didn't tell her.

But she moved away from him. "You knew, and you didn't say anything." She sniffed and wiped her nose with the tissue in her hand. "You lied to me."

He shook his head, trying to close the distance between them. "*Nee*, Moriah. I didn't lie to you."

"You weren't completely honest. That's the same thing."

Raking his hand through his hair, he said, "I couldn't tell you. What *gut* would it have done? I didn't want you to hurt any more than you already were." He dipped his head so he could look directly at her. "I wanted to protect you."

Her shoulders slumped, and he could see the strength drain from her. She gazed at him with weepy blue eyes, eyes that he had fallen in love with more than six years ago. "What else are you hiding from me, Gabriel? What other secrets do you have? Or will I have to wait until someone else dies to find out?"

He froze, as if her words had been a physical blow. "That's not fair, Moriah."

She took a deep breath and closed her eyes. "I know. I'm sorry."

"*Nee*, I'm sorry." A flash of lightning lit up the sky. "You're right. I haven't been honest with you. Not completely. And you have a right to know why."

His somber countenance stunned Moriah. She'd never seen him so serious, even when he had told her about Levi leaving her. Dread pooled inside her, and she wished she hadn't questioned him. Hadn't she had enough?

"There is something I need to tell you," Gabriel said. "It's something I should have told you a long time ago." He gestured to the sofa. "Can we sit down?"

She nodded, knowing they had both come too far in this conversation to turn back now. Outside a boom of thunder shook the house, much the same way her life had been rocked to the core. They sat down together, and she could see the sheen of perspiration on his forehead. The room had become unbearably hot and humid, the afternoon thunderstorm doing little to cool things down.

"Moriah, I only want you to be happy. You have to believe that. Everything I've done has been driven by that desire."

The irony of his statement struck her. She'd never been so miserable in her life.

"Remember when we were in school, the day you and I first walked home together?"

She nodded. "Levi was sick and stayed home. We were in fifth grade."

"Sixth. We took the long way home. Remember how we talked about everything?"

"We even went and sat by the creek for a while. Just talking."

"I got in trouble for being late." He grinned, but the expression was tempered with solemnity. "That's when I knew."

"Knew what? Gabriel, what does this have to do with anything?"

"It has to do with everything." He swallowed, his Adam's apple bobbing up and down. "I—Moriah, I love you." He let out a long breath.

"I know," she said wearily. "I love you too. You're my husband's brother, and the uncle to my child. Of course I love you."

He shook his head, his brown hair flopping against his ears. "*Nee*, you don't understand. I *love* you. Not like a *schwester*." He took her hand in his. "I love you like a man loves a woman. Like a husband loves his wife."

When his gaze locked with hers, her heart stopped beating. She could see that his words were true. It was evident in his eyes. As he looked at her with such warmth and love, she wanted to weep. It was obvious in the way he held her hand, gently, almost reverently, like he never wanted to let her go. "Gabriel," she said, almost unable to form his name. "I . . . I . . . ."

"Shhh." He brushed the top of her hand with his thumb. "Let me finish. I wanted to tell you, but I was afraid. Afraid you'd reject me, or laugh in my face."

"I would never have laughed at you."

"I know that now. But my twelve-year-old heart didn't. Then by the time I had found my courage, you were in love with Levi, and he loved you. I didn't want to stand in the way of that. So I kept my feelings to myself. At least I tried."

Moriah felt like a fool. How could she have been so oblivious to everything? Memories flooded her mind—how reticent Gabriel had become shortly after she and Levi were together. How kind he'd been to her after Levi left. How he had been so attentive to her since his brother's death, so loyal . . .

So loving.

"Did anyone else know?" she asked. "Did Levi know?"

"I didn't think so. I had tried so hard to keep it inside and thought I had. But the day I went to Johnston's Farms, I found out Levi did know. And that leads me to the second thing I need to say."

"There's more?" Her mind and emotions were swirling in a cauldron of confusion.

"In the hospital, Levi asked me to take care of you."

She jerked her hand out of his and stood up. "What?"

He stood and faced her. "He made me promise that I would take care of you."

"Why would he do that? He loved me and wanted to come home. Taylor told me."

Both surprised and elated to hear this news, Gabe asked, "She did? What else did she say?"

"That he was coming back to me . . . to home . . . to the Amish."

Gabriel smiled. "*Daed* was right. Levi had come back to God. And he was coming back to you."

"So why would he tell you to take care of me?"

"Because he knew he wouldn't make it. He knew I loved you, and he knew I would take care of you." Gabriel went to her and covered her shoulders with his large palms. "And he was right. Moriah, my love for you hasn't changed. It's only grown stronger over the years. I would care for you, and for this child"—he nodded at her tummy—"for the rest of my life."

Moriah couldn't speak. She couldn't think, and she didn't know what to feel. It was all too much to take in at once—too many secrets, too much betrayal. Too much confusion. She wrenched herself from his grasp. "Leave, Gabriel."

"*Nee.* I don't think you should be alone."

"I *want* to be alone." She looked up at him, a vortex of anger growing inside her. Anger at Levi for leaving, for dying, for putting her through all this. And anger at Gabriel for not telling her the truth about her husband or about his feelings. The blade of their betrayal cut at her heart and her soul. "Get out," she said, clenching her hands together.

"Moriah, please."

"I said leave!"

"What's going on here?" Tobias stood in the doorway of the front room, his clothes damp from the rain outside. Obviously he had entered the house from the kitchen and she hadn't heard him come in. "Moriah," her brother said. "Is everything all right?"

"*Nee*," she said, unable to hold back the flood of hot tears any longer. "It's not all right. I don't know if things will ever be right again!" With that she flew out of the room and headed for her bedroom upstairs, far away from Gabriel Miller.

"What did you do to her?" Tobias entered the room, anger sparking in his blue eyes.

Gabe didn't blame him for being upset. He wanted to kick himself for upsetting Moriah. He'd gone about it all wrong, he could see that now. He told her too much, too soon. Now he wondered if she'd ever speak to him again. "I made a mistake," he told her brother. "A huge mistake."

Tobias stared at him for a moment, his hardened expression softening a bit. "You want to tell me what's going on?"

Gabe started to say no, but then changed his mind. He needed someone in the Byler family to know his side of the story.

Maybe he would have an ally in Tobias. "I told your sister I loved her."

Tobias sucked in his breath. "*Ach*. That *was* a mistake, Gabe. What did you do that for?"

"You don't seem surprised."

He shrugged. "I heard *Mami* talking to *Daed* about it." Then he let out a small chuckle. "What can I say? *Mei schwester* is loveable."

The tension drained from Gabe's body at Tobias's levity, though Gabe also knew Tobias meant it. "That she is."

"I don't know what to tell you, Gabe. Feelings are funny things. You can't always choose who you love. Sometimes love chooses you, whether you want it to or not."

"You sound like the voice of experience."

"Eh, maybe. Let's just say I've learned a few things lately."

Gabe went to the table to get his hat, then nodded good-bye to Tobias. When he stepped out on the front porch, he saw that the rain had stopped. A bright rainbow arched in the sky for a brief moment, only to disappear behind the clouds.

A sign. Perhaps the flood of pain they'd all gone through would soon come to an end. At least he hoped.

Chapter 15

*A*s Rachel pulled her buggy up to Eli Yoder's barn, she could hear the hum of talking and laughter coming from the front part of the large white building. She hadn't attended a Sunday night singing in a long time, since she and Christian had started dating. But Christian hadn't returned from Charm yet, and it was the middle of summer. Maybe this was his way of telling her that their relationship was over.

Surprisingly, she was only mildly irritated with him and actually felt more than a small amount of relief. Truth be told, Christian hadn't been on her mind much lately. Not as much as Tobias had. She still couldn't get him out of her thoughts, and she couldn't help but look for him at church on Sundays even though they'd rarely said more than a couple words to each other. She seemed to pine for him more and more.

Her feelings didn't make sense. Christian was the perfect man for her, at least in theory. The other day she had taken out a sheet of paper and divided it down the middle, creating two columns. One she labeled Christian, the other Tobias, and from there she proceeded to list their positive points. Christian's list dwarfed

Tobias's, even with Christian being gone for so long. Logically she should be in love with him, not Tobias.

Love? The prospect of her loving Tobias was preposterous. And thrilling. And ridiculous. And dreamy.

She groaned. Even her thoughts were contradictory and confusing.

After tying up her horse to the hitching post, she jumped down from her buggy. The sun had started to dip in the horizon. The Yoders had set up a volleyball net and several young people were deeply involved in a game. She half expected to see Tobias in the midst of the action, and she was disappointed when she realized he wasn't there.

"C'mon, Rachel!" One of the girls yelled from the other side of the net. "We need you on our team."

Rachel shook her head. Normally she would have jumped at the chance to play, but she didn't feel like it tonight. "Maybe next time."

The girl shrugged, and the game resumed.

She walked into the barn, and several more friends greeted her. The scent of hay hung in the air, and against the wall she saw a table laden with cookies, potato chips, and peach and blueberry fry pies. She looked around the room and saw three of her girlfriends standing in the corner of the room, whispering and laughing. She started over toward them, eager to find out what was so funny.

Halfway to her destination, someone tapped her on the shoulder. Turning around, she was surprised to see Tobias Byler standing behind her.

"Hi, Rachel," he said in a soft voice.

"Tobias." A tingling sensation coursed through her stomach.

"Can I talk to you for a minute?" he asked, glancing at the door behind them. "Privately?"

She surveyed the large expansive barn, which had been cleaned especially for tonight's gathering. Square bales of hay were pushed against the wall, their sweet, dusty smell overpowering the scent of horses. The bales were used as seats, but there were also about a dozen or so chairs spread out in the room, a few of them already filled with people talking and laughing. Since she had arrived early, there weren't too many people inside. "We can't talk here?"

"I'd rather not."

His serious expression alarmed her, so she agreed. "Where should we go?"

"Just outside."

"All right."

When they reached the outside, they didn't stray too far from the barn. They had just enough privacy to be hidden from everyone else, but not so much that they wouldn't be discovered if someone walked to the back of the building. A waist-high, white fence surrounded the property. She turned around and leaned against it, looking up at him.

Without much fanfare he said, "I just wanted to tell you that I appreciated you visiting Moriah a couple weeks ago."

She lifted her brows. "How did you know about that?"

"She told me." He looked out over the pasture, where a small herd of black and white cows were feasting on the tender blades. The tangy scent of freshly mown grass drifted through the evening air. The *clip-clop* of a horse and buggy sounded in the distance. "My sister has been through a lot, you know. We're all pretty worried about her." Clearing his throat, he continued, "I'm glad you were able to be a friend. She needs as much support as she can get."

His appreciation elicited a smile. It hadn't been much of a sacrifice on her part, just a simple visit to an old, if not close, friend. But to hear Tobias talk, to see the mix of gratitude in his eyes, made her feel like she'd done something amazing.

"I'm glad I could spend some time with her." Rachel tried to keep the emotions bubbling underneath the surface from shining through her voice. "She's a *gut* listener."

"*Ya.* She is." He tilted his head at her. "How's Christian doing?" he asked, turning from her and leaning his back against the fence.

"I wouldn't know," she said, suddenly forgetting her practiced response for that very same question.

Surprise flickered in his eyes. "You haven't heard from him?"

"*Nee,* not much anyway. But I'm sure he's having a marvelous time with his aunt and uncle in Charm."

"Have you been down there to visit him?"

"What's with all the questions?"

"I'm just asking. Making conversation."

"Well, I don't want to talk about Christian." A warm breeze swirled around them, lifting up the ribbons of her *kapp*. She pressed them down. "Especially not with you."

"Suit yourself. I just thought *maedel* always liked to talk about their beaus. And I've been told I'm a good listener." He gave her a crafty look. "If you ever want to talk."

She didn't understand his sudden interest. She also didn't like the way his sly smile made her feel. All tingly and giddy inside. Actually she didn't mind the feeling; she just didn't appreciate that Tobias was the cause of it. "I'm a very private person. I'm not like the other *maedel.*"

He turned and faced her, his grin fading. "You're right," he said softly. "You are different from the other *maedel.* It's what I like about you."

Rachel's mouth almost dropped open. Did Tobias just admit he liked her? She gazed directly at him, noticing the short blond whiskers on his chin. He noticed, and his lips parted into a grin, one that made her heart melt like ice on a summer day. This couldn't be real; it couldn't be happening. The urge to touch his cheek with her palm almost overwhelmed her as his gaze held her in a gentle caress. "You like me?" she whispered.

He looked away from her, his expression a mix of surprise and confusion. For the first time she saw past his charming, careless façade; he was fighting to put it back in place. "I . . . I—"

"Rachel?"

She swirled around at the sound of her name and saw Christian standing behind her.

Tobias had never been jealous a day in his life. But when he saw Rachel run up to Christian, he turned green.

"Christian!" she exclaimed, going to him, but stopping short of throwing herself in his arms. Instead she put her hands on her hips. "You have a lot of nerve showing up here after all this time."

Christian, to his credit, appeared contrite. "Rachel, I'm so sorry. I wanted to come back earlier, but my uncle's injury was very serious. He came close to breaking his back, so they needed me to stay there until he could heal."

"And you couldn't tell me this in a letter?"

Tobias hid a grin. For once someone else was on the receiving end of her ire. And with good reason. Christian should have never been away from her for this long without giving her more of an explanation.

"I'm not much of a letter writer. To be honest, I was exhausted. I know I should have called and written more, but I kept thinking he would recover and I could come home soon. But it took longer than we all thought. He's still not a hundred percent, but I couldn't be away from home any longer."

"Oh, Christian, I'm so sorry." She took her hands off her hips and walked toward him.

Tobias's good humor disintegrated. He didn't like the soft way Rachel was talking to Christian, or the moony expression on Christian's face. Tobias cleared his throat and they broke apart, Rachel turning around and giving him an annoyed look.

Christian peeked past her shoulder. "Hello, Tobias. Nice to see you." He strode toward him and held out his hand. "It's *gut* to be back home."

"I'm sure it is." He shook Christian's hand, guilt striking him. He had no right to be jealous. Christian and Rachel had been courting long before Tobias had understood his true feelings for Rachel. Christian was his friend, and he had been so close to betraying that friendship by telling Rachel how he felt. He'd already let it slip that he liked her, and she seemed shocked by the revelation. He could only imagine how she would react if he told her how much he really cared about her.

Christian leaned forward, lowering his voice. "Hey, do mind if I have a few moments alone with my girl?"

Another wave of jealousy rose within Tobias, but he shoved it down. "Sure." He shrugged in the most nonchalant way he could muster, then looked at Rachel. "I promised Carol Mullet I'd sit beside her during the singing anyway."

Pain flashed in her eyes, and for the second time in five minutes, he wanted to kick himself. He'd made no such promise, even though he knew that Carol had liked him for a long time and probably wouldn't mind one bit if he sat next to her. He'd lashed out from his own envy and had hurt Rachel in the process, all because he couldn't handle how she made him feel—irritated, excited, interested, and most of all, confused.

Pulling down the brim of his straw hat, he headed inside the barn, needing to get away from both of them. He stood in the doorway and immediately saw Carol standing next to the refreshment table. She gave him a small wave and then smiled, her gray eyes shining behind her wire-rimmed glasses. Carol was a nice enough girl. Maybe he would sit with her after all. Perhaps she could help him forget about Rachel, who was now off limits since Christian had returned. He walked over to her and gave her his most charming grin.

"I missed you so much, Rachel."

Rachel pulled her gaze from Tobias's retreating form. "What?"

"I missed you." Christian smiled, more animated than she'd ever seen him. "I hated being apart from you for so long."

"Me too," she said absently. Why had Tobias promised to sit with Carol Mullet? Did he like her? If he did, then what kind of game was he playing, telling Rachel he liked her when he really liked someone else? Or did he just enjoy teasing them both?

"Rachel? Are you listening to me?"

She blinked and looked at Christian's face. "*Ya*, I'm listening to you." Irritation sparked her voice. "I'm standing right here, aren't I?"

Christian's smile faded. "I know you're mad at me, and you have every right to be. I should have called more, written more." He took a step toward her. "I promise, I'll make it up to you."

The sound of hymn-singing wafted over to them. Glancing around, she saw that the teens playing volleyball had already gone inside the barn. She and Christian were alone.

"I did a lot of thinking while I was gone," Christian said. He reached out and took Rachel's hand.

She jumped, surprised at the gesture. "Christian, what are you—"

"Shhh." He put his finger on her lips, and her eyes widened. "We need to talk."

Moving her mouth from his hand, she said, "I don't really think this is a *gut* ti—"

"I think we should get married this November."

"What?"

"Get married. I've thought about you every day while I was gone. It was like a part of me was missing without you. I believe God was telling me that we were meant to be together. Forever."

"But, Christian, doesn't this seem sudden?"

"I know it does, but I've been doing a lot of thinking while I was gone. When my uncle got hurt, it took a toll on my aunt. She thought she'd lost him. You should have seen how she took care of him while he was laid up."

Rachel couldn't believe his words. "You want to get married so I can take care of you?"

"*Nee*, it's not just that. I also heard about Levi." His expression sobered. "Life's too short, Rachel. And I don't see any reason why we should wait any longer to get married. You never know what might happen."

"But, Christian, you just got back. I need some time."

He took a step back, disappointment darkening his features. "Are you saying you don't want to marry me, Rachel?"

"*Nee*, I'm not saying that—" Before she could finish, he bent toward her and kissed her lightly on the mouth.

"You've made me so happy, Rachel. I know you'll be a *wunderbaar frau*."

Wife? Had she somehow agreed to marriage and didn't realize it? She didn't recognize the man in front of her. She'd never seen him so excited, so exuberant. It was as if he was a completely different person. And now she was going to marry him?

She didn't even know him anymore.

"Let's go inside," he said, putting his hand on the back of her waist as if he already possessed her. "The singing's started."

In a daze she walked with him to the barn. Thirty or so young people were sitting on wooden chairs, some in groups, some in pairs, surrounded by bales of fresh hay. When they stepped inside she expected him to drop his hand, but he didn't. Her cheeks turned red as she realized he'd all but shouted to their friends that she and Christian were more than just courting. Her gaze landed on the floor, wishing she could turn around and tell Christian that she needed to think about his proposal. When she looked up, she spied Tobias.

He was sitting next to Carol Mullet. Very close to her. She looked as if she would pop with glee. Glancing up from the hymnal, his gaze caught hers for a split moment, then he looked at Carol and smiled.

So that was it. The feelings she had for him were definitely one-sided. Good thing she found out now, before she had *really* started liking him. She should have known better anyway. Tobias Byler was only interested in himself. Soon Carol would realize that, just as Rachel had. Her initial analysis had been right— Christian was far superior than Tobias could ever hope to be. He wouldn't toy with her emotions, wouldn't make her feel like a fool. She didn't need to think about Christian's proposal any more. She had already made up her mind.

"Ready?" Christian whispered in her ear as he led her into the barn.

She turned to Christian and smiled. At least she tried to, but the burning lump in her throat made it difficult. Fortunately he didn't seem to notice. "*Ya.* I'm ready."

"Moriah, I think it's clean enough."

From her position on the kitchen floor, Moriah looked up at her mother. Emma crossed her arms, a stern expression on her face. Moriah turned her attention back to the spot she was scrubbing with a soapy rag. Sweat dripped from her brow onto the floor. "I just need to get this spot up," she said.

Emma crouched down and took the rag out of her daughter's hand. "I said, it's clean enough."

Unwilling to argue with her mother, Moriah moved to rise from the floor. The baby had grown quite a bit in the past month, swelling her belly and making her feel off balance. Emma reached out and helped her to her feet.

"You have no business scrubbing the floor," Emma chided. "Not when I can do it. Or Elisabeth and Ruth."

"You have enough work to do," Moriah said, wiping her slick forehead. August heat filtered through the house. "I'm only trying to do my share."

"You're doing more than your share. Sit down, Moriah." Emma gestured toward the kitchen table. "I'll bring you something to drink."

"*Nee*, I can get it."

"I said sit down. No arguments."

Moriah dutifully sat. Her mother returned with a cold glass of water, filled with ice cubes from the outside gas freezer. "Drink this. It will help cool you off."

The water felt refreshing sliding down her parched throat. She hadn't realized how thirsty she was. She had been so focused on getting the stain up from the floor, scrubbing and scrubbing until her hand ached. But it was no use. The stain had set in. Just as sorrow and loneliness had settled into her soul.

"I'm worried about you, Moriah. Your *daed* is too." Emma sat down, her own face rosy from the heat of the day. "You're working even harder at your chores than before, and you've been so quiet the past few weeks. You haven't even wanted to stay for dinner after the church services." She laid her hand on Moriah's forearm. "Please, *dochder*, tell me what's going on."

Moriah looked away. She didn't want to talk about her tumultuous feelings, not when she'd been trying so hard to cast them away. Levi's affair haunted her while Gabriel's declaration of love confused her. He had said he would take care of her for the rest of his life. That Levi asked him to do so. But she hadn't been good enough for Levi. What if she wasn't enough for Gabriel? What if she would never be enough for any man? She didn't want to find out. She couldn't go through this pain again.

"Moriah, honey, please. Talk to me. Is this about Gabriel?"

She jerked her head. "What makes you say that?"

"He used to visit all the time. I notice he hasn't been here in a while."

"He's busy."

Emma sighed. "I'm sure he is, but he always found time for you before."

"He must have realized I wasn't worth it."

"Now where is that coming from?"

Moriah rose from her chair. The truth was, Gabriel had come around, several times, but she had sent him away. She hadn't seen him for nearly three weeks now, except at church, where she avoided him. Evading him was easier than seeing the yearning in his eyes. "I'm going to take a nap, *Mami.*" Without waiting for her mother to respond, she left the kitchen and went upstairs, glad that Elisabeth was at her babysitting job so she could have their room to herself.

She lay down on her side and stared at the wall on the opposite side of the room. The bedroom was sweltering hot, but she didn't care. Her baby moved, and she put her hand over her belly. The babe's active movements were the only thing that brought her joy anymore. But even that was tempered by the knowledge that the baby would never know his or her father.

Next to her bed was a Bible, but she didn't pick it up. She hadn't read the book in weeks, not since the day Taylor had visited, that same day Gabriel had revealed his secret. Her prayer life had always been strong, but she couldn't bring herself to pray. What good would it do? She didn't even know what to pray for anymore. All her hopes and dreams had been shattered, and she didn't trust her own judgment. How could she, when she had completely believed in Levi's fickle devotion, but had never noticed Gabriel's love?

There was one thing she had decided on. After the baby was born, she would get a job to support herself and the child. Her parents would always have a place for her, but she didn't want to depend on them anymore either. She would never marry. She would never put her trust in love again.

Flipping over on her back, she closed her eyes, tired of the thoughts assaulting her, tired of feeling empty. Finally, she succumbed to her weariness.

Gabe stood in front of the blazing forge until his face felt like it was on fire. He welcomed the burning as it heated his cheeks, threatening to sear the skin. Only until he couldn't stand it anymore did he step back, his face tingling as his flesh cooled.

If only his resentment could be as easily extinguished.

Even though the shop didn't officially open for another hour, he came out here to think, to try to figure out what he should do. He hadn't seen her in nearly a month, and he was dying inside. Telling her he loved her had broken a dam of yearning inside him, one he couldn't repair.

Leaning against one of his work tables, he hung his head. "What did you expect?" he said aloud to the empty shop. "Her to fall in love with you?"

No, he hadn't expected it. But he had hoped for it.

He loved her so much—still did—but now it was even more difficult to hide that love than it had been before. When she had been married to Levi, when he hadn't confessed his feelings aloud, he could push them down. But now that she knew, his love increased each time he caught a glimpse of her, and it was compounded by the fact that she was still out of his reach.

Picking up a rod of iron, he held it in the fiery flame of the forge, watching it grow red hot. As the rod heated, so did Gabe's emotions. Yanking the rod prematurely out of the forge, he tossed it in the water bath and threw off his gloves.

"You're up awful early."

Gabe answered his father, but didn't turn around. "*Ya.* Thought I'd get a head start."

"By ruining that piece of metal?"

With a sigh Gabe said, "Sorry."

John came up beside him. "I'm not bothered about that, *sohn.* I'm worried about you."

"Don't be. I'm fine."

"That's what everyone says, especially when they're the exact opposite. I know your heart is hurt over Moriah, especially after you told her how you feel about her, but she needs time, Gabriel."

"*Ya.*" Gabe said, but the bitterness seeped through his voice.

"You can't force her into your life, *sohn.*"

"I'm not forcing anything!"

"You don't think telling her about Levi's request might make her feel pressured?"

"I didn't have a choice." He tossed his hat on the work table and hung his head. "She was upset with me about not coming forward about Levi's affair. She asked me if I had any more secrets." He glanced up. "I had to be honest with her. I wanted her to know I would never give up on her, that I would always care for her. I wouldn't be like . . ."

"Like Levi?"

"I would never hurt her, *Daed.*"

"She's already hurting, Gabriel. You both are."

"Even more reason for me to make her understand how much I love her."

"You can try. But you need to prepare your heart. Be ready to accept that you may never have her. God may have chosen another husband for Moriah."

Just the thought of it made Gabe's stomach twist in knots. If that happened he didn't think he could take it. He would never abandon his father, but how could he live with seeing her married to someone else again? "I thought you were on my side."

John put his hand on Gabe's shoulder. "I am. I always will be, no matter what. But sometimes, despite our best intentions, certain things aren't meant to be. And if you think you're letting Levi down, don't. If he were here now, he wouldn't let this go on."

"If it wasn't for me, he might be here now." Gabe sat in a chair and let his head drop in his hands.

As he sat down beside him, John asked, "What do you mean?"

"If I had told her how I felt a long time ago things would be different."

"You can't know that for sure. Moriah might have gone on to marry Levi no matter what you told her. Remember, God always has a plan."

"But what kind of plan is this? Levi's dead; Moriah's pregnant, left to raise her baby alone."

"Her family will help her. We'll all help her."

"You know what I mean. That child needs a father."

John stroked his beard for a long time. "What's the real reason you want to marry Moriah?"

"You know why. I love her. I love her more than anything."

He patted him on the shoulder. "Spend some time in prayer, Gabriel. Seek God through this. And above all, remember that sometimes the hardest thing to do when we love someone is to let them go."

The door to the shop opened and Aaron walked inside. He glanced at the two men, but didn't say anything. Instead he headed for the back of the shop and put his blue lunch cooler on the cluttered desk.

"Remember what I said." John stepped away. "Take it to God, Gabriel." He went to the front of the shop and flipped the Closed sign to Open.

Gabe worked steadily throughout the day, but his mind was consumed with Moriah and his father's words. He didn't have to pray about his reasons for wanting to marry Moriah. He loved her, and he wanted to spend the rest of his life with her. The thought of living without her made him weep. If that wasn't love, then he didn't know what was. But he did need to pray for her, for both of them. Only God could see them through this. Other than that, the only thing he was sure about was that he'd do whatever he could in his power to make her happy. Even if that meant staying away from her forever.

Chapter 16

*T*obias, what is your problem?"

Tobias looked at his brother Lukas, whose tanned complexion was florid with anger. Lukas tossed the piece of molding on the table in front of him. "This is the third time you've measured this wrong. It doesn't fit, and now I've cut too much off. If we don't get this armoire finished, *Daed* will have our heads."

"Sorry. I'll do it right this time."

"You better." Lukas was the most skilled woodworker in the Byler family, even better than their father. They all had natural talent, but Lukas's passion for the craft surpassed them all. As serious about work as he was about life, he brooked no careless mistakes from his brothers. He turned around and headed back to the opposite end of the long work table, where he had been gluing and nailing the molding on the side of the large piece of furniture.

Respect for Lukas's skill, combined with his own irritation at his lapse of attention, kept him from arguing with his brother. Instead he stalked to the very back of the shop where they stored the wood and selected another long piece of cherry molding. The wood was beautiful, as this particular Yankee customer wanted the best and had no problem paying for it. Lukas was right; if they screwed this job up, they would be losing a valuable customer, something that would upset their normally placid father.

He carried the molding back to the table and took out his tape measure. He intended to apply singular focus to his task, but as it had been happening all day, Rachel entered his thoughts. She was marrying Christian. Even though they hadn't announced it, everyone knew. Rachel's mother had been giddy with excitement, and he had over heard her and his *mami* talking about wedding plans a couple times during the church dinners. But the most telling sign had been the change in Christian. Before he had left for Charm, he had been a simple guy, not one to show too much emotion. Now, you never saw him without a smile. Of course who could blame him? If Tobias was marrying Rachel, he'd be walking around with a goofy grin too.

But Rachel's reaction confused him. She didn't act like a woman in love, at least how he thought one should be acting. He remembered how happy his sister had been when she and Levi had gotten engaged. Granted, that wasn't the best example, considering how their marriage ended, but at the time Moriah had been very much in love with Levi, and everyone could see it. Kind of like they all could tell with Christian. Yet Rachel had seemed more resigned than anything else. Resigned and apathetic.

Or maybe that was wishful thinking on his part. He hated the idea of her and Christian together, but there was nothing he could do about it. Declaring his feelings for her now would complicate everything. And Tobias hated complications. He liked being Amish in part because he enjoyed the simplicity and ease of life. Not that he didn't work hard, because he did. But he appreciated knowing what was around the next curve. With Rachel, he sure wouldn't have that. Better to let Christian deal with her temper, her need to always have the last word, her competitive nature.

Lucky Christian.

"Tobias, the molding?" Lukas shouted at him. "I need it now."

Shoving Rachel and Christian out of his mind, he ran the tape measure across the length of the molding and made the appropriate tick marks. Double-checking his work so he wouldn't experience Lukas's wrath, he took the molding to his brother, who put it up against the armoire. Nodding, he gave Tobias a half smile of approval.

At least someone was satisfied.

Gabe's palms grew damp as he pulled his buggy into the Bylers' driveway. It had been over a month since he'd seen Moriah, and he couldn't stand it anymore. He had spent every night on his knees, asking for God's guidance. The only thing that came to his mind clearly was that he needed to see her, but he didn't know if that was God's direction or his own overriding desires. Eventually he decided to take action, which had led him to try to visit her again.

He parked the buggy and stepped onto the driveway. His hat shielded his eyes from the glare of the bright sun. September had brought slightly cooler temperatures, mostly at night. Soon the harvest would begin. He had planted a small garden, and together he and his father would can the tomatoes, green beans, and beets the ground had yielded. Maybe one day he and Moriah would plant a garden for their own family, but he didn't dare dwell on that prospect for very long.

The door to the wood shop opened, and Gabe turned to his

right in time to see Tobias come outside. His light-blue shirt and dark pants were covered in sawdust. When he saw Gabe, he held up his hand and waved.

Gabe shoved his hands in his pockets and walked over to him. Tobias brushed off some of the dust from his black suspenders, but he was still covered in the fine wood powder. "Hello, Tobias."

"Nice to see you, Gabe."

"*Wie geht's?*"

"Fine, everything's fine. Just taking a break. You here to see Moriah?"

"*Ya.* Is she home?"

Tobias nodded, his welcoming expression growing sober. "She is. I don't know if she'll want to see you, though."

Gabe had expected as much. "Are you saying I should leave?"

"*Nee.* I'm not saying that at all. In fact, I'd be happy if you could talk to her. Maybe you can cheer her up a bit."

"I don't know. I really messed things up."

"Gabe, you didn't abandon her. You're still here. I don't think you're messing up at all." Tobias started toward the house, then motioned for Gabe to follow. "I'll tell her you want to see her."

"*Danki,*" Gabe said, grateful to have Tobias in his corner. He stood by the back door while Tobias walked into the kitchen. A few moments later he came outside, shaking his head. "She doesn't want to talk right now. I'm sorry."

Gabe nodded, drawing in his lips. "I'm not surprised."

Tobias looked irritated. "For the life of me, I'll never understand women. They do the opposite of what's good for them."

Suspecting he wasn't just referring to Moriah, Gabe said, "Having some lady troubles yourself?"

"Am I ever. Sometimes I wonder why I even bother."

"Because they're worth it." He said the words not only to convince Tobias but also to convince himself. "Listen, I don't know what you're up against, but let me give you a little advice. If love is within your reach, do everything you can to grab it. Don't let her get away." He looked up at the Bylers' house. "You'll only live to regret it."

Tobias cocked his head to the side. "That is good advice."

"Given from experience."

"I know." He smiled. "It's gonna take Moriah some time, Gabe, but I think she'll eventually realize she needs you. Don't give up on her."

Gabe looked at him. "I don't intend to."

"I think your wedding dress is coming along very well." Sarah carefully folded a small pleat in the waist of the dress and stitched it in place. "Don't you think so?"

Rachel stared at the dress in progress. They had cut the dress out of a lovely light-blue fabric a few days ago, and with both of them working on it, it was almost completed. She pushed her needle through the hem of the dress, only to stab her finger. "Ow."

"I told you to use a thimble." Sarah continued to sew, a shiny silver thimble on the middle finger of her left hand.

"They always slip off."

"That's because you're not used to using them. I'm afraid I waited too long to teach you to sew."

"I wasn't exactly eager to learn."

"True. You took to sewing like you took to cooking."

"Not very well." Rachel put her injured finger to her mouth.

"I wouldn't say that. You're adequate." Sarah smiled. "You'll have lots of practice after you and Christian are married. Good heavens, I can't believe the wedding is only six weeks away. We have so much more to do!" Sarah sighed with contentment and folded another pleat.

Rachel wished she could share her mother's enthusiasm about her upcoming nuptials. She also wished she could share her future husband's. Christian's excitement had yet to wane, and all their conversations now centered on their marriage. He had already decided where they would live, in his parents' *dawdi haus* until they found a home of their own. There were a couple of houses for sale in West Farmington, which wasn't too far from their families. They had already looked at one together. Rachel had hated it.

More than once they talked about children. Christian wanted a large family, at least eight kids. Rachel wasn't sure how practical that would be, considering how expensive it was to raise so many children. When she pointed that out, he gave his standard reply: God will provide. While she truly believed this, she still worried how they would make ends meet once they were married.

She was starting to think they had rushed things. As the wedding date neared, she became more and more anxious, and not in a good way. She'd even started dreaming about the ceremony. More than once she had awakened in a cold sweat when the groom in her dreams hadn't been Christian. It had been Tobias.

"Is Christian coming by today?" Sarah asked, snipping the blue thread.

"*Ya.*"

Sarah put down her needle. "You don't sound very excited."

"I see him almost every day now," Rachel said. "I guess the excitement has worn off."

Her mother gave her a dubious look, then picked up a spool of thread. "It's normal for brides to be nervous, Rachel. I was terrified when I married your father."

"You were?" She'd never heard her mother admit this before.

"*Ach*, I was. Like you and Christian, we didn't court long. And though I knew I loved him, I was still scared."

"How did you know you loved him?"

"Let's see. I'll have to think about that. We've been married almost thirty years now." She fingered one of the ribbons on her white *kapp*, and Rachel could suddenly imagine her mother as a young girl newly in love. "I thought your father was one of the most exciting men I'd ever met."

"Really?"

"*Ya*. He was so charming, quick with a joke, but very kind. I remember one afternoon he came by to help my *daed* with the harvest, and one of my cats had just died. He stopped working to sit with me. I cried like a baby over that pet, and when I was done I felt foolish. I was eighteen years old at the time, a year younger than you, and I was far too old to be crying like that. But Emmanuel never teased me about that. Instead he put his arm around my shoulders and I leaned against him. That's when I knew I would love this man for the rest of my life."

Rachel's sighed. "What a romantic story. I never knew *Daed* had it in him."

Sarah chuckled. "Your *daed* has a side he never shows you *kinder*." She reached out and touched Rachel's hand. "Marriage isn't easy, Rachel. It takes hard work. But the rewards and blessings are many. We couldn't be prouder of our *kinder*."

"Even Aaron?"

"Even Aaron." Tears sprang to her eyes. "Aaron has had a rough time of it, to be sure. But he's changed. God is doing a *gut* work in him, I can see that. Hopefully one day you'll see that too."

Her father suddenly came in the kitchen, covered in dirt from working in the barn. Sarah held up her hand and stopped him from taking another step. "Emmanuel! Off with those boots."

He grumbled as he pulled them off and set them outside the door. "Can I come in now?" he said, pulling off his hat, revealing the bald spot on the top of his head that had grown larger with age.

"*Ya.* Now you can come in." Sarah turned back to her sewing as he went to the cabinet to get a plastic cup. He took it to the sink and filled it with water from the tap.

Rachel regarded her parents for a moment. They weren't overly demonstrative with their affections, as was the Amish way. But she had never doubted that they loved each other. For the first time she thought about how their relationship had weathered raising six children, especially Aaron's drug abuse. She tried to imagine herself and Christian thirty years from now.

For some reason, she couldn't.

"Christian's coming," her father said, looking out the window. "That boy's like clockwork with his visits, isn't he?"

"*Ya,*" Rachel said, still unsettled by her lack of clarity regarding her future with Christian.

"There's someone coming behind him too. You expecting someone else?"

Rachel rose from her chair and started toward the window. "*Nee.* Only Christian."

"Then who's that?"

She recognized the vehicle right away.

Tobias.

Tobias wanted to throw up. Never had his stomach been so twisted up. For the past two days he thought about his conversation with Gabe Miller. He watched as Gabe stopped by their house and kept trying to visit Moriah, even though she refused to see him. The man said he wasn't giving up on her, and he was as good as his word.

But Gabe's visits weren't the only thing that had gotten Tobias thinking. Gabe's admonishment to grab love when it's right in front of you had echoed in Tobias's mind. He could see how miserable both Gabe and his sister were. How her marriage to Levi had been a mistake, and how both of them were living with regrets.

Tobias didn't want to live that way. He didn't want to regret letting Rachel go, even if he wasn't sure he ever had her in the first place.

He'd never been a man of risk, always playing things safe. Today, he would take the biggest risk of his life. If he didn't vomit first.

He pulled his buggy beside Christian's. He'd been hoping Christian wouldn't be here, but now he had second thoughts. Now he could talk to them both at the same time and hopefully make them both understand why he had to do this.

Christian jumped out of the buggy and walked toward Tobias. "Hello," he said, sporting that crazy lovesick grin he'd had on his face since returning from Charm. "What brings you by?"

His stomach coiled into another knot. He truly understood what Gabe had gone through, being in love with Moriah but not wanting to hurt his brother Levi. Tobias didn't want to hurt Christian, and for a split second, he thought about turning around and going straight back home. But he had come this far. There was no turning back now.

"I'm here to see Rachel," he said to Christian.

"Oh? What about?"

Tobias didn't like the possessive way Christian asked the question, as if Rachel were already his wife. "I just need to talk to her."

"Can it wait 'til later? We were planning to go look at another house this afternoon. I think she'll like this one, and the price is right."

"*Nee*. It can't wait." He looked past Christian to see Rachel coming out of the house. His stomach twisted again, but not with nerves this time. Good heavens, she was so beautiful. Fair-haired Rachel, with sharp blue eyes and tongue to match, along with a fiery temper that he loved to spark. He couldn't let her marry Christian. Not without a fight first.

"Tobias, what do you want?"

He could see she was annoyed with him, probably over the way he had treated her at the singing in August, where he had purposely flirted with Carol Mullet in front of her. Looking back on that now, he realized how immature he'd been. If he had only been honest with himself, and honest with Christian, then maybe Rachel would be his right now. Instead someone's heart would soon be broken.

He hoped it wouldn't be his.

"I need to talk to you, Rachel." He looked at Christian. "There's something you both need to hear."

Rachel couldn't imagine what Tobias had to say. He seemed uneasy. Disconcerted, as if he were about to jump out of his own skin. Instead of his usual relaxed stance, his hands were thrust deeply inside the pockets of his trousers, and his full lips were pressed tightly together.

Christian moved to stand next to Rachel. He put one hand on the back of her waist, which had been his habit whenever they were in public together. As if he were branding her as his own. The more he did it, the less she appreciated the symbolism. "What is it that you want to tell us?"

He took a deep breath and looked at Rachel. "I wanted to tell you I'm sorry. I acted like a *dummkopf* at the singing last month. I apologize."

She didn't know what to say. That had happened almost three weeks ago, and she hadn't thought about it since. Well, not too often anyway. Okay, more than she wanted to admit, but still, she had assumed he'd forgotten all about the incident by now.

Christian looked confused. "What are you talking about?" He glanced at Rachel.

Tobias held her gaze, and she could barely breathe. His eyes were filled with something she'd never seen before, an emotion that made her run hot and cold at the same time.

"Did I miss something?" Christian said.

She ignored him. How could she be expected to pay attention to Christian with Tobias looking at her like that?

Tobias moved toward her. "Rachel, I'm sorry for every dumb thing I've ever said to you. For all the stupid things I've done. I promise, things will be different from now on."

"How?" She could barely speak, her mouth had gone dry.

He took another step. "Trust me. I promise you, they will."

"Will someone please tell me what's going on here?"

Tobias glanced at Christian. "I need to apologize to you, friend."

"Apologize?"

"For what I'm about to say." He looked back to Rachel and leaned toward her. "You can't marry Christian, Rachel."

Her eyes grew wide at his unexpected words. "Why?"

"Because. I want you to marry me."

Rachel literally could not speak. She tried to form words, any words, but nothing came out of her mouth. Tobias asking her to marry him rendered her speechless.

Christian, however, was not. "I don't know what you're up to, Byler. If this is a joke, it isn't funny."

"It's not a joke. I'm sorry, Christian, but I'm in love with her."

"You're what?" Finally finding her voice, she had to fight to keep from swaying sideways. "What did you just say?"

"I love you, Rachel. I should have told you that night at the Yoders', but I chickened out. I should have asked you to marry me that night, but I didn't. I made a mistake, and I'm trying to fix it."

"Wait a minute." She held up her hands and took a step back. "You made a mistake by not asking me to marry you?"

"*Ya.* Because if I had, you wouldn't be with him." He gestured to Christian, who was glaring at him with open hostility. "Look, I'm not doing this to hurt you. You're my friend."

"Some friend. You're trying to steal my girl."

"I'm not trying to steal her." He faced Rachel. "I'm giving her another choice. Rachel, tell me you don't love me. Tell me you love Christian, and that you want to marry him. If I hear those words, I'll walk away right now, and I'll never bother you again. I promise."

Rachel looked at him, then at Christian. She didn't say anything for a long moment.

"Rachel?" Christian dropped his arm from her waist. "Tell him. Tell him you love me."

Turning, she faced Christian. "Do you love me?"

Christian gaped. "Of course I do. Why would you even ask?"

"Because you've never told me. I've never heard you say the words."

"Of course I've said them." He frowned. "Haven't I?"

She shook her head. "*Nee.* You haven't. And I need to hear them."

He lowered his voice. "I love you. I'll tell you that for the rest of our lives if you need me to."

"Why? Why do you love me? Better yet, why do you want to marry me?"

Christian backed away. "Wait a minute, why am I the one being questioned here? You should be asking Tobias this. *Nee,* you should be telling him to leave."

"I can't. Not until I have my answer." Her heart thrummed in her chest, threatening to explode.

"You already know why I want to marry you, Rachel. We've talked about this."

"We've talked about where we'll live, and how many children we'll have. But we've never talked about us, Christian. We've never shared our feelings." Her body shook with emotion. "I've never said I love you either. I don't think you even noticed."

Christian's eyes hooded. "Rachel . . . what are you saying?"

"I'm saying I can't marry you, Christian. Things don't feel right between us. They never have."

"Is this because of him?" Christian pointed at Tobias.

"*Nee.*"

"Then you don't love him?"

She gazed at Tobias. Handsome, charming, unpredictable Tobias. He drove her crazy, and she knew he always would. Yet she couldn't imagine living without him.

His mouth curved in smile, one that promised a life of passion, consternation, and love.

"*Ya*," she said. "I love him." Then she turned to Christian. "I'm sorry. I really am."

"That's how you really feel?"

Rachel nodded. "*Ya*."

Christian shook his head, his shoulders slumping. "I guess there's nothing more for me to say." Without looking at either of them, he spun around and went to his buggy. Tobias and Rachel moved out of the way as he turned the vehicle around. When he pulled up alongside them, he stopped. "I do care for you, Rachel. I just want you to know that."

"I know. I care for you too."

"But that's not enough, is it?"

"*Nee*. It's not enough."

He looked at Tobias, his eyes narrowing. "If you ever hurt her, you'll have me to deal with."

"I understand."

Christian slapped the reins on the horse's flanks and drove off. Rachel turned to Tobias, apprehension suddenly filling her. "Did you mean what you said?"

"About loving you? *Ya*." He leaned in closer. "About marrying you? Absolutely. I love you, Rachel. I know my past actions have shown otherwise. All I'm asking for is a chance to prove how much I want to be your husband. To fall asleep with you at night and wake up with you in the morning. To be with you for the rest of our lives . . . until death do us part."

His words etched themselves on her heart. That was what she needed to hear, and they were words Christian would have never been able to say, not with the sincerity and love Tobias had. Oh, how much she loved this man, more than she ever thought possible. More than anything she wanted to fall into his arms and accept his proposal. But she couldn't resist holding him off a little longer.

"Well, I do have a wedding dress that's almost finished." She tapped her chin with her finger. "Getting married to you would be the practical thing to do, since *Mami* and *Daed* have made so many preparations already."

"I just told you how much I love you and you're talking about being practical?"

"I can't help it. I'm a practical woman."

"And I've never done anything practical in my life."

Rachel grinned. "It's never too late to start." She took his hand, surprised by her boldness, yet the gesture felt completely natural. "I can't wait to marry you, Tobias Byler."

"Because it's practical?" Even though the words were said in a teasing way, she could see the faint glimmer of worry in his eyes.

"*Nee.*" She squeezed his hand, happy to see the joy suddenly reflected in his expression. "I can't wait to marry you . . . because I love you."

Chapter 17

$\mathcal{G}$abe stood on Moriah's front porch, hesitating to knock. Frankly, her rejection had started to wear on him, and he wondered if he should heed his father's advice and let her go. But something inside him refused to give up, not yet.

"Father God," he whispered. "Please, let her open the door to me. Help me to reach her. I can't do this without you." Bolstered by his prayer, he rapped on the frame of the screen door. Emma answered right away.

"Gabriel," she said through the screen. Although Emma hadn't always been home when Gabe stopped by, he knew she was aware of his frequent visits. Still, she didn't seem annoyed with his persistence. Quite the opposite. "It's *gut* to see you. *Wie geht's?*"

"*Gut, danki.* Is Moriah home?" His standard question, which was always met with Moriah's standard answer—she was too busy to have visitors. He fully expected to hear those same words from Emma.

"*Ya,* she is." Emma opened the door and stepped outside on the front porch. "Rebekkah put Moriah on bedrest this week," Emma said, her voice nearly a whisper.

His heart jumped with apprehension concerning the midwife's decision. "Is she okay? Is the baby all right?"

"The baby is fine. It's Moriah she's worried about. She's not getting enough rest, and she won't listen to anyone when we tell her to take it easy." Emma sighed. "I never knew my *dochder* had such a stubborn streak. Rebekkah told her flat out that if she didn't follow orders, the baby would be in jeopardy. Only then would Moriah listen."

"Maybe I should come back another time," Gabe said, even though he didn't want to leave. This was as close as he'd gotten to her in weeks.

"*Nee.* She's asleep on the couch right now. Go in and sit down, then I'll wake her. I must apologize for her rudeness, Gabriel. You must understand, she hasn't been herself, not for a long time."

"No need to apologize. I only want to talk to her for a moment. I won't bother her too long."

"*Danki.*" She smiled. "I know how much you care for her. I was concerned at first. After everything she's endured, I thought the last thing she needed was another suitor, especially so soon. But I can see that this is different. You're different. You're not like . . ."

"My brother?"

Emma nodded.

"You're right, I'm not. Somehow I have to convince Moriah of that."

"I know you will, just as you have convinced me. Come, let's go inside."

Moriah awakened from a fitful sleep and rolled on her side, trying to find a comfortable position on the couch. She had wanted to lie down upstairs in her room, but the heat of the day coupled with being in the last two months of her pregnancy made the bedroom unbearable. Even though the front room was several degrees cooler, she still felt too warm. Unable to relax, she sat up and started to reach for a magazine to fan herself with when she heard the front screen door close. Emma walked inside, Gabriel Miller following closely behind.

Her body stiffened as a fusion of emotions tumbled through her. Seeing Gabriel standing in front of her, his brown eyes consumed with hope and trepidation, made her realize how much she'd missed him. But the feelings were intrusive. She'd spent the past two months shutting them down. Why did it take him only a few short seconds for him to revive them again?

"Hello, Moriah." His deep voice—soft, gentle—sent a ripple of warmth down her spine, causing her to wince. She didn't need to have this kind of reaction to him. She didn't want to.

"Gabriel, why don't you sit down?"

Moriah looked up at Emma, betrayed. Her mother had known she didn't want to see Gabriel, yet she invited him in. How could she do this to her?

But Emma ignored her as she said, "I'll bring you both a glass of lemonade. Or would you prefer iced tea, Gabriel?"

"Lemonade is fine, *danki*."

As Emma disappeared into the kitchen, Moriah stared down at her lap, fingering the ribbons on her *kapp*. She heard Gabriel clear his throat, but he didn't say anything. An uncomfortable silence stretched between them.

"Moriah?" he finally said. "Will you please look at me?"

After hesitating for a moment, she turned. He had taken off his straw hat, placing it in his lap. He ran his long fingers through his brown hair, and not for the first time she noticed his muscular forearms. "Gabriel, I can't talk to you right now."

"Then when can we talk? Just name the time and place and I'll be there." When she didn't answer him, he added, "You can't keep pushing me away, Moriah."

"I'm not." She gazed at her lap again.

He let out a bitter laugh. "Oh really? Then what do you call refusing to see me?"

"I don't have to see everyone who visits me."

"Moriah, you know that's not fair."

She lifted her head. "Fair? You have no right to talk to me about fairness."

"I reckon I don't." He leaned forward in the chair, an intense expression on his face. "Moriah, I know I've made a mess of things. I should have told you about Levi and Taylor, but at the time I wanted to protect you."

"I don't need protecting. Not anymore."

"I disagree. You're vulnerable right now—"

"I've always been vulnerable, Gabriel. Idealistic. Always seeing the best in people, even when they showed me their worst. And what did it get me? Nothing."

"You have a baby," he said softly.

A stab of remorse ran through her. "*Ya.* I have a baby. And this child means more to me than anything." She looked directly at him. "My baby is all I need, Gabriel. I don't need your concern, or your protection."

Hurt seeped into his eyes. "That's not all I'm offering you, Moriah. I'm offering you my heart. My love."

"I can't accept it."

"Maybe not now, but in time."

She shook her head. "You don't understand. Time won't change anything. It won't change how I feel." She lied, for even now she could feel him melting her defenses with his loving words. "Find someone else. Don't waste your love on me."

"Oh, Moriah." He got off the chair and knelt down beside her on the couch. "I'm not wasting anything, especially my love. I wish there was a way I could make you see how much I want to be with you."

"Because Levi told you to."

"*Nee*, this has nothing to do with Levi. I regret telling you about what he said, but you asked me for honesty, and I wanted to show you that I will never lie to you, or betray you."

She closed her eyes. "You're making promises you can't keep."

He rose. "It's not going to work, Moriah. You can keep me at arm's length, but that won't change the way I feel. I will love you forever. But I can't, and I won't, force you to love me." He picked up his hat and put it back on his head. "It's up to you now, Moriah. All you have to do is say the word and I'll stay. And if you want me to go . . . I'll go."

She couldn't look at him. For if she did she would never be able to utter the words she had to say, for both their sakes. "Goodbye, Gabriel."

He didn't move right away, but then she heard his footsteps on the wooden floor, followed by the bang of the screen door. Only when she heard the faint *clip-clop* of his horse and buggy on their driveway did she let the tears fall.

Emma entered the room, carrying two glasses of lemonade. She took one look at Moriah and set them on the coffee table, then went and sat down next to her. Gathering her daughter in her arms, she said, "What happened?"

But Moriah didn't answer her. She couldn't tell her mother that she had just destroyed her last chance at love. Instead she leaned against her and sobbed.

Later that afternoon, after Moriah had cried herself into a restless sleep, her mother awakened her. "Moriah," she said softly. "You have another visitor."

Her eyelids, heavy with sleep, fluttered open. "Who?"

"John Miller."

Fully awake now, she pushed herself, with some effort, into a sitting position. What was John doing here?

"Do you want me to tell him to come back another time?" She brushed Moriah's forehead with her hand.

Moriah shook her head. "That's all right. I'd like to see him."

A few moments later, John entered the room, his battered straw hat in his hands. Other than at church services, she hadn't seen him in more than two months, and she realized how much she missed him. Even though she had to cut off any chance of a relationship with Gabriel, she couldn't do the same to his father. "Come in," she said. "Have a seat."

John shuffled inside, and then slowly lowered his body down on the chair. "It's *gut* to see you," he said.

"It's *gut* to see you. I've missed you, very much."

"I've missed you too." He looked at the mountainous bulge of her tummy. "How is my grandchild getting along?"

"Fine. Rebekkah said I'm right on schedule with the delivery."

"That's great news. I can't wait to hold him—or her. I remember when Gabriel and Levi were born . . ." He paused, then continued. "What a joyous day that was. Velda and I had never been happier." A smile appeared on his face, crinkling the corners of his eyes. "I'm sure you'll feel the same way too."

She nodded, relying on the joy of her child to block out her pain. "You know you're welcome to see the baby any time you want. And once I'm back on my feet, *Mami* and I will bring the babe over."

"Does that go for Gabriel too?"

Pausing, she said, "I wouldn't keep him from seeing his own kin."

"But you don't want to see him."

Moriah leaned back on the pillow, averting her eyes from John's.

"I thought you two were friends."

"We were."

"You're not treating him like much of a friend. He comes to visit you, you send him away. One of these days he won't be coming back."

"That would be a good thing."

John didn't say anything for a long moment. "I know how he feels about you, Moriah."

Her head jerked in his direction. "You do?"

"*Ya*. And I also know why you don't want to see him. You're scared."

Unbidden, tears welled in her eyes. "Don't I have a right to be?"

"*Ya*, you do. But you can't keep running away from your fear. And ignoring Gabriel isn't going to help matters."

She wiped the moisture from her eyes. "Did he send you over here to talk to me?"

"Absolutely not." John fingered the brim of his hat. "He'd be spittin' mad if he knew I was over here. And I probably shouldn't interfere, but I don't like seeing either one of you stuck on this merry-go-round anymore. Don't shut him out of your life, Moriah. You'll come to regret it if you do."

"But what if I regret letting him in?"

His smile was gentle. "I know you're hurting from what Levi did to you. Everyone understands that, including Gabriel. But that doesn't mean you have cut him out of your life completely."

"He wants so much from me. More than I can give."

"Moriah, for as long as I've known you, you've been a giver. You gave all your heart and soul to my Levi. I loved my boy, but I'm not blind to what he did to you. He ran your well dry, and maybe it's time for you to get filled up. We all have wounds from this, wounds that the Lord needs to heal. Sometimes He heals you Himself." John stood, his movements slightly stiff. "And sometimes, He sends others to bandage us up. One thing I know for sure, you can't be restored on your own." Picking up his hat, he gave her another smile. "Well, guess I've meddled enough for one day. I should be getting back home."

She noticed the fresh scar on his hand, the one he had injured on the forge. "Are you still drinking your tea?"

"Every night. Though I gotta admit, it tasted better when you made it. Maybe someday you won't mind making it for me again." He winked, then turned around and left.

Moriah stared out the window in the front room, mulling over John's words. Was God's hand in this after all? Since Levi's death she had questioned how any of this could be His will. Levi's leaving, his affair, widowed and left to raise a child alone—this was how God showed His love for her?

Then again, how had she shown her love for Him? By shutting Him, and everyone else, out of her life. By refusing to pray, refusing to seek Him in her pain. No wonder she was lonely and miserable.

The family Bible lay on the coffee table in front of her. She picked it up, letting it fall open in the middle. Psalms. She found the High German language a challenge to read, but she muddled through it.

"He healeth the broken hearted, and bindeth up their wounds."

Closing her eyes, she held the Bible against her chest, pouring her soul out to God. Her fear over letting Gabriel into her heart, despite her wanting to let him in. She beseeched the Lord to take away the loneliness and grief, her constant companions. A lump jumped in her throat. "My heart and spirit are broken, Lord," she whispered. "Please, healeth them."

Chapter 18

*M*oriah folded her hands across her huge belly as she listened to her brother and Rachel exchange wedding vows. Her due date was very near, and she hadn't felt well when she'd awakened. But she wouldn't miss Tobias's wedding for the world.

The entire community had been shocked when Rachel and Tobias had announced their engagement two weeks ago. Everyone but the Detweilers and the Bylers had assumed Rachel would marry Christian. To his credit, Christian didn't say a word against Rachel or Tobias. But he wasn't at the wedding either. Moriah didn't blame him. While she was happy for her brother, who everyone could see was completely in love with his soon-to-be bride, listening to the service was difficult. It was nearly a year to the day she had married Levi.

Her stomach lurched as the baby moved again, and she shifted in her chair. Then a squeezing pain seared across her abdomen. The pains had started yesterday, but they had been sporadic, more uncomfortable than anything else. But this pain was different, more intense. She glanced at her *mami* and *daed*, who were watching the service and beaming at the bride and groom. She didn't want to do anything to disturb their happiness, or her brother's wedding.

Over the past couple weeks she had been engrossed in wedding details, helping her mother and Sarah prepare for today. Yet she had taken time to rest, to read the Bible, and especially to pray.

She still didn't know what to do about Gabriel. She had felt God nudging her to talk to him, but her fear held her back. The few times she had seen him, he had kept his distance, honoring her wishes. She had seen him walk into the Detweilers' home earlier that day, but he had ignored her, instead walking up to Tobias and offering his congratulations right before the ceremony.

He looked so striking in his dark trousers, crisp white shirt, and black vest. He'd removed his black hat, revealing thick locks of chestnut-colored hair. Then he laughed, his smile illuminating his entire face, causing her breath to catch in her throat. An intense longing rose within her, one she had never experienced before, not even with Levi. When he turned from her brother, she inexplicably wished he would make his way to her, just so she could be near him. But he didn't give her a glance as he walked to the back of the room and sat down next to his *daed*.

The bishop pronounced Tobias and Rachel husband and wife, and the two of them turned and faced the congregation. Her brother nearly glowed as he looked down at his beautiful bride, her hand resting lightly on the crook of his arm, a radiant smile lighting up her face. Moriah said a quick prayer of blessing for their union, then another sharp pain stabbed at her midsection. Glancing at her belly, she saw it tighten beneath her gray dress. She winced and looked around, glad no one noticed her discomfort.

Everyone stood and started talking, anticipating the delicious meal to come. Moriah started to rise, but was assaulted by another pain, longer in duration and nearly taking her breath away. When it subsided, she tried to get up again, her protruding belly making her feel awkward and unbalanced, until she felt someone take her elbow and gently help her up.

"*Danki*," she said, then looked up and gasped.

"You're welcome." Gabriel let go of her arm. "I hope you don't mind, but you looked like you were having a bit of trouble there. Are you feeling all right?"

His kindness amazed her. Even after she had hurt him so deeply, he still cared. "*Ya*," she said. "I'm fine. The baby is very active today."

"How close are you to delivery?"

"A little over a week, according to Rebekkah."

"I'm excited to meet my new niece or nephew." Doubt crept into his face. "If that's okay with you."

"Of course you can, Gabriel. I would never keep you from seeing the *boppli*."

Relief washed over his features. "*Danki*."

His gentleness increased her remorse. She really had been horrible to make him doubt whether he would be a part of Levi's baby's life. She remembered those dark hours when she thought she had been protecting herself from pain. In reality she had not only perpetuated it, but she had spread it on Gabriel too. She had to let him know how sorry she was. "Gabriel, I—"

Her hand went to her belly as another burning wave tore through her. Fortunately this one had been brief, but it had brought tears to her eyes.

"Moriah, something's wrong." Gabriel moved closer to her. "Let me get your *mami*."

"*Nee*, she's busy with the meal. I'll be all right."

"I don't think so. You're as white as a sheet."

Perspiration broke out on her upper lip. "I don't want to worry my family. This is Tobias's day." She couldn't stand to ruin his wedding.

"Then let me take you home. I'll run and fetch Rebekkah afterward."

Moriah nodded. "All right."

"Where's your cloak?"

She told him where he could find her wrap, and he dashed off to retrieve it. The pain had subsided to nothing, but she was still worried. Her due date was a week away. Certainly she wasn't going into labor now.

Gabriel returned and helped her slip into her cloak. By this time most everyone had moved outside. The day was unusually warm for November, and at the last minute they had moved the meal outdoors. No one had noticed that she and Gabriel had stayed behind, and when he escorted her out to his buggy, she was relieved to see the guests involved in their own activities.

As he helped her into the buggy, another contraction came. He put his arm around her shoulders and she leaned against him, gritting her teeth against the pain. When it subsided, she took a deep breath. "*Ach.* That one hurt."

"What do you need me to do?" he asked, still holding on to her.

"Just take me home."

He assisted her into the seat, then dashed around to the other side of the buggy and jumped in. "Hang on, Moriah. We'll be home in no time."

She nodded, grateful the pain had gone away.

"Do you think you're in labor?"

"*Ya.*" She clutched her belly and exhaled, trying to calm the terror rising inside her. "I don't know if I can do this," she whispered.

Gabriel's hand slipped inside hers. He squeezed it lightly. "You can, Moriah."

Tears fell out of the corners of her eyes. "I'm scared, Gabriel."

"I know you are. But you'll be fine. In a little while you'll have a beautiful *boppli.*" His words and touch comforted her.

They made it to her house in quick time. When he pulled into the driveway, another contraction hit, and she waited for it to pass before she got out of the buggy.

Gabriel put his arm around her waist this time and helped her to the house. When she reached the front porch, her water broke.

"Gabriel!" she exclaimed, clutching his *reck.*

He glanced at the ground, unfazed. "It's all right, Moriah. Let's get in the house."

A few moments later he led her to her parents' bedroom, which was the only bedroom on the first floor. She sat down while another contraction, this time stronger, seared through her. Letting out a cry of agony she screamed, "Help me!"

With each of Moriah's cries, Gabriel's anxiety increased. He tried to remain calm for her sake, but inside he could barely keep it together. He hated seeing her like this, consumed with agony as the contractions became stronger and more frequent. When she was able, he laid her back on her parents' bed and brushed her damp brow with the back of his hand.

"I'm going to fetch Rebekkah," he said, amazed by the steadiness of his voice. "I'll be right back."

She clamped her fingers down on his arm. "*Nee!*" He held his breath as another contraction came and went. "Don't leave me, Gabriel. I can't do this alone."

"You won't. Rebekkah will be here to help."

"There's no time." Her gaze bored into his, her eyes holding a desperate combination of pain and fear. "You have to help me."

Gabriel's birthing experience was limited at best. He'd helped a neighbor deliver a calf when he was a teenager, but that in no way compared with this situation. Yet he knew she was right; the speed and the intensity of the contractions filled him with stark panic. He couldn't leave her to have this baby alone.

Yanking off his *reck*, he asked, "What should I do?"

She gripped the sheets as another contraction came. "I don't know!"

That wasn't what he wanted to hear. He flipped off his hat and rolled up his sleeves, his mind frantic. His mouth turned to cotton as he tried to figure out what to do. The next contraction forced her to a halfway sitting position. He could see her knees drop open to the sides underneath her dress. *Dear God in heaven, help me!*

"Moriah?"

Gabe breathed with relief when he heard Lukas's voice coming from the front room. "In here!" he yelled.

Lukas poked his head in the doorway. "*Daed* saw you two leave and he sent me to find out what's going on." His gaze darted from Moriah to Gabe. The color drained from the seventeen-year-old's face. "Is she having the *boppli*?"

"Go get Rebekkah Fisher! Hurry!"

Lukas ran out of the room, and Gabriel continued to hold Moriah's hand. "Rebekkah will be here soon," he said.

She gripped his hand, her face dripping with sweat and red from the pain. "Don't leave me," she said, gasping. "Don't ever leave me, Gabriel."

Without thinking, he lifted her hand to his lips and planted a kiss on the knuckles. "I won't." Her words sparked a tiny flame of hope inside him that she meant something other than him seeing her through the birth. "I'm not going anywhere."

"She's beautiful."

Moriah's eyelids opened at the sound of her mother's voice. She smiled as she saw her baby cradled in Emma's arms, only the very top of her head and face visible underneath the light yellow receiving blanket.

Every fiber of her being hurt, but the dull throb was nothing compared to the relentless pain she'd gone through giving birth. Exhausted, she had fallen asleep soon after she held her new daughter, barely remembering Rebekkah taking the baby out of her arms to wash her tiny body and wrap her in the blanket.

"Perfect in every way." Rebekkah's voice reached Moriah's ears, and she turned to see the midwife standing over her. "You didn't sleep for very long." She smiled. "Would you like to sit up and hold your *boppli*?"

Moriah nodded and allowed Rebekkah to help her to a seated position. The midwife propped pillows behind her back. A clean blanket lay across her lap, and her *kapp* had been removed at some point. The pain of childbirth had been so consuming that she barely remembered what had happened until she'd heard her baby's cry after the final push. Now her arms ached to hold the child she'd been anxious to meet for so long.

"Here she is." Tears welled in Emma's eyes as she passed the swaddled bundle to Moriah. "You should be proud of yourself, *dochder*."

"*Ya*," Rebekkah added. "You made my job very easy. By the time I got here the *boppli* was already crowning."

Moriah gazed down into her daughter's face. Her eyes were barely open, but she could make out their bluish-gray color. Her cheeks were round and pink, and her lips were full. Downy brown hair covered her head, the same shade as her father's.

"Do you have a name for the *boppli*?" Rebekkah asked.

"Velda," Moriah replied without hesitation.

Emma put her fingers to her lips. "After Levi and Gabriel's *mudder*?"

She nodded and looked up at her mother. "Velda Anne."

"After my *mudder*." Tears rolled down her cheeks. "*Danki*, Moriah. And *danki* for my beautiful *grossdochder*."

Moriah smiled. "Where's Gabriel?"

"He's in the front room." Rebekkah chuckled. "I think you scared about ten years off that man. I'd never come across anyone so happy to see me in my life."

"I couldn't tell." Then again, she had been more than a little preoccupied. Things were starting to come back to her now, and she remembered how he had stayed by her side, holding her hand, giving her words of encouragement until Velda Anne was born. He had still been next to her when she'd fallen asleep. "Has he held the baby yet?"

"*Nee*." Rebekkah looked at her. "Would you like him to?"

She nodded. "Please. Tell him I want to see him."

Emma went to get Gabriel while Rebekkah made sure Moriah was completely covered. Then she said, "I'll leave you all alone for a few minutes. Velda's asleep, but if she gets cranky, let me know and I'll help you get her fed." She left the room.

Moriah leaned back against the pillow, her baby tucked in her arms. A perfect miracle, she was a gift from God. As she marveled at her daughter, she realized that God had been with her through everything. She had questioned His plan for her life, especially after Levi's betrayal. But now she could see how going through the pain had made her stronger. Over the past few weeks, she had asked the Lord to heal her heart. He had done that not only through her child but through Gabriel as well. Even after she had hurt him, he stood by her.

"Moriah?"

Gabriel stood in the doorway, as if he didn't know whether he should come in or not. His gaze went to Velda Anne, and his smile, coupled with the tenderness in his eyes, touched her.

"Come see your niece," she said, smiling and lifting the baby slightly toward him.

He strode in and stood by the side of the bed, still appearing unsure. She motioned for him to sit next to her, and he did.

"*Danki*," she said, with all the sincerity and gratitude in her heart.

"No need to thank me, I didn't do anything." His brown eyes softened. "You, on the other hand, were incredible."

She blushed, then looked down at her baby. "Do you want to hold her?" He nodded, and she placed Velda Anne in his arms.

"She's beautiful," he said, staring at her. "Emma said you named her after *Mami*."

"*Ya*. I think it suits her."

"I think you're right." Gabriel smiled.

Moriah took a deep breath as an all-consuming wave of peace washed over her. As she watched Gabriel hold her daughter in his strong arms, she understood how right it all was. He had said he would love Levi's child, and she could see that love in his eyes as he gazed at Velda Anne's precious face. He had been by her side through everything, just as he'd promised, never asking for anything in return. He had been her rock through the dark times, and had shared the happiest moment of her life. His belief and love in her had never wavered, a shining example of God's own devotion to His children.

Tears filled her eyes.

"Moriah?" his voice covered her in a gentle caress. "Why are you crying?"

"I'm so sorry, Gabriel. I'm sorry for sending you away, for not trusting in you." She wiped her nose with the top of her index finger.

"Shhh," he said, tucking Velda Anne deeper in the crook of his arm. He reached out and wiped the tears off Moriah's cheek with this thumb. "It's all right."

"*Nee*, it's not."

"Listen to me, Moriah. I won't let you do this. We've all made mistakes, but those are in the past. The time of mourning is over." He pressed a kiss to Velda Anne's forehead, then smiled. "The time of celebrating has begun."

She grinned through her tears. "You're right. We have a lot to celebrate." Consumed with joy, she reached out and took Gabriel's hand.

He squeezed it and smiled, but didn't say anything. He didn't have to. She knew he understood her meaning completely.

Chapter 19

*R*achel snuggled Moriah's three-month-old daughter in her arms. She and Tobias were sitting on the Bylers' sofa in the front room while everyone else had gathered in the kitchen. It was Sunday, a day of rest and, in this house, celebration.

"Isn't she adorable, Tobias?"

"*Ya*," he said, looking at his niece. "Cute." He picked up a copy of *Family Life* magazine from the coffee table and thumbed through it.

"That's all you have to say?"

He cast her a sidelong glance. "What else do you want me to say? She's a *boppli*. They're all cute." He inclined his head and looked at Velda Anne for a moment. "Although I'll admit, she's prettier than most."

"*Ya*, she is. Hopefully we'll have one of our own someday soon."

"Maybe." He gave her a wicked look. "Until then, we'll have fun trying."

"Tobias!" Rachel admonished him, but only halfheartedly. "Your parents could walk in here at any moment."

Instead of behaving himself, he scooted closer to her and nuzzled her neck.

A chill ran through her entire body, and though she didn't want to—she really, *really* didn't want to—she pulled away. "Stop it!"

His sly grin made her toes curl. "Only if you promise we'll continue this later."

Rachel could barely breathe. Being married to Tobias had been everything she ever dreamed of—exciting, unpredictable, at times exasperating, and above all, filled with fun and love. They brought out the best in each other, and even though they hadn't stopped being competitive—she had just beat him in a game of washers last weekend—they also didn't mind losing, as long as it was to each other. They had also started their marriage on solid financial footing. Between what he made working for his father and her tips and pay at the restaurant, they had been able to buy a house last month.

"Let's get out of here," he whispered in her ear.

"You want to go home? We haven't been here that long."

"It's been long enough." He looked down at the baby. "Don't get me wrong, Velda Anne," he said. "I love you, but you're taking up *mei frau*'s attention. She'll tell you herself, I don't share very well."

Rachel laughed. "Fine. Let me take her to Moriah. Then we can tell everyone good-bye."

They walked into the busy kitchen. John Miller was seated at the table with Joseph Byler, the men engaged in a serious conversation. Emma and Ruth were at the opposite end, looking at a devotional book. She didn't see Elisabeth, Lukas, or Stephen, and assumed they had gone upstairs to their room. Finally, she spotted Moriah standing by the kitchen sink, speaking to Gabriel in low tones. The two of them had spent a lot of time together since Velda Anne's birth, and Rachel had never seen Moriah look so content. She smiled as she brought the baby to them.

"Tobias and I are leaving," she said, handing Velda Anne to her mother. "*Danki* for letting me hold her. She's precious."

"You're welcome." Moriah glanced at the baby. "Thank goodness she's asleep. She was up for most of the night."

"And here I thought she was the perfect baby," Rachel quipped.

"She is," Gabriel responded, looking at Velda Anne, then at Moriah. "She is."

Rachel and Tobias said their good-byes and headed for home. She leaned back in the buggy, tucking the warm lap blanket around her.

"You're awful quiet," Tobias said, as he led their buggy down the snow-covered road. There weren't many cars out today, adding to the peace of the Sunday afternoon.

"Just thinking."

"Want to let me in on your thoughts?"

"I was just thinking about Gabriel and Moriah, and how much has changed in the past year. They look happy together, *ya*?"

"*Ya*. I wouldn't mind having Gabe as a *schwoger* some day. He's a *gut* man."

"Do you think they'll get married?"

Tobias shrugged. "Who knows? I may have to warn him that marriage isn't as great as I thought."

"What?" She turned to him, gaping.

He grinned, then chucked her under the chin. "It's even better." Then he winked at her. "Gotcha."

"Tobias, when I get my hands on you—"

"I can't wait to find out."

She laughed, then scooted closer to him, leaning her head against his shoulder, more in love with him than she ever thought possible.

Shortly after Tobias and Rachel had left, everyone moved to the family room except for Moriah and Gabriel. She had transferred Velda Anne to his strong embrace. He never seemed to get enough of holding her. They stood by the sink and looked out the window as dusk descended on the horizon, her mind consumed with thoughts and memories. Velda Anne had taken on the features of Levi, and in essence, Gabriel's features too. But for the past couple weeks, she hadn't dwelled on the past. Instead she had thought and prayed about her future.

At one time she thought she wanted to face it alone, with only her child filling the space in her empty heart. Now she knew how wrong she'd been, how selfish and afraid. There was only one way she wanted to face her future, and only one man she wanted to spend it with.

But had she thrown away that chance?

She gazed up at Gabriel, willing him to look at her. Immediately, as if he sensed her silent pleading, he looked down at her, and smiled. "You look different tonight."

"Do I?"

He turned and faced her, Velda Anne asleep in his arms. "*Ya.*"

"In what way?"

"I can't put my finger on it." He searched her face. "You're just so . . . so . . ."

"*Ya?*"

"Beautiful."

She smiled. "There's a reason for that."

He quirked a brow.

"Because I'm with you."

She heard his breath catch. "Moriah," he whispered, his voice husky. Then he gazed at her. "Are you sure?"

"I'm sure. If you still want me, that is."

"If I still want you?" He groaned. "Moriah, I love you. I would marry you right now if I could. The question is . . . would you marry me if I asked?"

She stared at him for a moment, this man who loved her so deeply she could barely fathom it. Finally, she understood what love was, and she felt it nestle inside her heart. God had taken her brokenness, and through Gabriel's love, had made her whole again. "I would be happy to marry you, Gabriel Miller. *Nee*, I would love to marry you."

Such joy filled his eyes that Moriah felt like she was in a dream. Slowly he leaned forward and pressed his lips against hers, his kiss filling her with promise, with desire, with love.

Velda Anne stirred, breaking them apart. She gazed at her daughter, then looked up at Gabriel. "I love you," she said softly.

"I can't tell you how long I've waited to hear those words." His eyes glistened. "I can barely believe I'm hearing them."

"You can believe them," she said. "Because I'll be saying them to you for the rest of our lives."

Acknowledgments

*W*riting a novel set in an Amish community and featuring Amish characters was a challenge, one I wouldn't have been able to meet without the help of some very generous people. I'd like to thank Maria Byler and her family for their friendship and willingness to answer my many, many questions about the Middlefield Amish. I also thank Nick Fagan, head of Adult Services at the Middlefield Library for being so helpful and pointing me in the right direction for my research.

A special thank you to my editors, Natalie Hanemann and Jenny Baumgartner. Their invaluable expertise, encouragement, and patience played such a vital part in writing this book. Thanks to my agent, Tamela Hancock Murray, for being my cheerleader for so many years—thanks for not giving up on me! And a big thank you to my friends and fellow authors—Jill Eileen Smith, Tamera Alexander, Maureen Lang, Diana Urban, Edwina Columbia, Deb Raney, and Meredith Efken. Their support and encouragement means so much to me.

Above all, I thank my family—my husband James, my son Mathew and my daughters Sydney and Zoie. I love you all very much.

Reading Group Guide

1. When we meet Gabriel, he is struggling to hide his love for his new sister-in-law, Moriah. He also deals with the guilt of coveting his brother's wife. Have you ever wanted something you couldn't have? How did you handle those feelings?

2. Although Levi grew up in a community that values self-denial and loyalty, he has difficulty denying his impulses. Think back to a time when you were tempted. Did you give into that temptation? What was the result? If not, how did God help you overcome the temptation?

3. When Levi leaves Moriah, she blames herself for his abandonment. Why does she choose to believe she's at fault, instead of Levi? Is there such a thing as a "right" way for her to respond?

4. Rachel resents her brother Aaron. Is it justified? Why or why not?

5. After Levi's death, Gabe believes he gave up on his brother too soon. Do you agree? Is there anything Gabe could have done to convince his twin to come back to Moriah and the Amish?

6. Throughout the story, it's clear that Tobias and Rachel have feelings for each other. Besides Rachel dating Christian, are there any other reasons they didn't reveal how they felt?

7. Gabe loves Moriah, but he isn't honest with her. He doesn't tell her he loves her before she marries Levi, and he doesn't divulge the real reason Levi left. Gabe believes he is protecting Moriah by keeping these secrets. Can you think of some circumstances where hiding the truth might be for the best? Would God approve of that choice?

8. Gabe starts to think that if he had told Moriah he loved her before her marriage, Levi would still be alive. Do you agree with his assumption? Why or why not?

9. As a man of his word, Gabe vows to standby Moriah, even though she pushes him away. How does Gabe's patient faithfulness to Moriah mirror God's faithfulness to us?

10. Romans 7:18 says: ". . . I want to do what is good, but I can't" (NIRV). Despite being a woman of deep faith, in her darkest moment Moriah chooses to drown her misery in work instead of prayer. Why do we often choose the opposite of what's best for us, especially when it comes to seeking God?

About the Authors

*B*eth Wiseman has a deep affection for the Amish and their simpler way of living. She is the author of many bestsellers including The Daughters of the Promise series and the new Land of Canaan series. She and her family live in Texas.

*K*athleen Fuller is the author of the best-selling Hearts of Middlefield series. When she's not writing, she enjoys traveling and spending time with her family and farm pets.